A DARKENING FIRE

DENIS O'BRIEN

Copyright © 2020 Denis O'Brien
All rights reserved.
ISBN:
ISBN-13:

For GRÁINNE – Love Always

Contents

CHAPTER 1: MARCH 1911	1
CHAPTER 2: FEBRUARY 1913	4
CHAPTER 3: FEBRUARY 1913	10
CHAPTER 4: FEBRUARY 1913	13
CHAPTER 5: DECEMBER 1913	22
CHAPTER 6: DECEMBER 1913	31
CHAPTER 7: DECEMBER 1913	41
CHAPTER 8: JANUARY 1914	44
CHAPTER 9: FEBRUARY 1914	52
CHAPTER 10: FEBRUARY 1914	56
CHAPTER 11: MARCH 1914	62
CHAPTER 12: MARCH 1914	65
CHAPTER 13: MARCH 1914	69
CHAPTER 14: MARCH 1914	76
CHAPTER 15: MARCH 1914	85
CHAPTER 16: APRIL 1914	92
CHAPTER 17: APRIL 1914	100
CHAPTER 18: APRIL 1914	107
CHAPTER 19: APRIL 1914	114
CHAPTER 20: APRIL 1914	121
CHAPTER 21: MAY 1914	128
CHAPTER 22: MAY 1914	133
CHAPTER 23: JUNE 1914	138
CHAPTER 24: JUNE 1914	142
CHAPTER 25: JUNE 1914	147
CHAPTER 26: JUNE 1914	152

CHAPTER 27: JUNE 1914	156
CHAPTER 28: JUNE 1914	160
CHAPTER 29: JUNE 1914	165
CHAPTER 30: JULY 1914	170
CHAPTER 31: JULY 1914	176
CHAPTER 32: JULY 1914	183
CHAPTER 33: JULY 1914	191
CHAPTER 34: JULY 1914	197
CHAPTER 35: JULY 1914	204
CHAPTER 36: JULY 1914	212
CHAPTER 37: JULY 1914	220
CHAPTER 38: JULY 1914	228
CHAPTER 39: JULY 1914	236
CHAPTER 40: JULY 1914	240
CHAPTER 41: JULY 1914	246
CHAPTER 42: AUGUST 1914	267
CHAPTER 43: AUGUST 1914	272

A DARKENING FIRE

CHAPTER 1: MARCH 1911

'You have come to invade us, maybe?' Captain Brisse wiped the grime from the yellowish glass of the window and looked down at the convoy of peculiar mechanised vehicles drawn up on the parade ground below his office. 'If so, you'll find you've come into possession of about a million square kilometres of sand and rock. I hope you'll find the campaign worth your while.'

'As you will see from our papers,' Graf von Schwabe said, 'we have the authority of your Ministry of Colonies to conduct geological investigations in the Terere region. Nothing more martial than that.'

Still eyeing the dozen or so dun-coloured trucks that had brought the expedition to Fort Prouvost, the Captain appeared not to have heard. To have covered the long and hazardous journey from Dakar in them was, he thought, a technological feat that merited even his appreciation. Aware that the soldier's attention remained concentrated on his transport, the Count joined him at the window.

'It's none of my business,' Brisse said, 'but what exactly is the purpose of this expedition?'

'The University have asked me to conduct a survey of sandstone sites. And extract certain materials to take back to Zurich.'

The Captain picked up the sheaf of documents his visitors had produced and lazily flicked through them.

'Let me tell you this,' he answered. 'I am more than three hundred kilometres from any authority more senior than my own... So – please do what you want and go with my best wishes.'

Only half listening from a corner of the room the resident Ministry representative Vincent Garrou said nothing, and instead allowed the dusty air in the room to solidify into an unaccommodating silence.

'But,' Brisse continued, 'let me offer you a piece of advice. Turn round now and go home. You'll find nothing out there that's

A DARKENING FIRE

worth the risk.'

'The risk? As for the desert itself, we're well equipped to cope. But we were given to understand that this whole region was pacified a dozen years ago.'

Brisse shrugged. 'Please yourselves. But you might want to hear a little story first. Some months back I had a party of Europeans come through here. Looking for what was left of a giant lizard or something. Sergeant Heller and his patrol found these fossil hunters a couple of weeks later. Stripped naked, genitals stuffed in their mouths, bellies ripped open. Bodies laid out with their heads pointed in the direction of Mecca. Our Tuareg friends like to emphasise a point.'

'And the perpetrators were caught? Punished?'

'The deed didn't go entirely without reaction.'

'What does that mean?'

'It means that a few days afterwards Sergeant Heller's men left the corpses of twenty or so Tuareg rotting under the sun. For good measure they were angled in the direction of Rome. Unlike myself Sergeant Heller is a religious man.'

'So the guilty were made an example of?'

'That was hardly Heller's concern. We are soldiers, not policemen. So take my advice. Go back to Dakar, get on your ship, head back to whichever port you sailed from and go home to Switzerland with her watches and banks.'

Turning his eyes on the so far wordless Vincent Garrou, von Schwabe said, 'If I may appeal…'

'I regret, M. le Comte, that I am only a civilian administrator. Captain Brisse is the ultimate authority here.'

'Perhaps, but listen. We are here to determine the viability of mining significant quantities of pitchblende and its elements. I am not at liberty to explain the importance of this, but you can be certain that the University can be generous...'

Brisse waved a dismissive hand.

'I have no time for this. You should leave now before I suspect you of offering us a bribe.'

And Sergeant Heller, the post's munitions expert, who had been lounging by the door led the protesting delegation out into the stifling heat, jerked his head in the direction of the convoy and nudged the reluctant Count down the steep, unforgiving stairway.

A DARKENING FIRE

Brisse threw himself into his chair and tossed the Count's bundle of papers onto the floor.

'So, then, tell me,' the Captain asked Garrou, 'what was that about?'

'Pitchblende,' Garrou said. 'It was a throwaway line, but I'm pretty sure that he was supposed to keep that to himself.'

'Why? And what the hell is pitchblende? And why would he come all the way out to this hellhole to look for it?'

Garrou permitted himself to dwell on the resentment that had afflicted him for the past several months since he had been shunted off to this outpost of Hades. Previously he had been on a much-envied Foreign Ministry attachment in Berlin where in an unguarded moment towards the premature end of his tenure he had revealed to Helmut Protzman, an amiable acquaintance in the Prussian Civil Service, that he would shortly be posted to this miserable outpost of empire. And it had been in the course of a subsequent drink-fuelled conversation that Garrou had first heard any meaningful reference to pitchblende, though at this chronological remove the matter was cloudy.

Receiving no answer to his questions, Brisse gave way to an uncharacteristic bout of near-sympathy. Crossing the room he laid a friendly hand on Garrou's shoulder.

'This place is getting to you,' he said. 'I don't blame you for being down in the mouth. The minute you're back to civilisation you'll forget all about the dubious pleasures of Niger.'

In the parade ground below Sergeant Heller, explosives expert and committed Christian, was emptying his bladder on a supine Swiss with a bloody nose.

A DARKENING FIRE

CHAPTER 2: FEBRUARY 1913

In the spring of 1877 Joey Butler and his parents had left Donegal to settle in Glasgow and within six months the twelve year old found himself at the head of the family. On a Monday morning in October his father, along with 206 other men and boys of the early shift died in an explosion 900 feet down in Blantyre Number 2 coal mine. The transition to Scotland had proved devastating for the emigrants escaping wretched poverty in the west of Ireland.

Recovering from this trauma faster than his mother and two elder sisters who found themselves reliant on the services of the Barnhill Poorhouse, Joey soon set about supporting them. He juggled an array of occupations: thieving, errand running, delivering milk, smuggling poteen between illicit stills and seedy outlets, painting carts, tending horses and even on occasion attending school. Confronted by the hostility of many no less indigent Scots, he learned in short order to use his fists - and his head too, both as a weapon and a means of outsmarting the competition. And in this he had the advantage of coming under the protection of the biggest, burliest boy in the street who was rendered exotic by his being the offspring of an Irish father and a German mother, an aimless wanderer round Ireland's western shores. By his mid-teens Joey managed to undertake an apprenticeship that led to steady work in one of the city's shipyards. He might even have proved himself acceptable to the Board in time had he not, after almost a decade of philosophical acceptance of a foreman's verbal and physical abuse, surrendered to a bout of retribution which left his senior colleague a bloody and unconscious mess. After a brief spell in 'A' Hall in Barlinnie Joey emerged with his professional reputation strangely enhanced and obtained a position with the St Rollox Railway Works in Springburn.

Quick in the uptake, self-taught and absorbed by the dynamism of the flourishing technology, he was encouraged within a couple of years to shed his oily overalls, buy a suit and devote his energies to

A DARKENING FIRE

technical development in the drawing and design department. Glasgow had become home despite frequent public protestations that it was losing its identity to the Hibernian influx. All the same, Joseph Butler was Irish and remained Irish and it was in the company of his fellow immigrants that he spent most of his free time. The venues for assembly and exchange of confidences were numerous: weekend, evening ceilidhs, the terracing of Celtic Football Club, the National Halls in the Gorbals, Catholic Societies parochial halls and dozens of pubs across the city. Through these channels flowed a coagulating compound of instinctive kinship alongside an astringent enmity directed at the alien ascendancy over the water. At first none of this carried much weight with Joey, but lengthy reflection on the issue was encouraged by the aggressive vigour of its proponents – Ciarán Taaffe, Rónán MacInerney, Conor Fallon, Paddy Gormley and the others – persuaded him to their patriotic orthodoxy. Drawn into this seditious circle, Joey became someone else altogether. Revolving around highly complex engineering, his work afforded him expertise and knowledge that impressed the conspiratorial clique.

Discovering himself to be capable of being simultaneously secretive and conversable, Butler edged his way up the undesignated ranks of the Republican Brotherhood branch until he was regarded as second only to Ciarán Taaffe. His duties with St Rollox enabled him to make frequent contact with a number of Taaffe's euphemistically-termed "friends" in Liverpool and London. Toting a briefcase bulging with blueprints, contracts and rough sketches of machine parts, he wore the aura of the peripatetic businessman. And under this camouflage he carried instructions to the Sinn Féin branches of which Taaffe was the coordinator. Instead of drifting into middle age on a slow tide of alcohol, laughter and a brief, childless marriage, he was roused to a patriotic passion that consumed him. Living a double life became second nature and by his mid-forties he recognised that he was addicted to deception – it was what drove his adrenalin, gifted him purpose. And it was in that condition of suppressed excitement that he was making his way through the grey February snow falling into the muddy puddles of Gordon Street to Glasgow Central Station. This was a month that he hated, but the prospect of another clandestine

A DARKENING FIRE

assignation in London stirred him out of his habitual seasonal disaffection.

Ciarán Taaffe had advised him the previous day that the Special Branch were taking particular interest in Glasgow – hardly surprising given the acknowledged militancy of a section of the large Irish community. Entering the station through the small seven-pillared porte-cochere Butler snatched a glance over each shoulder before sauntering into the main concourse to note the general appearance of the half-dozen or so possible agents of the state who might be taking an interest in him. Finding himself alone in the first-class carriage ten minutes before the train's departure he used the moment of relaxed silence to reflect on the engagements of the next few days: first the official meeting with a representative of the Hohenzollern Locomotive Works; then on the following day he would conduct other prearranged meetings, one with a useful intermediary also from Germany and then at the Shaftesbury Tavern in Hornsey where he would get mildly drunk and collect a package. He was roused from this rehearsal by the arrival of a tall, slim woman whose two heavy bags Butler, leaping to his feet, hoisted onto the rack, casually noting the newcomer's neat figure and delicate, regular features. Gratefully acknowledging his gentlemanly assistance, the woman settled down opposite him to watch the hectic bustle on the platform as the guard's whistle answered to a hoot from the locomotive and clouds of steam and wisps of smoke came drifting past the window.

Feigning interest in the inside pages of the Catholic Observer Butler stealthily studied his travelling companion through half-closed eyes. He placed her in her mid-30s, moderately pretty, wealthy to judge from her clothes and jewellery, self-possessed and, he noted, wearing no wedding ring. At the Carlisle changeover to LNWR's blackberry black locomotive and purple lake coaches for the onward journey to London he volunteered to carry her luggage and was rewarded with a half-smile that confirmed that she was, in fact, on her way to Euston. Finding a first class compartment he deposited her bags overhead and ushered her to a seat which she took with an air of elegant weariness.

'Do you mind if I...?' Butler asked, indicating the vacant place opposite. She affected a gesture of refined assent. Not hurrying to

A DARKENING FIRE

deploy his Celtic wiles – he was, as always, confident in the attractiveness of his engaging nature – he took the opportunity of the woman's tentative gambit when she asked if she could borrow his discarded Observer.

'As a co-religionist or an ecumenical enquirer?'

'Midnight Mass at Christmas, occasional Easter duties,' she told him, letting the newspaper rest on her knees. 'Not lapsed altogether, just lacking conviction.'

They talked idly around the point for a time and when he gauged that the moment was right, Butler introduced himself.

'Tony Williams,' he lied with practised facility. *'En route* to some tiresome meetings before I re-join the regiment.'

Her interest piqued, she invited him to elaborate.

'You have no military connections yourself?' he continued, pretending a faint hint of surprise under cover of which he wanted to ensure that his mendacity wasn't to be readily exposed.

'None, I'm afraid. I come from a family of rather lazy country folk who would no more take the king's shilling than climb the Matterhorn in bare feet. One of those Old Catholic clans confined to the Recusancy in the part of the world we're chuntering through at this very minute.'

Reassured by her easy communicativeness and her lack of knowledge of things army he proceeded to add abundant colour to the phony outline of himself that he had sketched.

'Major Williams of the Scots Guards at your service,' he announced. 'Just returned with the battalion from two years in Egypt.'

'I never would have guessed it from your – well, your somewhat alabaster countenance.'

'One of those fortunate types,' he replied. 'Whether I lie supine in the sand or squirrel myself away in the shadows makes no difference. But I have to confess that as a Staff Officer I was mostly immured in a solidly built office and shielded from the desert sun by whitewashed walls a yard thick.'

The woman smiled again

'Harriet Nichols.'

'Enchanted, but please don't hesitate to dismiss my foisting myself on you. These train journeys can be demanding enough

A DARKENING FIRE

without having to bear the weight of unwanted company.'

'I shall keep that escape clause in mind, but until I have to resort to it I shall be delighted to entertain any diversion.'

'Then allow me to inflict on you the boredom of my accounts of my derring-do in His Majesty's service.'

And for much of that afternoon he amused his companion in tones far removed from his ordinary demotic with the convoluted fiction of his martial career until, with their destination only quarter of an hour off, he casually referred to his being lodged at the Grosvenor; and he tacked on that his engagements were not so rigidly ordered that he couldn't make himself free to offer her a break for lunch, a drink or dinner. It would, he said, be no great encumbrance for him to travel the breadth of the city to do so if necessary.

Harriet hesitated before saying, 'My cousin will be meeting me at Euston and I have to go on from there to visit some people in Camden. But I shall be staying in Vauxhall for most of the time. Perhaps if I can get away I could come to the hotel either tonight or tomorrow evening.'

'That would be wonderful.'

'Unfortunately I can't make that an absolute promise. It depends on my uncle's condition – he's been very ill for such a long time. But if I can slip away for a while I shall be delighted to see you again. I'll telephone the hotel if I can find the time.'

'Then I can ask for no more,' Butler replied with an air of genial optimism.

After a carefully staged formal handshake on the platform he watched her surrender her luggage to the fresh-faced young man who had greeted her; and saw them walk off towards the shiny new Austen 10HP, her arm hooked in his.

'You're getting old,' he reminded himself, 'but still, you never know...'

Relaxing in the lobby of the hotel after checking in he again took the precaution of surveying the human traffic trickling into the building and was able to assure himself that his tracks had been well covered. In fact the only activity in the place was an audible argument issuing from a group of five elderly men evidently on an excursion from the sticks who were debating which of the

A DARKENING FIRE

metropolitan fleshpots to plunder. Butler's sole official engagement of the day was due at four and exactly on time Herr Mirisch of the Hohenzollern Locomotive Works strode in through the front door of the Grosvenor, whipped open for him by a uniformed commissionaire.

Mirisch got down to business with an alacrity honed by the need to be on the boat train much sooner than he had hoped – other demands were being placed on him in a series of telegrams from Düsseldorf. This suited Butler well: although it was for this that his employers at St Rollox had dispatched him to London, he found the technical negotiations it involved both boring and predictable. Still, the connection with Hohenzollern provided the cover for his other activities in the metropolis should any inquiries after his absences from Glasgow were ever made. Mirisch had prepared well and presented his toneless commentary on the blueprint of the equipment St Rollox's Board wanted to consider. With care and dry clarity he answered Butler's probing questions and by five o'clock was gone. Butler left the lobby to the solitary devices of a florid-countenanced yokel mumbling into his goblet of brandy. When he awoke some long time later he was disappointed that no communication had been forthcoming from the pretty Miss Nichols and that he would evidently be spending the night alone. Major Williams, he decided, had to go.

In the lobby the abandoned, red-faced toper had lapsed into a comfortable, comatose condition; and alone in the dining room Butler was left to rueful contemplation of the inescapable passage of time.

A DARKENING FIRE
CHAPTER 3: FEBRUARY 1913

The next day Butler readied himself for the first of the two real, if furtive, purposes of the expedition. That morning he was due to see the representative from Berlin to discuss a matter too confidential to be conducted anywhere there was even the remotest chance of being overheard. The hotel lounge was deserted when the newcomer arrived – a cheerful man with a case full of documents relating to the most esoteric aspects of international trade, mind-numbing in their volume and impenetrable detail. Seating himself in the farthest corner of the vast room he signed to a waiter to bring him coffee and two cups and waited with inscrutable patience for Butler who arrived five minutes later. Far out of earshot of any eavesdropper the two men wasted no time on social niceties. At each of the preceding meetings with the man Butler had pressed the familiar case for supply of arms to the Nationalist cause in Ireland. There was, he had been told, no shortage of official sympathy for the request in Berlin, but the matter required a delicate touch. It was vital that good relations with the British were maintained at what had been described as a critical point in history. Any deal would have to be deniable by the German government. In short, the position was complicated and patience still had to be exercised.

'Aye – you lot have been telling me the same thing for months,' Butler reminded him, not hiding his exasperation. 'If Berlin wants the Brits kept too busy to interfere with whatever plans it has, the best bet is to set Ireland blazing with rebellion. I'm sick of saying the thing. For Christ's sake, it's the most obvious bloody answer to your problems and ours.'

Protzman was unmoved.

'Oh, we see that point, I promise you. But one wrong move and we are left with exactly the opposite effect to the one we want. Nevertheless, I haven't come here only to repeat this.'

'Well, show me that you're not fucking fobbing me off again. If this Home Rule Bill goes through there'll be a whole new situation to deal with. For you and for us.'

'I doubt if...'

A DARKENING FIRE

'It would mean that the Brits could wash their hands of us and we'll end up with a civil war. Ulster will be a scab we'll have to fix for ourselves and that won't be easy done. And if England's not looking out for us stabbing her in the back there'll be nothing to stop her having a damn good look at whatever's happening across the Channel.'

'Shortly we'll be in possession of so terrible a new weapon that no country will be capable of confronting us with arms.'

Butler registered a high degree of unconcern at what Protzman intended as a devastating revelation.

'What the hell good would that be to us? If the Brits aren't busy in Europe they're free to burn us to the ground. And your great big gun or whatever isn't going to help us.'

'Please believe me – we're on your side and that's where we'll stay. At the right time we'll give you everything that you need. Thousands of the latest rifles, millions of rounds of ammunition. But you must see that we can act only when the moment is absolutely right. If the critical point comes too soon,' Protzman glanced round to ensure that their isolation remained unimpaired, 'it could be very bad for us. And for you.'

'For us? Shite! It can't come soon enough. If you scare them off *your* doorstep they'll come and give *us* a good kicking instead. We may be in the right, but they're the ones with the army.'

Butler caught sight of the visibly hungover loner from the previous evening as he made his tentative way past the lounge's open door and collapse into a large leather armchair in the opulent vestibule.

'Trust me, Herr Butler. We're friends and comrades. When the time comes the British will find they're confronted by a well-armed insurgency.'

Butler issued an irritated sigh.

'Look, Protzman, show me there's some sharp point to this. If I go back to Glasgow and say that nothing's changed since the last time they'll tell me to go and fuck myself – and you.'

'You and your colleagues will not lose by this, I promise. Your people will hear more of it soon. For now I must keep my own counsel. You're clear where we stand?'

The still scowling Butler nodded once.

A DARKENING FIRE

'I can't yet set a date for another meeting,' Protzman continued. 'But when the time is ripe I'll find the means to let you know. Meantime you must say nothing – nothing – about this.'

Protzman stood up to go, but Butler placed a firm hand on his shoulder.

'Don't be a stranger,' he said in a tone that bore no hint of friendship.

A DARKENING FIRE
CHAPTER 4: FEBRUARY 1913

When Protzman had left Butler hurried over to reception and asked hopefully if there had been any message for him.

'Major Williams, isn't it? Yes, sir, a young lady telephoned while you were in conference. She asked if you could be contacted sometime after lunch. May I call her with a message from you?'

Butler brightened.

'There's an engagement I can't get out of but maybe you could give her this telephone number. I'll be there for most of the afternoon.'

Over several months he had used the Shaftesbury Tavern regularly as a meeting place and the number there was familiar to him. The pub was a long way from the Grosvenor but had some advantages. There were plenty of different routes to it across the city to make it hard for anyone to follow him and the place had been chosen by his metropolitan contacts because of its convenience to their stamping ground. These meetings were always fixed for the quiet time when few if any other clients would be in the place. Coincidentally, and somewhat to Butler's amusement, this timing tended to coincide with the brief appearance of a gang of thugs who made no secret that the purpose of their coming and going was to extract what Butler had overheard them describe as *"defensive readies."* On the way out of the Grosvenor he passed the sedentary figure of the old fellow he had caught sight of earlier, now perched on a low chair rocking back and forth, mumbling to himself and clutching what appeared to be a colossal glassful of gin.

'It's the only cure,' Butler told him, patting his arm as he passed.

'Too late for a cure, sir. Death would be a welcome visitant. Take my word for it: there comes a stage in every man's life when even a little is too much.'

Having shrugged on a capacious overcoat against the bitter cold outside Butler wound his way north across the city – first on foot through St James's Park, where he retrieved a small waterproof

A DARKENING FIRE

package from its usual hiding place and then carrying on by underground, by bus and by cab. Ninety minutes later, blowing on his freezing hands, he felt a great wave of relief to be embraced by the warmth in the unoccupied pub on Hornsey Road. With a nod to the skeletal tapster he ordered a glass of stout and a large whiskey and with a grunt of satisfaction settled himself in his accustomed place in one of the windows looking out over Shaftesbury Road, deserted for the moment beneath a sudden squall of hail. Hauling a newspaper from a side pocket he scanned the front page with affected interest, his edgy attention concentrated on the street door. Eoghan Gallagher was never late and he came in toting a carpet bag and shaking the shards of the storm from his head and shoulders. Without needing to be told the barman immediately devoted himself to dispensing with great professional care a pint of black stout which he carried to Butler's table while Gallagher shed his pea-jacket and scarf and a moment later joined his Glaswegian acquaintance, drank down half the Guinness, wiped his lips with an appreciative smack and leaned forward to shake hands. These perfunctory niceties out of the way neither man lost any time in prosecuting their business. The bag Gallagher had been carrying he nudged under the table until it rested against Butler's leg; and in return Butler shoved his identical case back to the other man.

'There's a bit more this month,' Gallagher murmured. 'Make sure it's wisely spent.'

These transactions themselves were hardly necessary but they conveyed an assumption of unified purpose as well as providing for the passing of coded messages. Butler had no objection to the errand-boy status this implied: he enjoyed London, the opportunity for philandering that the visits occasionally afforded, and the frisson that accompanied the expeditions. He liked Gallagher without knowing him, and they shared responsibility for collecting the written instructions and messages from the hiding place in St James's Park. The jangle of the telephone on the bar and the barman's signalling Butler to the instrument brought the reticent conference to an early conclusion. Tapping a mock salute to his forehead Gallagher picked up the bag resting at his feet, finished his drink in a single swallow, shrugged on his jacket and was gone into the filthy February weather before Butler had raised the BI &

A DARKENING FIRE

H receiver to his ear. His keen anticipation was quickly dissipated.

'Major Williams, it's Harriet. I'm so sorry, but my uncle's illness means I'm quite unable to see you today after all – and for a few days yet. Just a thought, though – my cousin has the telephone number of the officers' mess at Wellington Barracks. May I call you there sometime next week?'

Disappointed but not disconcerted, Butler earnestly expressed concern for the family and his profound regret that they would not now have the chance to catch up. And he tacked on glibly, 'Unfortunately I've been ordered to Aldershot tomorrow. No free time, I should think, for six weeks or so. Perhaps you have a telephone number where I could…'

The line went dead and mildly put out at the failure of his libidinous scheme he resigned himself to conducting a fresh campaign elsewhere in a month's time. Hanging up he returned to his seat primed to be entertained by the short, choreographed ceremony he knew was due to take place within the next half hour or so. He barely glanced up when a vast, lumbering figure entered the establishment, ordered a drink and sat down in shadow in the furthest corner. It was later than usual when Butler raised his eyes from the paper and witnessed the arrival of the party whose operations he had observed at these regular intervals for over a year.

There were three of them as always, their leader squat and dark with the over-muscled bulk of a weight-lifter. Known in the Archway area as the Turk, this thug had never been further east than Aldgate, but his swarthy appearance, heavy moustache and sinister reputation combined to create this exotic persona. For a decade he had led a small but efficient gang of hard men that derived its income from shops, pubs and other premises across North London, selling them protection from the depredations likely to be visited on them only by his own organisation. What caused Butler a hint of regret was that the affair in the Shaftesbury was always carried out with a minimum of ceremony and a complete lack of protest by the incumbent. Wedged between his two colossi, the Turk, hunched, bow-legged and enveloped in a greasy jerkin down which streamed channels of melting snow, banged without preamble on the bar and, wordless, held out an enormous hand. The

A DARKENING FIRE

lanky barman made a hasty, placatory gesture, retreated some steps and called for the owner who, expecting the unwelcome guests, appeared from the back room with a fat brown envelope. What excited Butler's closer than usual attention, though, was the trepidation with which the proprietor faced the Turk.

For several seconds nothing out of the ordinary happened; and then the Turk, slitting open the envelope with his thumbnail, paused and shook the contents on the bar – a bundle of blank paper. Incredulity was quickly replaced by apoplectic fury. Bending across the bar he lunged at the owner who had taken three or four steps out of range. Seething, the Turk hurled himself at a gap between the pumps and was swinging his leg onto the bar's surface when his career was brought to an abrupt conclusion. From the shade in the far corner a massive figure emerged with a speed that seemed to Butler to be impossible for such a leviathan. This unheralded arrival on the scene wasted no time or effort in introduction. Instead he brought a short cudgel crashing against the neck of the nearest of the Turk's lieutenants. The blow landed with such savage force that the man collapsed on the floor without as much as a groan. In the next instant the Turk himself, for all his brute strength, was lifted bodily from his interrupted scaling of the barrier between himself and the terrified owner and was tossed against the wall near the door. As he gave vent to a roar of pain and wrath, as well as to a generous spatter of blood, the second of his companions was being subjected to a hail of blows from the cosh and the callous flail of his attacker's boots. His wits still scattered, the Turk staggered back into the affray, too late to provide assistance to either of his now unconscious minders. He launched himself with an ape-like bound at his assailant only to be met with a flurry of kicks and punches that sent him reeling backwards to slide to the floor drenched in his own gore.

Admiring this display of calculated viciousness but simultaneously engaged by no overwhelming desire to draw attention to his thoroughly neutral presence, Butler waited to see what would happen next. He watched the big man casually step over the recumbent forms of his first two victims, haul the Turk upright by the throat and stuff something into his shattered mouth.

'You've got two minutes to lug the guts out of here,' Butler

A DARKENING FIRE

heard. 'Feck them out on the pavement, and yourself with them.'

And with something of a theatrical gesture the hulking mugger produced a fob watch, held it up for inspection and declared quietly but audibly, 'Your time starts now. If the three of you aren't off the premises in these two minutes I'll make sure you never walk again.'

With a cry of pain the Turk pulled from between his lips whatever it was that had been shoved there, glanced at it, tossed it aside and crawled whining to the stirring bodies of his accomplices.

'Two minutes, mind,' the giant repeated, waving to the cowering bartender to pour him a fresh glass of Guinness. And it was then that Butler felt the strange, unforeseeable jolt of recognition. Disbelieving, he concentrated on the man-mountain sipping his stout and eyeing the excruciating effort with which the Turk, on his knees, was slowly dragging his colleagues in crime out of the building and into the burgeoning snow storm. It seemed impossible to Butler, but the longer he examined the Titan the more persuaded he was, despite the passage of almost four decades, that this was the very same character who had been his mentor and protector in those far-off school days in Glasgow. *Two minutes, now.* Yes, it was in that accent, that tone of voice, its combination of Donegal and Glasgow dialects, its terse authority; it was those features, craggy now, but surely unmistakable; it was without doubt the mature manifestation of Leo McGarrity. While Butler was trying to come to terms with this discovery, the establishment's boss was surrendering to the imperturbable bouncer a bank note and some coins.

'You know,' he said in a confiding, half-whisper, 'if they come back they'll kill me. Or get somebody else to do it. Or burn the whole place to the ground.'

'I promise you, my friend, they'll never bother you again. My word on it.'

'Well, Jesus, I can't…'

'You can rely on it. I've taken steps.'

Yes, yes, Butler confirmed, there could be no doubt: this was the very man. Anxious not to provoke an instant, violent reaction, he made his approach with the utmost care. Extending a hand as an earnest of his amicable intention, he nevertheless paused a few feet from the behemoth, aware that a mistake on either side could have

A DARKENING FIRE

serious consequences for his wellbeing.

'"*Lug the guts*," eh?' he said, making sure that his fixed grin conveyed nothing other than genial intent. 'Aren't you the very man for the Bard?'

Swiftly pocketing his earnings, the brute bestowed on Butler a glower devoid of recognition or any hint of good will.

'I've read a bit,' he said softly. 'Not that it's any of your affair.'

'And that would have been in that noble seat of learning in Parson Street, would it?'

A flicker of surprise crossed the other's face.

'Maybe,' he answered, his eyes narrowing. 'And how would you know that?'

'St Mungo's forever,' Butler hastily embroidered his approach. 'Not that I spent that much time in the place. There was always somewhere else I needed to be. But…'

Another pause.

'But you were always on hand when wee Butler needed some defending, eh *Mag Oireachtaigh*?'

To his relief he saw the slow registering of acknowledgement on the big man's face.

'Joey Butler is it?'

And a second later Butler found himself lifted off the floor in a crushing bear-hug.

'Jesus, Mary and Joseph, it can't be. J P Butler grown to be a London toff is it?'

Prising himself free with a gasp, Butler grabbed McGarrity's right fist in both hands.

'Leo, man, I can't believe it. Come. Come on.'

And tugging his old school friend in his wake he retreated to his table and signalled for another round.

'A London toff you say? Christ, no. I'm still a Glasgow boy just here on business for a day or two. I'm at the St Rollox place. But you, big fellow, what in the name of God are you doing punching the lights out of yon crowd?'

McGarrity shrugged.

'It's what I do,' he said. 'There's a bit of money in it. Enough, just about.'

'But, Jesus, man, I thought you went off to the university.'

A DARKENING FIRE

'Aye. But a lot's happened since those days.'

'It's a fact. Are we strangers now or what? Tell me about yourself.'

'Nothing much to say after all these years. Got in with some hard cases down here. I was doing the same as the Turk and that bunch.'

'You? For fuck's sake, I don't believe it.'

'Still it's true all the same. Then I met Róisín. Married. She turned me sort of respectable. Started on the building sites. Worked up to foreman, then a manager.'

'Then what in the name of God are you doing kicking the shite out of the likes of the Turk.'

McGarrity summoned the still pale-faced barman and ordered more stout and whiskey.

'This is what happened,' he said, tapping one of the glasses. 'Róisín died four years ago. Without her… well…'

Another shrug.

'She was everything,' he went on after a minute of thickening silence. 'She made me new. And she's never gone away out of my head. I can't sleep at night without her. Can't get through the day. So… it's been the drink kept me going. Lost the job because of it. So I make a few bob with these.'

He raised his huge fists and stared at them.

Butler laid a hand on the other's heavy forearm.

'Hell, man, this isn't Leo McGarrity at all. I was right – you're a ghost. A stranger.'

McGarrity rolled his eyes and downed most of the whiskey.

'How are things with you anyway,' he asked. 'Are you still playing away at the patriot game?'

Butler glanced furtively in the direction of the bartender who was assiduously polishing the gantry.

'You're all right,' McGarrity went on. 'He's a friend.'

But Butler didn't believe in unmet friends and kept his voice low.

'I am that,' he answered. 'And I'll tell you something for nothing – there's plenty of room in it for you and all. You'd be one of us yet, wouldn't you?'

'Aye. But I'm a long time out of it.'

A DARKENING FIRE

'Homesick at all?'

McGarrity might have nodded.

'I miss the old place once in a while, but it's been a long, long while since I was ever up there.'

'You never met Ciarán Taaffe? Out of the Liberties. No – you wouldn't have. You're too long away right enough.'

'*Na Saoirsi*, eh,' McGarrity remarked but offered no further response.

After a lengthy pause Butler said, 'A lot of the Mungo's lads are with us, but we've a fair number of new faces now. From the Old Country.'

'And sitting around in pubs doing fuck all except boasting something about how "*beidh lá eile ag an bPaorach*"?'

'That's just the way you remember it. No – there's steel in them nowadays. And Taaffe's the man to keep things on the boil. We've money, too – and plenty else.'

'And how long have we been hearing that?'

'But it's time. And it's time for good men to rally. Christ, Leo, don't waste your life on... on this.'

Butler waved at their surroundings.

'And that too,' he added, indicating the array of glasses on the table between them.

'I'll not be lectured,' McGarrity told him quietly.

'And I'll not be the man to try it. All I'm saying is you're still the one I'd go down fighting for. You stood by me in the worst of days. Maybe I can give you something back.'

'There's no need for that, Joey boy. All you can give me is another pair of these.'

And he indicated the glasses in front of him.

Having obliged the big man with more drink, Butler returned to his tentative proposal.

'It's not a one-way thing,' he said. 'Sure we can give you money. A place to stay. The comfort of friends...'

Before he could go on, McGarrity interrupted: 'Friends? They're all strangers to me nowadays.'

They drank in silence for a minute until Butler carried on: 'It's good luck brought you in here today. Good luck for the both of us. I'm asking you to come home, Leo.'

A DARKENING FIRE

'Home? I've been here for nearly thirty years. A lot longer than ever I was in Donegal or Glasgow. And I can't leave Róisín on her own.'

'I thought you said...'

'She's buried at St Patrick's over in Leyton. She has nobody else. Niamh's away in the States so I'm the only one goes there.'

Butler recognised the delicacy with which he was going to have to promote his case.

'Look,' he said softly, 'you told me Róisín's in your head always. Well, she's not alone then, is she? And you neither. You need to be doing something more than beating the bowels out of yon Turk and his likes.'

The door of the pub swung open and three or four heavy-set men in rough jackets crowded in together, the snow dusted on their shoulders. From their noisy banter it was easy for Butler to judge them to be West Coast men – Clare maybe.

'What,' he asked, 'was yon bit of paper you stuck in your man's mouth?'

'Just three words.'

'Oh, aye, and they were what?'

'The names of his kids.'

In a final throw of the dice, Butler steeled himself to stare directly into McGarrity's eyes.

'Come home,' he whispered. 'There's work for you to do.'

A DARKENING FIRE
CHAPTER 5: DECEMBER 1913

A miserable early December had descended on Glasgow like a damp, dirty rag on an intake of breath. Between drifts of cold drizzle unconvincing appearances of watery sun withdrew to the ironic applause of rain on the puddles in the scrap metal dump behind the Tir na nOg on the Gallowgate. There was a dank, colourless selvage to the late Saturday afternoon that lay along the edge of the ill-defined season and the mood of the occupants of the nondescript, smoke-filled back-room of the undistinguished pub had barely been lifted despite the favourable outcome of the football match a few hundred yards away with Celtic's having played out a 3-0 victory against Third Lanark. Drink in large quantities was brought through regularly from the bar past the pair of sour-faced bouncers under instruction to control their own abiding affection for the hard stuff until the meeting had run its uneven course.

The conclave had been touted as a significant event with Ciarán Taaffe having returned after a lengthy absence in Dublin. But pending his arrival the conversation dawdled around the abrupt disappearance of Big Tommy Neil, a popular foreman at the Raglan Boatyard. The Clyde shipyards accounted for about twenty percent of the world's sea-going tonnage, but Raglan was a builder of small inshore vessels and private yachts. Tommy was an easy-going teller of elaborate tales. Like Taaffe he was a native of Dublin's Liberties and in his cups given to noisy pronouncement of his devotion to the aspiration of a free and united Ireland. These effervescent demonstrations had drawn the attention of the authorities, but so overt and rumbustious were they that no-one seemed much exercised by their pyrotechnics. His non-appearance on this Saturday was causing a ripple of puzzled inquiry which subsided only when Taaffe himself finally turned up on his customary waft of impelling self-importance.

A short, stout man with a doughy complexion circling a heavy moustache that blossomed beneath a roseate bulbous nose, he was

A DARKENING FIRE

considered – and considered himself – to be the moving intelligence behind Glasgow's large and active Fenian movement and he ruled the Gallowgate coterie with ostentatious rigour. His arrival this time was accompanied by a frisson of anticipation mingled with curiosity. They were, with the exception of Big Tommy, all there – Rónán MacInerney and Conor Fallon from the Southside; others from Edinburgh and Dundee; Paddy Gormley from Clare; and slightly apart from the others, Butler and the morose giant McGarrity, having already put away several pints and as many whiskies. Thick as thieves, these two, Taaffe thought, bestowing a disapproving grimace that was lost on them.

'Right,' he said – his peremptory call to order – 'never mind the football, will you, and let's get on. First there's this: welcome home to our own Leo McGarrity - a man,' Taaffe concluded briefly, 'who's served his sentence with dignity and resolve.'

Though McGarrity had emerged from his three months in Barlinnie a fortnight earlier this was the first chance the group had had to reintegrate him into their company, and Taaffe's remark drew a spirited response of table banging and throaty cheers. In the course of an *al fresco* affray in the late summer it had taken five burly, street-fighting Glasgow police officers to subdue him. The encounter between the Micks and the Billy Boys had amounted to nothing more than the traditional free-for-all, but McGarrity's vast physical presence and sheer ferocity had obliged the initially reluctant upholders of the law to intervene. Taaffe's attitude was ambivalent. The last thing he wanted was to have his lieutenants draw unnecessary attention to themselves, particularly when doing so involved the coppers and the courts. On balance, however, Taaffe found in favour of this Goliath. A punch-up on Glasgow Green was of little consequence – probably most of the city's activists had participated in such an event at one time or another. About to address this very point, Taaffe was pre-empted by a slightly-slurred call from Conor Fallon who had unaccountably been trying to keep pace with McGarrity's drinking.

'Where's Big Tommy the day? I never saw him not here before.'

'The very next item on the agenda,' Taaffe grunted.

The terse preamble served to damp down the embers of the

A DARKENING FIRE

sporting debate still being stirred by the afternoon's match.

'Tom Neil's been a good and loyal comrade for a long time and nobody's forgetting that. In fact, that's the only thing that's keeping him walking around – with a bad limp, right enough, but mobile in a way.'

'Never mind the fucking riddle-me-ree,' MacInerney called. 'Where's Tommy about and what's happened to him?'

'He's in Dublin and about now he's busy explaining to Shay Boylan and the Council why he's been playing a solo tune.'

'Jesus Christ, no wonder they call you False Taaffe back there,' MacInerney fired back. 'Can't you just say the thing true and simple?'

'Fair enough. Tommy's been using one of Raglan's yachts to run some old Martini-Henry rifles across to Larne without any say-so from me.'

'Good for Tom. It's time somebody got a fucking move on.'

'Tommy's been an idiot and he might have put the whole lot of us in the shite. The coppers here and across the water had an eye on him. If we'd let him carry on he'd have hauled the rest of us straight into Barlinnie. So Tommy's been given a wee lesson and now he's likely apologising to our pals in the Liberties. He'll need to hope that he's convincing them.'

'Well, what was the "*wee lesson*"?' Fallon asked, leaning forward and knocking over his glass.

'Tommy was warned a dozen times. A dozen times, for fuck's sake! So I had to get Leo here to have a serious word with him.'

McGarrity barely glanced up from his assembled drinks. Since his release from prison he'd altered his appearance and not, Taaffe thought, for the better. His hair was long, shaggy, unkempt and he had grown a beard which, combined with his massive bulk, created an image of unadulterated malevolence. It irritated Taaffe that McGarrity and Butler were continuing their *sotto voce* conversation while he himself was trying to impose order on the gathering.

'So keep it in mind,' he went on, 'that Shay Boylan is brooking no transgressions. Important things will be happening shortly and there's a line that's to be toed. It's Leo's responsibility to make sure there's no lapse in discipline. You can all rest assured he's got the backing of the Council.'

A DARKENING FIRE

Making as much as he could of McGarrity's enlistment as arm-twister and leg-breaker, Taaffe attempted to bestow a flattering gesture on the giant but was irked that the subject of his blandishment was too involved in his exchanges with Butler to acknowledge the approbation. Butler had somehow managed to have McGarrity appointed to head up the security detail at the St Rollox gates even though his problematic history ought to have been considered a severe disadvantage. Added to that was the fact that McGarrity was the only member of the group to have attended university, which served further to fuel Taaffe's antipathy, which he was careful to mute, partly because of the big man's usefulness and partly because there was an almost elemental air about him. And so Taaffe was resigned to accepting that McGarrity was likely to become his necessary locum. But there was something about Butler that irritated nowadays: his contribution to the Cause was undeniable: he had contacts and had made himself indispensable to the fraternity over the years, but increasingly Taaffe felt himself being undermined or somehow outmanoeuvred by him. In Dublin he had tentatively voiced his concern and was told that how he ran the Glasgow operation was his own business. Butler seemed sound and had done excellent work but if Taaffe had doubts about his loyalty it was up to him to unearth the evidence.

'Let's have a bit of order here,' he said, raising his voice enough to remind the assembly that it was he who was at the helm. 'Forget Celtic, will you, for one minute, and maybe Mr. Butler and Mr. McGarrity could spare us a bit of attention...'

A reluctant silence fell on the room.

'Now look,' Taaffe continued when he was satisfied that he had the floor, 'we're not far off a year since we had the promise out of Hamburg that youse all know about. I doubt we can hold our breath or our water much longer. So Joey Butler – it's about high time you had the news for us out of your Jerry pal.'

'He's not my pal,' Butler answered, getting slowly to his feet. 'If you want to know, we're strangers still and I won't claim different. I can't read the man's mind and no more can he read mine. It's as well that way.'

'That's shite,' Taaffe replied, 'and you know it. What's the good of us being left here dangling, waiting on something that might

A DARKENING FIRE

happen and might not, and us with hardly a flintlock among us.'

Butler had made Taaffe aware that Protzman's interest was no more in money for guns than in signing up assistance from the Brotherhood for some mysterious project; but the matter of when the weapons were going to materialise was preoccupying Taaffe.

'You think that all we have to do is slap the notes down on the counter and walk out with a few thousand rifles?' Butler asked. 'I have Protzman's word on this – the guns will be with us early next year, and they'll be Mannlicher, the best you can lay your hands on.'

'You're an idiot to have signed up for that,' Taaffe responded, raising his voice.

'For Christ's sake,' MacInerney complained, ' would the pair of youse ever take a hold of yourselves. There won't be a copper between here and Kilrush that won't be treated to every word off you.'

'Go and boil your head in a pot,' Fallon contributed in reply, 'and shake the bones out of it. We'd all like to see a bit of a barney. Go on, Joey – give him a fistful of teeth. He couldn't beat the snow off a rope.'

With the tenor of acrimony alternating with the rising clamour of rowdy entertainment the meeting was pitching towards a characteristically anarchic closure when McGarrity rose, shoved Butler back into his chair and lifted a hand in a gesture that instantly restored order, to the visible disappointment of half the congregation.

'If there's any here think this is a playground,' McGarrity said softly, 'they can clear out now. There's work to be done. People are going to get killed and maimed on the way and that's no fucking joke. And another thing – what in the name of God are we doing in a place like this? Do you think the Special Branch are half-wits? They probably have the name of every man here. Jesus, the place is called Tir na nOg with every fellow in the room first or second generation Irish. And a pound to a penny there's some of you with a pistol in a pocket. The hour for us is coming and right now isn't the time for us to be seen and heard.'

McGarrity had never said more than a word or two and the impact of his speech was palpable. For several moments no-one spoke and a pause compounded of smoke, the reek of stale alcohol

A DARKENING FIRE

and the smell of wet clothes settled over the place. Finally Gormley, uneasily taking the lead and hardly daring to catch McGarrity's eye, said, 'Fair enough, and there's been a lot more talk than action for too long. So what's next then?'

'We don't meet like this again in a hurry,' McGarrity told him. 'When we get in touch with all of you you'll hear what we're about. Now clear off, the bunch of you and be easy on John Jameson. He has a knack of loosening tongues.'

An uncomfortable ripple of resentment and inchoate dissent ran through the company until, grudgingly, Deehan lumbered round a table pulling on his coat, shook hands with Taaffe and McGarrity and waited by the open door for the rest to follow him out, quietly grumbling at the premature and inconclusive winding up of business. It was about five minutes before only McGarrity, Taaffe and Butler were left in the room along with Rónán MacInerney who stood apart, sheltering in the shadows.

'I'll thank you, Leo,' Taaffe said, making a full scale exercise of lighting his pipe, 'to leave me to run things in future. And I'll remind you, Joey Butler, that you're here to obey orders, not stir up a row.'

'Ach, *cradi* your *pi*, you *leath-dhuine*. Go and take a running jump at yourself.'

'I'll put the pair of you through that window,' the exasperated McGarrity warned, 'if you don't sit down and shut up.'

Exchanging a glower Taaffe and Butler settled back and waited. With a demonstration of thespian reluctance MacInerney took the floor.

'Leo said I should tell you this,' he said after a noisy bout of throat clearing and an approval-seeking glance at McGarrity. 'I spoke to him last night,' he persisted, 'because I thought he was the fellow who…'

'Get on with it and never mind the introductions,' Taaffe ordered. 'It's me you're telling now.'

'Aye. Well, there's a man Dalton works beside me on the Broomielaw not done grousing because he has to be locked up in the Clarkson warehouse at Finnieston all over the weekend before Christmas. He's a Sergeant in the Territorial Force. Used to be in the HLI, but nowadays he's our top store-keeper.'

A DARKENING FIRE

'And a great man, sure,' Taaffe put in, emitting a cloud of tobacco smoke that would have choked a charging rhinoceros to a halt, 'but I couldn't care less about his sterling service to the Crown or the kibosh being put on his seasonal festivities.'

'The reason he's been called up,' MacInerney pressed on doggedly, 'is there's a load of eight hundred short-magazine Lee-Enfields and two hundred Webley revolvers due for the army in Dublin. The timing of the thing has been fucked up so they have to be stowed at Finnieston from the Friday night till the Monday morning before they can be shipped out.'

Taaffe lowered his pipe and communicated a hint of interest and encouragement by opening his eyes wide and waving the fingers of his free hand.

'Dalton has to secure the place and do what they call an inventory and then spend the weekend guarding the stuff.'

'Not on his own, though, but?' Butler asked.

'No, no. There'll be six regulars too. Armed, and no mistake. So – what do you think? You've been going on about Big Tom queering the pitch with his wee bundle of guns; and you're just done bending your man Butler's ear about the Jerries not coming up with the goods.'

Taaffe sat back and reflected on this intelligence.

'Can we find out if this is the real thing and not just your man Dalton doing a bit of show-off?'

'I took the liberty,' MacInerney said, pleased with himself that he'd exercised his initiative. 'I told the foreman at Clarkson's we wanted to have his place for the Saturday night for a load of church pews. When he said he couldn't manage it I offered him a few bob if he'd squeeze us in and he blew up in a rage and showed me the army's bill of loading and told me to go and lose myself in the Clyde.'

'So,' Taaffe took his time over the response, 'this is the sixth. We've got a fortnight.'

Another long pause.

'It would be one hell of an operation, though. How do we get by locks and armed guards for a start? And then how do we move a thousand guns? And how do we get them safe across the water?'

'You're asking for trouble if you try it,' McGarrity said. 'First,

A DARKENING FIRE

it's maybe nothing more than a trap. Second, there's a good chance the boys could end up shot or hung. And third, you'd never get the guns out of the country. Every port would be watched and every copper would be on the lookout for them. And anyway what would you be doing with half a dozen soldiers? If you killed them you'd have every soul in the land against you – in Ireland as much as here.'

'Ah, now, Leo,' Butler said quietly, 'you've missed a thing or two while you've been... away. Twice already we've...'

'I don't give a fuck for your secrets,' McGarrity said. 'I've had my say and if the lot of you end up with a hemp collar it isn't going to keep me from sleep.'

Restraining his customary aggressiveness Taaffe opted to cool the rising temperature of discord.

'All right,' the newly emollient leader replied, ' you're in order to be canny, Leo. But I want you with me on this...'

'I'll tell you this. You're all eyes and no sight. The whole business stinks to high heaven and you're a *bosthoon* if you fall for it.'

'So what is it you're saying to me? That the law's digging a pit for us? Or is it that you're not up for the game when it wants more than these handy fists of yours?'

'I'll show you one of these handy fists close up if you don't guard your tongue. All I'm telling you is the thing is set up to put the lot of you in Barlinnie or you could land up on the Broomielaw with five tons of weapons that you couldn't move without a convoy of lorries.'

'Let me sort that out,' Taaffe said. 'All I want off you is that I can call on you to keep the boys on the straight and narrow if it's needed.'

'Meaning what?'

'Meaning if I hear a word spoken or hear of a note passed about this or see a nod or a wink out of place I can rely on you top put things right.'

'I'm your man still. But I don't want to know one damn thing about what you're thinking of doing. If you go ahead, trust me – I won't be there.'

'I'm not asking that. If a mouth has to be shut up I need to be

A DARKENING FIRE

sure you'll do the shutting. Nothing more.'

'Then I'll leave you to your shenanigans, but don't ever say I didn't warn you.'

'Look, Butler's right, Leo – a lot's happened since you went away.'

And Taaffe signed to MacInerney to join him in muttered conference, McGarrity and Butler dismissed by the gesture.

Strolling west through the murky onset of night towards the Trongate the pair mulled over the merits of the Finnieston project. In the face of McGarrity's hostility to the affair Butler countered, 'Taaffe isn't about to go blundering into this with his eyes closed. He'll do the thing right – check every detail before we lift a hand to it.'

'I'll take your word for it, Joey, but unless the Glasgow Corporation's going to lay on a lorry or three for the load I can't see how your man thinks he's going to get away with it all.'

'Well, let me tell you. While you were being entertained by His Majesty's authorities Taaffe and me and MacInerney have been busy.'

And talking quietly as they walked the nearly deserted streets, Butler explained how a new organisational dispensation had been painstakingly established across the country. There now existed a well-coordinated network embracing the clandestine cells of the Brotherhood in Manchester, Liverpool, Glasgow, Edinburgh and Dundee, while Butler himself maintained contact with these further south. An operation like the one Taaffe was now formulating could be supported by volunteers, money and vehicles drawn from across Scotland and the north of England.

'We've moved up in the world,' Butler concluded as they stood shivering on the corner of Candleriggs, the rising wind thrashing a horizontal shower of hail out of the east.

'It's why you had to dole out Paddy Ryan's supper to Big Tom Neil. We can't have a weak link anywhere now, or some idiot singing solo when the choir's getting its notes together. We're right professional these days, Leo, and we know what we're at.'

McGarrity shrugged.

A DARKENING FIRE
CHAPTER 6: DECEMBER 1913

Leo McGarrity had insisted that the Finnieston caper was in all probability a snare set by the police. But if he remained unconvinced that Taaffe was approaching the affair with care and suspicion he was wrong. Before the day was out Taaffe had posted Conor Fallon, Franny Deehan and Paddy Gormley on exploratory missions. Fallon's cousin was an alcoholic who miraculously had been able to go on holding down a job as shipping clerk at one of the quayside offices on the Broomielaw. While the company he served had no involvement in the irregular transportation of military equipment between Glasgow and Dublin he was on the best of imbibing terms with his opposite number at the line charged with that responsibility. By the following Tuesday he had learned that a joint police and army operation was to be staged on the 21st to ensure safe removal of encased and unidentified material from the Clarkson warehouse to the MV *Dunstan*. By the time this information was in Taaffe's possession Deehan had spent the weekend in Dublin and deployed his contacts there to confirm that a security alert was set for the North Wall for the afternoon of the 21st.

And Gormley had scouted the layout of the Clarkson building. The main goods delivery entrance faced the quay itself and at night was conspicuously bathed in the light of two nearby street lamps. The doors were heavy, made of thick oak panels reinforced by massive iron crossbars and hung on huge hinges that looked as if they would resist a direct hit by a howitzer shell. There were no windows at street level – all were located fifteen feet above the pavement and protected by metal bars over wire mesh. An office entry was set in an alcove off Burrowes Lane at the rear of the building with side walls, also with high windows, overlooking the access passage. Gormley noted that, night and day, a watchman was posted at one or other of these windows, and the door was constructed entirely of steel. The lane was little used by day and almost invariably deserted at night. It was unlit, though a pair of inset lamps illuminated the door from the moment darkness fell.

A DARKENING FIRE

While this reconnoitring was proceeding Taaffe and MacInerney were pursuing their own inquiries. Having invited the warehouseman Dalton for an evening session in a riverside pub – a not infrequent event - MacInerney introduced Taaffe as his uncle and as a recently retired army officer. In creating his persona as Major Williams, Butler had done extensive research on the Scots Guards and had hastily tutored Taaffe on the regiment's history and current standing. As it transpired, however, little of this background was required. By the time Taaffe himself had arrived at the pub Dalton's clarity of thought had been swept aside by the free flow of strong drink. Impressed by Taaffe's evident loyal attachment to the Crown – Taaffe making no effort to disguise a Dublin accent that would never desert him – and in the highest of good humours Dalton was readily coaxed in to a retelling of the unwelcome intrusion on his time that the military would be imposing in a couple of weeks.

By the middle of the week Taaffe had brought together all these details and, shutting himself away in his rented apartment in Clydebank, drew up his plan of action. Some months earlier he had toured the Fenian cells across Scotland and northern England expounding a policy of cooperation and coordination amongst them as the sole means of prosecuting a campaign and in the end the purveyors of coalescence had prevailed and Taaffe saw in the Finnieston operation the first opportunity to deploy the full resources of the new, more coherent organisation. For several days he had Franny Deehan drive him from city to city to explain the scheme he had developed and to push for agreement to putting it into action. The main objection he encountered repeatedly was that the risk entailed in making a play for a mere thousand guns was unacceptable. If the business went seriously wrong the consequences would be severe. And it was pointed out that it had been Taaffe, after all, who had made himself responsible for cultivating German contacts with the object of acquiring far greater numbers of weapons.

'And we'll get them,' he had insisted. 'You have to remember what's happening in the big world out there. The Germans can't be seen to be stirring up trouble for the Brits right now with all them treaties and alliances all over the place. But for us there's work to

A DARKENING FIRE

be done and this is the best chance we've had so far to get things moving. And I'll tell you another thing – those Prods in the Ulster Volunteers aren't sitting around on their arses waiting for us to get our game up.'

So after his hectic round of hasty and often ill-tempered negotiation Taaffe came away with agreement to his intricate plot. Three days before it was due to come to fruition he summoned Butler, McGarrity, MacInerney and Fallon to Clydebank to brief them. After his deft exposition only McGarrity failed to hail his strategy with enthusiasm.

'Tell me this,' he said. 'How many folk know about the thing now that you've burned up all that petrol charging round the hollows of Lothian and Lancashire? How many of them do you know for a fact are as loyal to the Cause as you and me and the rest of us here?'

'They're good men all,' Taaffe assured him. 'There's not a new face among them and every one of them has been with us from the start.'

'You'll have to let it go, Leo,' Butler said, trying to placate the big man. 'It's all in motion – let God guide it.'

'God? If there was a God the Guinness would be free. But all right, I'll let it go, as you say. But if the whole thing turns out to be a monumental fuck-up just remember that my door's not the one it's going to be laid at. I'll not be going back to Barlinnie or Duke Street for you or anybody.'

Acrimony was diluted in alcohol, but when McGarrity left the others to their confidently excited anticipation of the weekend's event his mood was no more publicly uplifted than it had been when he issued his final warning. And something else was playing on his mind. As Butler accompanied him to the door he confessed, 'Joey, I'm past trusting myself. Keep this to yourself and swear to me you'll not say a word to another living soul – when I got home last night I knew Róisín had been in the place. It was like she'd left just a minute before.'

Butler patted his shoulder.

'She's gone a lot longer than a minute, my friend, but that doesn't mean she's lost altogether.'

'Not a word about it.'

A DARKENING FIRE

'Rely on it – not a word.'

Back in the city and under a barrage of freezing rain McGarrity wandered the streets, apparently aimless, his collar turned up and his hat pulled down over his eyes. His instinct for suspicion led him beyond the shallow pools of bluish light shed by the increasingly rare street lamps and down narrow, unwelcoming byways. The filthy night presaged by the miserable day brought a cauldron of vicious weather tipping down on the claustrophobic lanes and closes of the Gorbals. Even the incipient snowfall was tinted with grey as it was hurled against the dirty windows of the tenements. Here and there a garish light escaped from a swinging pub door and an inebriated denizen came lurching out of the Stygian gloom, seemed to consider accosting the bulky figure of the hard-faced passer-by and instantly discarded the notion when the forbidding form came within reach. Half an hour into this random odyssey he was confronted by an elderly man wrapped in a threadbare, oversized topcoat with a torn collar and a length of lining dangling to the pavement.

'Here, big yin,' this creature muttered, visibly unsteady on his feet but nevertheless standing squarely in front of McGarrity to block his way, 'I've got a great wee treat for ye.'

And grasping McGarrity very tentatively by the sleeve he signed with his free hand in the direction of the shadows gathered at the mouth of an alley. A moment later there emerged a tall, slim woman whose dishevelled clothing could not conceal a neat figure.

'Nice, eh?' the man went on, still heroically trying to restrain McGarrity's onward march. 'What would you say to a rare wee quickie up the close there? I'll mind ye'll no' be disturbed. Yours for five bob.'

McGarrity stared down at the other, waited for a few seconds to see if his lack of enthusiasm for the encounter was communicating itself, then reinforced his position on the matter.

'Fuck off out of it,' he growled, shoving past and in the process sending the supplicant spinning into the street.

'Hey, leave him alone, ye big bastard,' the woman shouted, her voice carrying its convincing enmity a long way down the wind, and she threw herself at McGarrity. Momentarily pressed against him, she thrust her hand inside his coat, skilfully dipped her fingers

A DARKENING FIRE

in the inside pocket to extract the folded paper and allowed herself to be pushed aside as if she were no more than a drifting leaf. Waiting until McGarrity was several yards out of range the pair began bawling abuse at his retreating back to which he offered no response.

'Come on, hen,' the man said finally, and hooking his companion's arm led her across the way to the smoky refuge of a disreputable public house.

Three days later, McGarrity shut himself up in his single-end flat after having for the last time upbraided Taaffe for his determination to proceed with the raid. Meanwhile Dalton, the Territorial Force Sergeant and reluctant guard commander at the Clarkson warehouse, had spent most of the late evening quarrelling with the half dozen regular soldiers about the accuracy of his inventory and about the sentry rota. Angry at his own lack of proper authority and despondent at the prospect of another 36 hours of being cooped up in the place, he had finally reached an uneasy compromise with the troopers: while one would man the observation post at the rear door and one patrol the aisles of the warehouse, four would retire to the camp-beds set up in a dingy office on the first floor. Each shift would last four hours and Dalton left it to the men themselves to sort out the order in which they would take their turn. Shortly before midnight, as he was dozing at his lonely post by the main entrance, he was startled into full wakefulness by an imperious banging on the door. Not inexperienced in complying with the responsibilities of a security detail, Dalton slid his revolver from its holster and, holding the weapon ready at his side, he shot back the spy-hole cover and shone a torch directly at the perpetrator of the intrusion. In the beam of the lantern he saw two thick-set policemen chatting casually as they sheltered under the awning above the gate.

'Sergeant Dalton, is it?'

'Aye – what d'yez want?'

'Here.'

And one of the uniformed officers thrust a closely printed blue document through the small gap.

'What the fuck am I supposed to do with this?'

Dalton played the light briefly on the paper which was headed

A DARKENING FIRE

with the crest of the War Department.

'What do ye think? You're supposed to read the thing.'

'Haud on, then,' he answered, closing the spy-hole and, lips moving, he scanned the small print which informed him that the consignment of Lee Enfields should have contained a thousand of the weapons and not the 800 already deposited on the premises. The 200 missing guns were already on their way under military guard and he, Dalton, was to ensure their safe delivery and storage. Opening the slat in the door once again he said, 'Fair enough. I suppose the pair of ye better come in out of that weather.'

'Jesus Christ, no. Are ye aff yer heid? For all ye ken we could be Shinners. Do ye want reported, ye moron? Listen – all ye need to dae is be on hand when the army get tae yer back door. Keep yer guards at the ready when ye count the cases in, sign for them and get back to sleep. Or is that ower complicated for ye?'

'Fuck off and die in the Clyde.'

'Well can ye handle the job or should we get the General in?'

'I can handle it fine.'

And Dalton slammed the little window shut to the sound of jeering laughter from outside. Later when the two trucks pulled up in Burrowes Lane he examined them and their occupants from the observation window. Satisfied that the arrivals were, in fact, wearing the uniform of the HLI he nevertheless took the further precaution of ordering his guards to stand well back with rifles loaded and ready. He himself shot the several bolts on the heavy metal door and, his hand resting on the butt of his revolver, signalled that the crates being brought from the lorries should be carried in singly and taken no further inside than the narrow loading bay.

'It'll be twenty boxes,' the Corporal in charge informed him and two men toted the first of these inside. Relaxing at the sight of very ordinary military sullenness in the face of tedious duty, Dalton indicated to his men that they could stand easy and rest their weapons while the work went on. Conor Fallon, in his role as Corporal leading the squad of counterfeit troopers, wasted no time: within seconds Dalton and his two guards were staring in incredulous silence down the barrels of half a dozen pistols.

'Where are the others?' Fallon demanded once the unfortunate

A DARKENING FIRE

trio had been swiftly disarmed and bundled into the narrow sentry space. A moment of defiant heroism on Dalton's part passed rapidly when, impatient for a reply, Fallon cocked his revolver and placed it against the other's throat.

'Upstairs. There.'

With a nod Fallon sent four of his party hurrying up to the office where the rest of the detail was asleep. In less than five minutes the guard had been corralled on the first floor, the trucks had been driven directly into the loading bay and the first of the hundred or so crates of rifles and revolvers was being carted onto the vehicles. The work was completed in three hours, by which point every rifle, revolver and several thousand rounds of ammunition had been stowed away on the transport.

'Right,' the squat, malevolent-looking Donohue, a native of Cork long resident in Edinburgh, produced a pistol rendered unwieldy by its Maxim silencer, 'let's get this finished and be on our merry way.'

His purposeful stride in the direction of the stairway was brought to a sharp halt by Fallon.

'You know what's agreed. No killing unless it has to be done. Now get back in the cab before I boot your arse from here to Kinsale.'

While this minor altercation was being resolved some cases of stout and whiskey were being toted up to the first floor.

'Mind what you're doing,' Fallon counselled the trio who had volunteered as custodians of Dalton and his terrified men. 'Not a drop for you lot. Just keep them happy till tomorrow night, then tie them up and get away quiet as you can. The car'll be here for you at two o'clock on Monday morning. Clear?'

And a moment later the rest of the gang were aboard the vehicles and being driven off slowly and carefully east along Clyde Street towards the familiar territory of the Gallowgate and on through Shettleston in the direction of Edinburgh. At the drop-off point by a remote farmhouse near the Roughrigg Reservoir the caissons were perfunctorily painted over for transportation in small numbers to the *Ailis* moored far from human habitation on the shore of Loch Nevis while the stolen trucks used in the raid were to be driven up to Perthshire and set ablaze. When the guns and

A DARKENING FIRE

ammunition had finally been placed on board the boat they were to be taken to a cove on the coast of Donegal where they could be concealed until the means of distribution had been put in place. The entire undertaking had been designed in haste and was a tribute to Taaffe's organisational skill. The Brotherhood had pooled the resources of its disparate components to commendable effect. Three days afterwards – by which time even the drunken posse left behind at Clarkson's had long made its staggering, raucous escape – Taaffe summoned Butler, Fallon, MacInerney and McGarrity to his Clydebank sanctum. Still flushed with pride in his own achievement he conducted his retrospective on the affair while pacing energetically about the room, rubbing his hands with satisfaction and already laying plans for further similar work elsewhere.

'What do you think of it now, Leo?' Butler asked in one of the few pauses in Taaffe's loquacious oration.

'When those guns are in the right hands I'll tell you,' McGarrity replied.

'Jesus, man, they'll be landed at Munterneese in a day or two. Before you know it they'll be firing practice rounds in the Blue Stack Mountains.'

'I'll say it again – when that's happened I'll join in the general rejoicing.'

'Ach,' Butler protested, 'I can't make you out any more. You're turning into a right gloomy bastard.'

'I'm for the Cause and nothing more. If lifting a few guns off the army is going to help it, then I'm your man. But if it brings the coppers down on us and damn all else we'll be up to our neck in *glár*. And make no mistake – if that happens there's more than a couple of heads I'll be breaking.'

'You worry too much, Leo,' Taaffe assured him. 'The coppers will come knocking on our doors for sure. Who the hell else would they be looking for? But they'll not have one bit of evidence. The thing is done – and we'll do more of the same.'

'You're a trusting man, Taaffe, and you shouldn't be. I bet you can't put a number to the folk you've used for this, and it only needs one to take the king's shilling to send the lot of us away for life.'

'If there's a spy among us, we'll find him and you'll deal with

A DARKENING FIRE

him.'

'Did you ever hear such *spochadh*?' McGarrity asked Fallon and MacInerney. 'By that time you'll all be festering behind bars.'

'It's only just occurred to me,' Fallon said as the conference broke up, 'that it's Christmas. Is there not a Christian man among us anymore? It's the boozer for me.'

When Taaffe, a little the worse for celebratory drink, had reeled off upstairs Butler and McGarrity were left to close the place up. On the way out Butler tentatively broached the subject of the big man's refractory mood. The reply was terse: 'I've got more to think about than the Cause just now, but I'll not let anybody down.'

Head lowered, shoulders hunched McGarrity had taken only a few steps from the door when Butler caught him up.

'Jesus, Leo, you can't leave it at that. We're not strangers, are we? Tell me – what's the trouble?'

With a display of chilling irritation McGarrity shook off the other's hand, but Butler, wincing more from the bitter wind than the big man's hostile reaction, stood his ground and held his stare.

'It's Niamh – my daughter,' McGarrity said, allowing himself to be ushered into a nearly empty pub. Drinks in hand the pair retreated to the quietest spot in the place.

'Is she ill or what?' Butler asked in a tone of urgent concern. 'What is it?'

'She's been in America for a year and a half. Writes to me every week. Or she did till more than a month ago. Nothing since. It's not like her, Joey. And it's Christmas and all.'

'Well, where is she? Is it Boston? We can get somebody to go round…'

'I've had letters from New York and Chicago and Seattle and Los Angeles. Christ knows where she is now, and I'm scared for her. She's all I've got in the world. All I've got of Róisín.'

'Think about it, Leo – she's a young woman off on a great big adventure. I'd be mad with the excitement of it if it was me and, God, I'm your age. Give her time to settle for a bit. It's a wide world out there, and everything new to see. When she has the chance to come to rest you'll be hearing from her again.'

'It was a solemn promise she made me,' McGarrity growled, not raising his eyes. 'She's Róisín's daughter – she'd keep her word

A DARKENING FIRE

for sure. I can't sleep for fear for her, Joey.'

'First Róisín and now Niamh. You need to mind yourself, big fellow.'

'Aye, well, keep this to yourself and all.'

For quarter of an hour Butler did his utmost to reassure his friend but the effort went unrewarded and as they trailed after the rest of the gang McGarrity was as deeply enveloped in gloom as he had been all afternoon. And something was playing on Butler's mind too – something that had been tiptoeing around in his memory for days. After several celebratory rounds of hard liquor were dispensed McGarrity, Butler and Fallon were hustled into MacInerney's car and carried off to Glasgow, their noisy singing of carols, from which McGarrity omitted himself, trailing through a drifting snow-shower. The festive season saw a halt to much of the normal activity of the city and McGarrity chose to excuse himself from the incautious celebrations that were planned for the Tir na nOg and other venues. He had given over the flat in the Gorbals, he said, to distant relations of his late wife - a family from Kilcar who had asked for the place over Christmas and the New Year. As a gesture of gratitude for his somewhat conditional support Taaffe had obliged him with a hideaway apartment near the river and left McGarrity with the keys and a substantial supply of whiskey.

A DARKENING FIRE
CHAPTER 7: DECEMBER 1913

Draped in a muffling fog as dense as a dream of night caves, London was clinging dourly to the undefined reality its ghosts coasted through. Little of its substance emerged from the damp grey emulsion that coated the capital's etiolated angles and edges. Figures, lethargic and disconsolate, trawled the murk gathered round the looming, fissile outline of the buildings. From the window of his office on the Embankment Sir Derwent Hartington scowled at the enveloping gloom that was stirred now and again by the doleful whine of a foghorn or the dull murmur of traffic.

Turning back into the room, he nodded briefly at his barons – the heads of the Security Service; the Secret Intelligence Service; the Metropolitan Police; the Special Branch. He had outlined the matters he wanted to address: the women's suffragist movement; Trade Union protests; 'this damned Irish Home Rule affair – apologies to our two Irish colleagues' – this directed at Patrick Quinn of the Special Branch and William Melville, head of the Special Section of the Secret Service Bureau.

Each item was addressed at length and with careful nuance for more than two hours until Hartington turned to the combined issues that he indicated were troubling him most.

'The German Secret Service still seem always to be one or two steps ahead of us. Mr. Todd's set of eyes and ears in Berlin has gathered evidence that there is at least one spy within the principal Whitehall departments. The PM is deeply concerned. The source of the leaks has to be identified in short order.'

'And your Mr. Todd can tell us what sort of material they're collecting from us at Wilhelmstrasse?' Major Kell of the Security Service wondered. 'Surely that would narrow the field of enquiry.'

'Unhappily not. There appears to be extensive interdepartmental leakage. So tighten up we must – close cooperation, gentlemen, until this has been resolved.'

After some muted grumbling Hartington went on: 'I have just become aware of this operation against the Fenians in Glasgow. I gather it involves a Special Branch officer who's been embedded in

A DARKENING FIRE

the gang. I've heard nothing more about it since. It would be appreciated, Superintendent Quinn, if in future my office could be fully apprised of such measures. I was embarrassed not to be able to provide the Home Secretary with the details when he wanted them.'

'Of course – I'll ensure that will be done.'

'My Principal Private Secretary Dr. Ackroyd was told nothing of the officer: not his name, his role or his status. Only the fact of his existence. We really can't be keeping secrets from each other at a time like this.'

'You'll understand the need for absolute secrecy in this kind of case but I'll pass all these details on to Dr. Ackroyd.'

'And so – the next item of business: these reports that the Germans have been working to produce some sort "wonder weapon." Can the SIS shed any light on this?'

'My people in Germany have nothing more than rumour for us. The consensus seems to be that it's nonsense,' Captain Smith Cummings said. 'All the same we can't afford to be complacent. I've put such material as we have to the Home Office Science Branch but so far there's too little for them to make any sort of judgement.'

'I hope that consensus is right, but I can tell you there is some possibility that it's not. A few days ago Mr. Todd secured something of a coup in enabling one of Krupp's most eminent researchers to make good his escape to this country. This man's area of expertise is –' another glance at the brief – 'in something called the disintegration of radio elements. It's all very abstruse and means little to me, but it appears indicative of an extremely dangerous development.'

'What's this refugee scientist saying about his work?' Major Kell asked. As head of MO5 he felt entitled to be irked that this information was coming to him at second hand. 'Not much point in having the man if were not clear what his claim to fame is.'

'Let me say this – Mr. Todd has managed to assure me of this man's *bona fides*. Our government scientists have had several long talks with him, but for now the little that has emerged bears on the matter we've just been looking at – this mystery weapon. Our immigrant celebrity has been leading a group of scientists at the Krupp plant in Essen. Some of the people he has brought with him have been involved in the same area of work.'

A DARKENING FIRE

'So we have some idea of what it is, or would be? An aircraft? A gun? What?'

'They are being quizzed as we speak. Julius Fučić from Manchester University is critiquing the material that has been brought from Germany. That process is, I understand, ongoing. Meantime…'

'Well,' William Melville said, 'presumably Fučić will be happy to share findings with us – when he has any?' As head of the Secret Service the quiet Kerryman did not hesitate to let the query float on a low tide of sarcasm.

'Of course. Anyhow our German had to depart Essen in such haste that most of his research papers remain locked away at Krupp. So putting together exactly what he knows and how far his work has taken him is going to be a long process. Mr. Todd is toying with the notion of trying to get hold of these papers, but I have little expectation that that can be done. What do you think, Captain Cummings? Is that feasible?'

'Nothing is impossible. Only very unlikely in this case. You don't doubt this man is who or what he says he is?'

'As I've said Mr. Todd has confirmed that all he claims for himself is true – his expertise, his background, his history.'

'And why precisely are all of us here now privy – albeit somewhat belatedly if I may say so - to the existence of this mad scientist and his monster?' Cummings asked.

'Debriefing the man will be a protracted affair. During that time it will be essential that his long-term security is assured. He's been stored away meantime at a secret location under armed guard. There is every chance that the Germans will want our prize restored to them if they can find him. Or if the worst comes to the worst, who knows…?'

'And the name of this treasure?' Kell asked.

'Dr. Joachim Rupprecht. As to his whereabouts I prefer to say nothing more at this stage. Now whoever is stealing our secrets it's beyond question that he's going to be under urgent orders to discover where the Professor is. Find the person who goes rummaging for that information.'

A DARKENING FIRE
CHAPTER 8: JANUARY 1914

The raid on the Clarkson warehouse had figured prominently in the press in the days between the event and Christmas but what concerned Taaffe was the lack of information on the progress of moving the weapons as planned. Paddy Gormley had been delegated to act as go-between: he was to accompany the guns as far as the Roughrigg hiding place and when that first leg had been successfully completed was to report back to Taaffe who had chosen to spend a few days with a girlfriend in Dundee. He was then to return to oversee their onward journey in a couple of rented trucks. The *Ailis* would not reach the west coast of Scotland until sometime in the first week of January so the entire shipment would have to be kept concealed at Roughrigg until then. And yet there had been no word and Gormley remained absent. Puzzled but not overly anxious, Taaffe kept his own counsel. There was nothing he could do but wait. As a non-driver he was unable to make his own way to Roughrigg from the east coast and anyway he was in no doubt that he and others of the circle were under surveillance. By the fifth of January, though, he could no longer contain his disquiet and late that night was climbing the stairs readying to share his mystification with Deehan who had arrived in Dundee with his wife when there was a thunderous knocking at the door. Tucking his Webley revolver into a pocket he stood half way down the lobby and, raising his voice, demanded to know who was calling.

'It's me Gormley. Hurry up, for fuck's sake. We're all deep in the shite, do you hear me?'

Taaffe swung the door open, hauled his friend inside and pushed him into the seedy living room, angrily dismissing his girlfriend and Deehan's wife who had been wakened by the racket.

'What's going on, then? What the fuck's happened now?'

Flushed and sweating despite the bitter cold inside and out Paddy Gormley threw himself down on a moth-eaten sofa.

'Christ, get me a drink first.'

With a faintly shaking hand Taaffe dispensed two tumblers of whiskey and sat down opposite the other.

A DARKENING FIRE

'Well?'

The measure of spirits would have choked a horse but Gormley had downed it in a single gulp.

'It's Sheridan. He's dead. And two others with him and all.'

'What? What the fuck are you telling me?'

'The police – the boat's been put on fire – arrests everywhere. Your man Cafferty from Manchester was chased into a canal and drowned – Torley out of Glenties shot himself before they could take him – it's a complete... - we're all fucked, Taaffe. I was near taken myself out at Roughrigg. It's the jail or run for it.'

'Calm down, will you.'

Taaffe's mind had gone blank but on the surface he remained the man in charge.

'Now let's have it. From the start.'

Gormley's account – made coherent only after another couple of whiskies – conveyed news that was far worse than anything Taaffe could have expected. It was clear that the whole operation had been betrayed from the outset: the sole reason it had been allowed to go as far as it had was so that the police could identify and rope in as many of the participants as possible. As yet there was no way to count how many arrests had been made, but it was obvious that the opportunity had been taken to spread the net over the whole area of the cells involved. Men from Dublin, Cork, Glasgow, Edinburgh, Manchester and Liverpool had already been captured; some – very few – were on the run. Probably the police had meant to let the project run more or less its full course and seize the entire gang on both sides of the Irish Sea, but they had been spotted at Roughrigg and moved in sooner. The trucks and their occupants had been detained in Perth; the volunteers from the cities had been followed and detained; the guns were back in military custody; the *Ailis* had almost made it to open water but had been set alight by gunfire from an inshore patrol vessel. Gormley had gleaned all this from Fallon and MacInerney, the only two to escape from the Lanark farmhouse, and from a drinking buddy who was a civilian clerk at police Headquarters in Glasgow.

'It'll likely be just hours before the both of us are hauled in,' Gormley concluded, mopping his brow. 'Some fucker has set this up to bag the whole crowd of us, and there'll be plenty as think it

A DARKENING FIRE

was you. You were the one that pulled the lot of us together for this. We never done nothing like it before.'

Taaffe was in no doubt that if the police didn't know of his involvement already they very soon would, and the Glasgow force was not renowned for its sensitive approach to interrogation.

'What about Butler and McGarrity? Have you heard if they're taken?'

'I don't think so. Not yet anyhow. But they've no better chance than we have if they stay put.'

'Aye, well, give me a minute. I'll pack some stuff and we'll get going. You've got the car?'

'Sure, but the coppers'll know it for certain.'

'We'll need to chance it for a bit. I know where we can get a bed for a night or two till we can get across the water.'

'Well, it better not be far. The longer we're on this side the sooner we'll be run in.'

Snatching some clothes from the bedroom and stuffing them into a battered cardboard case Taaffe bid his furious girlfriend and the Deehans a hasty farewell, checked the load in his pistol, peered out of the window to confirm that the street was deserted and followed Gormley out.

At Taaffe's direction Gormley drove his ancient pickup towards Cathcart on the south side of Glasgow where Butler's sister Maeve lived. Taaffe knew it had been closer to decades than years since the siblings had had any contact – Butler had made no secret of his disinclination to have her involved in his life, especially since her husband was a Presbyterian and a policeman who would have nothing to do with any of the Brotherhood's means and ends. Leaving the car two or three streets away from Maeve's address, Taaffe and Gormley hurried through the driven hail and to their relief found Maeve alone, her husband being off paying a festive visit to a retired colleague. Astonished to find Taaffe calling on her, she ushered the two men in to a comfortably warm sitting room decorated with a small number of Christmas cards and a limp-looking tree. But before Taaffe could explain the reason for his visit Maeve was breathlessly forestalling him.

'You've just missed him,' she said. 'He was here an hour ago, whispering something to Davie. God, I hadn't seen him for so long.'

A DARKENING FIRE

'He?'

'Joey. And now you. What's making me so popular after all this time? Not that I'm complaining, but it's all, well…'

'Aye. Look, did Joseph say what brought him here this fine New Year? And what was he on about to your man Davie?'

'God, now, I couldn't really make it out,' she said finally. 'He was that excited – so pleased with himself. All he was after was that box of stuff he wanted me to hold onto – oh, so long ago I can't remember when it was. I left it in the loft and forgot all about it, but as soon as he mentioned it, it came back to me.'

'Box? And did he ever tell you what was in it?'

Taaffe was trying not to sound as if he were interrogating her, but a troubling voice was whispering suspicion at the back of his mind.

'Oh, I don't know. I never asked. It was all locked up and I never cared for his business anyway. Were you going to be meeting him here – is that it?'

Taaffe threw a glance at Gormley.

'Aye,' he said. 'That's it. But, Jesus, it's a shame we missed him. So did he say he'd be back?'

Maeve looked confused.

'No, no. He took his box of tricks and said he'd be sure not to leave it another twenty-odd years before we… God, now, we're a strange lot, aren't we?'

'Excited, you say he was? Like excited how? Excited scared? Excited happy? What?'

Maeve was becoming uncomfortable at the tone of the conversation.

'I'm not sure. Just excited maybe. That's what I said isn't it? You'll need to tell me if there's something wrong.'

'Something wrong? Good Christ, no. It's just we wanted to see him today. Where would he be off to, do you think?'

Maeve shook her head and spread her arms in a gesture of ignorance.

'I'm sorry, Mr. Taaffe. I'm sure you'd know better than I would.'

'Maeve,' Taaffe said getting hastily to his feet, 'it's been a rare pleasure to see you again, and I promise I'll be back as soon as I

A DARKENING FIRE

can. But you'll have guessed we have things to sort out – me and Joseph, that is. In the business line.'

'But not this early in the New Year, surely?'

'Aye – it's unexpected, is all. But very important.'

Ten minutes later Taaffe and Gormley, taking brisk leave of their bewildered hostess, raced back to the car.

'I thought we were going to get a bed there,' Gormley protested, starting the vehicle with some difficulty. 'Anyway, what's Joey up to, then?'

'What do you think, you fucking idiot?'

'You're never saying he's the one gave us up?'

Taaffe's fury could be read in the deep flush of his face.

'Get a move on, will you,' he ordered, banging on the dashboard with both fists.

'Where?'

'Let's see if Leo McGarrity's still out of the net. I'll tell you where he's at.'

The drive through the empty streets took less than half an hour but again precautions had to be taken. The car was left in a nearby *cul de sac* and both men approached the shabby tenement close by the river with wary watchfulness, their revolvers concealed in their coats. In the unlikely event that McGarrity had been apprehended it was almost certain that the police would have kept the place under surveillance – but there was no reason to think that they knew of it. The close was deserted – not surprising, maybe, Taaffe thought, given the noxious odour of urine and human and animal excrement that filled the air even in the freezing winter half-light. While Gormley hunched in the malodorous shadows with his gun at the ready Taaffe tapped on the door. To their instant relief it was McGarrity who answered, yawning and stretching as he did so.

'Is it drink you're after?' he muttered, allowing the pair to squeeze past him and stand shivering in the cold, cheerless, ill-furnished room. A tiny flame played round the edge of a lump of coal in the grate and a guttering paraffin lamp tossed convulsive shadows against the peeling walls.

'Mother of God,' Taaffe said, blowing on his hands, 'what a shite-hole.'

'Aye, well, since it's yours you should know. And you're

A DARKENING FIRE

welcome to fuck off out of it, then.'

'Christ, never mind that. Listen – our lads are killed or rounded up like sheep.'

Taaffe gave a quick account of the catastrophic failure of the arms smuggling as he paced the room swinging his arms in an effort to generate some warmth. McGarrity listened in unsympathetic silence.

'They're bound to say it's down to me,' Taaffe went on. 'This was the biggest thing we ever got going over here. The whole fucking lot was my idea. Can you believe any bastard could put me in the frame for it? Jesus Christ almighty, it's more than…'

'You'll be saying next I didn't warn you. You were right cretins, the lot of you.'

'Well, it didn't happen by itself. It was given away by a Judas that…'

McGarrity interrupted him.

'You can't blame anybody but yourself. It's you buggered up the whole thing no matter who spilled the beans.'

But Taaffe was beyond listening.

'I know the bastard who betrayed us. I want you to rip the guts out of him before the day's out.'

'Now why would I do that when I can be resting here in this luxury instead?'

'Because Cafferty and Torley and God knows who else are dead, Leo. And I don't even have a clue how many are taken. We've lost the guns and the boat. Everything's been blown away because of one man – and I want him killed, but not before he sees what's going to happen to him.'

The stark catalogue of the debacle appeared to have some effect.

'Cafferty and Torley? That's a filthy stain on *your* soul, Taaffe.'
'Not mine. On Joe Butler's.'

This time the response was far from muted.

'Joey? You're off your head, man. Joe Butler's the truest Shinner among us.'

'And I'm telling you he's fucked us all. Find him and beat the bastard to a pulp.'

'Will you not hear me? Joey's the one man you can be sure of.

A DARKENING FIRE

Maybe you've got some reason of your own for setting me against him, but I'm telling you – I'll do no harm to the best man we have.'

Exasperated, Taaffe recounted what the visit to Maeve had turned up.

He paused for no more than a few seconds, then wound up: 'You remember he never carries a gun, right? Well, he's kept one hid at his sister's place since God was a boy. I know because he told me about it years ago. And now he's collected it. Why would that be all of a sudden? And he was busy bending the ear of that brother-in-law of his that's a copper at Govan.'

'Now why would a man ever talk to his wife's husband? And why wouldn't he take the gun if he thought the law might come at him?'

'It's a miracle you and me are still on the loose,' Taaffe carried on, ignoring McGarrity's point. 'Likely it's because me and Gormley here were up at Deehan's in Dundee. And you – if you'd been at that place of yours in the Gorbals you'd be back in Barlinnie by now. But you'll be next on the list and that's the truth. I'm not waiting around for a knock on the door and you bloody well better not either. You find out where Butler's at, do him and then get your arse across the water.'

'Find Joey? How would I do that even if I wanted to?'

But Taaffe was too incensed to condescend on detail.

'Things will be hot in Dublin too,' he went on and signed to Gormley to follow him to the exit, 'but it'll be safer than here. You know who to go to.'

'I'm not going back there. Not yet anyhow.'

McGarrity yanked the door open and shoved his unwanted guests out into the close. Shaken by the exchanges and already convinced the street would be alive with police Taaffe busied himself with peering into the dank darkness, impatient to get away.

'You know everywhere Butler goes,' Taaffe hissed. 'I'm ordering you – find the bastard.'

'Ordering me, is it, General Taaffe?'

'All right. Look, it's the last thing I'll ever ask of you, Leo. Settle with that toe-rag Joseph Butler and you'll never hear from me again.'

McGarrity's stare would have gone through a stone wall, but

A DARKENING FIRE

Taaffe saw the beginning of indecision behind the big man's eyes.

'Find him, Leo, and finish him.'

And Taaffe and Gormley were gone in pursuit of the rapidly diminishing prospect of freedom. It was close to midnight when McGarrity, having finished off the whiskey, caught a scuffling sound outside. Cracking open the door he heard carried with brutal clarity along the still silence of the crisp air that had abruptly replaced the turbulence of the storm, the metallic click of a pistol being cocked.

'Come out and don't look at me, Leo,' Butler said softly. 'Just cross the road there nice and easy. And keep your hands right where I can see them.'

His head lowered, McGarrity lumbered out of the close and with a slow heavy tread covered the forty feet to the river's edge.

'You're a great man, I know it,' Butler whispered. 'But there's a war coming and you're too dangerous to us now.'

'What are you at, Joey?'

'Look away from me I told you.'

As if on some cryptic cue the gale picked up again and caught a whorl of snow, sending it spiralling down the night until it disappeared in the churning water below. Like a billion lives, McGarrity thought, staring down at the end of days.

'Róisín,' he mouthed, half-aloud. Almost catching the sound of the name Butler moved forward as if to confirm the word or hear a prayer, and placed the barrel of the gun against the big man's head.

A DARKENING FIRE
CHAPTER 9: FEBRUARY 1914

Half-Welsh and half-German, The Owl had for nearly forty years run an import/export business in Hamburg and a company licensed to sell mining tools, machinery and explosives in Starnberg. For the last decade he had operated these as a conduit for passing messages between London and British agents in Germany. Overweight, middle-aged, benign in appearance and polite and accommodating in all his relationships he had never fallen under the stealthy scrutiny of either the police or the security services in his adopted homeland. He needed to keep no physical records: a raid on his home or offices would have produced nothing more than an image of a respected German executive whose thriving enterprise contributed much to the economy.

His value to the man Todd was inestimable. With his natural talent for duplicity he was a hidden portal to the activity of the German military and its associated infrastructure. Tonight he was to meet his sphinxian colleague who would be posing as a potential client with verifiable connections to a Midland engineering firm. The rendezvous was fixed for the renowned Schifferbörse restaurant much used for the transaction or completion of commercial dealings. Arriving at the location even the cautious Owl was mollified –Todd seemed hardly to exist. Average in every respect and as nearly silent as it was possible to be in mulling over fictitious business, he lingered for no longer than was necessary. The wad of documents he passed to The Owl contained nothing that could not be checked positively against the affairs of The Owl's company and that which Todd appeared to represent. In less than an hour the barely detectable presence of the man was gone and The Owl was home, ploughing patiently through a dozen leather-bound volumes to decipher the lengthy list of his instructions.

Late the next day The Owl's go-between Bertram stood shivering next to his Mercedes on an almost deserted stretch of roadway on the left bank of the Süderelbe, having contrived to have a cloud of steam rise ominously from the vehicle's bonnet. As arranged Klausen's blue Podeus pulled up behind and a hurried

A DARKENING FIRE

consultation took place as the two men set about examining the recalcitrant engine by the light of a tungsten-filament lamp. Clutching a scarf round his neck Klausen's passenger Jacob Fenner looked on from the warmth of the car. Beyond them the scarlet flecked selvage of the darkening sky was rendered intricate by the distant silhouette of the city.

'Stars,' Bertram remarked. 'There'll be ice on the roads tonight. Dangerous. Maybe you should wait until morning.'

But Klausen shook his head.

'It has to be done tomorrow,' he said as they trooped back to the Podeus, a canister of water having been poured into the radiator of the Mercedes. 'I have to be sure Eckhart Fischer is on duty.'

'Ah, yes – your avaricious collaborator.'

'We trust each other. I told you. I don't report his drinking and he doesn't care about my coming and going on weekends. We never say a word to anyone about our... little oddities.'

'Well,' Bertram moved back somewhat from the car and turned up the collar of his heavy coat, 'we're in your hands. But take no risks – my concern is for both of you.'

'I'm sure,' Fenner said, leaning across Klausen as he took his place at the wheel and extending a valedictory hand, 'Herr Klausen is a most reliable driver.'

'One last word, then,' Bertram muttered. 'If things at Essen are not exactly as they should be, forget the whole affair. Come back here and we'll work out something else.'

'Please,' Fenner answered, 'for me this is quite an adventure. It's exciting.'

'Dr. Fenner,' Bertram concluded as Klausen finally closed the window and started up the Podeus, 'don't underestimate the risk in this. If you're caught the consequences could be fatal.'

And he watched the vehicle lumber into the wintry dusk, convinced that Fenner – a scientist with no experience of the sort of project on which he was now embarking with apparently only a juvenile enthusiasm for this intoxicating novelty to propel him into extreme hazard – that Fenner, for all his impressive academic credentials, was an uncomprehending, heroic idiot. Trembling with cold under the bare sky Bertram returned to his own car and drove back to his accustomed anonymity. There was, he felt, something

A DARKENING FIRE

awry, but conveying that vague, uncomfortable conviction to his master would serve no purpose. Klausen had been reliable in the past: his post at Krupp afforded him access to a range of invaluable information which hitherto had always been channelled through Bertram and through him to The Owl himself.

The Owl had always discarded those contributions from Klausen that looked to him as if they might lay even the faintest trail for the German security and intelligence apparatus. Traps for unwary travellers were its stock in trade, and he relied on the close-mouthed Bertram as his hands-on operative. Even at his secretive remove, though, The Owl too was for once assailed by an uneasiness he was unable to shake off. His long run of success lay as much in his scepticism as in his quiet competence and the constant reliability of Bertram who would never surrender The Owl's identity, even to the like of the regularly useful Klausen. And so it troubled him that a novice like Fenner had to be deployed on this mission. The problem, though, was intractable. Its solution required the technical understanding of a specialist in the esoteric field Todd had described. Still not persuaded that what the Krupp Company was up to was anything more sinister than its tireless production of standard weaponry for half the nations of the world, The Owl was under specific orders to establish the truth. These had percolated down, he had been assured, from the highest government level. And it had been Todd, trawling through the most recent report from Klausen, who had recommended Fenner as the man most likely to be able properly to investigate what appeared to be simply a rumour circulating in the darker corners of Whitehall and Westminster.

Fenner was a chemical physicist employed by the Vickers Group in England which, until 1911, had been cooperating with Krupp on the development of artillery fuses. Not only was he well-qualified to look into the business of the putative new weapon of which he and Todd had heard vague murmurings, but he was *au fait* with the structure and dynamics of the giant German company. The Owl tended to alternate between amusement and mystification at the apparent readiness of the British to resort to the cheerful amateur in circumstances that elsewhere would have demanded the recruitment of a hardened professional. And there was another

A DARKENING FIRE

problem – Fenner had confessed that his grasp of German was tenuous, and he would have to rely on document titles, sketches, equations and recognisable references to identify the papers he was after. Not only that – the window of opportunity would be small. There would be no time for leisurely trawling through files and Klausen was in no position to advise which to purloin.

All these potential difficulties crowded in on The Owl, but exasperation quickly gave way to resignation. At best he had limited faith in Klausen and his zealous greed and The Owl's internal voice persisted that there was some aspect of the latest revelations from London that should strike him as out of kilter. Inclined to trust his own intuition rather than SIS's dogged optimism, he telephoned a coded warning to Bertram and as a precautionary measure set about clearing the decks in case his foreboding proved to be well-founded.

A DARKENING FIRE
CHAPTER 10: FEBRUARY 1914

With great care Klausen drove south west on the treacherous road surface made glassy under the clearest night sky. His executive post at Krupp's headquarters office in Essen afforded him entrance to even the most secure areas of the vast site. Some six weeks earlier, as he had explained to The Owl, he had glimpsed what at first glance appeared to be a routine contract dated some three years previously for an enormous tract of land at Freimann just north of Munich. His curiosity whetted, he had uncovered a horde of associated material containing plans for the construction of some sort of munitions facility – a project so huge it would take some years to complete. A number of things had struck him about this – that the new establishment was to be built so far from the company's main base; that the architectural blueprints provided for a degree of security that was inordinate even by Krupp's demanding standards; and that his casually incurious riffling through the pile of these papers while awaiting the start of a meeting was brought to an abrupt and angrily decisive halt when the Chairman himself had swept them up and deposited them in his personal safe.

The Company's Chairman, the spectacularly named Gustav Krupp von Bohlen und Halbach, had made only a single reference to this programme by summoning his trusted executives – including Klausen – and telling them that the project which the Freimann complex had been constructed to accommodate had now been brought to fruition; and that this information was a matter of absolute confidentiality. Not even the most tangential remark about the location or the work undertaken there was to be passed either among themselves or to anyone else. This level of secrecy was being insisted on by the Most High – the Kaiser himself – and any failure to observe the injunction would have the direst consequences. When Klausen had reported his sketchy findings to Bertram the latter had initially hesitated to bring them to The Owl's notice. The whole affair seemed too vague to merit the attention of the Foreign Section of the Secret Service Bureau. However his subsequent diligent enquiries in Bavaria had confirmed that the

A DARKENING FIRE

fortress-like structure was so tightly guarded that not even a trusted official like Klausen would be permitted the slightest opportunity to pass through its gates, far less determine what was going on there. This in itself had been enough to persuade The Owl to communicate what he had learned to Whitehall Court; and the arrival in Hamburg of the poker-faced Todd appeared to confirm that his conjecture was being treated seriously. As an administrator rather than a scientist Klausen himself had made no bones about his own inability to make sense of the voluminous documentation on the operation that he had managed surreptitiously to sift through. There had been far too much to copy in its entirety and he would have had no idea what was most relevant. At best he had recognised plans for a metallurgical laboratory, some electro-magnetic equipment and a series of diffusion devices. But whether these, abstracted from the bulk of complicated notes and diagrams, would themselves be adequate to Bertram's purpose was something Klausen could not, he claimed, begin to guess at. However his description of the extracts of the plans he had seen and made some sense of was enough to suggest the field in which Todd's agent would need to be a specialist. Fenner had done a little work for him before though none of it had been accompanied by the extreme peril attaching to the Freimann assignment.

'Good Lord,' Fenner had told his near-anonymous handler, 'you've turned me into a real spy at last.'

Unhurriedly *en route* for Essen some 250 miles away Klausen's sanguine passenger produced for his edification what looked like a heavy timepiece.

'Behold,' he said with a chortle, 'the very latest Ticka Expo Watch Camera complete with a 25 exposure film.'

Lapsing into an uncongenial silence the pair watched the deserted road twinkle hypnotically as the beam of the headlights was caught in the net of icy crystals. The freezing air edged into the vehicle and though both men wore thick coats, scarves and gloves the journey was proving far from pleasant. A little before 2 a.m. on the Sunday they stopped in Hanover to find a solitary, largely unoccupied café where they drank coffee and ignored the argumentative drunks at the next table. By five o'clock they were through Paderborn and, having refuelled the Podeus, they travelled

A DARKENING FIRE

on through Dortmund, resisting the lure of yet another gaudily-lit all-night road house.

Klausen's timetable called for their arrival in Essen by around 8 a.m. He had explained to both Bertram and Fenner that the timing was critical. Security at Krupp HQ was always tight and even as a senior executive he couldn't ordinarily expect unfettered access to the main administrative block. However Klausen knew that at the ungodly hour of their reaching the complex on a Sunday morning the security team would be at its least attentive. And it would be headed by Eckhart Fischer, who, Klausen had assured Bertram, owed his promoted post mostly to the encomia offered up by Klausen. His elevation had not been wholly unmerited but his weakness for alcohol and emotional attachment to gain were, Klausen had gone on, a vulnerability to be encouraged and exploited. Klausen's generous bestowing of the best brandy and his frequent gifts of money and jewellery for Fischer's wife ensured a relationship uncomplicated by formality.

Having negotiated the double barrier at the main gate where the familiar vehicle was casually saluted by two yawning sentries, Klausen parked his car and with Fenner in tow headed straight for the security detail office which commanded from some height a panoramic view of the vast courtyard that lay behind the site's entrance. As he had anticipated only Fischer and one other guard were present, the rest of the team lazily patrolling the enormous spread of the near-silent plant. Jumping to his feet behind his desk Fischer greeted his visitors and hurried to conduct the formalities.

'Good to see you, Herr Klausen,' he said while his companion stared glumly out at the colourless dawn seeping into the city. 'Must be something special on to bring you in today, eh?'

'Afraid so, Eckhart. This is Mr. Fenner – don't know if you remember him from the days when we were working with Vickers.'

Fischer peered at the genial Englishman of whose career at Vickers he knew nothing.

'Of course,' he lied. 'Welcome back.'

'I have to confess I'm at fault,' Klausen went on. 'A great fat file that should have gone back to Vickers an age ago is still nestling in my office. The whole thing has become rather urgent, so sleepless nights for forgetful Klausen. Still – nobody to blame but myself. If

A DARKENING FIRE

you can let me have the keys to the block, Eckhart, we shouldn't be more than an hour or so while I make sure the package is complete.'

'Certainly, sir. But please – not over one hour. That'd be more than my job's worth.'

As Fischer reached down the jangle of keys from a wall cabinet his underling turned away from his bleak survey of the somnolent world outside.

'I'll take these gentlemen,' he said. 'It'll save you the trouble, boss.'

'Gebstattel, isn't it?' Klausen put in hastily as he stood up. 'That's all right, old boy. We wouldn't dream of dragging you away from the fireside on a day like this. Here you are, lads,' he went on, passing out a handful of huge cigars, 'that'll maybe help to keep the cold at bay. We *will* need you to escort us out, of course – can't rescue you from that. But we'll try to conduct the operation as speedily as possible.'

The four men shared a perfunctory laugh, Fenner having barely a notion of what was going on.

'Very kind of you, sir,' Gebstattel said, sniffing a cigar appreciatively and subsiding with a contented sigh into one of the chairs just vacated.

'Just one small thing,' Fischer said, giving the appearance of being slightly embarrassed. 'I do really need to have a look in your briefcase. Now and on the way out. And I'm afraid I'll be obliged to search Herr Fenner at that stage.'

'Naturally.'

The glance at the scant contents of the case over, Klausen and Fenner made their way along the echoing corridor past yet another guard who merely nodded at them and concentrated on maintaining a condition of semi-wakefulness. Having unlocked two heavy oak doors, and having carefully locked them again from the other side, Klausen led his companion at a fast pace to the suite – also locked, but quickly opened with a rapid fumble of keys – identified in its significance by a brass plate large enough to accommodate the Chairman's ornate name.

'There won't be a problem,' Klausen insisted. 'We have one hour. There will be no suspicion. But you must work quickly. Now…'

A DARKENING FIRE

He swung away from the wall a large painting by von Hunthorst to reveal a safe countersunk into the ornate stonework.

'A small confession,' Klausen went on, grinning at Fenner. 'I have a duplicitous side to me. Who would have thought it? I've watched this thing being opened and closed so often that it might as well be my own. Bear with me one moment.'

With a steady hand he spun the dial several times and a quick tug on the handle opened the armoured door.

'We should hurry now, I think,' Klausen said, glancing at his watch.

'Please,' Fenner objected, laying a hand on the other's shoulder. 'You said it yourself – we must be doubly careful that there can be no suspicion that the contents have been disturbed.'

And nudging Klausen to one side he began to remove the pile of documents one by one, scrutinising them with professional proficiency and speed as he did so. Rapidly as the process was performed it was more than half an hour before Fenner had satisfied himself that he had identified the 25 most significant notes and diagrams. Producing the watch camera and steadying his elbows on the leather inlay, he set about photographing each target form.

'For God's sake, man,' the German said, 'Eckhart will be sending Gebstattel to look for us any second. We've been here ten minutes over our time as it is.'

'Quite; quite.'

Fenner seemed pleased with himself.

'Here,' he said, passing the watch camera to Klausen, 'tuck that in your pocket while I tidy this up.'

Almost dancing with anxiety Klausen put away the camera, crossed the carpet and held the door ajar, listening.

'Oh, Christ, I hear someone. You've no idea what they'll do to us if...'

But before he could conclude his half-whispered warning Fenner had closed the safe, moved the painting back in place, switched off the lamp and was giving Klausen a friendly shove into the corridor.

'Keys,' he instructed and in a moment the office was secure behind them.

But it was true – footsteps were echoing beyond the passage

A DARKENING FIRE

door and the lock was being noisily turned.

'Which is your office?'

Klausen nodded at the door a few feet to their left. Betraying an unexpected athleticism, Fenner bounded to it and was hunched over the knob brandishing the ring of keys when Gebstattel came crashing into view.

'Just finished,' Fenner reported in atrocious German. 'Can you give me a hand to lock this... ah, there we are. All done. Sorry if we've overstayed our welcome a bit.'

Catching a bare hint of meaning from the mispronounced stream of ruined grammar the guard said, 'That's all right, gentlemen. Best just check, though.'

And he rattled the handle of Klausen's office door. Content that all was in order he concluded, 'If you'll follow me... '

Back in the observation post a few minutes later Fenner was calmly submitting to a brisk search of his person and then accepting Fischer's offer of a cup of coffee which Klausen declined with an air of irritation and gestured at the wall clock with some impatience.

'Are you all right, Herr Klausen?' Fischer asked, closely studying the other's precipitate discomfort.

'Unfortunately,' Fenner put in as smoothly as his limited linguistic ability permitted, 'we two have had words. The papers I've come all this way for are not here. We can only hope that they are, as Herr Klausen now seems to believe, in storage in Hamburg.'

His coffee finished at leisure, Fenner politely shook hands with the sentries and indicated that he would be delighted to have Gebstattel escort them back to the Podeus. It was now daylight and a trickle of weekend employees was being checked in via the main gate.

'Jesus,' Klausen managed as he turned on the engine, 'you're a cool one. I thought the game was up for us there. My compliments, Herr Fenner. You are a true professional.'

Fenner allowed himself a small smile.

'Not at all, old chap. Not even a remotely gifted amateur.'

And he was still smiling when the bullet shattered the windscreen and blew a gaping hole in his forehead.

A DARKENING FIRE
CHAPTER 11: MARCH 1914

Inspector Gordon Mitchell of the City of Edinburgh police had until now enjoyed an impeccable reputation and a career free of blemish. He had been an obvious choice to head the guard detail placed on Talbot House outside the village of South Queensferry. He had been informed of neither the names of the party lodged there nor the reason for their being sequestered there nor from what or whom they were to be protected. The house itself was not particularly remote. It sat on the margin of the Dalmeny hamlet and was surrounded by a generous walled garden. The place had been in constant use for years, occasionally as the venue for small-scale military or naval conferences or as a temporary residence for visiting dignitaries or apparatchiks. Its being regularly employed in this way ensured that there was no novelty to its being occupied and under guard.

Domestic staff were deployed through the day on housekeeping and kitchen work and left the building each evening; but the current occupants appeared to have little need for their assistance. The group comprised three men and two women, but their presence went practically unnoticed – the principal seldom emerged from the self-contained suite where he was billeted on the second storey, while the others spent most of their time either with him or in the tiny laboratory that was still in the process of being completed on the first floor next to the bedrooms leading off the landing. Each dusk Mitchell had made a habit of inspecting all the windows and making certain that they were locked and shuttered, that the rear door was double-bolted and could not be opened from outside. Occasionally, though, the bulky Karoline Petzold would wander out through it to breathe in the freezing air that lay on the protracted winter's last snows or, accompanied by guards, to stroll shivering along the bank of the River Forth. It emerged casually in the course of these excursions that the residents were Germans who, they said, had been invited to carry out some undefined scientific research on behalf of the British government. This work was described as largely statistical but also of a clinical nature and

A DARKENING FIRE

related to some obscure tropical disease. They had introduced themselves as Professor Joachim Rupprecht, his principal researcher Dr. Rheinhold Sauer; his personal physician Dr. Manfred Klein; his assistant Hanna Blindt; and Karoline Petzold who acted as a general administrator. But beyond a somewhat cheerless exchange of names there was little interaction between the residents and their security detail.

Working up a routine that would satisfy both his officers and his wards, Mitchell ensured that at no point, night or day, was the place without a sentry near the main door and an officer patrolling the corridors. Once in a while Rupprecht would send down a scrawled note of his requirements and bits and pieces of lab equipment for Dr. Klein which would be delivered by a local. Other materials were brought in discreet vehicles bearing officials with Home Office or War Office identity documents. In the small hours of Wednesday 18th Mitchell, having put in an unusually long shift himself, was wakened from a deep sleep by the sound of raised and frantic voices from the front hall. Grabbing his revolver he stumbled out into the pitch-dark passageway and felt a sudden, freezing blast from the rear entrance where the door, normally bolted shut, was open just wide enough for Mitchell to see a band of brilliant white stars beyond the eight-foot wall that enclosed the estate. From the opposite direction loud voices instantly gathered volume and urgency; and a moment later one of the guards carrying a lantern torch in one hand and a Lee Enfield in the other came rushing out of the gloom with Hanna Blindt in his wake.

'Where is he?' she kept demanding. 'The Professor – where is he?'

Mitchell held up a restraining hand.

'Where the hell is…?'

But before he could finish the question the front door of the building, nearly fifty feet down the corridor from where he was standing, burst open and, accompanied by two troopers, the Constable delegated to sentry duty in the hall appeared, shivering with cold, caped in snow and his rifle at the ready.

Much later that day, Mitchell, humiliated by his failure to ensure the protection of the Germans, stood flushed, flustered and at rigid attention in the office of Chief Constable Roderick Ross.

A DARKENING FIRE

Mitchell's embarrassed return to the city had been fraught – the night before and the following morning had seen a heavy fall of snow and it had been only with the greatest difficulty that the car journey into Edinburgh had been safely achieved. The Inspector was accompanied by the officer who had deserted his post at the urging of the military. The Germans were too visibly distraught to be of much use, besides which he was convinced that they could contribute nothing to the interrogation he was about to be subjected to. His hurried phone call to police HQ had brought a posse of armed police to Talbot House along with a team of bloodhounds which turned out to be of little help. By the time they arrived several inches of snow had fallen and the pristine splendour of the grounds afforded neither sight nor scent to guide them. A man accustomed to maintaining an air of calm in any circumstance the Chief Constable eyed the unhappy Mitchell for almost a minute before gesturing to him to sit down. That invitation was not extended to the fidgeting Constable. Mitchell made to embark on his account of the nocturnal events but Ross held up his hand and tapped the telegram that lay in front of him.

'The thing is out of my hands,' he said. 'I'm told others will be conducting this investigation. I have a wire here from Sir Edward Troup at the Home Office that informs me I'm to surrender all authority in this matter. I believe that... '

He was interrupted by a discreet tap at the door.

'The Branch man has just arrived, sir,' a secretary announced. 'Will I...?'

'Please... '

The Constable moved aside out of the way of the newcomer. Ross stood up and rounded his desk, extending a hand to his not especially welcome guest. Only the previous day Sir Derwent Hartington and his team had been cloistered with the refugees and now their most valued asset had been removed from the scene. Reputations, Ross knew, were lining up to be seriously injured.

A DARKENING FIRE
CHAPTER 12: MARCH 1914

With some justification Theobald Bethmann-Hollweg would complain to his senior colleagues that, despite his role as Chancellor he came a poor second – in terms of access to the Kaiser and the exercise of power – to Conrad Schweitz. This official was not only made welcome at the Stadtschloss where he counselled Wilhelm on every issue taking the Emperor's interest, but was granted the unique privilege of a private army which, though numbering only about twenty, consisted of a cadre of the most senior officers and their small support staff. It was to this mysterious figure that the British Embassy's First Secretary Sir Christopher Cresswell was now making restrained but irate representation.

'A most unhappy incident,' Schweitz agreed. 'But you must understand that our officers have an onerous and sometimes dangerous duty to perform.'

'Which appears to involve shooting to death an unarmed and completely innocent man,' Cresswell replied, making no attempt to disguise under his diplomatic urbanity a tone of acid incredulity.

'Unfortunately we have as yet no device that can measure the lethality of a suspect's intention. I'm assured that Herr Fenner was seen to reach for what, in that uncertain light, appeared to be a weapon...'

'Preposterous. Herr Fenner was shot in a vehicle at close range.'

'Yes. A vehicle being driven at high speed straight at officers signalling it to stop. Does it not tend to confirm the legitimacy of their action that the driver then fled from the car and has yet to be apprehended?'

'But since it wasn't the driver who was targeted I fail to see the logic of the action.'

'You will forgive me if I point out that when events are moving so quickly logic may not inform decisions.'

Having been ordered by Whitehall to establish the events surrounding the death by gunfire of a British citizen on a bleak Sunday morning in Essen Cresswell was all too aware of the

A DARKENING FIRE

impenetrable wall being erected between him and a successful completion of that assignment.

'It must have been evident,' he persisted, 'that Herr Fenner was doing nothing but sit in the passenger seat of the car.'

'But, my dear Sir Christopher, I'm advised that he had just broken into one of the most secure secret installations in our country; and we have good reason to believe that he had been taking photographs of highly confidential documents in the course of that trespass. Please feel free to designate Herr Fenner an innocent man, but the evidence hardly supports that contention. In fact, we here were of a mind to lodge a formal protest with your government.'

'But no camera was found on his person. He was accompanied by a senior employee of Krupp who had every right to be on the premises.'

'Not, however, in the office where he and Herr Fenner are now known to have been.'

'Ah, but, good God, a camera would surely have served as proof of wrong-doing and you have no such proof that it even exists.'

Schweitz sighed.

'It is hardly unreasonable to assume that the man Klausen made off with the camera itself.'

He spread his hands as if intending to upturn an invisible table.

'I regret that our police have not as yet succeeded in tracking down Klausen but you may be sure he will be found in due course. In any event you must understand that this incident has done nothing to improve relations between our countries.'

From the outset of his mission Cresswell had been under no illusion that whatever information he was going to glean it would shed no light on the real details of Fenner's demise. A few hours later Klausen, giving every appearance of a man already submerged in a tide of hysteria, was tapping with surreptitious urgency on the secluded back door of Bertram's home. Able to go no further than half-concealing his anger at this prohibited incursion, his reluctant host ushered the German into the plushly furnished lounge. Even as he reminded his visitor that such contact had been expressly forbidden Bertram spoke calmly, if not exactly reassuringly.

A DARKENING FIRE

'It puts us all in the greatest peril,' he said, dispensing a comforting brandy for his unwelcome guest.

'What else could I do? Fenner is dead. The police are searching my house. There are road-blocks everywhere. I got this far only by dumping my own car and stealing that thing I've left round the corner. And I fell into a damn stream in the dark – look at me. My clothes are ruined, I'm wet through and I'll probably die of pneumonia before the authorities catch up with me.'

'Perhaps we can both draw some consolation from that prospect, then.'

'Don't talk to me like that. I've risked my life… Listen… '

And Bertram sat in silence through a hasty account of the derailed operation.

'We were betrayed – that's obvious,' Klausen concluded. 'And that must mean it's only a matter of time before you're exposed too, so my turning up now is neither here nor there.'

'I agree. I've made my own arrangements already. To be frank I'm more than surprised that you made it this far.'

Wiping his damp forehead and raising his glass with a trembling hand, Klausen replied, 'It's true. More luck than skill, I admit it. I'm not cut out for this. But where do I go now? I have to look to you for help.'

'Yes. Well, we can both be gone by tonight if all's well. By separate ways, for certain, but by tomorrow evening we should be together again in England. But first – the most urgent thing I need to deal with: the camera. Is it with the police or did you…? '

With a triumphant flourish Klausen produced the item from the folds of his soaking coat. The watch was slightly dented and had clearly been immersed in water, but Bertram lacked the expertise to judge whether the film it contained was likely to be damaged. Meantime Klausen was evidently relieved to hear that his escape from the clutches of the police had already been considered. Aware of The Owl's early conviction that the mission felt wrong Bertram picked up the telephone, wound the handle, obtained the number he wanted, waited briefly for a reply and, without elaboration, uttered half a dozen words that might have been in Russian, Cymraeg or Greek so far as Klausen could make out, but which were actually in Welsh.

A DARKENING FIRE

'You'll be travelling as Frau Wagener,' Bertram told him, having received The Owl's instructions. 'Your transportation will be with us in fifteen minutes. All your documents will be in the vehicle together with your instructions. When you reach the port you will be welcomed by your husband. Please reciprocate his embrace – ' Klausen, wide-eyed with incredulity, made to interrupt but the effort was perfunctorily waved away – 'and link his arm going up the gangplank. The vessel is called *Selene*.'

Recovering momentarily, Klausen was compelled to be impressed by the other's calm and the astonishing speed with which the emergency was being met.

'And you?' he asked.

'It's better that you don't know.'

'And the camera?'

'Goes with neither of us. Don't worry – nothing has ever gone astray since the protocol was put in place. Packages are more easily dealt with than people.'

'Very good. Very good.' And Klausen again dabbed at his brow.

'Then follow me,' Bertram ordered. 'You have about five minutes to change your identity and your gender. I trust that an elegant blonde will be a satisfactory transformation.'

And several miles away The Owl also was preparing a hasty departure.

A DARKENING FIRE
CHAPTER 13: MARCH 1914

Taaffe's sense of injustice was mitigated, he grudgingly acknowledged, by the miracle of his survival. Escaped from the shambles of the Glasgow raid, he had made his surreptitious and circuitous way to Dublin leaving behind the wreckage of several cells of the organisation. Confronted by Séamus Boylan and a jury of his lieutenants Taaffe had feared the worst from the very moment of his arrival back in the city. It had been with an air of resignation that he had presented himself to the Brotherhood's Military Council prepared to mount an energetic defence of his actions but grimly persuaded that a sympathetic hearing was the last thing he would be granted. In this conviction he was hardly disappointed and, eliciting no response from Boylan and his glowering judges while he presented his case, assumed early in the proceedings that his reward would be a bullet in the brain and a shallow grave in the Wicklow Hills.

'You're either a right fucking idiot,' the thug Rogan had informed him when he'd paused for breath, 'or a traitorous bastard. Either way you've got guts coming here and putting your hands up to it. But guts won't save your stupid hide. You've lost us the best of men and every bloody penny that whole thing cost to put together.'

Taaffe had known better than to offer a response as he stood at near attention, his thumbs pressed against his thighs, sweat coursing down his spine. There had been a murmur of agreement from the row of hostile comrades behind the long table.

'Are you done?' Boylan had asked Taaffe. 'Have you another word to say on the thing?'

'I've finished. We were betrayed by a man I would have trusted with my life. If the fault is mine, then do what you want and then say a *paidrín* for me. But never doubt this – I'm your man through and through.'

'This isn't a fucking debate about whose fault it was,' Rogan had remarked. 'You've said it yourself – the whole *cíor thua thail* is down to you.'

And for the best part of an hour Taaffe had been obliged to

A DARKENING FIRE

listen to an increasingly rancorous argument about the severity of the judgement to be visited on him. Boylan had allowed the exchanges to flare to ebullition, observing from his patrician silence the gradual cohering of view.

'You've served us well enough,' he had agreed when the wrangling had subsided into a slough of reciprocal scowling and imprecation, 'but by Christ it'll take a longer time to repair the damage you've managed to preside over.'

There had followed a protracted interstice into which a brew of ominous suspense and minatory petulance was decanted.

'Maybe,' Boylan had finally gone on, 'what's left of your house is now in order. You can be sure I'll make it my business to find out the state it's in. But for now I need you. It was Butler, wasn't it, that did all our talk for us with Protzman?'

'Aye, Joey it was.'

'Well, the thing is this – you better get to your man Protzman and sort out a delivery of guns yourself, and in a damn hurry. Your *hames* on the Clyde cost us losses we can't afford so you get your arse over to Hamburg or wherever Protzman is and get some Mannlichers with whatever's left in your wee purse. And no more of his vague promises, mind. A sure date and place for them. And don't come back here without a copper-bottomed guarantee.'

'On my life.'

'Oh, aye – have no doubt about that. Now, I wouldn't want you to get too lonely on the trip or get lost along the way. So Antony and Brendan here will chum you there and back.'

Antony Breslin and Brendan Keegan – part-timers at the St Rollox works in Glasgow – had contributed nothing to the proceedings beyond their dead-eyed stare.

'I know where to find Protzman all right,' Taaffe had acknowledged, 'but that doesn't mean he'll listen to me. He only ever trusted Butler.'

'Aye, and very wise *that* turned out to be,' Boylan had observed sourly. 'Anyhow, Tony and Brendan can be persuasive enough. So get on with it.'

Still nursing a resentment directed against a generalised fate and the particular machinations of his betrayer, Taaffe now found himself lounging uncomfortably in Protzman's elegant apartment on

A DARKENING FIRE

the Agnesstrasse in the Winterhude district of Hamburg, conscious of his host's ill-suppressed exasperation at the intrusion. Half a lifetime of practised evasion had ensured that Taaffe along with his adherent companions had had no difficulty avoiding the nationwide notice of the authorities as they made their journey by fishing boat from Dun Laoghaire to a deserted stretch of coastline near Maen y Bugael on the north coast of Wales where the trio were collected by a car driven by Breslin's cousin. From Dover they had caught the ferry to Ostend. By the time they had reached Hamburg Taaffe's relationship with his posse had improved to the extent that they managed to exchange the occasional word. Protzman, however, made no effort to conceal his annoyance at being bearded in his den, especially by these pressing guests.

'You're lucky to have caught me here – I'm giving up this place tomorrow.'

'We have a problem,' Taaffe told his host. 'The Ulster Volunteer crowd in Belfast are near to having a big delivery of weapons from Denmark.'

'I know,' he said. 'My man Benny Spiro here in Hamburg is arranging it...'

'Then how the hell do you think us republicans are going to be able to fight our corner? You said you wanted to help *us*, not *them*.'

Protzman said nothing for a minute. The prospect of keeping the British occupied with violent unrest in Ireland was one to be encouraged, and Protzman's masters cared a good deal less for the cause of Irish independence than for promoting a possible civil war on the island which would absorb the full resource of the British military. That, though, was not the position he intended to convey to Taaffe.

'Then we have some alternative means to assist you.'

'Aye – the guns.'

'Of course. Let's discuss that in a moment. But bear this in mind.'

Protzman got up, strolled to the window and looked down at the almost empty street.

'Our scientists,' he began, talking as if he were examining his own words for their half-concealed significance, 'have succeeded in creating a bomb so powerful that it could devastate the biggest city.

A DARKENING FIRE

A single bomb, I say.'

He left the assertion to impact on Taaffe who combined sardonic disbelief with a shrug of indifference.

'Aye, so you told Butler. We kept that to ourselves for what it's worth.'

'The man most responsible for its development became so horrified at what he managed to create that he deserted us as soon as the thing was nearing completion. It appears that his intention was to make his knowledge available to the British. He thought if both they and we had access to the sort of device he had designed, neither of us would be so foolish – or perhaps I should say so suicidal – ever to deploy it.'

'Well, that's fine and dandy, isn't it? If you're telling me the truth, you're no better off with the thing than you'd be without it.'

Protzman tapped the ash from his cigarette.

'I'm pleased to say we've retrieved the situation. Luckily we have tracked him down before he had the opportunity to divulge much more than the most basic information about the thing. Of course their scientific community will even now be poring over that, but even if they have the knowledge or expertise to make sense of it, it would take them years, or even decades, to build their own version.'

Still unconvinced that all this could bring advantage to the republican cause, Taaffe responded with aggressive sarcasm.

'So these things will blow London into the Thames, is that it? Christ, you must be the only man in the world who has to get Holy Communion on a shovel.'

'What? Never mind – and I can't tell you how many of these devices we have. But I *can* tell you this – we won't need to fire it from a gun.'

Protzman turned back into the middle of the room.

'Most parts of these bombs are already in place. In at least one English city. I'll tell you no more than that. They've been put together piece by piece by our agents there. One by one and over many weeks. Subject to a simple process of completion we will be able to detonate the bombs at any time of our choosing.'

'Look, I don't give a shite what you do to London or any other bloody place. I couldn't care less. But it's obvious – the Brits will

A DARKENING FIRE

come after us if they're not traipsing down into France.'

'Have no concern on that score. When the time is ripe you'll have the German army by your side. And we can always use the threat of the bombs to persuade the British to give up on your small island. So if you want to go ahead with your little rebellion, of course we can supply you with weapons. We were always prepared to do that. If you want them sooner rather than later, Benny Spiro can accommodate you. He's already contracted to do so with others of your party – Casement and Childers. But in your case he'll have some unanticipated and pressing work to do which will require financial recognition.'

'Fair enough. Here...'

And Taaffe placed a sealed package on the arm of his chair.

'We're not rich, but that's my offer.'

Protzman nodded slowly, tossed his cigarette butt into the fire and slit the package open.

'No,' he agreed, 'you're not rich, are you? Still, I have one suggestion as to how you can make good the shortfall.'

Taaffe hesitated, his suspicions aroused.

'What is it?'

'Oh, a simple thing, but it will assure you and your comrades in Ireland of my good offices.'

'Go ahead.'

'When I told you that we would be in a position to explode the bombs concealed in England I should have made something clear. To do that we need our technicians there to insert a very particular type of material in a certain component – a sort of gun barrel.'

'You want me to give you a screw-driver, is that it?'

'Ah, you joke and I see you smile. But no. Obviously Herr Butler did not confide *all* the details to you. We had agreed, you see...' a pause accompanied by a sardonic smile. 'These pieces of equipment I mentioned are highly complex. Very sophisticated; very delicate. So I look to you to deliver them to my people in England.'

'Christ, you're a halfpenny short of a shilling. What do you think the customs at Dover would make of it? We'd be in Brixton before my arse was off the boat.'

'What?'

A DARKENING FIRE

Taaffe explained in unvarnished English.

'Not at all,' Protzman replied when the anatomically inconceivable was cleared up. 'The pieces have been designed and labelled to look like an item required by the St Rollox Company in Glasgow for their fireless locomotives.'

'Well?'

'I look to you to deliver these items.'

'*What?*' Taaffe was incredulous. 'Why don't your own folk take the damn things to England? You just said they took all the other bits and pieces.'

'Because,' Protzman said in a tone of pained patience, 'our network has become dangerously exposed. Most of our best agents are known to the British.'

Taaffe shook his head. He doubted that he was being told the truth but he was at a loss to know how to pursue the argument. And Protzman chose that moment to complicate the affair even further.

'Oh, and one thing more.'

Rolling his eyes Taaffe said, 'Oh, Christ, now what?'

'It appears that this man Gallagher of yours, useful as he has been, has proved a weak link in the chain of your interests. If your people find themselves – what shall I say – lacking in certain funds, it's because Gallagher seems to have been syphoning off a great deal of money from what's collected in London to support your efforts.'

'Eoghan Gallagher? Never. He's our man through and through.'

Protzman held up a hand.

'You must understand,' he said patiently, 'that all our plans – yours and mine – need to be very carefully coordinated and guarded. Neither can we on this side of the Channel nor your colleagues in Ireland countenance this betrayal. It's not just a question of theft; it's an exposure of deep failure in your organisation. So I trust you will understand that an early and permanent solution to the problem is necessary.'

Keegan stepped forward, no longer prepared to maintain his sullen taciturnity.

'Eoghan Gallagher is a friend of mine. I've known him since we were lads. You couldn't get a better man for the cause. You're a fucking liar, Protzman – you're up to something. Give me the nod,

A DARKENING FIRE

Taaffe, and I'll beat it out of him.'

'My only concern in this is my own security and yours too. Please don't let sentiment get in the way. From what I've heard you've suffered enough from traitors in your own ranks.'

'So,' Taaffe said, half to himself, 'Gallagher threw his lot in with Butler. Maybe we should have seen it coming, the bastards. They saw too much of each other.'

Keegan, his face pale with a draining emotion, retreated from the others and, turning his back, butted his forehead twice against the wall.

'We are agreed, then?' Protzman asked. 'It will be done? The fuses delivered and Gallagher dealt with. Gentlemen, let me get you to Bavaria. You'll like it. And things will become clearer to you there.'

'Look at that,' Breslin muttered, staring out of the window. 'Rain. Snow's going. They say it'll be a glorious summer.'

A DARKENING FIRE
CHAPTER 14: MARCH 1914

'Inspector McGarrity, isn't it?' Chief Constable Ross rose to greet the newcomer.

'Yes, sir. I believe London has been in touch with you?'

'I'm aware of the extent of your authority. A Dr. Ackroyd came rushing here to make sure I was going to be adequately complaisant. You've just missed him in fact. He shot off to Talbot House seething at our astounding incompetence and then demanded transport back to Waverley. Your Superintendent Quinn assured him his best qualified man was on the job but that didn't seem to mollify him. As I say, he's off to London nursing his metropolitan outrage.'

McGarrity glanced at the others in the room, then at Ross's signal strode to the chair which had been vacated by the sheepish Inspector Mitchell. Having for weeks been preoccupied to the point of boredom with the winding up of the Clarkson operation he was not averse to undertaking a fresh commission, and he wasn't surprised that Superintendent Quinn had put it his way. His being only forty miles away from the scene he was the perfect candidate.

'I've no intention,' he said, 'of usurping your position, sir. Any action you want to take in this business, any personal involvement will be fine by me. I haven't come here to throw my weight around.'

The Chief Constable resisted the temptation to remark on the man's menacing dimensions.

'Believe me, Inspector, I'm delighted to be relieved of this affair, especially after Ackroyd's fulminating flying visit.'

'Fair enough. I take it these gentlemen are here to report what they know about your man Rupprecht's disappearance. Are you content to hear what they have to say?'

'Inspector, unless you would prefer that I stay, I'll be more than happy to leave you to it. There is just one thing, though – if you don't mind satisfying my curiosity in front of these lads.'

McGarrity shrugged.

'Dr. Ackroyd had heard a rumour that you'd been shot and dumped in the Clyde. I assume from your presence that the report

A DARKENING FIRE

wasn't entirely accurate. Would you care to enlighten me…?'

'A man with a gun to my head got himself an inch too close,' McGarrity told him tonelessly. 'I broke his neck.'

And Joey Butler had disappeared forever into the coagulating waters of the Clyde.

What McGarrity learned from the witnesses in front of him was that in the small hours of the morning two breathless soldiers had arrived at the front door of the mansion and alerted the sentry to their having been in pursuit of two suspected terrorists. There had been a long-standing anxiety that Irish republicans would attempt to blow up the Forth Rail Bridge supports on the south side of the river. A permanent guard had been put in place and a small makeshift base had been erected close to the Hawes Brae to accommodate a detachment of KOSBs. The weather had started to deteriorate around midnight when a patrol had spotted what looked like a group of men clambering on the huge concrete block on which the end pillar of the bridge rested and trying to fix something at its juncture with the pylon itself. Visibility was too poor to be certain but the guards had challenged the intruders who took advantage of the swirling snow to make off up the hill in the direction of Dalmeny village. There had been the sound of something heavy being tossed into the river but so far there had been no sign of what that might have been, nor was there any indication of a successful effort to attach explosives – or anything else – to the bridge support. While the likelihood couldn't be discounted that the interlopers were either drunks or recalcitrant youths, the troopers had set off in pursuit. On the verge of abandoning the hunt the soldiers heard what sounded like a pistol shot which persuaded them that some kind of attack on the bridge really had been under way. By that time they were enveloped in a blizzard and it was only because they were equipped with lanterns and hot on the heels of their quarry that they managed to follow them, stumbling up the slope, through the trees and into vague sight of the great house.

The indications, becoming harder to determine with every step, were that the runaways had climbed the iron gate and disappeared into the vast garden. Wanting to ensure the safety of the occupants, of whose identity they knew nothing, the pursuers, also scrambling

A DARKENING FIRE

over the barbed wire laid along the top of the gate, had rapped at the door and finding themselves confronted by an armed policeman quickly explained their presence and enlisted his assistance as a guide familiar with the layout of the grounds. However the snow storm had become so violent that in a matter of minutes it was obvious that there was no prospect of finding any tell-tale tracks. It was when the officer and the pair of cold and exhausted troopers arrived shortly afterwards at the entrance to the building that they witnessed the turmoil in the hall.

Mitchell confirmed that a careful search had been made of the whole house and the grounds and that it had uncovered no clue as to what had happened to account for the Professor's disappearance. Every member of the household had been questioned, also to no avail. Even the rear entrance remained firmly bolted and there was no sign of any sort of struggle either in the house or grounds. No-one could offer an explanation for Rupprecht's sudden departure and no-one had witnessed his going. Despite the Germans' having been at the house for months Mitchell agreed that he had little idea what they were doing other than that they were said to be involved in some medical research. Why, in that case, they should have been provided with an armed guard and secure accommodation remained unclear to him except that he imagined that the material being researched was either itself potentially dangerous or the work was so valuable that it needed to be protected.

Not much enlightened, McGarrity summoned the Chief Constable's secretary and arranged immediate transportation to South Queensferry. Ross had already made provision for a number of officers to accompany him and to reinforce the effort already well in hand to secure a wide area around the village and to conduct house by house enquiries there and at the hamlet of Dalmeny. The snow had continued to fall heavily and without let-up and the short journey from the city took longer than suited McGarrity whose timetable was becoming tighter by the minute. An instruction to catch the 10pm sleeper to London struck him as an imbecilic diversion. By the time the party arrived at Dalmeny the wind was driving the late but unrelenting snow across the Forth and flailing the naked branches of the birches and chestnut trees that lined the high wall around the house. It was not hard to see why the

A DARKENING FIRE

bloodhounds, now whining in the confines of a black van, had been of no help in the search, and certainly any footprints that might have been revealing had long since been obliterated by the snowstorm. While the newly arrived body of police officers and military were allocated their duties McGarrity made a speedy inspection of the outside of the building which, not surprisingly, proved to be unrevealing, and then toured the inside of the house with Mitchell and one of his officers in tow. All the windows were locked and the shutters firmly in place as they had been, he was assured, since the preceding day. Before he could continue his inspection a figure emerged from the shadows of the stairwell and, waving a document identifying him as one of Major Kell's Home Section operatives, gave his name as Kavanagh.

'I've been in Rosyth for a couple of days, so it didn't take me long to answer the summons,' he announced, stifling a yawn. 'You might be interested in something I picked up over there.'

'And that is?'

'Not sure this is tied in with your evaporating academic, but I've been having words with a Sub-Lieutenant Drew over at Rosyth. The night Rupprecht departed our midst Drew was in command of one of these little inshore boats. Brand new patrol rota. It seems that the searchlight picked up what a matelot declared was a small submarine near the south bank of the estuary. The thing must have dived and fled or never really existed, because a search turned nothing up. Drew had reported this but it was left to fester on somebody's desk. Of course there have been all sorts of alarms and excursions around the fleet of late, so maybe this crew were a bit on edge and took a shadow or a wave or God knows what for a sub.'

On the way out Kavanagh turned and said, 'One other thing. I've come from a quick meeting with a strange sort of fellow called Todd who seems to know an awful lot about everything. You've likely heard about all these secrets going astray in Whitehall. I just wondered if you've had any dealings with this character. My boss Kell isn't too keen on this Todd digging around in every corner of government – and up here as well.'

McGarrity knew nothing of Todd and said so.

'Well, I leave you with those fragments of suspicion,' Kavanagh said. 'It's always a pleasure to do business with our Celtic

A DARKENING FIRE

colleagues. I'll be on my way.'

'*Slán go fóill, Caomhánach.*'

Kavanagh hesitated, frowned, shook his head and stumped out to where his car was waiting in the heavily guarded grounds.

With no knowledge of what form previous interrogations of the Germans had taken, McGarrity opted for the role of the amiable, bumbling officer compelled to tired compliance with orders. Months of careful questioning and secretive enquiries in Germany had provided all there was to know about the group's background, families and work so he saw no purpose in trotting round that course himself. Affecting an air of quiet sympathy he sat in front of Rheinhold Sauer, Manfred Klein, Hanna Blindt and Karoline Petzold and conducted in impeccable German a half-hour of apparently tedious and lazy questioning which taught him as much about the personalities and relationships and roles of the quartet as he needed. The sheer banality of his approach served its purpose, awakening at last an irritable reaction from Sauer.

'Surely your people must realise that our presence here has been exposed to German Intelligence. How else could this have happened?'

'Unless the Professor went of his own volition?'

'A ridiculous notion. A sick man setting off in these conditions? And why would he anyway? It was he who took the lead in bringing us here. Why would he desert you and us at this juncture?'

'Do you want to be set up elsewhere?'

'You have that authority?'

'Of course.'

Sauer looked round at his colleagues, hesitated, then said, 'That would hardly be reassuring if someone in your agencies is privy to such information and prepared to pass it on.'

'That's what you suspect?'

Sauer shrugged.

'And I suppose,' Hanna said, 'that if whoever took the Professor wanted to settle with the rest of us they could have done it at the time.'

'The guard has been reinforced if that's any comfort.'

'Bolting the stable door…' Klein complained.

A DARKENING FIRE

'Nevertheless,' Sauer went on, 'the facilities here suit us and it would be disruptive to transfer everything.'

'I leave it to you.' McGarrity intended that the words should convey a lack of concern on his part. 'Now tell me, if the Professor didn't go off of his own accord, why would he be spirited away at this particular juncture?'

The physician Klein was first with a suggestion.

'Since our whereabouts have clearly been betrayed it will be no secret either that Professor Rupprecht is, in my view, seriously ill.'

'So if he still has important information to impart your former employer would want to have it before it's too late?'

'Yes. Professor Rupprecht was determined to go on with his work at all costs. He expressly forbade any intervention by your British doctors, but I can assure you that he was displaying the symptoms of progressive anaemia even before we left Germany.'

'The condition is degenerative?'

'Almost certainly fatal in the longer term. The malady is indicative. I'm sure it's the result of his work with some of these materials he's been handling prior to coming here. Perhaps I should have said something about this sooner, but the Professor was adamant. And anyway I was under instruction – I was to provide your people with reports on his condition, but Joachim was quite specific: none of your medical staff were to be allowed to examine him. He was afraid that it could lead to his being forced to delay his work.'

'The nature of the work being what?'

'You must look to your own people for that. It's possible,' Hanna Blindt put in, 'that the Professor has been taken to ensure that his work can't be replicated here.'

Mulling over what he had obtained from the interview McGarrity strolled back into the hall and set off to find Mitchell. The latter, barking orders at some miserable looking Constables, was more than happy to turn his attention elsewhere. At McGarrity's request he recounted the details of his interrogation of the KOSB detachment. In short, a foot patrol had spotted some characters lurking at the south base of the bridge. When challenged they had taken off in the direction of Dalmeny. One of the troopers had claimed to have heard a shot and the two soldiers of the patrol

A DARKENING FIRE

had voluntarily set off in pursuit. There had been no clear indication of how many suspects were on the run but it had been reported that at least two of them had made it into the grounds of Talbot House, no mean feat given the height of the gates and perimeter wall and the treacherous conditions.

'It's all a bit queer,' Mitchell went on. 'I mean if the whole idea was to draw off the police guard at the front of the house I don't see how the runaways could have been sure the troopers would go banging on the door the way they did.'

'You spoke to that pair yourself?'

'The ones that came up to the house? No, I couldn't. They're on two days rotation rest.'

'They were let go before you got to the camp? Jesus Christ, that Commanding Officer should be shot. Hours after something like this and he lets the main witnesses piss off – to where, do we know?'

'Usually they spend their time off in the Hawes boozer in the village. I suppose he thought they'd be easy enough to get hold of there. We can cut along to the place now if you like. It's no distance.'

McGarrity frowned.

'I've got to be off to London on the sleeper tonight. Still, I've got the time to come with you if you can get me a lift to Waverley Station later on.'

'No problem with that. In fact these boys are probably in the pub by now. Apparently they're Campbell and Ironside,' Mitchell said, leading McGarrity down the icy driveway to the police car parked by the gate. 'The man Ironside has a bit of a reputation as a hard case. Heavy drinker, gambler, keen enough on the occasional punch-up. He's been up on the odd charge and spent a few days in the Glasshouse. Campbell's said to be a dour type – hardly a word to be got out of him, but a good record.'

'I was wondering if that KOSB Captain said anything to you about the pair of them. What I mean is – why were they the ones who went chasing after our mystery men?'

'Aye, he did. They'd volunteered for the guard duty, so it was up to them to rouse the others and get after the intruders.'

'Regular volunteers, were they?'

A DARKENING FIRE

Mitchell hadn't asked.

The light was already dying over the Forth with operatic ostentation, the Fife coastline on the far side a jagged etching against a seethe of scarlet and gold beneath a writhing drapery of smoky cloud. A bitter wind came coursing up the river and left the heart of the village almost deserted. As the police vehicle drew up on the promenade the only lights to be seen glowed from the windows of the Hawes Inn, practically under the rail bridge and only a couple of hundred yards from the KOSBs' makeshift base. The pub was almost empty and the gratingly cheerful barman was pleased to be diverted from his lethargic rinsing of glasses.

'Well, well,' he said to Mitchell, running his ironic eye up and down the officer's uniform and jerking his head at McGarrity, 'I hope you'll not be looking for a hand to run this fellow in. I've seen houses smaller than that.'

'Maybe you heard about the soldiers chasing after some roughs in the night?' Mitchell asked.

'I did that. Ironside and Campbell it was.'

He glanced round to assure himself that the shadows round the walls harboured no unnoticed visitors.

'If you wanted to see them they're in here most nights they're not on duty. But it won't be tonight – they're after that chum of theirs from the city. Why are you asking anyway?'

Mitchell hesitated but McGarrity, tossing some money on the counter, said quietly, 'Ah, it's nothing important. We just need them to give us a bit of a statement to confirm what happened. There's no hurry, though. And,' he nodded at the coins, 'I take it you're not averse to serving the law with a drop of the *cratur* even if we *are* on duty?'

'Not at all. Name it.'

'I believe that the lads are on a couple of days off. Pity – we could have got the thing done today and left them in peace, but they're off gallivanting in town, you say?'

'Aye. They're after yon Dyer. They've been seeing him in here off and on for weeks now. I don't think they were that pleased when he didn't turn up today. They were grousing that he was supposed to meet them so they hitched a lift to Edinburgh in one of the KOSBs' trucks.'

A DARKENING FIRE

'Dyer? Not a big bald fellow, is he, with an English accent?'

'Good God, no. A wee ginger-haired thing with one of these pathetic moustaches like two hairs and a freckle...'

'Ah, right – I thought I might have known – but not the lad I'm thinking of.'

'No. Well, he's only been coming here the last month or so. Willie Campbell knew him from the White Hart pub in the Grassmarket. That's where they'll be the now.'

He waved a hand at the furthest corner of the room.

'Mind you,' he went on, 'it must be pricy enough being in here as regular as that when you're on not much more than a bob a day pay.'

'The White Hart, you say?'

Back in the car McGarrity asked Mitchell if he knew the city centre pub the man had spoken about.

'I know it well enough.'

'Then do me a favour. Can you scare up a couple of lads in plain clothes and see if they can get their eyes on our threesome. Should be easy enough from that description of the fellow Dyer. And drop me off at Waverley on the way.'

'No bother. You want the lot of them locked up till you get back? Be no problem to find just cause.'

'No. What I want is for your ginger man Dyer to be followed. Likely there was nothing much going on in there except a fall out over the price of a few pints, but you never know. I'll be back here the day after tomorrow and you can tell me then what this crowd might be up to. Can you fetch me from Waverley when I get back?'

'Before you go tell me this. How was it that they found you out? The Shinners, I mean.'

'If there was a fault it was in my underestimating Joey Butler's powers of observation. At the time I passed on the details of the Clarkson raid he'd followed me because he was worried about my state of mind. My contacts were well enough done up to be a whore and her fancy man but Joey had had sight of them a year before on a trip to London. It took him a long while to remember – so he told me. Anyhow it cost us both dear – him more than me.'

A DARKENING FIRE

CHAPTER 15: MARCH 1914

Sir Derwent Hartington made no effort to disguise his preoccupation with the disappearance of His Majesty's prize defector from South Queensferry. To the meeting he had spent the previous hour chairing his Assistant Private Secretary Cecil Highway ushered in the chemical physicist Julius Fučić, the towering figure of Leo McGarrity, Captain Smith Cummings of the Foreign Section and a dapper figure of whose identity only Cummings appeared to be aware.

'This is M. Vincent Garrou,' Cummings explained, concluding a round of introductions from which, as usual, the shadowy figure of Todd, sitting silent in a corner, was excluded. Then, responding to the blank reaction from his host, added, 'Of the Deuxième Bureau.'

'Let's press on,' Hartington instructed. 'The Rupprecht affair must be dealt with as a matter of urgency.'

McGarrity outlined the direction of his enquiries. It was too early to know for sure whether Rupprecht had absconded. Further questioning the Professor's colleagues might provide more definite information but only if he, McGarrity, had a clearer picture of what the Germans were involved in. Some points had emerged: Dr. Klein had remarked on Rupprecht's potentially debilitating illness which ought to be communicated to the Government's own scientific advisers if that had not already been done. If, McGarrity concluded with an undisguised grimace, he could be left to prosecute his investigation without interruption he was confident that he could soon shed some light on the event.

'And Mr. McGarrity would like to be on the sleeper north tonight,' Superintendent Quinn said. 'In my opinion we shouldn't keep him any longer from his duties.'

Hartington turned to Fučić and said, 'For my own satisfaction as much as Mr. McGarrity's can you enlighten us on what all this means. In layman's terms, please.'

Fučić launched into his account of the circumstances that had

A DARKENING FIRE

brought them together. He omitted unnecessary detail and kept his explanation as brief as comprehension would allow.

'First you must understand – nothing has been going on at Talbot House that takes practical shape. All it's concerned with is a matter of calculation, equation and the most complex theorising. Now you are probably all aware that Mr. H G Wells and others – Mr. Winston Churchill at the Admiralty for instance – have entertained themselves publicly with the notion that quite a small bomb might be created that would have a destructive power far beyond anything that might exist today. This is what Rupprecht's work has been aimed at achieving.'

'Is there any substance whatsoever to all this?' Hartington asked.

'For the present I don't believe so. But if you wish I can offer you a postage-stamp description of how the thing might ultimately be constructed in, say, fifty or a hundred years.'

'Please indulge us.'

'Very well. I think that one day it might be possible to create a chain reaction in certain elements by somehow shattering its component atoms. If that reaction could be controlled, probably in a compressed state, the energy released would be enormous with matter being converted to gigantic amounts of energy.'

'So that I'm sure I understand you properly,' Hartington said, 'you're suggesting that the smallest particles known to us could be converted into a bigger explosive device than has ever existed? Forgive me if I intrude a layman's doubt.'

'To which, for the time being, you're entirely entitled. The difficulty of acquiring the necessary materials, manipulating them, encasing and controlling them is far beyond any present capacity that I'm aware of. And although I've said the weapon would be small I mean its dimensions would be modest compared to the immense damage it could inflict. Nevertheless it would still be a huge contraption. The means of delivering it are beyond any machinery I know of. And anyway in the end it could prove to be the case that the theory will have to remain just that forever.'

'And the means of translating this theory into practice is what Rupprecht claimed to be bringing us?'

'We need to be clear about this. Even if all the theory

A DARKENING FIRE

underpinning the work could be put into practice the actual construction of the weapon would require equipment and premises on so vast a scale that they would occupy acres of land.'

'Then what exactly was the gift he claimed to be bringing us?'

'We know the Professor and Dr. Sauer are among Krupps' most prominent physicists, but they've been only a part of the Company's technical circle. Still, given time Rupprecht should have been able to add enough to his own efforts to round out for us a theoretical construct of the thing for our benefit. It seems England would be the intended target.'

'Surely if Krupp have already built at least one of them the completed plans for it already exist?'

'Of course. And Rupprecht's contribution to it would have been essential. But a contribution is all that could be. However if Rupprecht could bring together sufficient detail of the entire programme then it might be possible at some point for him to replicate whatever Krupp have been working on. I have to repeat my opinion that, no matter how developed the theory may be, the science that would allow such a bomb to be made is decades away – probably more.'

'You don't think it even remotely possible that the Germans actually have harnessed these forces for the purpose of building some sort of bomb?'

'If evidence can be produced to which convince Ernest Rutherford and myself that their atomic theory can become a physical reality, then I will tell you that the world has changed.'

'I would prefer a direct answer,' Hartington said, 'though I understand your reluctance to afford us one. But if there is even the remotest possibility that this weapon has been, or is about to be, created I must include that in the calculus of my advice to the PM.'

'Very well. I will say this - Rupprecht's papers indicate that the necessary base component simply doesn't exist in sufficient quantity in Germany. And as I've said the edifice for laying the ground work for it would have to be so enormous it could never be built with any degree of secrecy.'

Cummings held up a hand. Vincent Garrou cleared his throat and made his tentative entrance into the debate.

'My friend Captain Smith Cummings was kind enough to invite

A DARKENING FIRE

me to join you and I am here with the consent of Colonel Dupont of the Deuxième Bureau.'

The Frenchman's unexplained presence and hesitant intrusion conjured a puzzled silence for several moments before Cummings chose to offer his reason for inviting Garrou without first consulting any of the others present.

'I've known Vincent for a long time,' he said. 'He has worn the mask of duplicity with aplomb – a gift I admire as you can imagine. He has plied his Machiavellian trade in many places and I suggest you hear what he has to say.'

And Garrou described how the "*Swiss*" expedition three years previously had obtained permission to extract large quantities of ore from a remote area of Niger. By a process christened heap leaching the material had been extracted, broken into pieces over-ground and leached with chemicals to tease out what transpired to be uranium. It had since then been established that the resultant supply had been transported to the port of Dakar and onward to Hamburg.

'Hardly enough to confirm its use as a base for the sort of weapon Dr. Fučić has described,' Hartington said.

'Nevertheless,' Fučić said, 'this is not good news. Rupprecht's theoretical work is predicated on the requirement for a substantial amount of this material. At best it seems the Germans are approaching the matter seriously.'

'And at worst?'

Fučić waved a vague gesture.

Sir Derwent brought an uncomfortable pause to an end by turning his attention to the little man who settled in the most inconspicuous corner of the room, his face barely visible beyond the pools of light spread by the shaded, wall-mounted lamps, lit against the darkness imposed by the blinds drawn as a barrier against the annoyingly untroubled world outside.

'Mr. Todd?'

Without preamble Todd described the unsuccessful attempt to copy from the Krupp plant in Essen the papers which Rupprecht had indicated would help him complete his work on replicating the putative device. The failed operation had resulted in the death of Jacob Fenner, a highly regarded English scientist, and the exposure of Todd's some of most reliable and long-standing agents in

A DARKENING FIRE

Germany.

'I leave it to your consideration whether material that is any less than pivotal should be protected by the Germans at such lethal cost.'

Before Hartington could respond, Todd continued, 'You've just heard what's said about the requirement for suitably extensive premises in which to hatch this monstrous egg. It's no secret that Krupp have created a huge industrial complex at Freimann outside Munich. Since its inception it's been so closely guarded that even my legendary powers have been insufficient to penetrate its defences.'

'Obviously,' Hartington put in, 'Professor Rupprecht's disappearance means either a radical change of heart on his part or a successful abduction by German agents. Whichever is the case it shows his importance to this affair, even if the sole objective of his going has been to deprive us of his expertise.'

'I'm not a medical doctor,' Fučić said, 'but Inspector McGarrity's reference to the Professor's condition suggests aplastic anaemia. There's no known relationship of that condition to exposure to what Madame Curie has described as radioactivity but it's quite possible that protracted such exposure may indeed cause damage to the bone marrow and result in a severe anaemic condition. And ingestion of uranium might result in problems with the kidneys and radium might integrate itself into the bones. I confess this condition of the Professor's along with what we're hearing now *could* go some way to weakening my conviction that his researches could have borne only theoretical fruit.'

'Wouldn't you say,' Kell suggested, 'that even so much as a threat to deploy such a weapon – however it might be delivered – would in itself be tantamount to an act of war?'

'Perhaps so, but acknowledging that would still leave us with the problem of defending against it,' Hartington replied. 'We need to discover what precisely is going on at Freimann but from what Mr. Todd says that will be more easily said than done. Meantime I intend to recommend that Ministers urgently seek to open talks with their German counterparts to define and clarify their respective positions on this matter.'

'I have to warn you,' Todd said, 'that that could have dire

A DARKENING FIRE

consequences for the Entente with France. If the information M. Garrou has brought here is correct Germany may be very close to entering into hostilities on the continent. In that case we should not be in any way properly prepared to support our ally. We would be hesitating on this side of the Channel awaiting the outcome of negotiations that might in reality lead nowhere.'

'That's true,' Hartington acknowledged. 'But if any of you gentlemen believe that a more appropriate approach would be to risk the lives of millions of our citizens and a catastrophic impact on the country from which we might never recover, then I suggest you speak now.'

'There remains the overriding difficulty that so far we've been incapable of plugging the leak of vital information to the Germans,' Kell said. 'If they get wind of our position on this they'll play an even longer game against us. This outflow of secrets has to be stopped.'

Todd sat back and scanned the faces of the others

'This hunt had best end soon,' he said. 'Morale is low because of the suspicion that's blowing up amongst every department in Whitehall. If none of you here objects I'll have a go at the investigation myself and use my own folks to do the digging.'

'Then report directly to me and no-one else,' Hartington told him.

As the meeting broke up Superintendent Quinn collared McGarrity.

'We're overstretched right now,' he said, 'but what I can do is offer a Sergeant to give you a hand, Leo.'

'Hughes is available?' McGarrity asked.

'I'll make sure he meets you at King's Cross tonight.'

A general movement towards the exit was forestalled by Hartington.

'This business of the man Gallagher here in London,' he said to Quinn. 'You told me that your Branch have been keeping an eye on the fellow. What's the latest position in the case?'

'You'll remember his name came up while we were tracking that fellow Butler that tried to put a bullet in Leo's mercifully thick skull. Gallagher has somehow been getting hold of some damn useful information and he's been passing it on – to the Fenians and

A DARKENING FIRE

to some undesirable Germans as well. I think we have enough of the goods get hold of him and gently persuade him to spill whatever beans he's been gathering.'

'And this material is of the sort we've been losing? Then clearly he could lead us to the person responsible for passing it to him.'

' I think,' Todd said, 'Dr. Ackroyd has suggested that it might be sensible to leave him at large for a while longer if that means we could bag our spy and the objectionable Teutons as well?'

'If you like I'll give it a bit longer on the off-chance we can haul in a bigger catch,' Quinn agreed, 'but it's a dicey game we're playing.'

A DARKENING FIRE
CHAPTER 16: APRIL 1914

'Edinburgh Waverley; Edinburgh Waverley!'

The disconsolate-looking official was still trawling the length of the platform announcing the sleeper-train's arrival, his ill-fitting uniform easily accommodating to the weary futility of his duty now that the relatively few passengers had already disembarked into the hesitant April dawn that edged uncomfortably down from the city centre. Inspector Mitchell, in plain clothes, welcomed the two Special Branch officers at the platform gate.

'Over there,' McGarrity said, hefting his travel bag over his shoulder and nodding in the direction of the largely deserted tearoom in the concourse. Small talk came readily to none of the trio and once settled at a table they drank coffee in silence prefaced only by McGarrity's brief introduction of Niall Hughes. Fifty yards away Mitchell's driver paced beside the muddy police car, pausing occasionally to stretch and yawn. A newspaper vendor was shouting a headline incomprehensibly and a short queue of taxis waited for some anticipated but unforthcoming increase in traveller numbers.

'I've got you rooms in the Sealscraig Hotel in The Ferry,' the Inspector told McGarrity when they had climbed into the waiting vehicle. 'We should go there first.'

Turning from his place in the front seat Mitchell contemplated the contrasting appearance of the two men behind him – the hulking McGarrity and the slim, quiet, unremarkable Hughes. Not for the first time it occurred to him that for an officer whose work so often involved concealing his identity McGarrity cut a conspicuous and far from anonymous figure. Mitchell's appraising look and hesitation in responding laid bare this familiar rumination to the shrewd Irishman.

'It's my disguise,' McGarrity said, apparently reading Mitchell's mind. Slightly flustered Mitchell stumbled over the opening of his report but by the time they were out of Princes Street and travelling through the city's west end he was again his professional self. For Hughes' benefit he provided more detail than McGarrity himself

A DARKENING FIRE

required, but he was left to complete the narrative unhindered by interruption. Ironside, Campbell and Dyer had been identified from the description provided by the barman at the Hawes Inn and Mitchell's detectives had had no difficulty in following the trio from their alcohol-fuelled gathering at the White Hart. Apparently having succeeded in extracting some funds from Dyer the soldiers had promptly chosen to deploy them on repairing relations with their benefactor after an angry initial confrontation.

'Anyhow,' Mitchell continued, 'my lads had no problem trailing this lot. Even if they'd been riding elephants and playing drums our KOSBs and their pal wouldn't have noticed them by that time. Ironside and Campbell went reeling off to one of these down-at-heel hostels in the Grassmarket for the night and Dyer got in a cab that took him to the Peacock Hotel in Newhaven. He's still there and we're keeping an eye on the place.'

'Anything known about it?' McGarrity asked.

'Oh, aye. It's still being run by a German-born fellow by the name of Francis Holstein.'

McGarrity looked out at the sunlit rolling fields on either side of the road beyond the city limit.

'Well, well,' he remarked, 'our German friends are being either very clever or very careless. You'd think that the last thing they'd want would be for this Dyer to be so easily connected to them.'

'You're becoming too devious yourself, Leo. Apart from its boss Gustav Steinhauer the Nachrichten-Abteilung folk are third rate.'

'Maybe. Keep this Peacock hotel under observation. Niall and I will get ourselves into the Sealscraig in South Queensferry and then I think we should have a quiet word with Ironside and Campbell. After that I'd like to sound out Rupprecht's people at Talbot House again.'

'What's the latest on Rupprecht himself?' Mitchell asked. 'Anything new that might put me in a better light with my masters?'

McGarrity shook his head.

'But the next day or two might give us a clue.'

'Well, I can tell you,' Mitchell said as they drew up outside the hotel, 'that the KOSB Captain is happy enough for you to quiz our pair of bob-a-day soldiers whenever it suits you.'

A DARKENING FIRE

'Good. We'll get along there as soon as our rooms here are sorted out. What about you?'

'The Chief Constable needs a report from me. Maybe we can catch up tomorrow?'

After Mitchell's car had gone the Special Branch officers checked in at the small hotel and, taking advantage of the newly spring-like weather, ambled along the riverside to the little military post at the south end of the rail bridge. They were welcomed by Captain Harrow whose demeanour gave away the fact that he had been reprimanded on the lax handling of his detachment and instructed to cooperate with the secretive authority that now confronted him. Brutally hungover Ironside and Campbell had returned to their post minutes before they were due to report for duty and McGarrity and Hughes were left to interview them in the relative privacy of Harrow's small wooden office. McGarrity wasted no time on preliminaries, or on sympathy with the soldiers' self-inflicted condition. He had no intention of either revealing the extent of his knowledge of their transgressions or of offering an easy exit from their situation.

'I can charge you,' he told them, 'with aiding and abetting a foreign power in undermining the security of the nation. Make no mistake – you'll both go to jail for a very long time. Obviously you'll be dishonourably discharged from the service, lose all your pension rights and after seven years in Saughton quite likely, if you're lucky, end up in that hostel you were in last night.'

'Fuck off,' Ironside replied. 'The only thing we've done wrong is get a wee bit pissed, pee'd in the street and nearly – nearly, mind you – missed the start of our shift out here.'

'Good,' the Inspector told him. 'I was hoping you'd make it that easy for us. The only thing that might have held me back would have been if you'd spilt the same lot of beans as your chum Dyer has. That would have meant you were cooperating with me and I'd have had to dream up some way of making things look less serious for you.'

'Who the fuck is Dyer? I never heard of nobody called Dyer.'

'Sure you haven't. That's fine. Sergeant Hughes, will you explain the charge to these fine examples of soldiery. I'll go and see Harrow and let him know they'll be in custody in Edinburgh before

A DARKENING FIRE

noon. And I doubt they'll be handled too gently.'

McGarrity had reached the door before Campbell stood up abruptly, his chair crashing back against the floor.

'Hold on a minute. I've a missis and kids to think about,' he half-shouted, shoving Ironside's restraining hand away. 'Tell me what you'll do for us if we... if we... if...'

'Will I help you? Not a chance. Why would I complicate my own life for a pair of scum like you?'

McGarrity opened the door and was about to leave when Hughes said quietly, 'You don't think we should give them a shot at getting out of the hole they're in?'

'Christ, no. I want to see their faces the day they're sent down. No more booze, no more women – nothing for them but a damn good hiding now and then from our more patriotic convicts. And warders, likely.'

'I don't care what Dyer told you,' the desperate Campbell protested. 'He never said to us it was to do with spies and that. It was just supposed to be a wee joke – a laugh. Just to scare the folk up at the big house.'

Catching McGarrity's contrived hesitation even Ironside now opted for some gesture of collaboration.

'He said to us they wouldn't pay him for work he did at the place. He just wanted to give them a bit of a scare.'

'That's the truth,' Campbell agreed, wiping his sweating hands on his uniform. 'It's lies he's giving you if he's saying we're fucking spies or any of that shite. He promised us a few bob for a drink and that was it.'

McGarrity easily conveyed the impression of snorting scepticism.

'Are you saying there never was anybody at the bridge that night? Because Dyer says there was a Fenian plan to blow up the support.'

'All shite, I'm telling you,' Campbell insisted, righting his chair and sitting down again. 'We were the security detail. We were supposed to say there were folk at the bridge. Maybe we could fire a shot to make it seem real enough. Then we had to chase up the hill and scare the daylights out of that lot in Dalmeny – tell them some fucking nonsense about men running around with guns.'

A DARKENING FIRE

'And Dyer's a lying cunt if he says different,' Ironside added.

'Aye,' McGarrity said, 'so you deserted your post for a joke, eh?'

'Harrow said we could go after... '

'After nobody at all.'

'All right,' Ironside concurred grudgingly. 'But what's that – stoppage of pay; maybe a few days in the Glasshouse. Never seven years inside.'

McGarrity pulled a face.

'This is a waste of time, Sergeant,' he said. 'Why would Dyer leave himself open to a long stretch in prison by giving us a pile of lies about German spies and Fenians? Your man would be a right idiot.'

Hughes nodded, paused and said after some moments of counterfeit reflection, 'I suppose you're right, sir. This pair will have to go down with him.'

'Jesus, we're telling you the fucking truth,' Campbell yelled. 'All we wanted was a couple of pounds.'

'A lot of money for somebody getting paid less than two shillings a day,' McGarrity pointed out.

Campbell was becoming clearly frightened.

'Dyer's just trying to get himself off and drop us in the shite,' he blurted out. 'I'll bet he hasn't said anything about his wee hiding-place in Corstorphine, has he?'

'We're asking the questions – not you,' Hughes reminded him. 'You tell me what you know about it. Maybe that'll help you. Maybe.'

'I never trusted the bastard,' Ironside said, 'so I followed him a week or two back then banged on his door to make sure he knew we could find him if he didn't come up with the money.'

'So what?'

'The place was stowed out with stuff the coppers would like to know about.'

'What stuff?'

'I'm only telling you this,' Ironside went on, ' if it's going to get us off all that spying shite and that.'

'It *could* help, right enough,' Hughes said slowly.

'Tell them, for fuck's sake,' Campbell muttered.

A DARKENING FIRE

'There must have been fifty SMLEs, and maybe that many Webley IVs. Boxes of ammo all over the floor. All good stuff – new.'

'You'll need to do better than that,' McGarrity said. 'You two – soldiers of the king involved in espionage and insurrection? These are testing times for crown and country.'

Campbell gave instant way to disbelieving protestation, but Ironside was less easily intimidated into acknowledgement of complicity.

'You thick Mick bastard,' he snarled, half-rising from the chair, 'Dyer's got you dancing to his tune and you hang on every fucking note.'

McGarrity smiled benevolently on him, leaned his head to one side and with his hand made a jerking motion in the air.

'If you're lucky,' he said, 'the noose breaks your neck, but there are times when the thing goes a bit... wrong. And you mess yourself while you're choking.'

'Gormley,' Campbell forced through his numbed lips. 'Dyer says he got them off a Mick called Paddy Gormley. They came off that Clarkson business in Glasgow.'

'And why,' Hughes asked, 'would the Fenians sell off guns they stole for their Volunteers across the water?'

'Jesus Christ,' Ironside protested, 'you think these Mick shites are great honest men whatever side they're on! They're lying bastards like everybody else. Gormley pinched the guns off his own lot, right? And Dyer will sell the stuff on to any fucker with the money – to the Prods in that Ulster Volunteer crowd in Belfast or any other bugger.'

McGarrity bestowed on him a long, sardonically appraising look.

'You're a born orator, Private Ironside. But I doubt the jury will believe you any more than I do.'

'So are the guns still sitting in some kip in Corstorphine?' Hughes asked.

'Christ knows where they are now. When I went back there, there wasn't nothing – not a gun or bullet.'

'You've no idea what happened to them?' Hughes asked.

'If you've got Dyer, ask him,' Ironside said.

A DARKENING FIRE

'And what good will that do you?' McGarrity asked. 'Your only chance is that we can say you cooperated with us. I don't care if you do or not – it's up to you.'

A stain had spread slowly across the crotch of Campbell's fatigues.

'17 Garthlock Terrace. That was the place. They could be near anywhere now. The only thing I know is that that bastard Dyer hasn't flogged them yet, because for sure we would have heard about it and he'd be too scared not to let's have the rest of the money he's owe us as soon as he's back in funds.'

McGarrity was minded to beat the daylights out of the pair of them and allowed the inclination to show itself in his demeanour and posture. The soldiers were fit, streetwise young men but, standing up quickly they recoiled in haste before the implied threat.

'Mick shites, is it?' McGarrity said, bunching his huge fists. Reading from instinct and experience, Hughes, concealing sly amusement, stepped in.

'I'm arresting you on a charge of sedition. The offence is so serious it's placed on you by the civil power and overtakes the claim of military justice. I will write down anything you may say to me now and will read it out in a court of law. You can surrender yourselves to my custody or Mr. McGarrity's'

And with a flourish he produced a pair of handcuffs and left it to the pair to manacle themselves together.

'Harrow won't like this,' Ironside protested. 'It's army discipline for us.'

And his not entirely mellifluous rant continued gradually out of hearing as Hughes led the prisoners into the care of the Constables standing chatting and smoking by the police vehicle.

'What do you think?' Hughes asked when he had re-joined the Inspector. 'This Garthlock Terrace next?'

'It might be worth getting the local lads to keep a hidden eye on the place. You never know what might turn up.'

'Right. And Dyer – do you want him picked up now?'

'No. We're after him for something else altogether. It sounds as if he's the one that set up Rupprecht's disappearance all right, but for all we know he's just a wee cog in a big machine. Leave him to me. I want you to sort everything out with Mitchell. See that

A DARKENING FIRE

Campbell and Ironside are kept well apart. I doubt there's anything more to get out of them but grill the pair of them until you're sure. I've got plans for our friend Dyer. At the least there's a chance that he'll lead us to some clue about what happened to Rupprecht if that lot up at Talbot House don't or won't.'

A DARKENING FIRE
CHAPTER 17: APRIL 1914

If nothing else Ciarán Taaffe was taken by the sheer scale of what he was looking at. For thousands of yards in all directions what had been a vast rural site of rolling meadows had been levelled to a plateau of heavily compounded earth on which were laid out in rigid ranks and files scores of enormous brick-faced and windowless square buildings. The broad avenues between them were patrolled by well-armed, grey uniformed infantry as was the fifteen foot high mesh- and barbed-wire periphery. At every hundred yards or so on this enclosure was a twenty five foot watchtower on which, in the bright spring sunshine, could be seen an array of searchlights machine guns and elevated observation platforms.

At the double set of gates Taaffe, Keegan and Breslin were, despite the authoritative presence of Protzman, searched by a pair of expressionless thugs.

'I can't stress enough,' Protzman said when these precautions had been negotiated, 'that I put more than just my reputation at stake by permitting you access to this facility. I argued with my masters that it is essential that you, my friends and colleagues, should be privileged with the knowledge that is to be revealed to only a select few.'

'Aye,' Taaffe answered, unimpressed, 'well, all I see is a bunch of stone huts and what might be in them would mean bugger-all to me.'

'Bear with me, Herr Taaffe. I need you to see that we are in a position to compel Great Britain to accept our position on two fronts – your own and ours. I want you to witness the reality of this for yourself so that there can be no doubt in your mind what we are capable of.'

'Aye, well, staring at a hundred brick shithouses isn't going to tell me a bloody thing.'

Protzman waved a hand at the immense installation and its forbidding defensive mechanisms.

'Tell the truth,' he said. 'Do you believe for a single second that

A DARKENING FIRE

what you see here is anything other than the best protected, most impressive operation you can conceive of?'

Taaffe merely grunted.

'These two fronts you're on about – what's that mean?'

'Just as I've told you already. To keep the British from becoming involved in any continental conflict; and to impress on them that unless they abandon their occupation of your country by a date to be agreed, well, it's their own country that will bear the cost.'

Taaffe shook his head.

'You don't think, do you,' he said, 'that any time soon I'm going to march into Downing Street with that wee message? Asquith's as likely to believe that the *murrúghach* is swimming up the Thames.'

Protzman smiled.

'I don't ask you to carry messages. We can do that ourselves. But I want you to be assured that the messages we *will* deliver have all the substance required to confirm their authenticity.'

Taaffe glanced at Keegan and Breslin in exasperation.

'You might as well, he said, 'give me a map with X marked on it and tell me that's where the rainbow ends. Did you take the three of us all the way down here to look at...?' he fished around for some other derogatory description of the Krupp site, 'a fucking great *buinneach* factory for all we can tell?'

Protzman placed a hand on Taaffe's shoulder.

'Obviously the first thing you need is to see behind these walls.'

'Never mind that,' Keegan replied. 'Get the stuff you want us to take and we'll be on our way. I don't give a wailing fart if they're milking cows or fucking nuns in them great bloody outhouses.'

The German caught Taaffe by the arm.

'No,' he said, 'Herr Taaffe is right. If I've taken you to the most advanced scientific location in the world it would be stupid of me not to allow you full and free access to it. After all, it's from this place that your country's future – its freedom – can be assured.'

Pleased with the outcome of his insolence Taaffe nodded at Keegan and jerked a thumb in the direction of the nearest of the nondescript buildings.

'You won't mind, I hope,' Protzman said as the Irishman stepped forward, 'if I don't join you. My health, you see...'

A DARKENING FIRE

'Your health? What in the name of Christ has that to do with anything?' Breslin asked, half closing a suspicious eye and extending a none-too-friendly hold on Protzman's lapel. Protzman threw his hands up in the air.

'Gentlemen, please – I don't doubt your familiarity with the technical processes of atomic fission. When you see how this machinery has been put to use you'll understand exactly how our weapon has been created. Am I correct?'

'Don't be so bloody smart,' Taaffe answered, pausing in front of a soldier struggling to restrain a salivating Doberman pinscher. 'Like Breslin says – how's your health got anything to do with this?'

Protzman made a dismissive gesture.

'I can show you if you wish, but what does it matter? It's your concerns that need to be met.'

The dog was baring its yellow fangs a foot from Taaffe's groin.

'Aye, well, show us and then we can get on with the business we're here for.'

Protzman offered a pout and ordered the guard to retreat a few steps with his hound.

'Very well, gentlemen,' he said, 'but I have to ask you to exercise the greatest discretion. Come – follow me.'

And the trio fell in sullen line as he led them to the only building, so far as they could see, whose walls, were not entirely blank. The ground floor windows were a greenish hue and it was only on the closest approach that it became possible to make out the shadowy interior.

'Feel free to stare,' Protzman told them. 'While we can peer in, no-one inside can see out.'

Exchanging ironic glances, Taaffe, Keegan and Breslin walked up to the glass and, shading their eyes, looked into the beautifully appointed room crammed with handsome furniture – an extensive library, luxurious furniture, some metal filing cabinets, a jumble of laboratory equipment. A man sitting at the desk appeared to be sifting through a pile of documents. His hands shook so conspicuously that even at several yards distance it was obvious that every movement was a challenge. The man's skin was as grey as his long, thinning hair. Every few moments he paused in his modest exertions to spit into the bucket.

A DARKENING FIRE

'That,' he told his reluctant guests, 'is Professor Rupprecht. He's been abroad but as you can see he's now settled back with us. It's mainly to him that we owe the success of our research. It was he, Herr Taaffe, who was largely responsible for designing the bombs we have distributed and almost completed.'

'Jesus, he's a freak,' Breslin said, moving close to the window and cupping his hands against the light. 'Is that it? You've brought a ninety-year-old back from his holidays?'

'Professor Rupprecht is 55. In a few weeks he'll be dead. That is what exposure to the atomic process has done to him. I certainly won't say that a single tour of the establishment will have that same effect. The simple fact is that at this stage we have no way of knowing why or how this has happened. But the Professor is now alone – his team have... gone.'

A pause.

'And so, gentlemen, I leave it to you to decide on the extent of you tour of inspection here. I say only that I shall not be coming with you.'

'If a wee look in your sheds is going to kill me,' Keegan said, 'who's in there now with his spanner or hammer or whatever the fuck he needs to break up this atom stuff?'

Their host spread his hands almost apologetically.

'I can't tell you that,' he said. 'I can say only this – a great number of our convicted criminals have thought it better to be employed here with the prospect of freedom after a brief term of labour. So far none has completed that term. But,' and Protzman conducted the others away from the garish glass, 'please do not allow any of this to deter you from a closer examination of our work. And if you understand what that reveals, then you will be able to better explain it to... whomever.'

'We came here for your bits of tin or whatever,' Breslin said. 'That's all that this is about. Give us them and we'll be on our way singing.'

But Taaffe was still scanning the grim location.

'Have a good look at me,' he told Protzman, 'and tell me if you see a moron.'

The German stopped in his tracks and asked where the rhetorical question was leading.

A DARKENING FIRE

'You're telling me,' Taaffe went on, 'that you've been planting bombs somewhere in England that are so fucking big that they'll blast whole cities to pieces – and that the folk who made them are dying because of them? Well, tell me this then – why is it that all these honest Brit citizens aren't dying of them already, or why won't we be dying of them if it's up to us to arm the fucking things?'

'I am a simple Civil Servant,' he replied. 'I can't say for sure. There is, though, someone else who might tell you what you want to know. All I can say is that you needn't worry about arming these devices – that's a technical matter that our own people will deal with. All you will have to do is deliver the necessary items to my agent in London.'

'Oh, fuck all this,' Breslin said. 'Just give us the goods; and I'll tell you what – give us a pound or two as well for a drink and you can forget all about the lot of us.'

Taaffe was cannier, though.

'Your man Rupprecht there,' he said. 'If your bombs are just about ready except for this stuff we're on about what do you need him for any more? Not just to scare us, is it?'

'It would be fine, wouldn't it,' Protzman answered, 'if science just stopped where we want it? But that's not the way of the world. I don't pretend to understand the Professor's work – only what it means to me, to us as Germans. We'd be foolish indeed if we were to allow him to make available to others the great advantage with which he has endowed us.'

Both Keegan and Breslin were becoming more impatient.

'Who's your man going to give us the lowdown Taaffe here thinks he wants?' Breslin asked.

'He'll welcome you, I'm sure. But have you made up your mind – do you want to scour the facility for your own edification or do you not?'

'Never mind that,' Taaffe said. 'Let's hear your man for a minute or two and we'll leave it at that.'

With a nod of satisfaction Protzman led them back out through the gates to a small wooden house remarkable only for its Bavarian ordinariness. The two sentries on the door saluted Protzman and waved his party through. From the velvet half-dark a man rose from an enveloping wing-chair and extended his arms in a curiously non-

A DARKENING FIRE

Germanic greeting.

'This,' Protzman told the Irishmen, 'is Graf von Schwabe – Count, if you like. He will explain to you in detail what my government required of him some years ago and why they did so. He is a geologist and a sort of adventurer. Please remember his name and what he has done for your country as well as mine.'

'I don't give a rat's fart,' Breslin said, 'about your Princes or Counts or what the fuck. Come on, Taaffe, we've seen all we need. And you – give us your bullets or fuses or gun barrels or whatever they are and show us the door.'

'Very well. Come with me.'

'This is what you will do for us,' he said, having turned abruptly on his heel and confronted the trio, leaving a disappointed von Schwabe to commune with himself.

'First Herren Keegan and Breslin will set up at Mrs. Fogarty's boarding house on Crouch Hill in London – you will all know it already, of course. You, Taaffe, will find safe accommodation at an address nearby that I shall give you and make contact with Herr Keegan three days later. And you will deal with the traitor Gallagher, take possession of his apartment in London. And there you will wait. Clear? Simple?'

Despite harbouring real doubts now about Gallagher's trustworthiness, Taaffe was irritated and cautious and said, 'Listen, Gallagher's been a good man and we'll do fuck all to him without the proof he's gone from us.'

'You will find the evidence of his treachery in his possession,' Protzman replied, raising his voice and both hands. 'And that you can take back to Dublin if you like, but for you that's not the point. We work together or not at all. Gallagher's reaching into your purse – I've told you you'll find the evidence where he keeps it.'

After a pause of accumulating significance, he added with some emphasis, 'The shortfall in what *you* can pay Benny Spiro for guns is going to be made up by delivering these trigger devices. And by the way you entertain Herr Gallagher.'

Content that he had made his case adequately the German conducted the party beyond several guarded metal doors to what looked like a sterile store-room the walls of which were lined with an array of large locked iron boxes labelled with complex serial

A DARKENING FIRE

numbers.

'These,' he said after fussing with keys and dials and swung open a handful of these containers to extract five chrome devices with the appearance of weighty oblong tubes, 'will be collected from you in London. As they are they are harmless, but a piece of advice: don't in any circumstances try to open them – the effect would be devastating.'

As he had explained earlier the metal was stamped with the name and crest of the St Rollox works in Glasgow and a folder of copiously detailed paperwork from the Hohenzollern Works described them as components for use in an experimental range of fireless locomotives.

'As you can see,' Protzman concluded, 'the sole risk attaching to delivery would be for anyone to prise the casing apart. And no Inspector is going to be interested in innocent and delicate industrial items.'

'And how are we going to know who the fellow is that we're supposed to hand these over to?' Taaffe asked.

'Nothing complicated. He'll tell you his name is Klausen and he'll ask for his parcels.'

A DARKENING FIRE
CHAPTER 18: APRIL 1914

Norris Dyer was a cautious and suspicious man accomplished at watchful, surreptitious but usually venal wheedling, never given to doubting his own pecuniary motives and well aware of the pitfalls of dealing with his own ilk. So when Arend ten Berge had approached him with a proposition involving little personal risk and financial reward disproportionate to the effort entailed he had viewed this display of generosity with his accustomed scepticism. First he had asked how he had come to the attention of the visitor and was informed that the proprietor of the White Hart had recommended him as a useful contact in matters of business in the area. This was perfectly credible – Dyer was a regular in the place and over many years had made his dubious services available to owner and clients. Nevertheless, he had taken the precaution the next day of confirming that the boss of the pub had indeed been extolling his virtues. From his acquaintances in the *demi-monde* of small-time felony he had gathered that his new friend had a reputation as a smuggler of alcohol, tobacco and a wide range of assorted goods which he transported via his boat between the ports of Holland and various locations along the east coast of the United Kingdom.

This encomium had been enough to recommend him as a reliable colleague and Dyer had had no hesitation in responding positively to the proposal that had been put to him – that, relying on his ruffian boozing pals from the military, he should clear the ground for some foreign gentlemen to extract a colleague from closely guarded tenancy of a house in nearby South Queensferry. Whether this was a matter of kidnapping the party in question or setting him at liberty had been of no concern to Dyer, although The Dutchman, in order to lend weight to his proposal, had gone so far as mentioning a highly-placed contact in London whose name at the time meant nothing to him, but who was concerned with the matter and not to be crossed. The extent of the profit to be had was so considerable that it had blinded Dyer to the matter of how his relationship with the recalcitrant troopers had become known to ten

A DARKENING FIRE

Berge.

The fact was that Dyer was no master criminal – he had no expertise in the more sophisticated aspects of professional dishonesty, but he was endowed with modest ambition and prodigious greed. A few evenings poring over his own rough sketches of the location and sounding out Ironside and Campbell on the extent of their rapacity had provided him with the conviction that he could mount a diversion of sufficient effectiveness and duration to allow The Dutchman's anonymous clients to whisk their countryman from the clutches of the law. But all had not gone to plan – whoever was supposed to effect the rendezvous on the snow-covered bank of the Forth had failed to materialise The following day he had sought out The Dutchman who, with a great show of ire that his plan had gone awry, had completed the evacuation on his yacht the *Ineke*.

It was some days before ten Berge had reappeared during which time the furious Dyer, in hot pursuit of his fee, had hunted around the docks and bent the ear of every one of his shady acquaintances in the area – all without turning up even a hint of the man's whereabouts. It had been the failure to find and share the promised spoils that had led to the spat with Ironside and Campbell that the barman at the Hawes had witnessed. In a final throw of the dice he had barged off to the Peacock yet again determined to extract from the German proprietor any clue as to where The Dutchman could be found. On discovering his quarry seated calmly in the lobby, his reaction was a comical combination of relief and fury that neither terrified nor amused the other.

With his loot safely stowed Dyer had felt himself better disposed to his companion and had agreed without hesitation to making himself available for further cooperative endeavours when called upon. It was in response to this invitation that he had hurried off once more to the hotel after his encounter with Ironside and Campbell in the White Hart under the covert eye of Inspector Mitchell's officers.

'I've another small commission for you,' ten Berge had told him. 'The fee will hardly be as generous as the last one, but that's because there's nothing much to it.'

Dyer had listened to the suggestion that he use his network of

A DARKENING FIRE

disrepute to distribute a small amount of contraband – spirits, mostly, but some tobacco and other goods – to the pubs, shebeens and traders around the docks. Carefully calculating Dyer's enthusiastic reaction The Dutchman had told him to return to the hotel on the next Wednesday to conclude the deal.

'I hope,' he had wound up, fixing Dyer with a long stare from his narrowed eyes, 'that we can trust each other completely.'

'Aye, well you can rely on me,' Dyer had answered. 'I done you fair work in The Ferry, didn't I?'

'You must understand,' The Dutchman had gone on, 'that my friend in London is a powerful man. When you are in my employ you must on no account confuse his interests with your own.'

'Aye, well, I couldn't care less what your pal's up to, so don't you worry about me spilling any beans. But, look, I'm in funds right now and I think I'll give myself a wee treat and book myself in here for the couple of days until you need me again.'

'Suit yourself, Mr. Dyer. I'll be here late on Wednesday evening and we can have our little talk then.'

When, early on the Wednesday evening, Dyer returned to the unaccustomed luxury of his temporary accommodation he was a little unsteady from a drinking session in a nearby pub. Not a man given to acts of any form of charity, far less of heroism, he was sufficiently emboldened by liquor to take frank interest in an altercation in the lobby. An attractive young woman was being berated by a much older man whose condition seemed to approximate Dyer's own. Red-faced, his speech slurred, the man was waving an unimpressive fist in front of the woman's eyes and apparently complaining that the money he thought he had invested in plying her with food and wine had brought him no return. Mrs. Holstein had retired behind the reception desk and betrayed no enthusiasm for intervention, and ordinarily Dyer would also have made himself scarce. But on this occasion, glowing with interventionist rectitude, he cast himself as Galahad.

'What the hell's going on here?' he managed to demand with only a hint of the difficulty he felt in piecing the rhetorical question together.

'Mind your business, short-arse,' was the prompt response, but even in his cups Dyer could see that the other was in no mind to

A DARKENING FIRE

provoke a physical confrontation.

'Mrs. Holstein,' he called, 'if this character isn't out of your establishment in one minute you have to call the police. And I'll make sure he...'

But before he could conclude the laboured harangue the man embarked on an unsteady retreat in the direction of the front door, issuing imprecations over his swaying shoulder.

'And you, you bastard,' he bawled in Dyer's direction. 'I know you. You and your foreigner pals and yon lorry you're aye shifting stuff about in. It's you the police'll want to know about, not me.'

Caitlin Hagan and her partner had performed similar scenarios so frequently that their respective roles had become second nature to them. Her present act was unoriginal and hardly opaque but given her quarry's relative befuddlement she was confident that the lure would be taken. When The Dutchman appeared she and Dyer were comfortably seated in the residents' snug chortling over large glasses of red wine. The new arrival was far from delighted to find his intended colleague in unexpected company and significantly the worse for wear – and, trembling with rage, he was fulminating about something else.

'Those goods of mine need to be taken ashore quickly,' he said without preliminary. 'But some swine has just slashed the front tyres of my truck, right there in front of my eyes. You must have seen him – he came out of here not a minute ago.'

'What? Aye – we seen him,' Dyer muttered. 'He was pushing this young lady around.' A dramatic pause, then, 'I rescued her.'

'And I'd like to know why he did that to my truck,' the irate Dutchman demanded. *'My* truck.'

'His name is Plunkett,' Caitlin told him. 'You were lucky it was only your vehicle that he took his knife to. And I'm lucky Mr. Dyer was here, or God knows what might have happened to me.'

'Never mind that,' the furious Dutchman snarled. 'We need a vehicle. I have to be away from the port in four hours at the most. And I won't have some stranger sit here and listen to my business.'

'Hold on,' Dyer rose from his seat and waved both hands in a gesture that combined apology with self-justification. 'Caitlin here is just a pal. She's staying in the hotel for a bit. On holiday from...' He shook his head as if to dislodge the impediment to recollection –

A DARKENING FIRE

without success.

'From Kilkee,' Caitlin provided. 'It's in Ireland.'

'Is that so? That so?' The Dutchman fixed her with an oblique look, rubbed his chin thoughtfully and sat down beside the couple. 'And you're a friend of Mr. Dyer's?'

'He's my guardian angel. But please – don't let me interrupt your talk. I'll head off to my room and leave you fellows to get on with it.'

'No, no, lass,' Dyer insisted, restraining her with a tug on her sleeve and a glassy, pleading stare. 'There's nothing to it – just some bits and bobs to be brought up to my wee store in Newhaven. No more than a few minutes away, I promise. We'll find a way.'

'Well, it's been so nice to meet you,' Caitlin assured The Dutchman as she made to break free of Dyer's anxious attention. 'But I mustn't hold you up at all. If I could have been of any help to you both... Well, my car's at your disposal if you need it. Just bring it back in one piece is all I ask.'

'Ah, now,' Dyer said thoughtfully, 'what do you think, Mr....?'

'I'll take the car, thank you,' ten Berge said grudgingly. 'But I can't say I'll bring it back here. As I say I have to be at sea before one o'clock. Dyer, will you...?'

Dyer wriggled in his seat.

'The wee thing is this,' he said. 'I can't drive.'

'It's no matter,' Caitlin put in. 'Leave it at your store and I'll collect it in the morning. Or I can drive for you'

The Dutchman and Dyer exchanged a brief glance.

'If you could do that, that would be excellent,' The Dutchman said impatiently. 'Then you can come directly back here. If that's not taking too great advantage of your time?'

'Not at all. Let me get my coat. But I'd be happier if one of you could make sure Plunkett is gone from out there.'

The operation to remove Dyer's contraband from The Dutchman's yacht was conducted in darkness and without incident. Caitlin gave every impression of being flushed with excitement as the various boxes were unloaded, shipped in her car to Dyer's miniature warehouse and locked safely away pending illicit distribution.

'I can't tell you,' The Dutchman said as she dropped him off on

A DARKENING FIRE

the pier and wished him *bon voyage*, 'how much I appreciate your help, Miss Caitlin. If ever you would be interested in working with me in the future our friend Dyer can get in touch with me.'

'Well,' Caitlin replied, 'it'll come as no surprise to you that an Irishwoman like myself would be happy to do anything to twist the tail of the Crown's servants.'

'I thought as much when you told me where you come from. Now, may I offer you some recompense for your efforts tonight. Without you we would have been lost.'

'If Mr. Dyer can see his way clear to buying me a little drink before Mrs. Holstein closes her bar that would be more than enough reward.'

With a courteous little bow The Dutchman folded the paper with Caitlin's phone number into his pocket and disappeared into the night.

'A bottle of your best red,' Dyer called to Mrs. Holstein who was betraying signs of wanting to call an end to the evening's proceedings, 'and have a little something for yourself while you're at it.'

The landlady let him have the drink, turned down the lamps and announced that the pair would have to content themselves with that as she was off to bed.

'And keep your hands off that gantry,' she admonished, lumbering out. 'I know the stock like the back of my hand.'

'Do you think Mr. ten Berge would do some work for Irish friends of mine if we asked him very politely?' Caitlin asked.

'I would think maybe so. Did you have anything specific-like in mind?'

Caitlin affected circumspection and took her time in answering.

'Well, I hope I can trust you not to say a word about this beyond our two selves,' she began, and Dyer, expansive, offered her every assurance of his discretion.

'It's just that sometimes we need to be able to get some items moved across the water.'

'My lips are sealed. And anyhow I do the odd wee service for the Irish myself, so you're in good hands.'

'And The Dutchman? Would he ever go, say, as far as Hamburg to collect or deliver… well…? For the right sort of fee, of

A DARKENING FIRE

course.'

'He's the very man for it. In fact, it's no time ago that… '

'That…?'

'Let's say that he knows the way well enough. Now,' and Dyer was already reflecting on the commission he might extract from future dealings, 'all you have to do is come to me and I can make all the arrangements with The Dutchman that you'll ever want.'

And he was in the process of putting his glass to his lips when his cocky bumptiousness was overwhelmed by a tide of dread.

'You little weasel,' the lurching Plunkett snarled, bursting back on the scene, clearly no more sober than before, but detectably more belligerent, waving an open razor and stumbling in drunken haste towards the seated couple.

'I'll let you two sort out your differences,' Dyer announced hurriedly. 'Mrs. Holstein can always get hold of me if you… '

And fired by a fierce anxiety to abandon the possibilities he had foreseen for the night he made good his disorderly retreat up the stairs feverishly searching his pockets for the key to the safety of his room.

A DARKENING FIRE

CHAPTER 19: APRIL 1914

On the train journey north through Germany Taaffe, sullen and tired of the repetitive debate between his two minders, closed his ears and concentrated his attention on his own plans for reaching their London destination. He had no doubt that the authorities in England would still be on the lookout for him and Protzman had provided him with the name and contact details of The Dutchman who could arrange to take him across the North Sea to wherever he wanted to be put ashore on the British east coast. He had also provided the name of a contact in Edinburgh – one Norris Dyer – should Taaffe be landed near there which was what Protzman advised. But there were conditions, the German insisted. Keegan and Breslin would travel by ordinary ferry. Given that the authorities in England would still be on the lookout for Taaffe himself it would be unwise for him to attempt to negotiate customs at the English ports.

'It's more than a precaution,' Protzman had pointed out. 'This is the surest way of getting as many of the things through as possible. God forbid that a boat should go down or run aground or be stopped by the Royal Navy or the coast guard. Of course none of that will happen. But my masters will be happier if they can be sure that at the very least one of these devices reaches its destination.'

Taaffe had baulked at all this, but Protzman had been adamant.

'These items are complex and they are all we have for the moment. If by some foul stroke of misfortune we were to lose them all it would upset our timetable of operations. So long as one is successfully installed we can proceed.'

In the end it was agreed that Keegan and Breslin, each with two of the devices, would make their way to England by a circuitous route – from Hamburg they would move on to Esjberg in Denmark where they would catch the *A P Bernstorff* to Parkeston Quay in Harwich, making no secret of the fact that they were carrying the priming devices.

'Hidden in plain sight,' as Protzman put it. 'Nothing looks more

A DARKENING FIRE

innocent than a thing offered up at every chance for careful inspection.'

Taaffe would pack the remaining item in a trunk that would accompany him on the lengthy voyage to Scotland from where he would make his way to London. Protzman assured him that this would be the most secure means of reaching his destination. He would be put ashore at a time and place well out of the purview of any interested police or excise officers. Taaffe spent most of the rest of the rail trip pretending to doze, aware that his two travelling companions were still more his captors than his bodyguards.

Much that they had witnessed in the course of their excursion mystified him and he felt a burgeoning suspicion that somehow they were being made use of rather than aided by Protzman who, for all his volubility, remained as hard to make out as the most tight-lipped stranger. And the entire expedition to the Bavarian site seemed to Taaffe to have been unnecessary and punctuated by diversionary occasions that had been made to bear some inexplicable weight. Presumably it would have been a simple matter for the components to be brought to Hamburg; and his involvement in the whole affair felt over-elaborate, even if it was construed as a *quid pro quo* for the inadequacy of the funds for the cache of weapons to be routed to Ireland. What was no less puzzling was the parading of the ailing Professor Rupprecht and the aborted confrontation with the man von Schwabe – a meeting that appeared to have been planned in advance but which was discarded by Protzman without demur. And, finally, it was hardly evident why Taaffe and the others should be interested in the fact that the Krupp site was being at least partly manned by convicted criminals.

The following day Keegan and Breslin sat out their voyage with of a pair of whiskey bottles in their modest third class cabin on the *A P Bernstorff*. Slightly seasick and suffering from the protracted bout of inebriation they stumbled ashore at Parkeston Quay in Harwich the next morning, and were discovered by the brilliance of an English spring. They sauntered through the customs hall in the direction of the exit to the town and to the welcome, they assumed, of some traditional pubs before heading for the metropolis.

'One moment, gentlemen,' the uniformed officer called from

A DARKENING FIRE

behind a rickety wooden table. 'You have the look about you of honest men, but would you be so kind as to let me have a bit of a rummage in your bags there?'

'Take your time,' Keegan said, shoving the luggage in the man's direction and settling down casually on a bench to light a cigarette

'No contraband in these, is there?' – a rhetorical question accompanied by a cheery smile.

'Just stuff for the factory in Glasgow,' Breslin assured hastily. 'You'll see the name on the side.'

'And their purpose is what?'

'Not sure, *mo chara*. Something to do with locomotives, I think, but we're just the delivery boys. Is there a problem? We've got all the paperwork if you want to see it.'

'Not at all, gents. We had word about some chap trying to bring in some sort of exotic firearm – somebody got sight of it on the boat. So – nothing for you to worry about. Sorry to hold you up, but we're going to have to hold all luggage here until we have the time to check it properly. Be about two, maybe three hours. Have a ticket, chaps, and come back then. You might want to see the inside of the pub across the street.'

Folding the shabby ticket into his pocket, Keegan led the way out of the hall and led the way to a bench that gave a view over the harbour.

'What do you think?' Breslin asked. 'Should we just get the fuck out of here and head back to Glasgow or even Dublin. All this stinks.'

Keegan was no less cautious, but it was obvious that everyone coming off the ferry was being dealt with in the same way.

'Look at all these poor bastards,' Keegan remarked, waving a hand at the milling around them. 'We've not been singled out, have we? And I'll tell you this – if somebody's on to us, they're not going to let us make a run for it now. Fuck it – we'll hang on and take our chances.'

And a couple of hours later they found their bags neatly repacked by harassed customs officers compelled to continue their weary routine of going through the belongings of everyone who had come off the ferry, apologising to the apoplectic and trying to

A DARKENING FIRE

return the contents of several hundredweight of baggage to their pristine condition. While Keegan and Breslin possessed themselves in patience waiting for their bags they had the opportunity to bend the sympathetic ear of one of the invigilating officers who was happy to encourage their humorous account of the excursion that had brought them to this inconvenience. Resuming the nonchalant air with which they had attired themselves when the heart-stopping search had got under way, the pair strolled out of the building with a cheery wave at the policeman patrolling the pavement at the dock gates. But the proximity of exposure had had effect, and they soon repeated their resort to shelter in the nearest pub before heading to the railway station where they caught a train for Liverpool Street. For the duration of the journey they kept a watchful eye for any unwanted observers, but, in a mood improving with each stage of the trip, arrived in London satisfied that they had survived the hazard of the expedition intact.

Meanwhile Ciarán Taaffe, laden with the chunk of metal bearing the St Rollox stamp and making no effort to find his sea legs, was crouching in the cabin of ten Berge's yacht as it sped north west across the North Sea. Being a regular client of Benny Spiro's and of the Nachrichten-Abteilung, The Dutchman had made the voyage between Hamburg and any number of ports on the east coast of Scotland and England on more occasions than he could recollect. The small crew were former navy men on whose loyalty and silence he could rely. As a precaution he always carried a cargo of legitimate goods as well as any unauthorised merchandise or personnel whom the German intelligence service wished to be transported between the continent and the British Isles. He liked Leith because the bribes he had spread around among customs officers and dock workers ensured that his affairs remained private. This time, however, he had been told to put his passenger ashore on a remote part of the Fife coast as he was, apparently, much sought after by the authorities.

Left to his own devices, Taaffe continued to struggle with the order to assassinate his friend Eoghan Gallagher. He had to conclude that Gallagher and Joey Butler had given up the Cause in favour of lining their own pockets with the King's gold or had simply chosen to take the Brotherhood's money and make a run for

A DARKENING FIRE

it. Lending weight to this suspicion of collusion was the fact that Gallagher had sometimes shared with Butler the collection of instructions from the location in St James's Park. If only, Taaffe thought, there was some way of getting hold of McGarrity – he would have snapped Gallagher's neck without turning a hair. But a vast silence had fallen on events after the Glasgow disaster and those of the organisation who had survived it seemed to be lying low. There was Gormley out there somewhere, but few others now. How, he wondered, had it come about that a few months back he was near the top of the tree, surrounded by men he could call his own, and now he was on a mission that bewilderingly seemed to him might damage the Cause. It was late afternoon when ten Berge's yacht *Ineke* arrived in Silversands Bay and Taaffe was rowed to the deserted beach in the tender with a sketchy map of the route to the nearby small town of Aberdour from which he would have to make his own way first to Edinburgh and then on to London.

While Taaffe was stumbling ashore several hundred miles away Superintendent Quinn of the Special Branch was pondering the reports on the activities of the man Gallagher that had been accumulating on his desk for some days. It had been his intention, as he had agreed with Hartington, to postpone an arrest for a bit longer on the chance that some further useful material might come to light. But Gallagher had spent most of that time lying low in his dingy flat, contacting no-one and leaving the building only to buy food or to down several pints in the Shaftesbury Tavern, where he had sat in solitary, scowling isolation conveying the impression of someone either resigned to some irretrievable downturn in fortune or waiting for some long-overdue occurrence. The single deviation from this tedious routine was an uneventful trip to St James Park where, after a slow, slouching tour of the place he settled on a bench and spent half an hour feeding the ducks.

'You think he knows we're on to him?' Sergeant Halligan asked as he eyed his boss with the anxiety of a man about to be subjected to intemperate inquisition. 'We've been well up to the mark on this. I would swear there wasn't a chance that he's spotted us.'

'No. Your man would have made a run for it before now if he had.'

A DARKENING FIRE

'Do we give him a bit more rope or do we haul him in now?

'Yon Dr. Ackroyd tells me the esteemed Hartington thinks that sooner or later we'll land a bigger fish or two if leave him be for a bit longer. Todd reckons that Berlin has been getting no more of our secret stuff for quite a while now so my inclination was to run the bastard in, but let him be for a while yet. Now, what about Herr Klausen – that fellow that The Owl managed to sneak out of the Germans' clutches?'

'So far he's been fine, but let's face it – he's not been here any length of time. Until now he's been keeping himself to himself. Been set up in a place in Islington. He *has* been given a good once-over by Todd's people – even the lovely Miss Nichols found nothing to his discredit for all her wiles. Everybody seems to think he's above board and you know how short we are of officers for other things. I'd say we can leave him be now.'

Left to his own devices the Superintendent flicked through a confidential report from Dr. Fučić indicating that work at Talbot House had become sporadic as Sauer had already suggested was inevitable and the consensus was that without Professor Rupprecht any further progress was going to be slow and quite possibly unreliable. Increasingly irascible in the face of apparent inertia, Hartington's PS Ackroyd had turned up at Talbot House again to berate in private and at length the remaining Germans, which intrusion had annoyed Fučić and his small posse of other specialists. Two full days of poring over the documentation Rupprecht had left behind and quizzing his companions had borne only a modicum of useful information. It seemed that Klein was from the outset the one medical doctor whom the Professor had insisted on having with him since his own health had begun to deteriorate in the course of his researches. Rheinhold Sauer had already proved himself an accomplished theoretical physicist who was well able to hold his own in debate with Fučić's eminent professionals, but his knowledge was circumscribed by limits imposed by the absent Professor's regime of rigid secrecy. Nevertheless, as it was the Germans' view that the new weapon was quite probably complete and ready for use, the still sceptical Fučić was content to let the Talbot House project take its now leisurely course although he recommended some more resolute prodding.

A DARKENING FIRE

Disappointing news was that Fenner's Ticka Expo Watch camera had suffered serious water damage while in Klausen's possession and had provided only almost indecipherable photographs of the papers Rupprecht had declared he wanted from Essen. In the moments set aside from venting his wrath Ackroyd had drafted a note to Home Secretary McKenna recommending that Sir Christopher Cresswell, the First Secretary at the embassy in Berlin, should try to tease some information out of his regular sparring partner Conrad Schweitz. This approach and the terms in which it should be couched would be delayed until further reliable information could be obtained. Fučić for the time being concluded his lengthy review of events by opining that there was little more on the technological front to be extracted from the Talbot House tenants, but he understood that McGarrity was on track to identify the means by which Rupprecht had been removed from the scene and those involved in it. Quinn leaned back in his chair and, studying the unrevealing ceiling, visualised the many pieces of the puzzles in front of him, and how far they interlocked.

A DARKENING FIRE

CHAPTER 20: APRIL 1914

Norris Dyer couldn't believe his luck. Having just dismissed the driver Hawke whom he had enlisted to deliver the contraband stored for a day or two at his warehouse in Leith, he was painstakingly counting the loot he had accumulated in the course of that operation. A tap at the door of his musty office prompted the hasty concealment of his gains as the figure of Caitlin Hagan appeared.

'We are alone in the building, are we?' she asked. 'I shouldn't want to be overheard.'

'Quite alone. Please – sit down. So, my dear, what can I help you with? Nothing will be too much trouble.'

When Caitlin had explained what she required Dyer's practised caution was mitigated by her production of a large bundle of bank notes which she described as a down-payment.

'You'll need to understand, though,' he told her, 'that there are certain precautions that I have to take before I can accommodate you. Just a few enquiries.'

'I quite follow. And if you are not in that market you *will* return the money, won't you? My friends would be very displeased if it wasn't put to the use they intend.'

'I'm sure there will be no problem, my dear Miss Hagan. Leave things with me for, let's say, two days. Will that be all right for you? We can meet here again then.'

When Caitlin had gone, Dyer took his time about counting the money she had left with him, and, rubbing his hands with satisfaction, he wound up the telephone and called Hawke. There was a long pause before the driver responded to his summons. Finally Hawke muttered that he had been back home for less than an hour and couldn't Dyer have spoken about this while he was at the warehouse. Irritated, Dyer insisted without explanation and again there was a protracted silence on the line.

'Well?'

'The wife'll no' let me,' Hawke reported. 'But I'll get you

A DARKENING FIRE

somebody else. A good reliable man.'

'I've no time for this,' Dyer told him in exasperation. 'I need to be away somewhere this very afternoon.'

'He'll be with you in an hour if that'll do you.'

'Just make sure he is, or you can forget about the work I give you.'

Hawke's nominee turned up in thirty minutes and proved to be an excellent driver of the rattletrap truck. Following Taaffe's directions the man took the road along by the Forth as far as Stirling and on towards Perth. Even though darkness was falling the new recruit handled the lorry with confidence as Dyer, peering out at the night, called out for stops or sudden turnings when they had passed the village of Balbeggie. After a long tour of the area, he let out a cry of triumph and pointed the driver to a narrow, rutted path quarter of a mile long and breathed a sigh of relief when the swaying truck was brought to a halt in a stony yard in front of a single storey dwelling from which the merest flicker of light emanated through a curtained window.

'Good man,' Dyer conceded. 'Hawke would never have got us here in one piece. I'll not be long and we'll be on our way back.'

'Aye,' the driver said, 'but you wouldn't mind, would you, if I made use of the jakes? My bowels have been real shaken up in this thing.'

Dyer hesitated and then grudgingly agreed on condition that the urgent excursion was concluded with all reasonable dispatch. A tap at the front door produced minimal response. Through a gap no more than a few inches the resident peered at the new arrivals with suspicion while his eyes accustomed themselves to the encroaching darkness. When Dyer announced himself and was recognised the door was opened wider and the occupant, shoving something under his jacket, signed to him to come in, but held up a hand when he saw the second figure.

'He'll be in and out in a minute,' Dyer assured him. 'He just needs the bog, and he'll wait in the lorry.'

'Be quick about it, then,' the Irishman grumbled, and indicated with his thumb where the lavatory was. 'And you, Dyer, what the fuck brings you here at this ungodly hour? I might have blown your face off.'

A DARKENING FIRE

'Never mind that, Gormley, you big dunderhead. We're in a way to make a right pile off of some of your Mick pals, but I'm not falling for any tricks. I have to know if you can check up on a woman who's come to me with a grand offer for the stuff we've got lying up in Gorgie. We need to be sure she's what she says she is.'

Gormley shot a glance in the direction of the toilet door and indicated to Dyer to keep his voice down.

'Maybe I can. Tell me.'

'Name's Caitlin Hagan. She told me she's out of some place called Kilkee.'

'Handy enough. I've family from there that are in Dundee nowadays. They'll know for sure if she's what she says. What's the money like if she's the right thing?'

'It'll get you to Peru like you want.'

'Aye, good. I'm sick of this fucking miserable hole of a place. How soon do you want the lowdown on her?'

'I'll need the news in a day or two, no more, so I'll get you on the telephone and…'

The toilet flushed noisily and the bathroom door opened. Dyer tossed a pack of cigarettes to his much relieved driver and telling him to wait in the truck, said nothing further until he was well out of hearing.

'There's one thing, though,' Dyer went on. 'Can you rely on these folks of yours? I mean they won't bring the wrath of your man Taaffe down on our heads will they?'

'Christ, man, even Taaffe himself doesn't know I *borrowed* the stuff. The whole bloody thing turned into such a fucking shambles there's likely guns and ammo lying around half the country.'

Relieved to be free of the sullen and uncommunicative Taaffe, The Dutchman had dropped anchor half a mile offshore and late the next day made for Leith where he hoped that Dyer could put some business his way. Unable to find the Scot at his warehouse he paid a brief visit to the Peacock Hotel to collect one or two messages Holstein wanted delivered to Germany and spent much of the night on board drinking schnapps with his crew and with a pair of corrupt employees from the docks. On the following day he caught up with Dyer who was uncharacteristically preoccupied and reluctant to leave his telephone unattended.

A DARKENING FIRE

'Listen,' he told The Dutchman, 'there's a good chance that I'll be able to get you a real money-maker of a job if you can hold on in Leith for a while. Maybe today, maybe tomorrow. I guarantee it'll be well worth your time. But I can't say a thing about it until I know the story myself.'

On returning his employer to his base in the Scottish capital, Dyer's replacement driver – a Glasgow police officer named Simmonds recruited for the task with the certainty that Dyer would never have encountered him – had reported the details of the excursion to Sergeant Hughes of the Special Branch. Simmonds was a first class driver, so it was in the early hours on the day after Dyer had had his meeting with Paddy Gormley and well before the dawn had broken that a car carrying Simmonds himself and a heavy-set stranger had drawn up outside the isolated cottage in the of Perthshire. The niceties of introduction were dispensed with in the chilly dark as the two men pulled on balaclava masks.

'Knock, knock,' Simmonds whispered with a sly grin before tacking on, 'No answer, then,' and standing to one side to allow his passenger to dispose of the door, the full weight of his muscular body behind the savage kick that sent it crashing off its hinges to catch Gormley coming down the lobby to investigate the soft sounds that had wakened him. Pinned under the door and gasping for breath, he tried to grab the revolver he had dropped but the combination of shock and the inconvenience of being crushed beneath the considerable mass of the door and its assailant prevented his reaching the weapon. The subsequent struggle was short-lived, and Gormley was dragged, his legs flailing vainly, into the dingy sitting room where he was tossed onto a chair, choking under the grip of a powerful hand on his throat.

'What the fuck...' was all he managed to say before he felt the long, cold blade of a knife probing the skin over his carotid artery. And then, 'There's not a damn penny in the place if it's money you're looking for.'

'So,' the bigger of his two attackers began, the accent undeniably Northern Irish, 'you're in the guns business, are you? Well, my friend, you can do yourself a big favour and maybe walk away from this, or I can open up your throat like a wee tin can and stick your head on a post out there.'

A DARKENING FIRE

'Jesus Christ, leave me be, you bastard. Just get that bloody sword off me.'

'A wee word from you to yon Mr. Dyer is the length and breadth of it. So we'll just sit here for an hour or two and work at your phone call. But you better hear this loud and clear – if you make a one little mistake it's your cock that goes first, if you get my meaning. And it'll not get any better after that either. Are you with me?'

'I'm with you. Just tell me what you want.'

Had the disembodied voice been carried on any accent other than the one he was hearing, Gormley would have had no problem resisting, but he knew too well that there would be no quarter given by an Ulster thug if he failed to comply. So until mid-morning he studied and read out several times the script that had been prepared for him, and by the time he was making the call to Dyer over the crackling telephone line he was fluent and convincing. It was entirely to his surprise, then, that shortly after noon a police wagon rolled up outside the house and he was hurried out into it, unhurt and still having difficulty in understanding how easily he had fallen for the trick. As the posse with Gormley in its charge drove towards Edinburgh Norris Dyer was sitting back in his chair beaming across at ten Berge and rubbing his hands with satisfaction.

'We're in the money, you and me,' he announced. 'That's the call I was hanging on for. My client will be here sometime today and once I've cleared the air with her we can set about the job. Are you on for shipping a fair load from here to Erin's Green Isle?'

Never one to be discouraged from making a profit regardless of looming difficulty, The Dutchman contented himself with a slight inclination of his head. It would not be the first time that he had run illegal cargo either from the Continent or from Scotland to Ulster or further south. In financial matters he trusted Dyer no further than he could toss a caber, but he intended to be present when the anonymous customer turned up so that he would be privy to all the subtleties of any agreement.

Gormley had taken issue with Dyer over the lack of security in storing the guns and ammunition that had been liberated from the Clarkson haul. Having the stock of rifles, revolvers and ammunition casually piled up in a vulnerable flat in the west end of the city

A DARKENING FIRE

struck him as ridiculous. Carting the stuff elsewhere in an aged vehicle had been done in several trips and by concealing it in large pieces of furniture or under canvas covers he had deposited it an unobtrusive terraced house in a back street in the Gorgie area. The problem this left Dyer with was how to arrange clandestine transport of the merchandise across the city to the docks at Leith – his usual driver Hawke, who had proved tight-lipped and dependable, was still not answering the telephone and when Dyer dispatched a street urchin to stir him the boy had found the house shuttered and silent. Cursing his own inability to drive or to raise Gormley on the phone it started to feel as if what should have been a routine swap of goods for money was starting to shape itself into one fraught with hazard. It crossed his mind that the safest course was to abandon the thing altogether, tell Caitlin Hagan that another dealer had pre-empted her and ward off The Dutchman with a promise of more lucrative work in the near future.

Dyer was shortly to regret not responding to the cautionary chimes at the back of his mind, but the instant that Miss Hagan reappeared in his office he surrendered to her feminine charms. And when he had explained his predicament she immediately undertook to drive his lorry, stressing the urgency of her cause. This amicable accord had just been concluded when The Dutchman ushered himself into the building and made certain that every line of the financial arrangements was presented to him. Irritated that his grasp on the situation had been so loosened, Dyer contemplated one last opportunity to pull out. With The Dutchman's being privy to the details his own share of the loot was going to be substantially diminished; this Irish woman, though commended by Gormley, was an unknown quantity who was going to know precisely where his favoured hideaway was; and his usual accomplices seemed to be out of contact.

'I don't like it,' he confided to ten Berge, but made no effort to explain what it was that he found unappealing; and Caitlin Hagan was too impatient to pay him any heed. The result of this unhappy negotiation was that the guns and ammunition were moved without incident to the *Ineke*, the money was produced without query and by midnight Dyer was relaxing in his office, bathed in the sweat of anxiety and fatigue but triumphant that the affair had been carried

A DARKENING FIRE

off without incident. It remained only for him to decide how much he would tell Gormley had been realised by the sale. What small injustice was going to be perpetrated by a white lie?

A DARKENING FIRE
CHAPTER 21: MAY 1914

Back in London Helmut Protzman looked and sounded very different from the man Vincent Garrou had met in Germany.

'We've become strangers,' the German said when the pair had exchanged greetings in the pub off Leicester Square, and he might almost have avoided recognition by his long-time acquaintance had they passed each other in the street. 'And I fear that you might be drawing a great deal of trouble down on yourself just by agreeing to see me. You know that the British security service are aware that I've had dealings with the Irish separatists?'

Garrou nodded.

'But they have done nothing to apprehend you?'

Accepting with a wave of his hand Garrou's added remark that anything he said could not be treated as being entirely between themselves, he launched into the tale he had been working on since his last meeting with Conrad Schweitz.

'It seems a Professor Rupprecht absconded to England with some colleagues. It's not clear to me why,' he went on, 'but what I do know is that he has been working with Krupp on just the sort of weapon we're all so exercised about. This is a genie can't be put back in the bottle. From what I've heard in Berlin I'm convinced that at least one of them has been… misappropriated by a cabal of disaffected officers. If that's the case you'll be aware already what their objective is.'

'I need to be clear about all this. If what you're saying is correct, where do you believe the bomb is now? And what do your… treacherous military intend to achieve by taking it?'

'My guess would be that it has, or they have, been hidden away somewhere in London or some other city to be detonated if England complies with her Entente agreement if your country should go to war with mine.'

Garrou shifted in his chair.

'Then why bring this to me?' he asked. 'Why not directly to the British? Or to my own government?'

'I can't pretend to be in possession of the whole story. You are

A DARKENING FIRE

my friend and I'm offering you only what I've been able to glean or guess. Look, my own status is problematic. Should I be divulging any of this? Does that make me any less of a traitor than those I'm talking about?'

'I have to be frank – you put me in a difficult position. The best I can do is convey what you say to the British and to the Élysée.'

'Then do so. The British Security Service know me for what I am. I've taken a great risk to come here as it is. My motive is simple – this affair is beyond all countenance. I can't calmly accept responsibility for the death of millions of innocent civilians.'

'My friend Mansfield Cummings has advised me that something of this kind is already suspected by the British. Whitehall has in mind to make some kind of official representation, I think.'

'And that would be very well. But the situation may by now be beyond the state's control. Pass on my concern as you see fit. There's nothing more I can do or say.'

Then he leaned forward and placed on the table a sheaf of papers and said, 'This is an extract of documents held in the office of the Krupp Chairman in Essen. I know from our own security people that the British tried to obtain a copy themselves; and that that effort met with no success. What I can give you is limited because I couldn't run the risk of obtaining more without giving myself away. But on top of what I think the British government will already have learned from other sources it will add weight to what I say.'

As Protzman took his leave Garrou watched two other customers, men over-dressed for the season, set off immediately after him. There was, then, no attempt being made to conceal the fact that Protzman's presence was recognised and being monitored. Why he had not been apprehended was of no concern to the Frenchman but he assumed that the British were up to something that was either hopelessly inept or artfully conceived to achieve an end that was lay outside the span of Garrou's curiosity. For another half-hour the Frenchman sat on in the pub reflecting on what he had just heard. One glance at the documents Protzman had left with him was enough to make it clear that none of their contents meant anything to him. They seemed to be a precis or summary of far

A DARKENING FIRE

more than they contained – diagrams, equations, incomprehensible text. But Garrou was concentrating more on what the German had been saying, and why he should have chosen to communicate it to him rather than directly to the British. Stuffing the pile of documents into his briefcase he left the pub, shading his eyes against the sudden onslaught of the brilliant spring sunshine, and made his slightly hesitant way in the direction of Watergate House in the Strand.

Having travelled down on the sleeper from Waverley, McGarrity reported mid-morning to the same office to find the usual cabal, presided over by Home Secretary McKenna, already ensconced along with Sir Derwent Hartington and the newly arrived Vincent Garrou of France's military intelligence agency. He listened with interest to the Frenchman's account of his curious meeting with Protzman and to Todd as he reported in his customary quiet monotone that the fugitive Ciarán Taaffe had been identified by agents in Germany. Although it had not been possible to keep track of him while he was in that country it seemed likely that he had been approaching arms dealers in Hamburg. To keep these under surveillance, though, would be a problem since Todd's organisation there had been compromised and had not yet been regenerated.

'There's another side to this Irish business, though,' Todd went on. 'It's clear that the revolutionaries have got themselves tied in with the Germans on something on an altogether different scale from a few hundred rifles.'

And for some minutes he outlined events that had brought him to that conclusion. Two suspected rebels named Keegan and Breslin had come ashore at Harwich carrying equipment designed to activate at least one of the so-called atomic bombs.

'They've been detained, I hope?' McKenna asked.

'No, Minister. If the tip-off from Germany is genuine our best hope of locating any bombs already planted in our cities is to follow this pair. We have to find out where these tube things are going to be married up to the rest of these bombs.'

'Anything more on Taaffe?' McGarrity asked. 'He's the one I'd like to nab.'

'My people came close to laying hands on him recently. I

A DARKENING FIRE

gather he was brought back to this country by a fellow called ten Berge. One of my female colleagues is currently keeping watch over *his* activities. If he ever makes landfall himself down here we have an address in Lambeth that he'll use.'

'There's no doubt as to the purpose of these articles Keegan and Breslin were toting?' McKenna asked.

'Our information is reliable. They were examined at Harwich by Dr. Fučić. It wasn't possible to prise them open without giving the fact away, but our enquiries at the St Rollox plant in Glasgow confirm that these things do not belong to them and mean nothing to them.'

'But are we then in a position to say unequivocally to the Prime Minister that this atom bomb does exist and has been placed somewhere in England? Most likely here in London?'

Todd explained that there had been no attempt by the two Irishmen to conceal from Customs officers the fact of their journey to Freimann. Replying to the cheerful, informal but subtly probing questions from one of these officials Breslin and Keegan had taken the line that telling as much of the truth as possible was the best way to disguise a lie. They had complained about the intimidating nature of the security at the Krupp place; had unaccountably been shown a sick and dying scientist called Rupert or a name like that; had been told the place was manned mostly by criminals; and that they had been introduced for no reason they could see to some kind of prince called Swab; and that the Germans had taken to using forced labour. All this, McKenna told the meeting, served to confirm that it had been the correct course to have Sir Christopher Cresswell at the embassy in Berlin put to Conrad Schweitz in the strongest diplomatic terms King George's grave concern. In response Schweitz had assured Cresswell that the government Berlin would never countenance any kind of operation directed at Britain. If there were any substance to the report it had in all probability been generated by some party determined to drive a wedge between the two countries who, after all, were natural allies. Schweitz had gone so far to hint that, in current circumstances, it was France that had most to gain from a rift between the United Kingdom and Germany.

'Any other remarks, gentlemen, before I take these bleak

A DARKENING FIRE

tidings to the PM?'

'The man Protzman,' Todd said, 'is a low-level and not particularly competent spy. So far as we're concerned he's pretty harmless, but let's not discount the thought that he might simply be spreading disinformation. It's his stock-in-trade. Who do we believe? Protzman with his mutinous military or Schweitz and his dark hints about France or whoever?'

'I hope that...' Garrou began but was quickly interrupted by McKenna.

'Of course not, but I have to put this matter before the PM and the Cabinet. It will have to be raised again with the Germans at the highest level but we can hardly wait in hope for a satisfactory outcome.'

'Now,' Hartington said after the Home Secretary had bustled out, 'one other detail before we round this item up: Superintendent Quinn, you and I have spoken about this at some length. I gather you intend to corral yet another of our Irish dissidents – Eoghan Gallagher.'

'The man is a danger,' Quinn remarked. 'It's time we had him in. And since we're confident he's been the go-between passing on leaked documents I assume you yourself would want him detained and questioned now that the leak appears to have been plugged.'

'Well, the advice I have is that, given a little more time, he will lead us to others whom we would otherwise let slip. Please hold off for a little longer.'

A DARKENING FIRE
CHAPTER 22: MAY 1914

A couple of days later the city of Edinburgh was bathed in a benign evening light and even in the untidy little garden behind Norris Dyer's unkempt ground-floor flat there remained enough warmth of the cloudless May day for him to sit on a moth-eaten chair and contemplate the possibility of his moving up in the world thanks to the success of his recent commercial manoeuvring. As he reached for his glass of cheap red wine Dyer saw a shadow fall across the battered deal table. Shocked out of his pleasant reverie he made to grab the wooden cudgel he always kept to hand as a precaution against the intrusion of unwelcome, disappointed patrons. But the move was anticipated by the interloper and the club was dashed out of his reach. Looking up he was surprised to see only an undistinguished, somewhat portly man, neatly dressed and carrying a heavy bag on his shoulder. Although he conveyed an air of calm he spoke with captious urgency.

'Why the fuck are the police watching your place?' he asked and Dyer recoiled in alarm at the harshness of tone in the quiet Irish accent.

'What? The police aren't interested in me,' he spluttered before thinking it would have been indicative of more confidence if he had demanded first to know why this stranger was standing uninvited on his premises.

'There's a plain clothes copper over the road. I had to wait for him to go for a piss in the pub before I could get in here.'

'What makes you think it's me he's watching – if he is a copper? Anyhow get the fuck out of it or I'll call your man if he really is the polis.'

'I've an eye for these things,' the man told him, unburdening himself of his luggage and dropping down into the vacant chair on the other side of the table. 'Whatever you've been up to, you're in the *puiteach* for sure. So give me what I want quick as you can and I'll be on my way before the pair of us are run in.'

Dyer stared at him disbelievingly.

'*Give* you what you want? I might be able to *sell* you what you

A DARKENING FIRE

want.'

'I want a car. Nothing fancy – and cheap too.'

'A car? Why would you come to me for a car? I'm not a garage, am I?'

'Oh, I know who you are,' Taaffe assured him. 'But that's a long story and I've better things to do. Give me a price and I'll let you have the money now. Get somebody to leave the car in the lane behind the Old Docks by first thing tomorrow morning.'

'Well, Christ, you're a trusting sort of fellow, aren't you?'

'Am I fuck! You put one foot wrong and my friends will burn you out of trade and home – and then rip the lugs off your head. You know I'm telling you the truth.'

'I believe you, pal. Look, I can do what you want,' he said. 'There's a three year old Tin Lizzie I can get hold of tonight. I can't drive myself but I'll get somebody to leave it where you want.'

'Good enough. Just remember: the boys will be watching you.'

And with that Taaffe, seeing for the first time that there was a deserted alleyway at the back of the building, was off scrambling over the low wall and into the thickening evening light. Badly shaken Dyer finished his wine and made his unsteady way to his cousin's lockup a few streets away, haggled over the asking price for the Model T, counted out the pile of banknotes from his greasy jacket, told the hand-rubbing owner where to leave the vehicle for collection and, back at home, polished off the rest of his supply of red biddy and headed for bed. Hungover he woke early the next day and was slowly recovering from the unfocussed drama of the previous night when The Dutchman came calling.

'I have very little time,' ten Berge told him. 'I've been carrying those guns around for days now, and not only is that ridiculously risky, your Miss Hagan is becoming extremely impatient for delivery.'

'Well, get them to her.'

'Patience. Hear me out. I know a certain party in Rotterdam anxious to unload a supply of sprits – gin, schnapps, whisky, cognac, vodka, rum; and that this cargo is ours for the taking, so, well...'

'I'm with you,' Dyer butted in hastily.

'Good. The only condition is that you help me with unloading

A DARKENING FIRE

these guns of Hagan's. She wants them landed at a place just outside Kinsale on the south coast.'

'In Ireland? Are you mad? I don't drive and I don't sail the seven seas. And I don't go anywhere near Ireland either.'

'Then I bid you goodbye, old boy,' The Dutchman said with a sneer, turning on his heel and making for the close. 'It would appear that our partnership is dissolved.'

'Fuck, all right. I'll do this for you; but, Jesus, make sure this is the first and last time.'

Shivering with anxiety at the prospect of the voyage, Dyer had to be helped on board the *Ineke* which was berthed at a quiet corner of the Leith docks. Never had he been at sea, and the novelty of watching the shoreline slip away behind them did nothing to reassure him that all was going as it ought. With an oath, he plunged down into the darkness below deck, falling on a bunk, clutching a pillow in both hands and emitting a series of low-pitched moans. The weather on the Forth was bright and calm, with visibility excellent – the sort of day on which The Dutchman felt most completely at one with the universe. The engines which sounded to Dyer like the tireless grumbling of those long-consigned to hell, lulled the skipper as if they were the gentle humming of the spheres. With these two men in their separate and different soporific condition it was the first mate who was startled by the appearance of a grey-hulled little vessel coming towards the *Ineke* at some speed. Alarmed that the oncoming cutter was out of control the steersman took early evasive action – enough to bring The Dutchman hurrying to the bridge and to dredge Dyer from his refuge below and to propel him into the eye-narrowing brightness over the firth.

'What the fuck's going on?' Dyer squealed, grabbing the binnacle for support and security. 'Are we sinking? Christ, I can't swim, you bastards.'

The Dutchman scowled at him, but continued to concentrate his attention on the nearing speed-boat. Seconds later he could make out that the oncoming vessel was a 40-foot coastal motor boat armed with a pair of Lewis guns. Even a confirmed landlubber like Dyer was afflicted by the palpable tension that accompanied The Dutchman's crew. Once again he shut his eyes and moved his lips

A DARKENING FIRE

in a silent prayer to a God in which he had not even a vestigial belief. Gradually adjusting her speed to that of the *Ineke* the naval vessel edged closer as the boats continued downstream until the patrol suddenly built up pace and cut across her.

'This is His Majesty's Ship *Callista*.' A pause, then a peremptory, 'Stop.'

The Dutchman cupped his hands and yelled back, 'We are the *Ineke* and we're *en route* for Rotterdam to collect perishable goods. I hope you need not detain us for more than a few minutes.'

'My bowels,' Dyer moaned. 'Oh, my bowels.'

For a handful of seconds nothing more passed between the boats, and then, without further warning, a Lewis gun loosed off some very audible rounds well wide of The Dutchman's vessel. The message they conveyed was clear. And to ensure that there wasn't the remotest possibility of misunderstanding, the broadcast voice opened up again.

'This is Lieutenant Drew of HMS *Callista*. Heave to or I will fire on you.'

Signing to the helmsman to stop, ten Berge busied himself with the grim reflection that it could hardly be a coincidence that, on the one occasion on which he was carrying so incriminating a cargo, the authorities were on hand to waylay him. As he had expected a cutter was being lowered from the patrol boat and at a distance of less than fifty yards he could see that the ratings were sporting rifles. The chance of talking his way out of the situation was slim but he had to trust to his own ingenuity and adroit duplicity.

'No-one talks to them but me,' he told the mate who rushed among the crew members to relay the injunction.

Meanwhile Dyer had been watching and listening with growing horror. Even more than The Dutchman he foresaw plainly the outcome of this confrontation. Surrounded by an aquatic environment that represented the intransigent hostility of the world, he gave way to a blind panic. Fully aware of the unfortunate condition the incident had provoked in his underwear, and of the sheer injustice of fate, Dyer dashed from the cabin as the cutter pulled alongside the *Ineke* and, with no idea what he hoped to achieve, picked up a heavy metal wrench that had been lying on the deck and, yelling gibberish at the top of his voice, charged straight

A DARKENING FIRE

at the first sailor clambering aboard. Taken aback by the ferocity of his assailant the matelot toppled backwards, dropping his rifle as he fell. The weapon went off with a roar that was magnified by appalled silence and Dyer, stopped in his tracks, bent double clutching his belly and collapsed in a heap, screaming and writhing in agony.

For some seconds nobody moved, until the boatswain in charge of the boarding party, acting with commendable coolness and speed, signed his men to take possession of the *Ineke*, ignored ten Berge's protestations and pleas to be heard, instructed the yacht's medic – a hastily obliging retired nurse – to tend to the injured Dyer, and ordering the traumatised helmsman to make full speed back to Leith. The Dutchman's rehearsed outrage went ignored. His cargo of arms did not.

A DARKENING FIRE
CHAPTER 23: JUNE 1914

Taaffe was exhausted by the 420 mile drive from Edinburgh to London, taken at a speed low enough to ensure that nothing untoward happened to draw attention to him. After dozing in the car for a few minutes he drove to the boarding house in Muswell Hill where he was able to lock the car in a shed, perfunctorily acknowledge the landlady who was expecting him and retire to his room in a state of very pronounced unease.

The day before Taaffe arrived in the metropolis Todd's favourite home-based agent had passed to a colleague the task of continuing on the trail of Keegan and Breslin. Switching between the identities of Harriet Nichols or an unsteady Gorbals prostitute or Caitlin Hagan or any number of other personae was second nature to her and her invisible presence at Harwich and on the train south had gone entirely unremarked by even the cagy Volunteers with years of experience of avoiding the attentions of the law. But she had recognised that she would be pushing her luck if she and her clandestine retinue continued on their tracks after they had reached Liverpool Street station. Once there she had retreated from her lead role, giving way to a squad under the Colonel, her elderly colleague – formerly a soak at a hotel in Victoria, a Glaswegian pimp and the apoplectic Plunkett – to pick up the trail.

The Colonel shared with Harriet the curious ability to be seen without being seen, and tracing Keegan and Breslin to the Fogarty *pension* on Crouch Hill had presented him and his posse with no problem. There seemed to be so few guests in the place that it crossed his mind to book himself in at the same address, but a moment's thought was enough to dismiss the notion. He found a suitable base at another boarding house across the street and explained to his landlady that as a travelling businessman he would probably have quite a number of callers if that was all right with her. For a day and a half there was no sign of his quarry going any further than the pub at the end of the road or of any new guests being accommodated at Mrs. Fogarty's; nor was there any indication of Keegan or Breslin making any effort to pass on the

A DARKENING FIRE

bulky metal tubes they had arrived with in their luggage. Nevertheless the job was carried on with the usual exacting care and the Colonel was able, on handing over to Harriet and her team, to report that no contact had been made with the Irishmen. As Todd and Major Kell were anxious to hear about progress the Colonel took it on himself to keep his boss apprised; and Todd in turn passed the information on to Hartington.

Ticketed for that night's sleeper to Edinburgh, Inspector McGarrity had arrived at the Colonel's observation post an hour earlier and had spent that time being briefed by Todd's elderly agent and a Special Branch Constable dressed as a street cleaner. There had been no sign of either Keegan or Breslin that morning. McGarrity enquired after the disposition of the Branch men still on duty and was told that both the front and rear of the house were under tight supervision. It was a late-morning visitor who finally provoked interest. One of Todd's men thought that the face of the visitor was vaguely familiar. Unable to put a name to him and not certain that he had come across the man, the officer had consulted the other members of his team, describing in detail the features that had drawn his attention. With no confirmation of his tentative belief that the stranger was known to the police, he had reported the encounter to Harriet Nichols and the Colonel, both of whom had been stationed on watch in the house on the other side of the road. At that remove it was impossible to make out much of the man's appearance and acknowledging that to do so was a risk, Harriet elected to take up a position near the house and left her post beside the Colonel to stroll in the same direction as the target on the opposite pavement.

Harriet would, McGarrity and the Colonel knew, be too professional to give any indication that the man was known to her, but they watched from the curtained window as she drew level with him, her attention seeming to be fixed on the frontage of a little row of shops. She glanced quickly towards him and as he reached out to tap at the door to the Fogarty place he turned, presumably by chance, to look directly at her. For a second nothing appeared to pass between them, and then, with an unhurried movement, he produced a revolver from his pocket, extended his arm with sedate care, pulled the trigger twice, and set off at a run down Crouch Hill

A DARKENING FIRE

towards Sparsholt Road. The sound of the shots brought the Branch officer in front of him to a halt. He spun round to block the man's escape, reaching for his truncheon as he did so, but was felled immediately by a third bullet. Crumpled on the ground, his body jerked once or twice and lay still in a pool of blood. Two further officers took up the pursuit while a number of passers-by huddled behind a low wall and more policemen hurried to the aid of Harriet and their comrade, shedding any attempt to conceal their presence from the occupants of the Fogarty house. The Colonel let out a strangled cry and, close behind McGarrity, raced from the room and into the street to tend to Harriet.

What then and later impressed the posse was the speed with which the gigantic Inspector sprinted down the Hill, overtaking the two other pursuers in seconds. Losing ground to the hurtling colossus, the assassin stopped in his tracks, spun round and aimed his pistol with the same degree of calculation as he had shown already, but with almost twenty feet still between them, McGarrity loosed off his baton which, thrown with all the brutal force he could muster, caught the other full in the face. Rocked by the blow the man was unable to control his actions and his gun arm flailed to one side, sending the shot wildly into the air. McGarrity's pace remained undiminished as he bore down on the disorientated marksman and when the Inspector's great bulk charged into him he was sent crashing onto the pavement, his head catching on the edge of the kerb. Breathing heavily, McGarrity planted one boot on the groin of the prostrate assassin and with the other kicked the revolver far out of reach. By the time the other officers had arrived on the scene a pool of blood was spreading under the man's skull and there was no sign of movement from him. A quick check on his pulse indicated that he was at least still alive, though his prospects for longevity were less than glowing.

'Get some kind of help for this bastard,' McGarrity instructed. 'We need him alive if possible.'

And with that he was off again, dashing up the street to where the two casualties lay. The Special Branch Constable was badly wounded but alive and being cared for by a confident-looking colleague while another officer, familiar with the area, was a hundred yards away pounding on the door of a medical practice.

A DARKENING FIRE

Barging across the roadway, the Inspector joined the group that had gathered round Harriet. As he approached the Colonel, his pale face streaked with tears, turned to him and shook his head. McGarrity knelt by the woman and found her hardly conscious, blood coursing from two gaping holes in her chest. He clasped her hand and yelled for the doctor who had been brought in haste from his consulting room. Feeling Harriet's grasp tighten on his, McGarrity leaned over her as her lips moved and blood pumped from her mouth.

'Klausen,' she whispered. 'Tell... Todd.'

'Klausen?' the Colonel repeated. 'She interviewed him once.'

A moment later the doctor, waving the onlookers away, spent some desperate but vain effort in tending her. Police whistles were blowing all around, truncheons were banging summonses on the walls and pavements, and in the frantic confusion people were shouting for or offering help and everywhere was the sound of a chaos of vehicles. But ignoring the uproar, the incensed McGarrity broke away from the throng and headed for the Fogarty house, his massive fists clenched by his side, and it was only with the greatest difficulty that two of the Special Branch officers succeeded in restraining him as a first floor window was thrown open and the barrel of a Hembrug carbine was pushed through the gap.

A DARKENING FIRE
CHAPTER 24: JUNE 1914

Perched on the steps outside the soon to be consecrated Sacré Coeur in Paris Vincent Garrou watched a small group of uniformed *poilus* laughingly shove each other about, bawling coarse insults and tossing caps in the air. Harmless as it all was, it struck him, even as a confirmed atheist, an inappropriate venue for the rumbustious behaviour. I hope, he told himself, that there really is no celestial overseer to take umbrage at this irreverence, or something's going to happen to bring work on this basilica to a sudden halt. Spread out below the Hill of Montmartre the city itself was bathed in the pooling gold light of the early summer evening, stretching away to the hazy horizon. As soon as the soldiers had moved on, an air of tranquillity settled on the scene and even the *gosses* with their skipping ropes and hoops and bouncing balls joined in the hush that had fallen quietly through the deepening twilight. Having returned from London some nights previously Garrou had reported to the Rue Saint-Dominique the confusion that had been sown in British security circles by the apparent melding of potential Irish insurrection with the mysterious German initiative which, if it were genuine, presented a truly horrific prospect.

On arriving back in France he had wired an acquaintance at the office of the newly appointed War Minister Adolphe Messimy and discovered that Captain Brisse, commander of the Legion's outpost in Niger, was on leave in Paris. A wryly worded telegram to Brisse's address in Le Marais that morning had produced an amiable answer and an agreement to catch up on the steps at the Sacré Coeur. When the officer arrived well into Garrou's bout of uncomfortable cogitation he was dressed in plain clothes but no-one would have taken him for anything other than a colonial soldier. After a friendly exchange of greetings Garrou led his companion to an *auberge* in the Place du Tertre, ordered wine and beef bourguignon and turned immediately to the subject. After some hesitation he decided that he might as well spread all his cards on the table.

'I think,' Garrou concluded, 'that the Germans see themselves

A DARKENING FIRE

parading down the Champs Élysées someday soon; or charging across the Steppes; or maybe doing both. So as I read it they see these bomb devices as assurance that the British will stay on the side-lines or risk the destruction of London or other cities.'

Brisse poured himself another glass of wine, assumed an air of sardonic distance and waited to hear more.

'Well,' Garrou said after a lengthy pause, 'that's it. As things stand who in Westminster is going to run such a risk?'

'And so,' Brisse asked, 'you think you can find out one way or the other whether this bomb is the real thing? Surely our universities are full of people who can do that? I can say for sure it's not work for the Legion.'

Garrou splashed another large measure of wine into the Captain's glass, glanced round to make sure once more that nobody could catch what was being said, and replied, 'Is your magnificent Sergeant Heller still out there pissing on passing strangers?'

Brisse sat back, wiping his mouth and permitting himself a slow smile under the dawning of comprehension.

'This place that Krupp have set up – you tell me it's near Munich, eh?'

'Yes, at Freimann.'

'And Sergeant Heller is…'

'Is a Bavarian gentleman.'

That same evening Sergeant Hughes of the Special Branch was sitting by the bedside of Norris Dyer in Edinburgh's Royal Infirmary. The patient's face was deathly pale and only occasionally did he demonstrate any signs of life by issuing a long, whining breath and fractionally flicking his eyelids.

'Be gentle with him,' the stout nurse instructed, 'and don't take too long.'

Still heavily sedated Dyer moved his head only slightly in a faint effort to take in his surroundings, then with a grimace of pain he shifted his unsteady gaze in Hughes' direction. The Sergeant placed a friendly hand on his shoulder, bent forward and casually and succinctly reminded him about the ill-fortune had brought him into the scrupulous care of this hospital.

'You'll be fine in a while. We all want you to rest, get your strength back and get better. Just let me know if there's anything I

A DARKENING FIRE

can get you. OK?'

Dyer managed a weak acknowledgement.

'Now then – I'm here to help you out of the jam you're in, but I can only do that if you let me have the answer to some questions I'm going to put to you. After that, well, you can go back to sleep for as long as you want.'

'What are you asking about?'

Dyer decided that a teary whine was the appropriate tonal mode.

'There's a few questions I need to ask about your pals Ironside and Campbell. If you can fill me in on them, who knows? It could go a long way to knocking a lot of years off your time inside.'

'Time inside?'

The very thought of incarceration for a matter of hours was anathema to the injured man; the rearing up of ghostly and ghastly years in Saughton was too much to confront.

'I'll say anything you want me to say,' he muttered, 'but, Christ, it'll take more than a bit of time off.'

'It's the best I can offer. Now, this South Queensferry trick of yours…'

'That's all finished with.'

'Not exactly. We need to find out who set it up. We can't have folk doing that sort of thing with a war maybe coming.'

'War?' Querulous.

'So you tell me exactly how it was worked and I'll make sure that your cooperation will make a difference. What you need to tell me is what happened after that chap was got away from the place.'

'The Jerry? I had to wait for them in the vennel and…'

'Them?'

'Aye – yon wee fellow with the beard and two others that had him by the arms.'

'What? Like taking him prisoner or just helping him?'

'Jesus, I couldn't tell you. He couldn't stand just about, it was that cold and he looked like he was at death's door, so, no, I didn't have a clue if they were wrestling him or carrying him. And nobody said nothing to me.'

'All right. What happened after you met them in the lane?'

'The plan was I had to take them down to Whitehouse Bay. It

A DARKENING FIRE

was snowing like fuck. The balls were near frozen off me. But when we got down to the river they did a wee dance, the two of them that was hanging onto the wee fellow, they was that angry. There was supposed to be somebody waiting for them – a boat or some bloody thing. But it never turned up – no fucker turned up.'

'The plan? Whose plan?'

'The Dutchman's, you idiot – ten Berge. Who do you think? He gave me the money for myself and Irey and Campbell and told me what I had to do.'

'So there was nobody at the rendezvous?'

'The what? Oh, aye. No, nobody.'

'So you improvised?'

'What?'

'You had to make the thing up as you went along.'

A long, whining sigh, a flicker of the eyelids and then Dyer went on, 'Aye. And your little man's face is kind of grey and green; he looks like he's on his last legs. Then one of the other pair says to me, "You better get us away from here or I'll cut your throat." So we get going along by the river. It's pitch black and snowing like buggery, and the wee Jerry looks like death on a plate. My teeth are falling out of my head with the cold, but we get the three or four miles to Cramond. I never thought I'd manage.'

Hughes was making sporadic notes, and glanced up when Dyer came to a breathless halt in his barely audible narrative. The Sergeant made an encouraging movement of his hand and waited some minutes before Dyer felt up to continuing.

'I've a pal has a wee house there and he took us in. I told him we'd been too long at the drink. He'd seen that plenty before.'

'I'll need his name.'

'Aye. Well, Tommy Beckett. So the next day I get down to Leith and give The Dutchman the fucking tale of woe and he takes his lorry and we bring Jerry and the others down to the *Ineke*. And The Dutchman's cursing the whole time and going on about how much this is going to cost somebody.'

Dyer tried to wipe some saliva from his chin, but gave up the effort.

'Well, then, what about the guns on ten Berge's boat?'

A long pause.

A DARKENING FIRE

'Irey and Campbell are one thing, but crossing these fucking Micks is another altogether.'

'You don't have to. It'll all be down to ten Berge. And we know where the guns came from anyway. Listen, you're still in the mire and we know where the guns were being taken to.'

With another wounded sigh Dyer said, 'There was some fucking Irish wife called Caitlin Hagan. That's all I can tell you.'

'Sorry, Norris. Miss Hagan is a figment of somebody's imagination.'

'Fuck off.' Dyer managed to raise his voice in protest. 'I saw her myself.'

'I mean Miss Hagan wasn't really Miss Hagan at all.'

Dyer's eyes filled up.

'She's a copper?'

'Something like that.'

'Oh, for Christ's sake… '

'There'll be a bobby here to make sure nobody bothers you. Keep well.'

A DARKENING FIRE
CHAPTER 25: JUNE 1914

Eoghan Gallagher read through the manuscript notes which he had collected from the dead-letter drop in St James's Park and which he intended to exchange for funds adequate enough to take him to America. He had to recognise that his mark could almost certainly call on a candidate to deal with the inconvenience of his extortion, and he had spent some weeks in a state of cautious anticipation every time he had embarked on a round of his usual north London haunts to collect the regular donations. There was no shortage of hard cases in these venues who might have been recruited to silence him. His insurance was with the purloined papers which he had insisted would fall into the hands of unforgiving authority if anything happened to him, but his nights had become more sleepless as the agreed date for the exchange of currency for the incriminating hand-written documents he had salted away. The flat off Seven Sisters Road was cramped and none too clean, but it suited. Gallagher never thought of himself as a violent or dangerous man, but now he kept a .455 Webley near at hand. The life of a revolutionary had taken a toll of his nerve and his body. Gaunt and on edge he realised that he had brought this excessive discomfort on himself. At this rate the affair was going to turn him into an aggressive paranoid. He hated the long summer days and yearned for rain and darkness, a more natural habitat for a man of his disposition.

In the foul-smelling kitchen Gallagher ate some none too fresh bread and drank a bottle of stout, watching the shadows thicken in the untended garden at the rear of the building. Because he was sitting in the darkness he could see quite clearly all the way to the high wall surrounding the rubble-strewn patch of ground but it took him some seconds to make out the shape of a man haul itself cursing and yelping over the broken glass *cheveux de frise* and falling in an ungainly heap on the ground. The kitchen window was protected by solid iron bars and there was no other way into the house from the rear, but, taking no chances, Gallagher grabbed the Webley. By the time he had returned a pair of bleeding hands was

A DARKENING FIRE

grasping the bars and a pale, familiar face was emitting a wheedling sound in his direction.

'Let me in, for fuck's sake,' Taaffe seemed to be saying but the sight struck Gallagher as sufficiently entertaining to be left to run for a while longer. When the plea became more urgent and more audible he approached the window and with ill-suppressed amusement explained that the intruder would have to retreat in the direction he had just come in and apply himself to the front door.

'You might want to be a wee bit careful going over this time,' Gallagher sniggered. 'Catch your balls on our defences and you'll be transferring to the dis-Taaffe side.'

Tossing his jacket onto the top of the wall Taaffe, cursing still, scrambled out into the twilight and a minute afterwards was pounding at the street door with a bloodied fist.

'Ach, you'll be fine,' his host insisted, ushering his stricken guest into the cabbage-scented hallway and on into the no less unappealing atmosphere of the flat. 'Pick the shards out of your arse and have a wee *deoch an dorais* before you get on your way. Christ, you look like a *fear bréige*.'

'Aye, you're as funny as itching piles,' Taaffe muttered as he examined his palms and fingers, letting the blood drip dramatically on the bare floor. 'Jesus, I can see there's no expense spared here,' he added, glancing round at the mouldy walls barely visible in the dying daylight.

'I hear the cops are keen to have a few words with you,' Gallagher told him. 'Is it sanctuary you're after in this holy of holies?'

Still flexing his injured extremities and cursing, Taaffe sank into a moth-eaten armchair and made some effort to adjust to his surroundings, recoiling slightly from the musty scent that assailed him.

'I've business here in London,' he said. 'Have you seen Keegan or Breslin? We're due to meet up.'

Edgy and suspicious of the motive behind his unwelcome guest's arrival, Gallagher said, 'I didn't know you were pally with that pair of toe rags. It's bad company you're keeping. And I see you've got a wee friend there in your jacket. Not like you to be carrying a gun, is it?'

A DARKENING FIRE

Taaffe was uneasily aware of his difficulty in maintaining the casual air of a long-term acquaintance, and for the moment he was at a loss to know how to deal with the situation. He had purposely delayed this visit for a day in the hope that his two minders would already have attended to Gallagher, and he had intentionally kept away from Mrs. Fogarty's place for the same reason. Anyhow, he thought, I'm doing nothing until I see what this proof is that Eoghan's been screwing us.

'What do you expect?' he replied as Gallagher at last chose to turn on the spluttering oil lamp. 'They'll not be taking me without a fight. But I've a question for you now. Where's the Glasgow money we've not been collecting since January?'

'Oh, aye. I heard about Butler. But don't you worry – I can put my hand on your share whenever you want it.'

For two men who had had such close ties for so long they were hardly behaving like old friends pleased to be back in each other's company. Taaffe was in a quandary – for a start Gallagher was sitting directly in front of him with a revolver an inch or two from his hand and Taaffe had no intention of engaging in a gun fight. And even if the opportunity suddenly presented itself he wasn't about to put a bullet in the man and spend the rest of the night ransacking the place in the remote expectation of discovering the evidence of betrayal that Protzman had claimed was there to be found

'I'll have that dram now,' he said, playing for time to decide on his next move.

'You're not yourself, Ciarán,' Gallagher observed, getting slowly to his feet and, without turning his back, reached for the bottle and a greasy glass and passed them to his visitor.

'I'm not exactly going to be on the pig's back with every copper in the land on my tail.'

Inspecting the half-full tumbler and noting that Gallagher himself was for once not imbibing, Taaffe made up his mind abruptly to shed all pretence that this was either a debt collecting occasion, a plea for refuge or simply a call by an old chum.

'Did you hear I've been in Germany? About the guns. Maybe Boylan let you in on it?'

'They tell me damn all nowadays unless the money's a day or

A DARKENING FIRE

two late. It's dicey for them to be too close to me nowadays.'

'I've handed over just about every bloody penny my outfit's got so that your man Spiro will get us some Mannlichers. Nothing to do with the shipment Casement and the rest are after for the Council. Boylan told me to spend what we've got left ourselves on a load to go to Leith. But the money wasn't enough. Me and the boys had to sign up to do some dirty work for the Jerries over here.'

Taaffe gulped down his whiskey and held out the smeary glass for another.

'What's this dirty work the Huns want you to do for them?'

'What? Oh,' Taaffe was annoyed at himself for letting this slip unnecessarily, 'a wee bit of smuggling is all.'

A brooding silence welled up in the fusty room for several minutes while Taaffe absently swished the dregs of his drink around the opaque glass and again turned his attention to his wounded hands.

'Where the fuck are Breslin and Keegan I'd like to know? It's the three of us got landed with doing the Huns a favour.'

'You're not telling me the whole story, Ciarán. I can feel it.'

Taaffe's eye strayed to the Webley still lying close to Gallagher's free hand and suddenly the whole ludicrousness of their circumstance came pounding out of the fetid shadows and rammed him in the chest. He gave way to a spasm of candour.

'Listen to me, Eoghan, and keep the hair on your head when you hear me out.'

In an access of sentiment Taaffe, forgetting about the pain in his hands and the more serious damage to his credibility, recounted briefly the gist of what he, Keegan and Breslin had been instructed to do by way of sneaking the final components of the bombs into the country.

'The idea was supposed to be,' he wound up, 'that if we did that the Jerries would make up the shortfall in what we could pay for the guns.'

'Let me get this straight. Your German *rifineach* has smuggled in all the bits and bobs of some kind of great big bomb and built them up somewhere in the English cities, right?'

Taaffe held out his glass for more whiskey, a request which Gallagher ignored.

A DARKENING FIRE

'And you and your jackeens were bringing in the one last part to set the things off when the time came – whenever the hell that was going to be?'

'Aye, that's about the strength of it. But you can see the profit for us. And the Brits get the shite scared out of them so they'll not gang up against the Germans.'

'Not gang up against the Germans? And what good's that to us? So their fucking army can do what it likes in Ireland without the worry of sending it across the Channel to help the Frogs if it comes to that.'

'Jesus Christ, Eoghan, give me some credit. That's exactly what I said, and your man Protzman… well, he told me that we needn't bother on that score. Once the bombs were set up the Jerries would tell the Brits to get the fuck out of Ireland, or else. And if that wasn't the way of it, the German army would be on our side anyway.'

Then seized by a sudden conviction that the Germans had all along seen him and his fellow smugglers as a trio of useful idiots he spilled out to Gallagher in a rush of unfamiliar veracity the other chore allocated to them.

'Ciarán Taaffe and his wee gang have been sent here to do me in, is that it?' Gallagher asked with a sour smile when Taaffe had exhausted his narrative and splenetic vocabulary. 'And for what mortal sin was I to be consigned to the eternal flames?'

'I've told you the lot,' he said, 'and you're alive and kicking. Point is, what are we going to do now? I mean – you and me?'

Gallagher stood up slowly and by the dull, flickering light walked off into the bedroom and emerged again after five minutes with a bundle of small sheets of paper covered in fine, spidery writing.

'I'm likely putting my life back in your hands,' he said, 'but maybe we're both where we belong again. I can't tell you what this stuff means to the Cause, but you'll see for yourself that they put somebody else in the deepest shite if they ever see the light of day.'

A DARKENING FIRE
CHAPTER 26: JUNE 1914

As the darkness rolled out of the summer sky and brought haloed lights on in the buildings and streets of north London the Fogarty house on Crouch Hill was surrounded by plain clothes and uniformed police officers armed with Bull Dog revolvers, shotguns and small bore rifles; and by a detachment of better armed marksmen from the Scots Guards. Since the Hembrug had been brandished at the window McGarrity and his colleagues had taken cover behind the low garden walls on the far side of the street, but not a single shot had been fired and the gun had not reappeared. It had been McGarrity's inclination to barge into the place regardless of hazard, but with the arrival of Assistant Commissioner Thomson the operation had taken a less precipitate direction.

'They'll be going nowhere,' Thomson had counselled. 'We'll wait the bastards out.'

Towards midnight Todd arrived on the scene, his face as usual inscrutable but no-one doubted the depth of his reaction to the news that Harriet Nichols had been killed. Crouching beside him McGarrity gave him the name Harriet had whispered to him.

'Klausen?' Todd muttered. 'I warned The Owl about that scheming…'

'The Owl?'

'A colleague of mine. This Klausen had already cost us dear. I'll be dealing with him myself when we get hold of him.'

'Maybe not,' McGarrity replied. 'His skull is split wide open and he probably won't see out the night according to the Holborn Union Infirmary.'

'Shame.' As usual, Todd's voice gave little away. 'How did that come about?'

'I ran into him. Accident.'

'Things happen,' Todd said. 'Anyhow, you and I willl likely meet up in Scotland tomorrow. There's still work for me up there too.'

Before McGarrity could embroider his account the air was filled with the reverberation of a muffled explosion from the other

A DARKENING FIRE

side of the road. Peering over the wall McGarrity could see in the encroaching dark that some of the windows of the Fogarty house had been shattered and thick smoke was pouring from the ground floor. There was a shout from the building, the Hembrug rifle was tossed into the street, the front door swung open and the stout figure of Mrs. Fogarty emerged shrieking with the stumbling Brendan Keegan close behind, his hands held high. In a moment both were surrounded by officers and handcuffs applied none too gently.

'Get these people out of here,' Thomson ordered. 'I want them at the Yard in an hour, and keep them well apart. Right, lads, let's see what or who's left over there.'

And he led a swarm of police and soldiers into the still juddering building while hundreds of curious onlookers materialised out of the night shouting complaint as they were held back by a rigid cordon of officers. The air inside was hardly breathable, filled as it was by dust and smoke, and lanterns had to be produced to show the way through the wreckage beyond the entrance. Weapons at the ready half a dozen Scots Guardsmen led the way into the dense, choking cloud of soot, ash and dross. Gaping holes had been opened over the cellar space and the walls of the hall were cracked and peeling. Proceeding with nervous care the advance guard hesitated at the huge opening that had been blasted through the floorboards. The bluish beams of the torches caught the sworl of drifting strands of lath and plywood, and picked out the wreckage below where pieces of metal mingled with the bloody remains of a human body strewn around the basement. Shouts from above confirmed that there was nobody else in the building.

Signalling one or two of his least unnerved men to accompany the sapper provided by the army Thomson directed the sealing off of the house, sent officers out to find engineers who could advise on the safety of the place and for medics who could deal with the gory mess clinging to the walls and ceiling of the cellar.

'Mr. Breslin's last act of revolt,' McGarrity murmured. 'Made sure that stuff they smuggled in wasn't going to give us any more clues to what they were really for. Brave fellow.'

Booked on that evening's sleeper to Edinburgh the Inspector spent a short time looking round the rest of what remained of Mrs.

A DARKENING FIRE

Fogarty's home. Aside from a discarded pistol on the first floor there was little of significance to be found. Shortly before he was due to be driven to King's Cross Superintendent Quinn turned up and the two Special Branch men spent some minutes in quiet conference.

'It looks like Breslin died to protect this secret they were toting around with them,' Quinn said. 'And that leaves us with a big problem. God knows how we're going to find out where the unarmed bombs are now, and it's a safe bet that more of these fuse things or detonators or whatever they're called will get through one way or another.'

'Maybe you'll get something out of Keegan, but I doubt it. For all their *claon chun oilc* they're hard men who believe in their cause.'

'Maybe you and I do, too, but we're not about to go about killing folk over it. Anyhow, *slán abhaile* and good luck to you now up there in sunny Scotland while I see what our patriotic miners, dockers and transport workers are planning for us next. Oh, aye, and our well-bred suffragettes, our Fenians and our German spies.'

'Ah, you're a poor and hard-done-by man, Pat. And here am I taking to the heather and leaving you to it.'

No such reflection was diverting Todd as he was driven the short distance to King's Cross. Never one to betray any emotion other than ill-humour, he had been profoundly shocked at Harriet's death. Such extreme outcomes had not been his experience and with his network of agents in the darker corners of both England and Europe so badly impaired who aside from the tireless and resourceful Owl, he wondered, was there still to trust, and who trusted Todd himself?

At the station he caught brief sight of the giant McGarrity lingering over a pint of stout and a large glass of whiskey and toyed with the idea of joining him, but as he stood in the concourse his instinct held him back for a minute and he let his wary alertness concentrate on a shabby figure pretending to read a copy of yesterday's Times, but mostly peering surreptitiously into the almost empty bar. Either there was something vaguely familiar about the man or Todd himself was beginning to see enemies where

A DARKENING FIRE

none existed. He had told his bodyguard to return the car to the office and take a couple of days off, so it was a slight inconvenience not to be able to share the observation of the observer – he knew too well that if he could so easily spot a Watcher then he too could just as readily be picked out. And he was unable to shake a grinding sense of guilt that he had been responsible for putting Harriet in danger. Without a glance in the other's direction Todd passed through the barrier and headed for his compartment, hesitating only when he was confronted by a newspaper vendor waving a copy of the day's Times opened to the leading article headed "The Tragedy of Sarajevo." He had made a profession of attending to the undercurrents competing beneath Europe's relatively tranquil surface, and had long ago been persuaded that they were shortly going to hurl a wave of calamity onto the shore of the prevailing complacence.

A DARKENING FIRE
CHAPTER 27: JUNE 1914

Within hours of the news from Sarajevo becoming public Vincent Garrou, having tucked away for early reference the secret arrangement he had made with Captain Brisse of the Foreign Legion, had been summoned to the headquarters of the Deuxième Bureau and charged by his boss Colonel Dupont to proceed urgently with the previously agreed mission to London. Left a little bewildered by his sudden elevation to the status of confidential go-between endowed with almost plenipotential authority he nevertheless was pleased at the prospect of dipping his oar into the waters of furtive diplomacy. And along with a set of formal credentials and specific matters to communicate he went armed with an agenda of his own. He travelled with all possible speed by train and ferry, reaching Whitehall Court in time to catch Sir Derwent Hartington's grim-faced PPS Ackroyd arriving in haste for the day's labours.

'I thought Mr. Todd might be with you. There's no sign of him at his own place,' Garrou explained without taking a breath.

'Unfortunately Mr. Todd has taken himself off northward on some undefined mission. However I have our security heads here this morning. No doubt they will be happy to consult with you after my business with them is complete. You have no objection to a short delay?'

'Of course not. Aside from Mr. Todd I was hoping to see my friend Captain Cummings.'

'I'll have him join you when this little conference is over.'

And leaving his assistant Solomon to take charge of the outer office and its vaguely embarrassed French occupant Ackroyd gestured impatiently, and marched into Hartington's suite where Major Kell of the Security Service, Captain Smith Cummings of the Secret Intelligence Service and William Melville of the Secret Service's spy-hunting section were assembled.

'Gentlemen,' Ackroyd said, settling at the head of the table, 'I find myself in the most delicate position and I have to rely on both your forbearance and your discretion. As you are aware I'm nothing

A DARKENING FIRE

more than a humble civil servant and if you find me to be exceeding my authority I shall have to throw myself on your mercy.'

'A humble civil servant?' Smith Cummings repeated from an armchair by the window. 'What's the word for that again? Oxymoron or something.'

'Sir Derwent will be at the War Office and then at the Home Office until this evening. In his absence yesterday I was instructed to provide Number 10 with some extremely sensitive material relating to our relations with Sazonov and Hartwig. Because the summons was urgent I asked Mr. Solomon, in Sir Derwent's absence, to search his office in the hope that what I required had not been placed in his private safe. I was in luck – Sir Derwent had been called away by Mr. Churchill at the Admiralty. The First Lord brooks no delay and Sir Derwent left without his customary attention to wardenship of his domain. The safe was closed but he had been in so great a rush that he had omitted properly to lock it.'

'Aye, well,' Melville remarked, 'it seems we're doomed to live in exciting times.'

'I must ask that you all treat this matter as for your eyes only for the moment.'

The note he dropped on the desk was hand-written clearly and boldly enough to be read where it rested. Kell picked it up, glanced at it and handed it to Melville who tossed it across to Cummings.

"I know that your Casement. If anything happens to me it all gets past on to police. I'll let you know what's next."

'No gold star for syntax. If this is what you called us in for I suppose you can tell us what it means?'

'I'd hoped *you* might tell *me*.'

'Have you any idea who wrote it?'

'None. And no idea what the "*all*" is.

'But obviously you believe there's something to be read into it or else you wouldn't have brought us here.'

Ackroyd nodded.

'It just seemed a little strange,' he said, 'that such a curious little note should suddenly turn up like this. It says nothing but suggests much. It occurs to me that it's been conveniently planted for discovery by me or one of my staff.'

A DARKENING FIRE

'To what end?' Smith Cummings asked. 'I see nothing damning or even specific about it. And what's this Casement thing supposed to mean?'

Kell ran his hand over the back of the sheet of paper.

'I'm inclined to agree with Dr. Ackroyd,' he said. 'It's maybe just enough to sow seeds of suspicion at a time when we're all busy looking at each other as potential traitors.'

'My view exactly,' Ackroyd replied. 'The purpose of the thing might be to divert suspicion in the direction of the very man the PM has charged with uncovering the spy in our midst.'

'Well,' Melville put in, 'at least you can tell us who would have access to Sir Derwent's safe.'

'In normal times and aside from me and Sir Derwent himself only Sebastian Solomon and Cecil Highway. But over the last day or two there has been more coming and going than ever. I'd like to claim the safe has been locked whenever the office was unoccupied but it would be foolish of me to insist that has been the case. And anyway much of the time there has been little or nothing confidential in it. Secret papers are kept in the larger safe in the outer office.'

'Much as I'd like to dismiss the thing,' Kell said, 'I think we must follow this up in some way.'

Ackroyd looked uneasy.

'You mean to confront Sir Derwent? With a scrap of paper that means nothing to any of us. Perhaps you'd give some thought to my own position – how would Sir Derwent react with the knowledge that I'd been responsible for setting this hare running and there is a simple and entirely innocent explanation?'

'I'd have thought he might be impressed by your concern for security. But how about this – tomorrow I'll let Sir Derwent have a Strictly Personal about the new security arrangements are being planned for the Channel ports. If that turns up in Berlin we'll know where we stand. I suggested something of the sort a while ago but nothing came of it then.'

'But until then we can hardly omit Sir Derwent from the usual circulation of secret papers,' Ackroyd objected.

'I believe we can,' Melville said, 'via your good offices. Surely you can delay or mislay anything of real importance for the few

A DARKENING FIRE

days it should take to do as Vernon has suggested? You mention Mr. Todd. I take it that he's still a regular visitor?'

'Of course. As you know Sir Derwent has left it to him to flush out the spy in our midst.'

After the meeting Cummings accompanied Garrou out of the building past the gloomy doorkeeper Tolley and into the brilliant sunshine of the month's end. The Frenchman was pocketing a note passed to him by Kell and addressed to McGarrity.

'Well, now, let me arrange a cab for you in an hour or so, M Garrou. Then while we here are busy sorting through each other's dirty linen you can be on your way to Bonnie Scotland to collar the sinister Mr. Todd. But first let's have a few minutes to mull over whatever it is that your Colonel Dupont is prepared to contribute to our collective endeavours. He has anxieties about our ability to keep confidences so let's keep this between ourselves for the time being.'

A DARKENING FIRE
CHAPTER 28: JUNE 1914

Conrad Schweitz was contemplating the mysteries of the world from a window of his base in Berlin. War was coming to the continent: the components of the conflagration had been long in the contriving and now that the lighted taper had been applied to them in Sarajevo that candescent event could not be far off. There could be no more suitable eyrie for contemplating this imminent occurrence than the ancient tower from which he studied the inescapable trundle of history. There was, he was convinced, a historical inevitability to the coming conflict.

His admiration for the British acquisition of their mighty Empire had mutated into the belief that this ramshackle conglomerate was on the wane, that by a Darwinian process Germany would rise to dominate first the whole of Europe and then replace moribund England as the greatest colonial authority. Am I a fanatic, he asked himself, to hold to this vision? In his most sober moments he would reply that perhaps he was. Terrifying the British into neutrality would be only the first step. The second would be taken when Germany's position on the continent was assured by force: the prize would be a world divided between the two nations, related by blood and culture. And when that protracted phase had run its course it would be succeeded by a German ascendancy as the British Empire subsided into irrevocable decadence.

And to ensure this outcome a jigsaw of evidential pieces had had to be assembled with sufficient skill to show that Rupprecht's atom-fracturing bombs possessed an earth-shattering potency. English scientists were far enough advanced in the field of natural philosophy to persuade their political masters of the appalling destructive power of the devices, even if their own practical work lagged far behind. This part of the operation Schweitz had mapped out with the assistance of Helmut Protzman, a mid-level intellect who, Schweitz believed, could readily be manipulated into the conviction that he alone was contriving the whole affair. The dispatch to Britain of the alleged fugitive Rupprecht and his subsequent retrieval had been a masterstroke, of course, though

A DARKENING FIRE

Schweitz, looking back on the gamut of tortuous machination, could no longer be completely sure who had proposed it and who had conducted it to a satisfactory outcome. It had been a colossal risk but if Kaiser Wilhelm was determined that none of the bombs could be exploded to evidence their prodigious power every stratagem was necessary to compel the English to recognition of their louring vulnerability. But these were matters to be pursued as expediency.

More demanding of careful planning was the handling of British reaction to the reality facing them. It was here that Schweitz prided himself on having properly guided the Kaiser's hand. It came as no surprise to him that the issue had reached King George himself and even before it had been raised in the diplomatic forum he had formulated a draft response on which the Kaiser had commented favourably. Its terms were designed to confirm the line already taken informally by Protzman posing as an informer. Only at the apposite moment on the eve of war with France would a formal reply be sent expressing the Kaiser's horrified discovery that a cabal of disaffected military had indeed succeeded in misappropriating the weapon. That communique would go on to explain that it was the intention of the guilty men to detonate these terrible weapons only if the British entered into hostilities against Germany. Every effort would be made by the counterintelligence services to identify them and discover where the bombs had been placed. These details would be passed to the British security services. The Kaiser would conclude by pleading for King George's patience while the perpetrators were traced and dealt with. Minister of War Frankenhayn and others had been consulted and agreed with Schweitz that the line adopted would afford sufficient time for the French to be routed while the English hesitated. But if the worst came to the worst and the British were not to be deflected from coming to the aid of their Entente partners the detonation of a bomb combined with the threat to use yet more of them would quite enough to deter the British from further involvement in the conflict. Schweitz's response to the earlier approach by Sir Christopher Cresswell would help promote the stealthy ambiguity that the Kaiser's reaction was intended to serve.

All in all, Schweitz confided to himself, his commitment to this

A DARKENING FIRE

complex and dangerous project was likely to be the crowning achievement of his illustrious career. It was true that he had made use of people like Protzman without their knowledge, but the value of the prize was inestimable – which the Kaiser himself recognised. Rubbing his hands Schweitz viewed with quiet satisfaction the news from England. He could now be confident that Protzman's betrayal of Keegan and Breslin to the customs authorities in Harwich had ensured reinforcement of the belief that the bombs – the *atomic* bombs as Rupprecht's shorthand designated them – were already in place in the cities of the United Kingdom and that all that was required for them to be fully primed was the addition of the sort of devices that the Irishmen had been carrying. What remained was for a second tranche of the fuses to be put in place. If handled properly there was nothing in all this which could be attributed to the government in Berlin. And a destructive fissure was being opened up between the Entente powers that at the very least would create a period of such uncertainty in Whitehall that it would detain beyond the critical point any intervention by the English on the coming western front.

There was something pleasingly nightmarish, he thought, about Rupprecht's definition of the weapon: *atomic bomb*. Probably not original, but so esoteric, so haunting, so fearsome. The unspeakable power of such devices sent a shiver coursing down his spine as he tried to imagine the fabric of the world blasted apart in a holocaust of uncontrolled ferocity. The sweltering June evening was declining into a peaceful wash of deepening shades which daubed the window of his office and cast his hunched reflection back at him. Scowling at this cruel image of an elderly, tired man he shook his head at the chronological reality it conveyed. Now over seventy he remained, he tried to assure himself, a dynamic thirty year old in his head. With a shrug he discarded these ruminations and turned his attention to the remains of the day.

It was his habit to stroll by the river for an hour before returning for a late dinner at his palatial home near the Friedrich-Wilhelms University. Schweitz was by nature a solitary man, professionally secretive and personally distant. His wife and daughter – the latter coming to him late in life – were dear to him beyond words and as the world became a grimmer place under the

A DARKENING FIRE

broiling sun of that summer he had grown more reticent and more pessimistic for their future. In addition the fear that his intellect and perhaps his memory were deserting him was becoming an obsession, eclipsing even his untiring service to the Reich. Plunged in that clandestine gloom further darkened by the onset of night he found himself ambling aimlessly along the Reichstagufer. Having paused to watch the river become a ribbon of heliotrope velvet he crossed the street and, leaning more heavily on his cane after the long walk, followed the Neustädtische Kirchstrasse back down to the Dorotheenstrasse. As was his custom he stopped at the neo-baroque Splendid Restaurant and drank a couple of glasses of Schnapps, just another nameless customer in the busy, upmarket establishment. Slightly irked by the noisy, jovial banter of the wealthy clientele ignorant of the parlous state of a once-civilised world he gathered up his redundant overcoat, hat and walking stick and went out into the welcome coolness and quiet of the night air.

The streets were deserted early and Schweitz hesitated on the kerb to allow a solitary horse-drawn cab to trundle past him on the corner of Charlottenstrasse. Now only a few hundred metres from his home in the University quarter he felt at last that he could put the wearying events of the past several days behind him and it was this absorption in the prospect of the welcoming comfort of family, chintz, flock-paper and friendly shades that concealed from him for a moment the presence of the other man standing stock-still in the recessed doorway of a building almost within touching distance. With a start Schweitz recoiled from this ungainly figure, relaxing only when he realised the man was even shorter and less physically imposing than he was himself.

'Do you remember,' this stranger asked, stepping forward to block Schweitz's advance, 'the name Fenner?'

Caught by surprise Schweitz recoiled and raised his weighty horse-head hazel cane, more as a token of apprehensiveness than defiance or defence.

'Go away,' he said hoarsely, 'or I'll call the police.'

And Schweitz peered into the stifling murk in an effort to identify the source of this confrontation and saw only a plump, pale-faced little man wearing spectacles so large that they conveyed the impression of a startled owl.

A DARKENING FIRE

'Let's walk a little together,' The Owl said, 'so that I can explain myself.'

And hooking his arm in Schweitz's he led his reluctant companion along the deserted pavement and continued to talk in an amicable, subdued tone.

'Doctor Fenner,' he said, 'was a good friend of mine. A harmless chap – very clever, much to offer the world.'

Schweitz pulled away from his insistent companion and moved a hand to the handle of his walking stick. The Owl barely glanced at him.

'Please,' he said, 'I know you have a sword in that, but make no mistake: I could shoot you dead long before you could draw the thing.'

And, pausing, The Owl whispered, 'Magda and Lotte.'

'My wife's name. And my daughter's... I hardly need to be advised of them.'

'It would be most unfortunate if some unforeseen incident should befall them if the head of the family failed to comply with certain instructions.'

Schweitz stared down disbelievingly at the little man.

'I understand your revulsion,' The Owl told him, leading him off again into the gathering twilight. 'But we live in cruel times. Of course you are already thinking that as soon as you return home you will arrange for your very efficient security service to spirit your wife and daughter to safety, but I'm afraid that even if you could do so in the next few seconds you would be too late.'

Staggering slightly Schweitz leaned against a wall for support, his hostility transformed to mind-numbing fear.

'What is it you want from me?' he demanded hoarsely.

'I'm coming to that,' The Owl assured him. 'We can talk as we walk. May I use "*du*" – like old pals. A little cooperation and in a few days I'm told you will be rid of us forever. A little too lenient in my view, but I'm a man who obeys orders.'

A DARKENING FIRE
CHAPTER 29: JUNE 1914

At Waverley Station in Edinburgh McGarrity was again collected from the sleeper by Inspector Mitchell who had elected on this occasion to drive the police car himself. On the journey west out of the city McGarrity reported laconically on what had transpired in London and Mitchell outlined the measures the local force had taken in an effort to find out if any of the occupants of Talbot House could have succeeded in communicating with the outside world. It was possible that Karoline Petzold had somehow managed to convey details of the security and other arrangements at the House in the course of her regular walks by the river. She alone of the group had ever left the building and the grounds, but even so she had been under constant supervision. No mail or any other means of passing on messages had been permitted at the estate itself.

'You think it's worth following any of this up now?' Mitchell wondered. 'Bolting stable door and all that.'

'There's still something to be got out of them. And this Sarajevo affair means we need to get this thing resolved in short order. There's no telling what's lying just over the horizon. If there's some party here that can magic people out of our sight we need to lay hands on them – if they're still in the country.'

After Mitchell had set off back to Edinburgh Hughes and McGarrity had dinner in the Sealscraig Hotel and watched from the window of the dining room as they dying sun bled across the unruffled surface of the wide estuary.

'You might want to hear this,' Hughes told McGarrity when they had adjourned to the bar. 'I was having a few earnest words again with Campbell and it seems he's been minded to shed a little light on our darkness. He'd like to talk to you.'

'I'll see him tomorrow. What else has been going on up here?'

The two men sat on in conversation until the barman, bereft of other custom began to sigh audibly and stare at the clock.

'I believe,' McGarrity said as they finished a final drink, 'that I'll take a stroll before I turn in.'

A DARKENING FIRE

'You want company?' the Sergeant asked, but McGarrity shook his head.

'I've a wee bit of thinking to get out of the way,' he answered. 'And I want to get back south soon enough, so let's pull things together in the morning, make up our minds about what we do next and aim for me to be back in London by the end of the week.'

The summer days were long in this part of the world but even so night was starting to fall by the time the big man set off along the deserted High Street that ran parallel to the waterfront. Pausing for a moment by a guttering streetlamp he leaned on a railing and peered out at the angular, elegant complexity of the great bridge edged against the vast, starry sky; then he ambled the hundred or so yards past the Jubilee Clock Tower and turned into the lane that led down to the harbour. Here the shadows were thick and heavy, gathered in silence between the buildings on either side, and even his vast bulk quickly became invisible in the almost tangible gloom. His pursuer came by small, careful steps, testing the cobbles to avoid discarded odds and ends that might betray his presence. The only light was the distant reflection of the moon on the river and the only sound was the quiet lapping of water and the occasional nuzzling creak of timber from boats in the port. Holding his breath and hesitating every few feet the man moved slowly, giving himself time to accustom his vision to the dense darkness. This painstaking progress was suddenly interrupted by a violent impetus from behind that sent him careering against the unforgiving surface of a stone wall. Left stunned, breathless and bleeding from his nose and forehead he made an ineffectual effort to turn and confront his assailant but found himself held immobile by brute force, his neck clamped in an iron grip and his arm twisted agonisingly against his back.

'I thought we might have a word before you go for a swim in the harbour there,' McGarrity said quietly. 'So I'd like to know what brings you creeping around at my heels and all the way from King's Cross.'

'Get your hands off me.' The reply was muffled and plaintive. 'I'm only here to…'

There was a lengthy pause before it gathered pace.

'I'm here to look after you. My orders…'

A DARKENING FIRE

Keeping a firm hold on the other's collar, McGarrity patted at the man's jacket pockets and extracted a small revolver. Snapping open the chamber he held the weapon vertical until each of the six rounds had clattered on the ground.

'Look after me, is it? And how would you propose to attend to my wellbeing with this wee thing? Not a bullet in the back of my head, I hope, for it's been tried before.'

'Christ, no. I mean it – Sir Derwent Hartington sent me. He's worried about you.'

'Well, that's damn decent of him. And why would that be?'

'I'm not supposed… Look – can you let me go now? I'll tell you what I know.'

'Aye, it'll be better for the pair of us if you do.'

'Let me…' and with some trepidation the man drew out an identity card which he passed to the policeman with a trembling hand. The document indicated that he was Terrence Edwards, an agent of Hartington's small, secretive organisation. Releasing his hold, McGarrity spun the man round and stood looming over him, his face expressionless.

'This has to go no further,' Edwards began, but McGarrity's grim non-reaction encouraged him to skip the preliminaries. 'You will have heard of Sir Derwent Hartington, of course?'

'Get on with it.'

'You're in Scotland to interrogate some folk at Talbot House, right? Sir Derwent says you could be in some danger here, from some Jerries or more likely Micks – begging your pardon, I mean Irish.'

'Hartington told you this?'

'That's all I heard and nothing more. I'm just supposed to make sure you come to no harm while you're here.'

'Well, you're a reassuring presence right enough. Anything more that needs to be revealed to me for the good of my health?'

Edwards shifted uneasily in the murk, his eyes fixed on McGarrity's clenched fists.

'All I'm at,' he said finally, 'is passing on what I've been told by Sir Derwent's Private Secretary Ackroyd. He's worried that something could happen to you because of your… well, whatever it is you're doing here. He says there are people that…'

A DARKENING FIRE

'And these *people* have names?'

'I don't get told that kind of thing. Just what to do.'

'And Dr. Ackroyd explained why he thinks I'm in such a parlous condition?'

'Well, he said, you know – all that undercover stuff for months... that kind of thing. And these... visions... your late wife... it must be...'

Again Edwards's voice tailed off into embarrassed intermission.

McGarrity shook his head in mild amusement.

'So our esteemed masters think I'm bound for Bedlam, do they?'

'They need you safe, that's all.'

Left to reflect on the limit of the support as manifested in the unhappy Edwards, McGarrity handed over the empty gun and started off back up the lane.

'One more thing,' he called over his shoulder. 'Where are you and Todd staying? I might want to have a talk with him shortly.'

'Todd?'

'I saw him at King's Cross and he was sneaking around at Waverley trying to escape notice too.'

'Sorry, Inspector. I never heard of the man.'

McGarrity pondered this and said, 'You hear that, Mr. Todd? Can I trust this fellow?'

Todd emerged from the place he had concealed himself while following McGarrity's follower.

'Very good, Inspector. And here was I thinking all the way from the Great Wen that you might be unaware of this chap dogging your footsteps and in need of my assistance. Where Mr. Edwards is billeted I couldn't say, but I've a room at the Hawes Inn. Maybe we could adjourn there for a brief conference. I doubt, though, if we need detain our mutual friend here.'

'Then I'll be off back to London tomorrow if you've no use for me here,' the sheepish Edwards grunted and stalked off into the night with hunched shoulders and an air of resignation. Ten minutes later McGarrity and Todd were closeted in the latter's room at the small hotel and sipping whiskey from tooth glasses. McGarrity wanted to know why Todd had come traipsing up to Scotland.

A DARKENING FIRE

'For a quick word with the Gormley fellow you have locked up in Edinburgh. This whole affair is being handled with too much regard for official sensitivities.'

'And did you prise anything useful from his culchie *béal*?'

'Maybe. Meantime I can tell you I've been letting loose my predilection for reprisal. My initial instinct was to have a Berlin fellow called Schweitz killed. I know he was behind our chap Fenner being shot at the Krupp place in Essen. But instead I'm having him gently waylaid.'

'*Tá plean ar bun.*'

'That Frenchie Garrou has come up with an idea that he thinks will appeal to the sense of fair play I lack. He's on his way here: I wanted him well away from our London coterie. Smith Cummings is the only other fellow we've enlisted.'

'And so the next thing is what?'

'We all know the answer to this whole sordid affair is to be had in that place in Bavaria called Freimann.'

'An expedition, then?'

'First there's something you should hear about our esteemed Sir Derwent Hartington, and I'll be interested in what you think about it.'

Todd briefly outlined the gist of Ackroyd's revelations which William Melville had conveyed to him earlier in the day by encrypted telegram.

A DARKENING FIRE
CHAPTER 30: JULY 1914

'Keegan's a good man whatever you say,' Ciarán Taaffe told Gallagher when news of the siege at Crouch Hill and Breslin's suicidal defiance was displayed in dramatic headlines in the newspaper Gallagher picked up from the front step. 'You can be sure they'll give him a rough time, but he'll hold out long enough for the rest of us to get well out of the way.'

'Aye, maybe,' Gallagher said, already setting about packing the few belongings that would accompany him to Liverpool and on across the Atlantic. 'But tomorrow I'm off to collect my dues and you won't see my arse back in this fine city any day soon. And, Christ, you've been here long enough yourself.'

Taaffe watched these hasty preparations dispassionately then switched his attention to the revolver on the table and now well out of Gallagher's reach.

'So you *are* running out on us?'

'If that's what you think there's fuck all I can do to change your mind. But let me tell you this – I've put in as many years working for the Cause as you've done, and I've not been the one brought the coppers to my door.'

'*Anois atámid I sáinn*. But don't put the blame for the Clarkson midden on me. We were given away by your pal Butler, remember.'

'So you say. But where is he now? And where's your man McGarrity that you set on him? And what about yon fellow Gormley? I heard he lifted half those guns from under your nose? Aye, you've been a great success yourself, eh?'

'I'd say Butler is at the bottom of the Clyde where he belongs. And if it's true what you say about Gormley I'll deal with him myself when the boys find him out.'

Gallagher sighed with exasperation.

'I don't *want* to walk out on the Cause,' he said. 'But things have got buggered up lately. The coppers are getting too close to me now. I'm tired and I need to get out for a bit.'

Once again Taaffe glanced at the Webley, measuring the time it would take for Gallagher to reach it if he drew his own weapon.

A DARKENING FIRE

'Eoghan, I'm a right fucking bastard for what I'm thinking,' he confessed, slumping back in his chair.

Gallagher looked at him, debating whether to ask him to elaborate and settling for silence. Taaffe rolled his eyes.

'The boys will find you one day,' he said quietly.

'Like enough, but that's better than getting banged up in Brixton in a day or two.'

'Where will you go exactly?'

'Best for both of us if you don't know.'

Taaffe stood up and grudgingly offered his hand. Slinging his bag over his shoulder he nodded once, tapped Gallagher's arm and without another word led the way down the corridor to the front door of the building. The air smelled of a rancid combination of rotting vegetables and urine.

'You'll miss this,' he muttered as he opened the door. The dawn spilled into the space to illuminate the foul debris that had accumulated in the passageway. He had covered three steps when the shot cracked against the draping silence. Turning by instinct he was confronted by his friend's open-mouthed confusion as he clutched his chest, the blood pumping between his fingers and with a strange rattling sigh Gallagher collapsed on the stone floor. Impelled by years of experience Taaffe reacted without thinking. Discarding his travel bag he went racing from the scene, dodging back and forth along the deserted pavement expecting to feel the impact of a bullet in his back with every erratic stride. Covering a hundred yards before he was confident that he was either out of range or left to make good his escape he slowed at the corner of the street gasping for breath, the sweat pouring down his face. The sheer ordinariness of the warm July morning closed around him like a suffocating dermis. It seemed impossible that so traumatic an event had gone unnoticed even at that ungodly hour but not a soul had appeared in the road or been roused by the sound of the gun. Fear and a crushing despair bundled him into a weed-strewn lane and catching his foot in half-hidden pothole he was sent sprawling on the ground, the scent of damp grass and earth suddenly having a calming effect on him.

For several minutes he lay breathless, clearing his mind in the lee of a high stone wall. There was no sight or sound of pursuit and

A DARKENING FIRE

he estimated that even his bobbing and weaving retreat would hardly have saved him if he had been a second target. The time to reflect on who the sniper had been and on whose orders he had acted was not now, though, and Taaffe forced himself to make his way up the narrow backstreet, passing half a dozen exits and casting repeated glances backward, until he reached a busy city byway where he felt he could merge anonymously into the crowd. He found a place in a seedy café from which he could watch the coming and going outside through a grimy window, his hand shaking as he tried to convey the impression of a casual coffee drinker *en route* for a normal working day. It was only now dawning on him that he had dumped the holdall containing the detonating device. And the evidence of Gallagher's treason which he had meant, he said, to go to the police in the event of his demise was now lying scattered on his table and, like the detonator device, ready for retrieving by whoever had pulled the trigger.

With diminishing financial resources Taaffe was in a quandary. He still had contacts in London and in Liverpool and Glasgow, but if the Council back in Ireland still had marked him out as a dangerous incompetent or, given recent events, a Judas he could expect short shrift at their hands. He had no way of discovering whether that estimate of his compatriots' disposition was accurate, but an error in computation would in all probability cost him an excruciating conclusion to his life. But just maybe things could be set right if he could track down Protzman. The Brotherhood's prospects were tied tightly to their German contacts and if the *quid pro quo* for a supply of guns to what remained of his operation in Scotland was getting another tranche of the fuses for the bombs back into England many broken fences might be mended. If that notion was a faint hope dangling in the gale of adversity it was better than any alternatives he could dredge up.

Over a third cup of coffee Taaffe reviewed his options. The Germans were hardly likely to welcome him, and more likely to be in favour of disposing of him as an inconvenience. Protzman alone might be prepared to lend a sympathetic ear, especially if he could be convinced that Taaffe could, after all, safely deliver a new set of fuses. But Protzman could be anywhere. As he'd told Taaffe he had given up the place in Hamburg. The Freimann site in Bavaria was a

A DARKENING FIRE

long and dangerous way off but at least there he might get news of the German's whereabouts. Only one opening occurred to him: that sly little Scotch bastard in Leith who had got hold of the car that he had driven to London. He knew from idle conversation on the *Ineke* that Dyer was a pal of ten Berge's who was working for the Germans, and Taaffe was confident that Dyer could put him in touch with his yacht-owning mentor to get him across the North Sea. He would have preferred to dispose of the Ford which Dyer had provided and find some other vehicle to take him north, but funds were low. Travelling by public transport was out of the question – the police and MO5 were almost certainly still on the lookout for him, and it was quite possible that he would now be suspected of being implicated in Gallagher's death.

The trip to Scotland was without incident, but by the time Taaffe arrived on the outskirts of Edinburgh his nerves were frayed. Exhausted, he took a room in a guesthouse in Portobello for the night before taking a cautious drive as far as Seafield where he abandoned the Ford in a side street and walked the rest of the way to Leith. He knew that Dyer had been the subject of interest to the police but he suspected that their concern was with the smuggling of the relatively harmless contraband that seemed to him to be the limit of Dyer's ambition or capacity. He was satisfied that he could identify and elude any surveillance still in place, but when he reached the unprepossessing building near the docks there was no sign of any official interest. The door to Dyer's flat displayed an array of deep gouges around the handle and what looked like a temporary hinge and padlock secured the door to the frame.

Taaffe tapped and, eliciting no response, shook the heavy lock with enough force to dislodge it from the rotting wood it had been attached to.

'The police was here,' he was informed by a stocky, sullen figure coming unsteadily down the close, reeking of drink and finding support from the crumbling wall coursing with damp. 'Dyer's gone somewhere. Fucker's owe me five bob.'

Taaffe eyed the newcomer for a long moment and decided that he could buy an ally for a few shillings.

'I'm supposed to wait for him here,' he lied, and then, judging the extent of the other's affection for the forces of law and order,

A DARKENING FIRE

went on, 'Here's the money he owes you, but if you could use another quid...' And he extended a palm with a sovereign coin in it, 'you might want to say nothing about me being here. You know how canny Dyer like to be.'

The man's bleary eyes lit up.

'No' a word out of me,' he agreed.

'Will the police be back, do you think?'

'Doubt it. They was here a whole day, then they shut the place up.'

'Another pound for you when I go if I'm left in peace. You know what I mean.'

'Aye. You'll get me at the North Star across the road or at the flat over it. Name's Higgins, but ask for Brandy.'

Ripping the lock from its mouldering base Taaffe let himself into the dark, squalid room that reeked of must and stale alcohol. The sunlight made only a wavering entrance through the filthy window, but it was enough to illuminate the shabby furniture, the threadbare carpet and the peeling wallpaper. If there had been anything of use or interest it would have been removed by the police and Taaffe was left to contemplate the folly of his panicked escape from London. As a temporary hideout the place was far from satisfactory, with no guarantee that he would remain undisturbed by the authorities or nosy neighbours. It looked likely that Dyer had either been apprehended or was on the run, so there was no chance of succour from that quarter. Taaffe spent the afternoon touring the local stores for food and drink, and in the evening he wedged a chair against the insecure door and fell asleep on the malodorous sofa. No closer the following morning to formulating a plan he lay low in the semi-darkness invoking a curse on every human being on the planet. His preferred resort would have been to make his peace with Boylan and his people in Dublin, but it was certain that he was unfairly but irredeemably tainted there. Having devoted his waning energies to this overnight, he opted for the least promising of the avenues left open to him, and far from confident of any successful outcome he emerged blinking into the shimmering July day and crossed the street to the pub.

Brandy Higgins was ensconced alone in a corner booth evidently making good use of the money Taaffe had given him and

A DARKENING FIRE

his eyes lit up at the Irishman's arrival and with it the promise of more to come. Ordering for Higgins a large measure of the cheapest brandy he could see on the gantry and a small beer for himself, Taaffe joined the tipsy skiver and prefaced an exchange of pleasantries by slipping onto the table a handful of coins he could ill afford.

'Are you a pal of Dyer's?' he asked.

'Near enough.'

'Was he arrested when the police came to his place?'

'No. He's no' been around for a wee while.'

'Do you know where I could find him?'

Higgins shrugged, his fingers twitching as they hovered over the cache.

'Your best bet would be the Peacock Hotel. Does a lot of business there. Usually with a big foreign gadgie. But if it's the police are after him I wouldn't be too sure where he is.'

Yet another sovereign later Taaffe set off to follow Higgins' directions to the two storey hotel facing on the north side directly out to the Firth of Forth. The bar was unattended and empty of clients but a rap on the counter brought Mrs. Holstein ambling from her cubby hole wiping her hands on a greasy apron.

'Norris Dyer?' she repeated in answer to his question. 'You've not heard then? The poor bastard's been shot. They say he'll pull through but he'll not be around here for a bit. If you're a friend of his, though, maybe there's something I can do for you.'

And for a sum that was near to ruinous she undertook to arrange clandestine passage for him to Germany. Despite rising tension on the continent there was as yet no shortage of vessels plying between Leith and Hamburg, and her husband had, she said, plenty of contacts who would be happy to accommodate the sour-faced but not ungenerous Irishman. At least the voyage would get him out of the purview of the law in Scotland and give him a slight chance of repairing the damage by which he was beset.

'It won't be the *Ineke*?' he asked

'Sorry, sir. Don't know what's happened to her.'

A DARKENING FIRE
CHAPTER 31: JULY 1914

On arrival at Schweitz's opulent home The Owl had followed his reluctant host into the beautiful but clearly deserted property.

'Where are they?' the white-faced Schweitz had demanded. 'What have you done to them?'

'In the safest of safe-keeping. And now we can have our little chat so that your family can be reunited.'

Schweitz had collapsed in a chair overcome by fear. He had married late and his devotion to his wife and daughter was, he had protested, the sole preoccupation that figured larger in his psyche than his fidelity to the State.

'What do want from me? I'll tell you whatever you want to know. But please… '

In the tone of a doctor conveying good news to a patient expecting the worst The Owl had explained what he expected from him.

Within a short time of this encounter the British government's scientific adviser Fučić was instructed to appear before a secretive Cabinet committee. On the basis of his continuing contact with Rheinhold Sauer Dr. Fučić set out before the uncomprehending members what he had gleaned about the formation of deuterium oxide, fissile material and the consequence of detonation. The paper provided to Vincent Garrou by Protzman was indicative but in reality added nothing of substance to what was known. Wherever a bomb of this nature was set off, he explained, would be as dangerous to an invading German army as to the surviving population. Its lethal detritus would mean that only England was a potential enemy suitable for targeting. Ministers were left to ponder how the concealed threat to destroy the nation's major cities could be properly dealt with. In the end it was agreed that until the diplomatic and investigative processes were complete it would be at best unwise and at worst dangerous to reveal its existence to the wider world. The ensuing panic could have indescribable effect.

Since Cresswell's approach to Conrad Schweitz had produced only sly obfuscation PM Asquith had drafted a message which the

A DARKENING FIRE

King had sent to his cousin Wilhelm. A telegraph response had not been long in coming. It replicated the line Schweitz had taken and elaborated only by asserting that if there were proved to be substance to the threat and that it was the work of some disaffected party they would quickly be identified and punished and, of course, any explosive devices located and rendered harmless. The Home Secretary was left to observe on the dangerous paralysis the situation was inflicting on Whitehall.

While frenetic deliberations on how to pursue matters continued in London McGarrity and Hughes, still installed in the modest hotel in South Queensferry, turned their attention to the register of visitors to Talbot House which one of Mitchell's officers had brought them. The list of names was shorter than the voluminous document suggested since the same officials had turned up there frequently. McGarrity found his own name and the date of his first arrival, hot on the heels of Hartington's secretarial entourage. With a grimace he turned his mind to the information that he and Mitchell had elicited from Private Campbell in his less than comfortable solitary confinement. He had made no secret of the expectation that his enthusiasm for imparting any intelligence might mitigate the effects of his transgression.

'It was easy enough,' he had told the McGarrity. 'Yon big Hun wife used to smoke like a lum. So when she was out walking past our camp at the side of the river she was never done throwing away her empty fag packets. Or sometimes she just gave us a ciggy – me and Irey, that is. The cops that was with her wouldn't let her speak to us and they never let her out of their sight, like.'

'And so?'

'There was some kind of writing in the empty packets or in the fag papers. Just letters or numbers. Never made any kind of sense. All we had to do was hand them over to yon Dyer and get a few bob for our trouble.'

'But how did Petzold know it was you pair she had to pass the stuff on to?"

'Dyer give me and Irey a thing we had to do when the fat one come past the camp first time round.'

'A thing?'

'Aye – like this.'

A DARKENING FIRE

Campbell had placed his pinkie finger against the corner of his mouth with an expression of embarrassed amusement.

'So that was it? How was that tied in with the idea of a joke you were supposed to be playing on the folk at Talbot House?'

'Never thought about it.'

'And how did Dyer come to be the one sorting this out?'

'How the fuck would I know? Likely The Dutchman told him.'

'I'll bet,' McGarrity had remarked as they left Campbell to his solitary devices, 'Petzold was keeping an eye on the patrols on the river. What she couldn't have known, as Kell's man Kavanagh told me, was that the rota had changed the day before Rupprecht was to be got away.'

Joined by Inspector Mitchell and leaving Hughes to put together a report on what had been turned up so far he set off along the waterfront in the direction of the Hawes Inn, pausing to take in the dramatic view over the estuary. On the distant north coast they could with some difficulty make out the great building works nearing completion at the Rosyth navy base, and, in front of them the intricate structure of the Forth Bridge. The sun had spread a pellicle of silver confetti on the surface of the river and around the bustle of small, grey-hulled ships. From a window of the Hawes hotel Superintendent Quinn, fresh from London, watched the brooding giant and his companion make their way through the crowds of holiday makers, for the most part unconcerned with events across the Channel or implied by the traffic on the Forth. Todd had ensured that a room had been set aside for the brief conference he had arranged with the Superintendent and the recently arrived Vincent Garrou who surreptitiously passed to McGarrity the closed note Kell had given him. Giving a brief account of The Owl's rendezvous with Conrad Schweitz Todd added, 'The next step's plain enough, but the snag is that somewhere in Whitehall there may still be a leak, and, if it's too widely known, Berlin could know about that step before it's even taken.'

'Somebody with the right technical know-how has to get into the Freimann site,' Garrou said.

'And the only way we can have a shot at that is for the thing to be done in total secrecy and before our own Government gets

A DARKENING FIRE

around to trying it.'

'How do you propose to manage that?' McGarrity asked.

'I've taken precautions,' Todd told him. 'I believe we can rely on Cummings. Asquith will look to him to run the operation and I've agreed with him that he'll dismiss the idea as far too risky with no chance of success for the time being – impractical until our resources on the continent are back to full strength – all that kind of stuff. He'll ask for a couple of weeks to work out a plan and see if agents can be put in place. He'll plead that nothing – not a thing – is done until he can figure out the practicalities and put the result of his cogitations to the Cabinet. So we can get the business done before anybody's the wiser.'

'And now…?'

'M. Garrou would like to explain what he and I have in mind.'

Despite their caution Todd and Garrou had elected to share with Quinn the scheme they had devised for an expedition to the Krupp site in Bavaria. It would have to be implemented quickly and carried a good deal of risk because it required hasty organisation. Todd had, via his contacts in Germany, prepared the ground for infiltration of the site. Conrad Schweitz had been roped by The Owl into the operation. Compelled to surrender to The Owl's brutal blackmail he had been forced to alert the army detachment at Freimann to his intention to inspect the site along with a small group of his personal military. Garrou, an excellent German speaker, would join this small party on a tour of inspection. Since it was clear that Irish seditionaries were implicated in the German project there was a strong possibility that they would be represented at the Krupp location with the intention of obtaining another set of fusing devices. With McGarrity's reputation as a violent insurgent still intact his presence on the expedition could be invaluable.

'You'll all need to play this by ear, Leo, but two things you might want to think about,' Quinn remarked. 'First, this isn't an order. I can see why the rest of you have reasons for thinking it would be advantageous for him to go, but it's something that's a long way outside his responsibilities. And second, if nobody beyond these four walls has any inkling about this – not the Commissioner or Kell or the others – you'll be acting *ultra vires*. If something was to go wrong you'd be in the biggest sucking turf bog

A DARKENING FIRE

if any of them found out you were mixed up in it.'

'I've already got all that, Pat. I'm your man,' McGarrity said. 'Have we decided who else is coming on this wee trip?'

'With me,' Garrou said, 'a fellow called Heller. He has the advantage of being a true Bavarian – and something more. We need some convincing scientific representation and expertise so Dr. Fučić has volunteered. One of Mr. Todd's mysterious accomplices is already making the arrangements for our regal process to Freimann.'

'And when does this all come off?'

'Time can hardly be on our side,' Todd said, 'if we're to be in a position to advise Ministers properly. If you and M. Garrou can leave tonight and be in Paris by tomorrow evening my people will collect the pair of you and Dr. Fučić and get you to on your way. So if you chaps want to push off for the Great Wen I'll see if I can get us all a lift into town.'

'I know it's a long shot, but if that fellow Protzman happens to be billeted at Freimann he'll rumble us as soon as he sees Vincent.'

'That would be a problem, I agree. But the French are financing a large part of this operation on condition that M. Garrou is involved, so we have to run the risk – which is small anyway. After all, Germany's a big place.'

'The French are putting up the readies for this?'

'Who has most to lose if the Entente is messed up?'

In less than an hour the both Sealscraig Hotel and the Hawes Inn were emptied of the various deputations that had descended on them. Before McGarrity, Quinn and Garrou had boarded the train for London Todd had collared Inspector Mitchell and used his offices to gain access to Paddy Gormley's cell at the police station in the Old Town.

'This is the only offer you're going to get,' Todd advised him. 'We need to find out how and when the main load of guns is going to be sent to that so-called Council of yours in Dublin. Taaffe's little consignment we can keep an eye out for – if he ever gets them. So we need you to get to Hamburg and persuade Herr Spiro that you've been sent to double check that the arrangements are properly agreed.'

'And me getting the King's shilling is it? You've lost your mind

A DARKENING FIRE

altogether.'

'Colleagues of mine will be with you all the way – tell Benny Spiro that they're your bodyguards. Once we have the information we're after you can be on your merry way and I'll be happy to put enough loot in your pocket to get you away somewhere sunnier than Monto or Tallaght.'

'And what in the name of God makes you think I'll go along with that? Jesus, I wouldn't give the boys away for all the money in your overloaded Treasury.'

'Well, in that case I think we can agree that in current circumstances your avoiding the noose is an unlikely outcome.'

'Fair enough. You do what you have to, and so will I.'

'Maybe the rope doesn't frighten you,' he said. 'But think about those guns that you filched from your dear friends in the Brotherhood after they'd gone to the trouble of removing them from that warehouse in Glasgow.'

Gormley's casual reaction hardly concealed his unease.

'So far,' Todd went on, 'only that incompetent little thief Dyer and his Dutch friend ten Berge know what you were up to. But if Boylan in Dublin was to find out I believe he'd have a fate rather worse than a rope waiting for you.'

Gormley sat very still for a moment, then asked, 'All right, but suppose I say I'm going along with your wee idea and just take off for places unknown.'

'Ah, that would be unfortunate. I can say with confidence that there won't be a single step you can take when you leave here without its being dogged by my minions.'

'Then why can't your minions do the business for you?'

'As I've said, Mr. Spiro will feel able to trust you. After all, he's well aware of your impeccable credentials as a murderous Fenian.'

'You bastard.'

A long silence.

'And you'll put me in funds? Enough to get me to some far-flung outpost of your shitty empire?'

'It would be my pleasure.'

'And how am I supposed to get to Hamburg? The way things are going I can't see the Jerries putting on a big welcome for some wandering Irish lad and a couple of hulking Sassenach thugs in

A DARKENING FIRE

tow.'

'Rely on me. Your safe passage is guaranteed. And you'll find my lads aren't exactly Sassenachs.'

A DARKENING FIRE
CHAPTER 32: JULY 1914

Dumped ashore in Hamburg where he was treated with suspicious disdain by the port authority and warned that he would be closely questioned at various stages of his planned journey, Ciarán Taaffe ploughed a generous proportion of his depleted funds into buying a train ticket that would take him via Lüneburg, Göttingen, Kassel and Nürnberg to Munich. Everywhere there were signs of military activity – cavalcades of horses, sidings full of carriages being inspected by Train-Battalion officers in field grey uniforms, hordes of reservists and anxious relatives milling about on crowded platforms, and on roadways horse-drawn artillery pieces throwing choking clouds of dry dust into the shimmering summer air. As yet Taaffe had formulated no plan of action for his arrival in Bavaria. If Protzman happened to be somewhere other than Freimann he had no idea what his next move could be. Nodding off intermittently Taaffe caught an occasional image of the cheerfully thronged pubs along the Dublin quays and waking with a start would curse the melancholy reality that, through ill luck, bad judgement but no disloyal intent, his home had become a foreign, hostile country. Almost in a trance he watched the landscape of Lower Saxony and Hesse trundle by, ate as cheaply as possible in the dining car, drank a bottle of red Riesling, returned to his seat and dozed badly for much of the rest of the trip. At Munich he found a grim *pension* for the night and next day, after many barely understood requests for directions and help, succeeded in making the relatively short journey to Freimann, going part of the way on foot and part supine on sacks of ill-smelling vegetables on a rattling mule-drawn cart.

While Taaffe was executing this navigational feat Conrad Schweitz was slumped behind his desk in Wilhelmstrasse looking every second of his 73 years.

'You look tired, Conrad,' Augustin Steinhoff told him, glancing at yet another tray full of files requiring urgent attention. 'I suggest you go home now and leave all this to me. You must rest while you can so that you can be at your most alert when…'

A DARKENING FIRE

'Yes, yes,' Schweitz responded irritably, 'but I have work to do that can't wait. Will you please arrange for my car to be ready in half an hour to take me to Hamburg.'

'Of course. But it's 350 kilometres, the weather is hot and you're far from well as it is.'

'Please don't patronise me,' he answered curtly. 'There is much to be done in the next day or two. These papers –,' indicating the pile of documents Steinhoff was still carrying, '– you will please deal with them until I return. And ensure in particular that my orders for Freimann are complied with to the letter.'

'For Freimann, Herr Schweitz? May I ask which and where orders these are?'

Schweitz waved an angry hand as if berating his most loyal adviser for not being aware of something that he himself had handled with impenetrable confidentiality. Recovering, he offered a terse apology and produced a copy of the coded message he had sent to the Bavarian site.

'I've decided that we must be absolutely certain that everything there is progressing as it should. These orders require security of the site and the progress of the work to be inspected by my own delegation. The inspection will take place in the next day or two and I will be taking personal charge of it. I can tell you now that Professor Rupprecht himself has been there for some weeks. Please ensure his absolute comfort and safety continue to be provided for.'

'Then perhaps it would be helpful,' Steinhoff said, 'if I travel there myself today to make sure all preparations will be made for your arrival.'

'Oh,' irritably, 'do as you see fit.' Then, more evenly, 'I'm sorry, Augustin, yes, please do as you suggest.'

His voice trailed off and after an embarrassed pause he brought the discussion to an end with a nod.

'My car,' he reminded Steinhoff as he left.

"Twenty minutes.'

As soon as Schweitz had departed for Hamburg, Steinhoff sauntered to the high-powered Mercedes 37/90 allocated to him. The 600 kilometre journey would have to be taken at high speed if Steinhoff were to be at the Krupp site by that night, but he had his own reasons for wasting no time on the way. Given the haste with

A DARKENING FIRE

which Schweitz's order was to be implemented, no-one in the building or elsewhere queried Steinhoff's loading of an extraordinary amount of official luggage in readiness for the trip. When Schweitz issued a command nobody below the rank of Chancellor dared to challenge it.

Paddy Gormley had spent the voyage to Hamburg on the *Ineke* commiserating with ten Berge on his capture by the Royal Navy, exchanging barbed badinage with Todd's two thugs Coyne and Rutter and smoking a huge number of cigarettes with the recently recruited crewmen. It had been Todd's idea to enlist The Dutchman, offering him the chance to free himself of the prison service's shackles and rehabilitate himself if he successfully carried out the mission. Todd had made it clear that ten Berge's role in Rupprecht's flight was now known to the police and that, combined with his inept gun-running, could not otherwise guarantee his future well-being or liberty.

'Just remember,' Todd had advised him,' like Gormley you will be under the eye of some disreputable colleagues of mine who will not hesitate to shoot you dead if you fail me in even the tiniest fashion.'

'And if I do all that you ask?'

'I'm a generous man. All will be forgiven and you may sail into the sunset undisturbed by His Majesty's navy.'

'You'll put this in writing of course?'

Todd sniggered. The Dutchman was well known to the gun-running fraternity in Hamburg and the sole reason for his presence was that it would help further to confirm endorse the expedition's authenticity.

As soon as the *Ineke* put in at the Free Port of Hamburg the Dutchman and his unwanted entourage trailed into the Speicherstadt to find Benny Spiro in the anonymous stall that passed as his office when he was conducting business at the harbour. After a falsely amiable exchange of greetings Gormley and ten Berge between them offered the agreed explanation of their unanticipated presence. The Irishman had been delegated, he said, either to confirm the arrangements for delivery of the load of rifles bound for Dublin which had already been paid for; or, preferably, for The Dutchman to uplift the shipments and therefore to make it

A DARKENING FIRE

unnecessary for Sir Roger Casement and his friends to take the risk of falling foul of the Royal Navy or the British customs on the way back.

Spiro heard them out with a forced display of patience, then advised them that a very careful strategy for the movement of the weapons to Ireland had been worked out and that there could be no question of altering it unless permission to do so was granted by the high official from Berlin who had given his consent for the operation. Underpinning the transaction, he pointed out, was the urgent need to distract the British from coming events on the continent, and so every aspect of the plan was subject to rigorous oversight. The senior representative from Wilhelmstrasse was already on his way to Hamburg to ensure that the business was conducted as scheduled. If Gormley and his party would be kind enough to wait until later in the day they would have the chance to put their alternative scheme to him. At this Gormley turned to the heavyweights watching over him and opened his hands in a gesture intended to elicit instruction.

'We can wait,' Coyne said, 'but we have to sort this out today.'

Spiro inclined his head and suggested that his four visitors find somewhere near the port to spend the next few hours until Herr Schweitz reached the city. Gormley made to reach for Benny with a fraternal handshake but Rutter stepped quickly between them and, with a cheerful wave at Spiro, conducted the delegation through the commercial bustle and out of the vast neo-Gothic red brick building.

'Don't mistake me for your kindly old uncle,' Coyne advised as the group crossed the bridge over the Kehrwiederfleet in search of a restaurant or bar. 'If you're after a shortcut to Paddy's paradise I'm the man to get you on your way.'

Gormley ignored the injunction and instead hooked his arm into The Dutchman's and said over his shoulder, *'Droch chrich ort.'*

'Mallacht mo chait ort,' Coyne replied casually.

Though the Freimann site was only a few miles from Munich it was late in the afternoon before Taaffe reached the fortified entrance to the rambling establishment. Tired, dishevelled and covered in dust he was distracted by belated reflection on the rash decision that had brought him to this sinister location. Looking like

A DARKENING FIRE

an impoverished itinerant he found himself at a loss to know how to respond to the half-amused challenge issued by the gate guards in the uniform of the 13th Royal Bavarian Infantry. Having not a single word of German and faced with five or six youthful soldiers without a word of English among them, Taaffe could think of only one approach.

'Mr. Protzman,' he said, and called out the name several times, raising his voice and pronouncing the name with an incremental increase in the number of syllables with each repetition until, bored with the performance, one of the troopers stepped forward, grabbed him by the lapel of his unkempt jacket and tried to push him back into the roadway. Taaffe was not a big man though he carried too much weight around his middle and his mendicant appearance did little to promote him as someone deserving of careful handling. Taken by surprise at the swiftness and skill of the Irishman's reaction, the soldier was instantly deposited on the ground and in a moment was struggling for breath with a boot bearing down on his throat. This was not how Taaffe had intended to make his presence known, and it was hardly conducive to amicable response. Before the incident could escalate into a more violent confrontation a second sentry had swung his rifle butt-first into his stomach and Taaffe went down with a long, low moan. Helping their comrade to his feet, the guards gathered round their stricken visitor, debating how they should conclude the encounter. Through a vapour of pain Taaffe did make out from their indignation that his immediate future appeared less than rosy. Hauled roughly to his feet, he was gripped by the arms and the soldier he had felled aimed a kick at his shin that left him yelling so pitifully in agony that an officer came hurrying from the guard post demanding to know what was going on.

Freed from the excruciating grasp of his captors Taaffe, breathing heavily and fighting off the pain of the assault, prodded his own chest, yelled, 'Irish. Me Irish, you gobshites. I'm here for your man Protzman. *Protzman*, for fuck's sake. *Protzman* – you hear me? Is he here?'

'Contain yourself, please,' the Lieutenant said in English. 'You've come to see Herr Protzman? Very well, come with me.'

'That's more like it,' Taaffe muttered, picking up his battered

A DARKENING FIRE

suitcase and brushing grime from his crumpled clothes. Trailing after the officer he cast a baleful glance on the soldier he had been unceremoniously tangling with and mouthed the insult *'Cac ar oineach'* which might as well have meant an invitation to the opera. Passing through the entrance to the site close on the Lieutenant's heels he stalked in the direction of a solidly built gatehouse.

'You will wait here,' he was informed and before he could take issue with the brusque diktat he felt himself edged into a stone-walled room containing only a rough wooden bunk, a three-legged stool and a pail. The late sunshine threw a beam of white light along a diagonal from a solitary window close to the twelve-foot high ceiling onto the unforgiving concrete floor. When the door was swung shut behind him he heard the click of the lock. Inured by years of contention with authority he responded to incarceration with a shrug, settled himself on the bed and waited for the summons he expected to hear within a short time. It was not until the sun had declined sufficiently for the light to become uncertain that he began to give way to impatience and then to a deeper concern. When by his estimate some three hours had passed he jumped from his place and beat on the door until his fist ached. He accompanied this racket with a volley of clamorous Gaelic oaths that faded away only when the door was unlocked and swung open to reveal the figure of Helmut Protzman standing between two uniformed guards.

'About fucking time,' Taaffe grunted, his voice hoarse on the dryness of his throat. 'Get me some water and get me out of this shitehole.'

Protzman nodded to one of his companions who disappeared for a moment and returned with a bowl in which some not particularly clear water was sloshing. Taaffe sat down on the stool and drank greedily, eyeing his captors with undisguised ill-feeling.

'Right,' he said, 'I need to speak to you about…'

'Oh, I know what you want,' Protzman told him. 'You want to excuse your failure, explain how it came about that your comrades were no more successful than you. Then you want to be given yet another chance to trade delivery of the bomb fuses for weapons for your cause.'

'Right enough, but don't you fucking speak about me and the

A DARKENING FIRE

others like we just made some big mistake and got caught. Somebody gave us away – Keegan's banged up in jail and Breslin's dead. I'm not saying we were great pals, but the three of us were doing exactly what you told us. Either you've got a traitor here or the Brits were anointed.'

'Anointed?'

'Got so fucking lucky that only God was responsible. Never mind that – I'm here now and I'll set it right. There's only one thing I want from you and that's to let my folk in Dublin know that I'm still their man and that they'll be getting the guns you promised once I've done your business.'

Protzman looked at him for a long time, rubbed his chin to dispel a twist of humourless amusement from his face and said, 'You are not welcome here, Mr. Taaffe. We hold you responsible for the delay in activating our weapons and for the losses incurred.'

'What the fuck are you on about? I'm here to get some more of your fucking fuses or whatever they are and get them to England. And hear that my guns are going to be on their way.'

'I do believe you're lying to me, Mr. Taaffe, but I suppose we are all guilty of that kind of thing in our profession – like the late Herr Gallagher who imagined that he could slip into Butler's place. But did he continue Butler's work? Not at all. He was going to betray our contact unless he was paid a large sum of money. And you know what happened to him – you were there.'

'I'm not lying. And… wait a minute. How did you hear that I was…? So you bastards shot Gallagher.'

'I haven't said so. Not at all. But what Gallagher was up to had a great deal to do with our agreement to deliver those guns to you. *Quid pro quo*, you see. The rifles in return for valuable information and delivery of the bomb fuses. And disposal of Gallagher himself. You do recall, don't you, that the money you were able to raise for the guns fell far short of their worth? So you understand our displeasure that your side of the bargain was not kept in either respect.'

Taaffe sat in bewildered silence while Protzman stared expressionlessly down on him. Finally he said, 'Well, at least you *will* be letting Spiro send the guns to Dublin that Boylan's *Fianna Eireann* folk have paid for.'

A DARKENING FIRE

'That's nothing to do with you but I expect so. They'll be useful enough so long as they have something to keep the British army busy with. Whether they're loyalists or rebels makes no difference to us.'

Taaffe continued to puzzle over what he was learning.

'Gabh transna ort fhéin. Look, if you get me out of this place and let me have another crack at taking your fuse things to England will you hand my rifles over then?'

'Mr. Taaffe, we wouldn't trust you with a pot of paint.'

Taaffe cast around for some adequate response – something that would persuade his host of his sincerity and reliability, but nothing came to him. It was obvious that to continue the argument was going to be futile.

'Then what?' he was reduced to asking with an air of crumpled resignation.

Protzman looked down at him for a long moment, shrugged and said quietly, 'The British want their hands on you; your friends in Dublin want their hands on you; and my masters in Berlin are *very* unhappy with you. Perhaps you have a preference?'

A DARKENING FIRE
CHAPTER 33: JULY 1914

The declining summer sun was casting London in a fluorescence of muted gold and hectic red as Sir Derwent Hartington was bringing to a close a conclave of his senior staff.

'The condition of the Balkans,' he said, 'has moved beyond critical. I can't say where the Government will position itself when the situation has crystallised, but what is clear is that we must put our own house in order. We have to accept that the information already garnered from us by Berlin is beyond recall. What cannot be accepted is that the traitor or traitors responsible might avoid detection.'

'I take it that Mr. Todd is still investigating,' Ackroyd asked. 'He hasn't bothered to keep me informed.'

'Yes. Like you I have heard nothing further from him.'

Ackroyd's face betrayed nothing beyond his usual urbane demeanour, but Hartington caught beneath that smooth surface a hint of artful reserve. For a moment the two men held each other's ambivalent stare until Sir Derwent announced that he would be occupied with other matters away from Whitehall Court.

'You will be out of the office for some time?'

Hartington nodded as Highway and Solomon hurried out.

'You will be careful, Sir Derwent – we are at a critical point and there is concern…'

Sir Derwent waved an impatient hand but Ackroyd pressed on.

'In the circumstances you will appreciate that I must insist that your new bodyguard will be with you at all times.'

'I beg your pardon. What I do and where I go is hardly your concern.'

'I apologise – the instruction is not mine, Sir Derwent. It comes from No. 10.'

'Then I leave business in your capable hands, Dr. Ackroyd. Meantime what progress is this Inspector McGarrity making on the Rupprecht affair?'

'Like Todd he hasn't confided in me but I gather he is pursuing a definite line of enquiry. I do wonder, though, whether he really is

A DARKENING FIRE

the best man for the job.'

'Because?'

'I don't dispute his reputation and his record, but he's been under the most intense pressure personally. For one thing his daughter is missing in America and, of course, he's Irish. I know that...'

'I'll have a word with him myself, but it's properly an operational matter for Superintendent Quinn.' A pause, followed by a tacit reprimand. 'Who's also Irish.'

'Of course, sir. I apologise. You will be contactable if circumstances demand?'

This time Hartington chose to devote his attention to sorting through the pile of papers in front of him.

'I shall,' he said at last, 'have a word with you before I go.'

While this meeting in London was drawing to a close Conrad Schweitz was emerging from his vehicle in the unfamiliar and uncongenial surroundings of the Speicherstadt in Hamburg. It was not his custom to concern himself with the practical mechanics of the machinations he set in train. It was impossible to tell how far he could trust in The Owl's undertaking to deliver his wife and daughter unharmed in return for this hurried excursion, but not even his passionate and undivided loyalty to the Reich could trump his fierce fidelity to Magda and Lotte. The Owl's injunction to arrange inspection of the Freimann site might have dire consequences but no price could be too great to ensure his family's safety. And anyway he envisaged little more coming of the enforced visit than exactly the sort of confirmation of the establishment's work that it had always been his intention to disseminate.

Schweitz saw nothing to commend the Speicherstadt. It was crowded, Spiro's sectioned-off cubbyhole afforded practically no privacy and the building was alive with traders, wasters, watchful thieves and, worst of all, in his estimate, the uproarious working class. Having dispatched Brockmann his driver to summon Spiro he told the arms dealer to bring his party – which had trudged back to his cubicle – across the bridge to a discreet coffee shop in the lee of the Katharinenkirche. Awkward introductions were speedily disposed of and ten Berge had explained with some mechanical haste that his friend Gormley had been ordered by his organisation

A DARKENING FIRE

in Dublin either to confirm the details of arrangements for supplying Casement's hoard of Mauser rifles or alternatively taking delivery himself. Unhappy with this intrusion into his timetable, Spiro replied that he himself had no desire to accept responsibility for divulging or altering the plan. The decision could only be for its mastermind Conrad Schweitz. Listening to all this in silence and aware that his own hands were invisibly but effectively tied Schweitz understood that he had no choice other than to agree to the weapons being diverted to the taciturn Gormley

'You come to me with this,' Spiro complained to Gormley, 'hours before the guns are due for shipment. Whatever decision you arrive at it has to be made very damn quickly.'

'You say Casement and Childers have already paid?' Schweitz asked, pretending that the issue was still to be resolved in his mind.

'It's all in my safe,' Spiro told him. 'Except for the government's share, of course. That's ready for you to collect from the Speicherstadt. By any standards, though, it's a good deal of money and we shouldn't leave it there in my desk for too long.'

'It's being guarded, surely?'

'Naturally. Nevertheless…'

'Then,' Schweitz turned to Gormley, 'I have no problem with your uplifting the rifles today if you wish. That can be done easily?' he asked The Dutchman.

Distracted by the invidiousness of his position and still casting around for a way of escaping it, The Dutchman could only nod, acutely aware of the fact that the man Rutter was clutching a revolver in his pocket and that it was aimed at his substantial but vulnerable belly.

'I make no secret of the fact that I am irritated at being brought all this way to sit in judgement of such a trifling matter,' Schweitz said, and turning to Spiro added, 'And so – please make any necessary arrangements with Mr. Gormley and his friends. Now if there is nothing further to detain me I have much else to deal with. Have someone collect the money for Berlin and bring it to my hotel within the hour. Please let me have your report when all is settled.'

As Spiro, smarting from Schweitz's display of rancour, wordlessly led the others trooping back across the Zollkanal, Gormley was searching with increasing desperation for some

A DARKENING FIRE

means of forestalling the loss of the cache of Mausers to the British authorities. Though he had misappropriated a few hundred guns from the Clarkson raid he had never intended to betray the Cause itself. Now he had been pressganged by his rapacity into that very position. There had to be some way to redemption, but with Coyne evidently ready to draw and use his concealed pistol at the first sign of disobedience he was struggling to work out how to salve his conscience and simultaneously retrieve the situation.

It was now late evening and the buzz of activity in the Speicherstadt had faded to a sporadic hum. Lamps were going on, a few distant shouts could be heard and most of the traders were closing up or had already gone home. In Spiro's enclave a skinny young man sat with his feet up on the desk emanating an air of surly importance having apparently convinced himself – not without reason – that he represented the whole of the gun-runner's security department. Wearing a much-decorated and entirely homemade uniform of dark green hessian that provoked him into a ritual of twitching and scratching and nodding at the gun lying in front of him he bestowed on his boss's guests a look designed to inculcate fear and compliance. Benny Spiro reacted to this display with impatience and snapped his fingers for the set of keys his minion had been tossing from hand to hand, and set about unlocking the drawer where he had deposited the contribution to the Reich's coffers brought by the sale of the elderly rifles to the Irish revolutionaries. Unimpressed by the patent vulnerability of this cache, Gormley shook his head and muttered an audible imprecation.

'You deserve to be hung,' he said, watching Spiro heft the heavy canvas bag onto the desktop. 'By the look of him this idiot' – pointing a thumb at the uniformed watchman – 'couldn't be trusted with a handful of pennies.'

'He can be trusted,' Spiro agreed, nodding at the weapon resting on the table, 'with only a single round in that gun of his – enough to raise an alarm but not enough to do any great harm. I don't deny it but he's my sister's son.'

To demonstrate his credentials as a reliable guardian the youth swung his feet off the desk and made to stand up squarely to the Irishman but in enacting this dramatic if apprehensive gesture

A DARKENING FIRE

caught his ankle on the Parabellum 1908 which was intended to impress and discourage intruders. The gun crashed to the floor, distracting everyone in the cramped cubbyhole except Gormley who chose in that brief moment to expiate his unpatriotic sins.

'They're British spies,' he yelled at Spiro. 'Don't give them the guns. They're…'

Before he could elaborate Rutter had smashed the barrel of his revolver against his forehead and sent him tumbling backwards into Spiro's feckless watchdog. The pair collapsed in a welter of curses and thrashing limbs. Dazed, Gormley was reaching for Rutter's pistol when Coyne expertly brought the edge of his hand brutally into his throat. Frozen into inaction by the suddenness of the affray Spiro and The Dutchman watched open-mouthed as the men tangled in a furious melee that lasted no more than a few seconds, after which Spiro's guard was left whining and cowering, Rutter, now upright, bleeding profusely from the nose and Coyne reaching down for the dropped Luger a moment too late to prevent Gormley seizing the weapon, pressing the muzzle against his own head and pulling the trigger. The noise in the constrictive space was ear-shattering and instantly drew the frantic attention of the small number of merchants and tradesmen still in the market.

'Fuck this,' Coyne snarled, gathering up the bulging satchel, hauling the unsteady Rutter to his feet and waving Spiro and The Dutchman aside with his revolver. Already he could hear whistles sounding outside and the shouting of officialdom closing in on the building. With his injured companion in tow Coyne dashed for the exit leading to the cobbled street at the east end of the market, shoving away the one or two traders who made a reluctant attempt to block their way. Some distance behind them Coyne and Rutter could hear the shouts of the small posse of police who had come barging into the market from the opposite side and a single, apparently aimless shot was fired a long way off.

'Jesus, now what?' Rutter panted and wiped at the blood pouring down his chin.

'Just don't stop,' Coyne called over his shoulder. As they dashed into the darkness of the deserted street an Ansbach Tourer came rattling round the corner to the south and squealed to a halt in front of them.

A DARKENING FIRE

'Do get in, gentlemen,' the stout little man at the wheel ordered, peering at them through the thick lenses of his spectacles. 'I fear you've rather irritated someone. Time to be off.'

Not waiting to debate the wisdom of complying the two men leapt into the car which set off with an agonised screech combined out of the racket of an inept gear change and spinning tyres. As the vehicle careered across the bridge and north into the maze of streets between the canal and the Jungferstieg boulevard in the Neustadt quarter the breathless Rutter, still trying to stem the flow of blood, made an effort to clear his mind by demanding an explanation from the driver who gave the impression of alarming over-confidence in his ability to manoeuvre the speeding car.

'Don't worry, chaps,' The Owl told them. 'I've lived more than half my life in this city. Know it like the back of my hand.'

'I asked who the fuck are you,' Rutter grumbled and moaned as a lurch in the vehicle caused him inadvertently to rap his broken nose with his bloody knuckles.

'A friend of your master Mr. Todd. I'm afraid you've both made a bit of a mess of this operation if you don't mind my saying so. Lucky I've been keeping a benign eye on you. I think I recognise the item that you've purloined.'

And he nodded at the bag Coyne continued to clutch.

'Where are we going now?' Coyne demanded, making no effort to reply.

'I have another car parked just off the Gänsemarkt,' The Owl said. 'We'll leave this one there and I'll get you chaps down to the port post haste. Obviously our friend ten Berge isn't going to be at your service but I have an alternative on hand. But I'm afraid you're going to have to bequeath me that hefty bag of loot – I'm sure Mr. Todd would disapprove of your misplacing it.'

'You're welcome to it. Just get us out of this bloody country.'

'And what of the guns bound for Erin's green isle? I trust that at the least you found out where, how and when that little affair is to take place?'

'Fuck,' Coyne said and stared glumly out through the car window and foresaw the deeply unpleasant debriefing that lay ahead.

A DARKENING FIRE
CHAPTER 34: JULY 1914

Furious at having been dispatched back to South Queensferry, Terrence Edwards repeated to himself that recent events had rendered his instinctive misanthropy wholly justifiable. The town recalled to him only his humiliation at the hands of McGarrity and the encounter with the sinister little man Todd who had dismissed him as an irritating nonentity. And now he had been summoned by Sir Derwent Hartington's Assistant PS Cecil Highway who had been ordered to pass on a message from Hartington himself.

'I've no idea what this means,' Highway confessed, 'but I gather the terms will be familiar to you.'

With a glower Edwards stepped aside and with the aid of an annotated notebook decoded the telegram instructing him to "*tidy up*" the arrangements for the German party at Dalmeny, and to attend to the immediate needs of Norris Dyer and his friend in the Cramond area of Edinburgh.

'I'm supposed to meet up with some fellow called Thomas Beckett,' he told Highway. 'Can you find out where I can get hold of him? He's a mate of this Dyer character that's been such a fucking nuisance.'

'I expect the police will be able to tell me,' Highway said. 'I'll leave a note for you here.'

Leaving the uncomfortably puzzled Highway with a brief nod of compliance he set off in sullen haste towards Talbot House in Dalmeny. To his chagrin, though, he was met there by the combined police and military guard unimpressed by his obscure credentials.

'I'm on urgent War Office business,' Edwards insisted.

'Aye, well, fuck off with your Sassenach bits of paper,' the surly Private Brandon told him, 'and come back in about ten years.'

Retreating under a cloud of irritation, he gauged that there would be a chance to gain entrance in a few days' time if the military component of the guard were summoned elsewhere as the agitation on the continent suggested was likely. Back at the hotel Highway had had no difficulty in obtaining an address for Beckett

A DARKENING FIRE

and within a couple of days Edwards had duly introduced himself to the unfortunate Beckett on his return from lending Norris Dyer what should have been a helping hand. The next day he was *en route* for Waverley to catch the mid-morning train to King's Cross.

By then Vincent Garrou, Dr. Fučić and Leo McGarrity had arrived in Paris where they stopped only long enough to rendezvous with Sergeant Heller on special leave from the Foreign Legion. The purpose of the clandestine excursion had been run through again in light of intelligence brought to Todd from Berlin and agreed without further reference to anyone beyond the participants. From Paris they were driven in a Peugeot 145 Tourer the 460 or so kilometres to the small town of Pontalier where they spent the night in a discreet *pension* to finalise their itinerary with a quietly-spoken newcomer dressed as a customs inspector. This man's demeanour and careful exposition suggested that he lacked no experience in the navigation of the byways of Europe's state-sponsored underworld. The following morning the party was collected at an unguarded crossing on the Swiss border and transferred to two anonymous local vehicles which made their separate way via Neuchâtel and Bienne to Zürich. There they took a short break at a seedy backstreet hotel to acquire various sets of documentation and change into the uniforms of the IV Army Inspectorate. Within an hour they set off for Konstanz. At a secluded clearing close to the German frontier they were switched to a pair of Opel staff cars bearing General Officer pennants. Their counterfeit papers indicated that they had been engaged on a series of training consultations with the small cadre of officer instructors of the Swiss Army, but the display of martial ostentation ensured that they endured nothing more than the merest glance, a prompt salute and a submissive wave.

Some thirty kilometres beyond the border they were delayed for a couple of hours waiting for Schweitz's arrival from Hamburg before setting off in convoy for the 230 kilometres towards Munich. Schweitz's driver Brockmann was accompanied in the front by a cheerful stranger whose role was to make sure that Schweitz embarked on no diversion from the plan put to him by The Owl. The IV Army Inspectorate was based in Bavaria, and as a precaution flags, uniforms and documentation were discarded and

A DARKENING FIRE

replaced by those of the special unit reporting directly to Schweitz. For the greater part of the trip Dr. Fučić, faint with anxiety and silently berating himself for his folly in agreeing to undertake the expedition, sat glumly bathed in sweat reciting equations from the 18th century through to the latest in the new science of quantum chemistry. Along the way they were greeted by salutes and cheers from groups of troopers and officers of the First Bavarian Infantry Division, but otherwise they proceeded unhindered to Munich. The drivers of the three cars appeared to be perfectly familiar with the route and Garrou's expression of appreciation was met with a polite but uncommunicative response.

It was late evening before they reached their destination and McGarrity was taken with the efficiency with which someone somewhere had constructed the arrangements when the vehicles pulled into a concealed courtyard and their occupants were welcomed into an elegant mansion beyond the vast *Englischer Garten*. Whether the owners were aware of their guests' nationality or their mission, or whether instead they assumed them to be a high-powered caucus of the German military went unaddressed. Early the next day the group were making their way to the secreted cars when they were met by a small, stout man wearing a pair of huge spectacles and the slightly embarrassed grin of someone who had intruded on a party at which he was unwelcome. The Owl wasted no time in introductory niceties.

'Here,' he told Garrou well out of Schweitz's and Brockmann's hearing, 'is the route you should follow when you leave Freimann. Your stopping places along the way have been marked. You will find colleagues of mine there who will ensure as far as they can that you will be conducted without incident all the way to Venice.'

Fučić's jaw dropped.

'Venice? Good grief, man, every policeman and soldier between here and Italy will be on the lookout for us.'

Garrou gave the scientist a reassuring pat on the shoulder.

'Please don't concern yourself, sir. Our friend here will see us through.'

'One other thing,' The Owl added. 'This,' handing over to McGarrity the case of money appropriated from Hamburg, 'is not something I want to be responsible for. No doubt I can rely on you

A DARKENING FIRE

to deal with it properly.'

'What happens to Herr Schweitz when we're done at Freimann?'

'Something better than he deserves.'

And a moment later The Owl was gone, leaving behind only the suspicion of a sardonic smile to linger in the hushed summer air. By mid-morning the little cavalcade had made the short drive to the Krupp site where its arrival had clearly been anticipated with a combination of disquiet and ostentation. The gate at which Taaffe had presented himself some days earlier was manned by a dozen troopers, their activity directed from a brick tower rounded off by a glass dome from which the barrels of two machine guns protruded.

'I am Lieutenant Wasser,' the duty officer announced, addressing himself to Sergeant Heller who was very much at home in the uniform of a Lieutenant General and sporting a huge and very weighty official-looking valise. 'We have been expecting you, gentlemen. Your Herr Steinhoff from Berlin has been waiting for you in the barracks. You'll find him now in the Commandant's office.'

Garrou and McGarrity exchanged a quick, puzzled glance, but disguised any abrupt disquiet accompanying this piece of news.

'May I say it's an honour to have you call on us, Herr Schweitz, sir,' Wasser continued as he led the five men into the compound leaving the drivers lounging and smoking beside the cars at the roadside. 'Will you,' he added, addressing the "General", 'be conducting the interrogation, sir?'

'You might entertain that lot,' Heller rasped, ignoring the question and nodding in the direction of the abandoned drivers. 'Nothing too much – a bottle of beer and some Bratwurst. And smarten up these lazy-looking wasters on sentry duty. Unless they're in better shape by the time we leave you'll be lucky to be a Corporal.'

Garrou, dressed as a Major, caught McGarrity's eye with a faintly amused incline of his head. The Inspector, posing as a Sergeant First Class, remained impassive, and Fučić, without understanding a word, peered at the ground as if it was strewn with mantraps. Just beyond the barrier was a single-storey building with two sentries posted at the door. Presenting arms as the Lieutenant

A DARKENING FIRE

threw the door open and the new arrivals entered they were visibly intimidated by this imperious procession. Inside the air was cool and smelled of cologne. Emerging from the shadows a tall, lean, aristocratic figure presented itself with a formal click of the heels of painfully burnished jackboots.

'We meet again, Herr Schweitz. You remember me? Colonel Klieger at your service, sir. I command the security unit here. It's my privilege...'

Before he could embroider the greeting Heller dismissed the introduction with a snort and a gesture of condescending impatience.

'Herr Schweitz's time is limited,' he pronounced. 'I assume you are familiar with the work of Herr Professor Fučić here?' Heller indicated the ashen scientist with a casual jerk of his thumb.

'Er... yes, naturally.'

'Like me he is concerned with the development of ordnance. He will be conducting the technical inspection of this establishment.'

'As for the technical inspection of the site you'll be aware many of those employed here are not the most reputable. They are closely guarded but I recommend an escort...'

'We all have our orders, Colonel,' Garrou said. 'And yours, sir, are to comply with ours. Lieutenant Wasser mentioned the business of the interrogation...'

'Of course, Major. You will know that Herr Steinhoff has insisted that the... interview be prepared for, and we have ensured that is the case and that you are left in peace to conduct it. As for any tour of inspection, naturally you may go where you please.'

'The interrogation...' Garrou said, and waited for an informative response.

'Will be entirely at your leisure, of course. I've had strict orders from Herr Steinhoff that none of my people must approach the... the guests except to provide for their immediate needs, and then only under close supervision.'

'Very good,' Garrou replied, still with no notion of why his delegation was assumed to be present with the purpose of questioning somebody of whom they knew nothing. It was evident that Heller was beginning to enjoy his role and Garrou feared that

A DARKENING FIRE

he was on the verge of overplaying his dissembling hand. Fučić's documentation described him as a Croatian physicist, an identity that would barely stand up to scrutiny since he would certainly have been required to be fluent in German before achieving the eminence attributed to him. However, this *alter ego* was the best that could be made available in the short time the mounting of the operation had permitted, and it had been calculated that it was adequate for the degree of engagement he was likely to encounter.

'Please let me know if I can do anything further to assist you and your people, sir,' Klieger said to Schweitz who merely waved him away and maintained what was taken for an aristocratic silence. 'You'll know that my orders have been simple: to keep the whole complex safe from prying eyes, and make sure my boys say not one word about what goes on here – not that there's even a remote chance that they would comprehend any of it.'

'I'm sure you do sterling work,' Heller remarked dryly, having waited for a moment to see if the near-catatonic Schweitz would offer a response. 'But my own orders are clear – Dr. Fučić is to be permitted unrestricted access to every part of the installation. Only I will be accompanying him. You will appreciate that Berlin is testing you and your men as much as the Krupp workings.'

Klieger's inchoate protest was swiftly dealt with.

'I'm confident you know where your duty lies,' Heller continued in a lazy tone. 'But I won't hide from you the fact that if we detect anything untoward being done or said by your detail there will be consequences – for yourself and your command.'

After a short pause the Colonel gave ground with as much dignity as he could muster.

'Understood, General. May I entertain you before you carry out your tour of inspection or do you want to proceed right away?'

'Need I repeat that time is of the essence?' Heller said, assuming an air of patrician perfunctoriness and dropping in the translation of a phrase he had once heard Captain Brisse use in French. 'My own commission is to escort Dr. Fučić and Herr Schweitz. The Major and his bodyguard are here to carry out the interrogation you spoke of.'

'Ah, yes – of Professor Rupprecht. And the others too, I assume?'

A DARKENING FIRE

Heller was becoming more lordly with each exchange and went on, 'It's for us to choose who we will talk to. Now, if you will be so kind as to point us all in the right direction we won't keep you away from your post. You can provide an orderly of some kind to show me and Dr. Fučić whatever we want to see?'

As Lieutenant Wasser held open the door and was directing the visitors to their designated destinations McGarrity took it on himself to nudge Heller.

'You remember, sir,' he said, 'that we were to ask if Professor Rupprecht has been made aware of our calling.'

'I thought it best,' Klieger said, 'to say nothing to anyone apart from Wasser and the duty NCOs. And I promise you that no special arrangements are in place – their quarters, as requested, are constantly kept in the excellent condition in which you will find them.'

'Very good,' Heller approved as he moved towards the exit, one hand on Schweitz's elbow and his bulging case in the other.

But before any of them could make their way out into the daylight their way was barred by a figure silhouetted against the brilliant early afternoon sunshine, and a mocking voice said, 'Well, well, is that my old friend General Heller I see?'

A DARKENING FIRE
CHAPTER 35: JULY 1914

Feeling somewhat restored Norris Dyer had lain propped up on the pillows of his hospital bed to contemplate the means of avoiding imminent and protracted incarceration. Miraculously the point-blank shooting that had brought him to his current sorry state had missed every vital organ and had done a great deal less damage than had seemed possible. All the same, the pain had not gone away and any movement promised a further onset of acute discomfort. The consolation of a private room had been more than offset by the presence of a police guard at the door and the realisation that every passing day brought him closer to the ministrations of the justice system. And what had served until recently to add to his woes had been the accumulating pile of books that his friend Tommy Beckett had foisted on him as if he was an aficionado of Jack London, Edith Wharton or E M Forster, not one of whom meant a thing to him. But the most recent addition to his burgeoning library – which with the passage of routine had been permitted to expand without inspection – had lifted his spirits incalculably. As Beckett had confided to him a pencilled entry at page 89 of Chesterton's "*The Ball and the Cross*" had advised him that an outfit of clothes along with a modest sum of money had been stored in the laundry basket in the nearby toilet. Dyer would have to get himself into the suit just before eight the following evening, at which time the basket was regularly emptied; and he was to make his escape at that time when Beckett would be waiting in Lauriston Place with his Hazelwood motor-cycle.

The details of the arrangement had been worked out in whispered exchanges over the past three days. The police guard had given up on the regular and uneventful propelling of Dyer's wheelchair to the bathroom for his nightly ablutions for which he was permitted twenty minutes, enough time for him to don the outdoor clothing and make his sedate way to the exit via a corridor well out of sight of his gatekeeper. Some extra apparel was stowed in an official-looking briefcase which would lend an implied professional appearance to his presence in the infirmary at that time

A DARKENING FIRE

of a late but still-bright summer evening. Beckett would transport the fugitive to Waverley Station in time to catch the sleeper to King's Cross in London, unaware that in a little over an hour later he would, on his own doorstep, be face to face with Terrence Edwards.

Bathed in sweat, as much from a combination of anxiety and excitement as from the unrelenting pain in his stomach, Dyer now found himself breathless but triumphant aboard the night-train to the metropolis. Mercifully alone in the wagon-lit he lay curled up in the bunk clutching the dressing that covered his wound, half-expecting to find blood seeping copiously between his fingers. So far all had gone well, it seemed. An hour earlier the alarm would have been raised and the grounds and echoing interior of the hospital would be being searched by a posse under the aegis of a furious Inspector Mitchell who would also be ensuring an officer's career took an abrupt turn for the worse. Tommy Beckett would be back in Cramond with an elaborately constructed alibi, and it was safe to assume that no-one would be on the lookout for Dyer himself on his journey south. The only contacts of his that the authorities were aware of were to be tracked down in Edinburgh, and Dyer had never ventured beyond Hadrian's Wall. By that time, though, Mr. Beckett was in no position to speak up on his – or anyone else's – behalf

Too wound up to sleep despite an overwhelming fatigue, he distracted himself from the nagging ache in his abdomen by working out how to approach the figure on whose aid ten Berge had long ago advised him that, *in extremis*, he could rely. Dyer realised that he was about to enter a circle so elevated that he had no idea how to set about representing his case and obtaining the help that would ensure his removal to a distant place of safety. Maybe, he thought, the evidence of his wound would suffice when taken with the details of the various assignments he had undertaken since falling in with The Dutchman. At least his appearance – sporting what he had admired in the mirror as a handsome beard and wearing an almost new suit – was not going to count against him, and his account of his spectacular escape ought to enhance his image. The most immediate problem was going to be finding this benefactor. London was a far country to him and its very vastness

A DARKENING FIRE

loomed out of the dark like a threat. While he had no doubt that any cabbie would be able to conduct him to Whitehall Court he was at a loss to know how to gain access to this *eminence grise*. Dyer had inhabited a simple world where the complications of conspiracy had been handled by others and he fell asleep at last to dream of effortless flight.

He was awakened by the bellowing of the sleeping-car attendant as the train came to a hissing, lumbering halt in the bewildering bedlam of King's Cross. Gathering his belongings and his scattered wits Dyer joined the throng on the platform, suddenly aware of a renewed spasm which caused him to press his hand against the location of his injury. To his horror his withdrawn fingers bore clear signs of blood. Close to tears he hobbled to a bench and sat down, doubling over more in despair than actual pain. A tide of fear washed over him, a conviction that he was facing death here in a strange place surrounded by strangers and a pall of indifference. Gingerly he felt again at the area of the wound, found a sticky patch of deepening red in the material of the suit. Pale-faced and faint, he remained unmoving for several minutes unable to clear his mind enough to decide what to do. To be taken to a hospital would lead to his quickly being apprehended again – no doctor was going to mistake the cause of his injury. Bent almost double he made his unsteady way to a waiting room where, enveloped in the seasonal heat and an irresistible fatigue, he fell asleep for several hours. Waking in the late afternoon he concluded that he was quite likely to die a slow, undignified death without the comfort of the familiar or sympathetic unless he could stir himself to action. Finally he persuaded himself that the only realistic alternative was to make for Whitehall Court in the hope that there he would be tended to and protected.

Bracing himself, Dyer half-walked, half-staggered to the rank of Unic cabs, shoved past the outraged phalanx of elderly women at the head of the queue, managed to utter his destination and collapsed in the rear of the vehicle hanging onto his briefcase, the extent of his disguise as a civil servant or respectable city clerk. All along Euston Road and down Tottenham Court Road and Charing Cross Road and through Trafalgar Square he crouched forward over his knees, ignoring the sights and sounds of the city he had planned

A DARKENING FIRE

to take in like an enthusiastic tourist he was at last deposited at the address he had given the driver.

'You all right, guv'nor?' the cabbie enquired as his sickly passenger handed over the fare with a trembling hand and issuing a protracted groan as he did so. Ignoring the query he reeled across the pavement and barged through the door of the building to be confronted immediately by Roland Tolley the eternal guardian of the entrance to Sir Derwent Hartington's particular domain in the corner of the vast building. But before Tolley could come to Dyer's aid a short, nondescript man who, despite the sweltering end of July day, was wearing a light-coloured raincoat dappled with unidentifiable stains, came hurrying from the side office from which he had been keeping watch on the comings and goings. Catching Dyer just before he fell, the little man led him to a moth-eaten wing chair in the foyer, drew open the jacket of Dyer's suit and stared expressionlessly at the widening blood-stain.

'My dear chap,' he said, 'we must get you looked at in a great hurry. You won't need me to tell you you're in rather bad shape.'

Dyer made a weak, sweeping gesture.

'No doctor,' he muttered. 'I was sent by The Dutchman to see...'

But before he could complete the sentence he was racked by a violent surge of pain that left him gasping for breath.

'The Dutchman? Ah, yes. Well, any friend of his... And Mr. Beckett did a fine job of getting you here, didn't he? You must leave things to me. Don't concern yourself – I know how to take care of you. Utmost discretion, old chap, utmost discretion.'

'Tommy? You know Tommy?'

'Oh, in a sort of way.'

And turning to Tolley the little man said quietly, 'Official business, Roland. Leave it to me to handle, and not a word to anybody about this.'

Accustomed to obeying this nondescript but autocratic colleague who had arrived from King's Cross minutes earlier, Tolley merely nodded and retired to his sanctum. The next hour or so was lost to Dyer in a welter of agony alternating with bouts of blessed semi-consciousness. He was vaguely aware of being propelled into the dark interior of a vehicle that smelled of carbolic

A DARKENING FIRE

acid; of lying down on a narrow, hard bunk and of low voices drifting past him on a waft of unconcern, and finally, after what seemed like an age, of a mask of some sort being placed over his nose and mouth and inhaling a slightly sweet odour. When he came to, he realised after a lengthy pause that he was sprawled on a damp, uneven surface of wooden boards and that he could move neither his hands nor his feet. Some foul-smelling water lapped against his face as he tried to turn over, and someone growled, 'Fuck, you didn't give the bastard enough.'

'Never mind,' someone else said in the pitch darkness, and through a fog of pain and incomprehension Dyer made out the sounds of gentle, relaxing waves nuzzling against what appeared to be the side of a boat. 'Never mind, I've just about finished here.'

Dyer tried to raise his head to see what was going on around him, but the effort was met with a bare-fisted punch that split his lips and loosened a couple of teeth. Too weak to protest or give vent to the paroxysm of agony that rent his body he collapsed backward and lay still, distantly aware that somebody was wrapping something around his ankles.

'What's...?'

But his hoarse whine was cut short by Terrence Edwards.

'Lie still, old man, will you. This won't take a minute – just have to tighten this – ' a sharp intake of breath '– oh, caught my thumb. Nasty. But there we are... Albert, give us a hand here.'

It was too dark for Dyer to see what was going on, but he could feel a heavy weight at his feet making it impossible to raise his legs more than an inch or two. Scrabbling frantically with his hands he found them sticky with blood from his open wound.

'I need a doctor,' he managed to utter through his swollen mouth.

'Not necessary,' Edwards assured him. 'Soon be clear of all that.'

'We should have let him bleed out somewhere,' the other voice said. 'This is a damn nuisance.'

'I agree, Albert,' Edwards answered as he continued to tighten the weight attached to Dyer's ankles, 'but the boss insisted he shouldn't be found lying around making a mess of our streets so there you are, and here we are.'

A DARKENING FIRE

'Help me,' Dyer pleaded. 'I'm cold.'

'Never mind,' the anonymous voice told him. 'Soon be over.'

And with a nod Edwards enrolled his impatient colleague in the perfunctory task of tipping the unfortunate Dyer into the depths of the Thames.

While Norris Dyer was dying in the silent river Sir Derwent Hartington was sitting at his desk plunged in gloom. The permanent presence of the lugubrious, grim-faced bodyguard higher authority had insisted on imposing on him did nothing to ease his discomfiture. In the face of Hartington's resistance to this intrusion Todd, like Ackroyd, had claimed that the PM would brook no refusal – it had to be assumed that the Judas was still in place somewhere in Whitehall even if his activity appeared to be on hold; and a small number of officials, Todd insisted, were thought to be at risk of attracting the attention of German operatives as the political and military tensions built up across Europe. Todd kept to himself the real reason for the enlistment.

At Kell's headquarters at Watergate House in the Strand the cryptographer seconded from the War Office was sitting, tetchy and impatient awaiting the promised coded telegram from Bavaria. And even as far north as Edinburgh the long warm summer day had drifted into muggy night. Sergeant Hughes was escorting Inspector Mitchell on a tour of the whisky-laden gantry of the lounge at the Sealscraig Hotel where Cecil Highway was had remained installed.

'I'm surprised to see you both here,' Highway remarked. 'I suppose you still need to close down the machinery that magicked Professor Rupprecht away but I shouldn't have thought that there would have been much of it left to discover here.'

Irritated, Mitchell turned his attention away from the inviting array of spirits.

'You have some expertise in the field?' he asked.

'Oh, God, I'm sorry. That didn't convey what I intended. But those four Germans up at Talbot House surely can't have much more to tell anyone. As it is one of these nasty little characters from Whitehall Court was sent up there recently, so...'

'That fellow Todd, was it?' Hughes asked.

'No, but not unlike him. I've seen him hanging about at reception in Whitehall Court.'

A DARKENING FIRE

Hughes put his glass down.

'That bloody Edwards. I wonder what he's up to now.'

Reading the other's mind Mitchell made for the telephone in the foyer and was back five minutes later to confirm that Edwards had been turned away from the House by the security detail.

'You think Sir Derwent sent this fellow up here?' Hughes asked the half-interested Highway.

'I imagine so – the instructions came in a coded wire. He was to visit Talbot House and then get in touch with some chap called Beckett.'

'Beckett? Well, it's probably nothing to worry about but I think we'd best get up to the House and see what's going on.'

Taking the car that had been left at their disposal the officers were driven the short distance to the outskirts of Dalmeny village. At the gates of the House they were greeted by an acerbic Private Brandon who had long since learned to loathe the guard-post he had been relegated to for an earlier act of insubordination.

'Aye,' he muttered, 'the wee man in the raincoat. Just the thing in weather like this. I told him to go and lose himself and he did.'

In the vestibule of the manor Hughes and Mitchell collared the youthful Lieutenant in charge of the detail and were informed that with the imminent threat of action on the continent it was probable that the military contingent would be heading south within a day or two.

'That was supposed to happen already,' he said. 'Instructions from London, but Major Keeley wasn't happy. He wanted the order to come from Redford Barracks, not from some Civil Servant who was up here from London a few days back.'

'A Civil Servant?'

'I think so. Some posh bloke anyhow.'

The upshot had been that most of the KOSBs would be withdrawn a day or two later than had been designated by the visitor from London and only a handful of police officers and a couple of troopers would be left to look after the place.

'If the Jerries over there in Berlin want to have this lot back –' he nodded in the direction of the House '– they can bloody well come and get them. From what I can gather they're not much use to anybody now that their boss has jumped ship.'

A DARKENING FIRE

'Let's have another quick word with that fellow Tommy Beckett since our friend Edwards seems to know him,' Hughes suggested to the Inspector. 'There's something not right about this.'

A DARKENING FIRE
CHAPTER 36: JULY 1914

Sergeant Heller of the French Foreign Legion, temporarily promoted to General in the German army, screwed up his eyes against the shimmering light behind the silhouetted figure who had greeted him as he, McGarrity, Garrou, Fučić and Conrad Schweitz emerged into the sun that bathed the Freimann estate. For a moment he was persuaded that the game was up and that the only alternative was going to be for them to try to shoot their way out. But as he reached surreptitiously for his holster the newcomer emitted a prolonged chortle and, leaning forward, patted him cheerfully on both arms.

'General, a delight to see you again, my old friend,' Augustin Steinhoff brayed. The effect of this greeting on Schweitz was stunning. He was already lost in a fog of anxiety about his family, the paralysing conviction that he was betraying his country and a present fear that his own life was in immediate danger. What Steinhoff was up to he could only hope was some off-the-cuff subterfuge. Quickly recovering his baronial calm and without the faintest notion of the other's identity Heller was in a moment wringing the stranger's hand and chuckling with a great display of bonhomie.

'It's been so long,' he said, continuing to hold the other in his powerful grasp.

And turning to Colonel Klieger, Steinhoff, apparently on familiar terms with the officer, prattled something about the lengthy duration of his acquaintance with the incomer General.

'Herr Steinhoff, always a pleasure,' Klieger beamed. 'How are things in Berlin? Do you have anything for me? Am I finally to be rid of this abominable posting and see some action?'

'Naturally, if that is your wish. But for now I'm obliged to attend to some mundane matters affecting the integrity of this establishment. General – perhaps we can rendezvous here when you have completed your duties?'

'At your service,' Heller replied crisply. 'Meantime you'll forgive us if we press on? Herr Dr. Fučić and I have a tour of

A DARKENING FIRE

inspection to carry out. My colleagues have other work to concentrate on.'

And linking his arm through Fučić's Heller led the quaking scientist out in the direction of the nearest barn-like structure accompanied by an intimidated Corporal bearing a set of enormous mortise keys. Exchanging a half-concealed, wholly-puzzled look, Garrou and McGarrity, with the frozen-faced Schweitz in tow, followed another suitably servile trooper past two armed sentries and into the block to which Colonel Klieger had directed them.

'Leave us,' Garrou ordered their guide as soon as they were inside the luxurious hallway which was blanketed from wall to wall in a beige shag pile. A decorated oasis of peace resembling the gallery of a stately home, this otherwise aesthetically pleasing atrium was disfigured by the bars on the high windows, an imperfection compounded by a guard station in the middle of the wide floor-space. Acting the officious underling, McGarrity marched to this station and demanded to know where Professor Rupprecht was to be found.

'Names are on the doors, Sergeant,' he was informed by the soldier who indicated the row of doors at the far end of the hall. Rupprecht was closeted behind the nearest, and McGarrity, rapping on the door and throwing it open, stood back to allow Schweitz and Garrou to enter first. They found themselves enveloped in the benign atmosphere of accommodation akin to that of an upmarket hotel. The walls were hung with tasteful water-colours and the room was filled with extravagant furniture: wing-chairs, a *chaise-longue*, a sideboard bearing an array of crystal glasses and decanters, a large table spread with technical drawings and a heavy oak desk piled high with printed documents and newspapers. While Garrou and McGarrity looked around at this handsome environment a door at the far end of the room clicked open and a slight, hesitant figure came in. Rupprecht was a small, intense man whose most spectacularly distinguishing features were hirsute: his face, glowing with health, was encircled by a shaggy halo of long, wildly unkempt grey hair, and divided horizontally by a vast, dense moustache that clung to his now podgy cheeks, dangled heavy strands over his mouth and at the ends burrowed into the impressive Victorian sideburns. Previous symptoms of anaemia were almost

A DARKENING FIRE

gone.

'Conrad, my friend – at last!' he said, embracing Schweitz with undisguised emotion. 'I've been hoping for this for so long.' Then, waving in the direction of a pair of distressed leather wing chairs, told Garrou and McGarrity to make themselves at home. 'The stress of it all, you know... '

Garrou and McGarrity settled into the chairs as Rupprecht and Schweitz sat down opposite them. The Professor was clutching to his chest a thick folder from which a mass of papers protruded at odd angles. Garrou kept his voice even, his tone neutral.

'Your confession, Professor?'

With no clear plan of how they would proceed, Garrou and McGarrity intended simply to follow whatever line was thrown to them by the Professor. Finding him ensconced in these most congenial of surroundings was the first unforeseen contingency; and now it seemed that Rupprecht had been preparing some documentation of his clandestine activities. Neither of the inquisitorial visitors found it necessary to betray the slightest sign that any of this came as a surprise to them, and both sat unmoved and unmoving waiting for the Professor to continue.

'Look, Conrad, please understand me: it was never our intention to mislead you – you of all people. We've assumed all along that all the technical side of the project was delegated to us. God knows, you have more than enough on your plate without being...'

He leaned across to touch his friend's shoulder. Again denied a response he asked simply, 'How do you want me to go on?'

'I'm sure,' Garrou said, 'that there will be no need for the Sergeant here to exercise his enthusiasm for his somewhat aggressive approach to questioning.'

Rupprecht freed one of his hands from their interlocked hold on his papers and wiped a sudden bead of sweat from his forehead.

'No need whatsoever,' he agreed.

'Then I suggest,' Garrou went on, reading between the other's words, 'that you do no more than provide us with a brief oral account of your role in this project. Not the one which, because of your failure to report to Herr Schweitz, has led to confusion in the Reichstag and the OHL. Such failure at this critical juncture is

A DARKENING FIRE

unforgivable. I must stress the severity of the consequences for yourself and all the others concerned if you continue to prevaricate.'

'But it was the Kaiser himself who agreed that...' Rupprecht protested. 'Conrad, tell them! You insisted always that you wished to hear nothing more of our work. I don't understand why you've come here at this late stage. What has changed?'

Schweitz restricted his reaction to brief nod of the head and a long, hard stare at Garrou, who directed his synthetic fury at the scientist.

'I'm the one asking the questions, not you. Is that entirely clear?'

Rupprecht, shaken, accidentally dropped his file and scattered its contents on the floor. With a profuse apology he fell to his knees and set about reassembling them while his trio of visitors looked on.

'From the beginning if you please,' Garrou instructed, switching to the epitome of benign patience. For the next two hours Rupprecht stumbled through his long and labyrinthine association with the bomb plot until, having responded to all questions, he passed over his voluminous portfolio and sat back exhausted with a look that combined relief with anxiety. The accuracy of every detail of the Professor's tortuous tale could hardly be confirmed without access to sources elsewhere, but Garrou was confident that it had not strayed from the truth.

'You realise the seriousness of what you have confessed?' the Frenchman asked. 'If I may speak for Herr Schweitz it's plain that he has not been kept properly informed. On the other hand, though, I can quite see why you would regard the operation as successful.'

'Krupp and Kaiser Wilhelm insisted we proceed on the basis that the utmost secrecy was maintained.' And as an afterthought Rupprecht went on, addressing Schweitz, 'I hope that I may now leave this damn place and retire to Trier as was agreed many months ago?'

But before Schweitz could offer an endorsement of this ambition the cell door was thrown open and "General" Heller and Dr. Fučić were ushered in by a uniformed guard.

No longer toting his vast valise and hardly bothering to glance at Rupprecht Heller declared, 'Dr. Fučić confirms what Colonel

A DARKENING FIRE

Klieger told us – this site must be preserved with the greatest care, and some of its workers need the most vigilant supervision. In particular the power plant needs at all costs to be maintained to the highest standard.'

'Just what I was saying,' the Professor said, nodding emphatically at both Schweitz and Garrou. 'But I have to repeat for the project to be successful total secrecy must be sustained.'

'Please don't try to advise Herr Schweitz or Dr. Fučić on all this,' Garrou replied. 'You know the extent of your role. Do keep within it.'

Rupprecht blanched.

'Of course, of course,' he muttered. 'I apologise.'

'When I report I'll be careful to stress the extent of your co-operation. Now I see no reason for us to delay – the sooner we're back at Wilhelmstrasse the sooner your position can be reviewed – favourably, I should think, Herr Schweitz?'

Schweitz again nodded dumbly, Rupprecht mistaking the vacant stare as one of irritated boredom.

'I have to say it again,' he said, 'the Kaiser himself...'

'Our work here is complete,' Heller interrupted and turning to the guard who was hovering by the entrance to the suite bellowed, 'Please arrange for us to say our goodbyes to the Colonel and to be escorted back to our vehicles.'

The trooper clicked his heels and McGarrity, still clutching his briefcase and strutting with martial gait was leading the unnerved Fučić away from the constant danger of linguistic confrontation when, emerging from a studded door some yards away, smoking a disconsolate cigarette and staring directly at them, was the unmistakable figure of Ciarán Taaffe. For some seconds McGarrity was tempted to carry on regardless, trusting that Taaffe was either no more likely than he to credit the coincidence or to recognise him in the German uniform. But as soon as the tubby little Fenian scrambled to his feet and started in his direction McGarrity knew that the well-honed powers of observation sharpened over years of energetic dissembling had not deserted the man. In a low tone that conveyed an evident note of urgency he instructed Fučić to make for the vehicles parked outside the main gate.

'Try to look annoyed,' he advised. 'If the guards speak to you

A DARKENING FIRE

give them a physicist's glower, whatever that might look like. And don't even break step.'

Before Taaffe could approach him more closely he was tackled by a slow-moving sentry who thrust a rifle against his belly and herded him back to where he had been sitting. While this guard was still devoting his sullen attention at his wide-eyed prisoner McGarrity, striding towards him, put his finger to his lips and shook his head. Taaffe's capacity for self-containment was severely tested by this turn of events but he succeeded in concealing his astounded disbelief as the giant figure loomed over him and the guard who, turning leisurely, snapped to attention at the sight of this Herculean NCO.

'This is the man Taaffe?' McGarrity rasped. 'He is to be shot.'

The guard responded with open-mouthed incredulity at this abrupt announcement of imminent annihilation and the non-German speaking Taaffe, sensing something ominous was in the immediate offing, dropped his cigarette and, caught between the Scylla of almost hysterical hope and the Charybdis of instinctive and abject fear, half-stood up and then sank back on a stone bench.

'Now? By me?' the sentry gasped.

'Don't be an idiot,' McGarrity told him. 'The man is a spy. He's to be interrogated in Berlin and then dealt with by firing squad. You have his papers?'

'Papers? I don't understand, Sergeant.'

'Never mind. I'll handle it for you, but in future you'd better be sharper than this or you'll be trudging up the Zugspitze with a 25 kilogram pack on your back.'

'Yes, Sergeant; thank you, Sergeant.'

'You,' McGarrity growled in English, 'come with me.'

And jerking a thumb he indicated to Taaffe to walk in front of him. Pushed and jostled the entire hundred yards to the gate the little man stumbled several times to the amusement of the lounging detail stationed at the barrier.

'One moment,' Lieutenant Wasser called from the guard room and came hurrying out to remonstrate with Taaffe's captor. 'What exactly do you think you're doing with my prisoner?'

'Take it up with Herr Schweitz or the General,' McGarrity answered. 'I have my orders. This man is to be taken to HQ in

A DARKENING FIRE

Berlin for questioning and execution. I suggest you respect the General's wishes. He's not in the best of humours.'

And tucking the briefcase more tightly than ever under one arm while continuously nudging Taaffe with the other he marched out through the gate and taking his captive by the collar yanked him into the rear of one of the waiting cars.

'Christ almighty,' Taaffe gasped when the door was closed after them and they were alone and out of earshot, 'you're a genius, Leo. How the fuck did you ever find me in this *carn aoiligh*?'

'Say as little as you can to these folk,' McGarrity told him. 'And remember – you never met me before; you've been hiking around the countryside and you're an innocent who's been held on a trumped-up charge of spying for the Brits just because you came wandering past this place.'

'Leo, man, you're the very God come to earth. You're a miracle worker. No, you're a miracle.'

'Dún do chlab, you idiot. Now sit there and wait.'

And, clambering out, McGarrity stood by the rear door of the vehicle watching Heller salute Klieger, berate one of the sentries for his slovenly appearance and lead the rest of the expedition out of the compound accompanied by Schweitz and the stranger Steinhoff whose own Mercedes stood glinting in the brilliant evening light. As the others climbed into the cars while the drivers revved the engines Steinhoff strode up to the Inspector and said quietly, 'We don't know each other but with some good fortune we should meet again in London before too many days have passed.' A pause, and then, 'The new security measures at your ports are known in Berlin.'

McGarrity offered no reply and Steinhoff attended to his reticence.

'In London, then. As soon as possible. I'm afraid I'll no longer be welcome in Germany.'

McGarrity shook his hand, turned away and settled in beside Garrou and Taaffe, but before the he could close the door Heller came hurrying from the lead car and placing a hand on the roof said, 'There might be some trouble coming in a minute or two so I'm telling you – now's the time to bugger off in a hurry. Oh, and here – I've liberated his portfolio for you. Maybe that's why he's so

A DARKENING FIRE

fucking upset.'

'Trouble? What trouble?' Garrou asked, leaning across the Inspector.

'The fellow had been watching you with binoculars from that communications room, which was where I lifted his bag. And now he's out there bawling at Klieger and pointing in our direction.'

Garrou's glance back at the assembled military was enough to confirm that some unpleasantness was in the immediate offing; and a closer look had the effect of his issuing an urgent demand to the drivers to set the cars going at full tilt. Though the Frenchman had so far escaped recognition, by a belated stroke of ill-luck Helmut Protzman had caught sight of him at this last moment. It was the cruellest coincidence, Garrou grumbled to McGarrity as Heller sped off to the lead car, calling over his shoulder, 'We're not the only ones in the shit.' And as the convoy went racing down the dusty roadway, a plume of smoke accompanied by the reverberations of an explosion filled the air in the middle of the operations block, and this was followed by a conflagration that was visible even at this distance.

'The power to the whole place knocked out,' Heller was shouting exultantly as he climbed into the car beside Taaffe and Fučić. 'Terrible accident.'

And Garrou noted that the legionnaire was no longer carrying his own enormous valise. Turning in his seat he could make out Steinhoff's Mercedes travelling at top speed close behind them.

'Who exactly is this Steinhoff at our heels?' he asked in a tone that failed to conceal a conflict of excitement and trepidation.

'Seems to be one of The Owl's chicks,' McGarrity said casually. 'I hope somebody knows the road to Italy.'

'And our new travelling companion?'

Taaffe was content to leave his description to McGarrity.

'An innocent abroad.'

With the cars juddering and emitting noisy complaint at the demands their top speed was pressing on them McGarrity watched as Steinhoff pulled out close behind them.

A DARKENING FIRE
CHAPTER 37: JULY 1914

The Dutchman brought the *Ineke* inshore in one of the many small inlets on the Essex coast south of Dengie Flat and east of the village of Tillingham. It had been a great relief to escape unscathed from Hamburg but much of what had happened there and even more of what was happening on the borders of his life was beyond confusion. Fleeing Germany without a single item of cargo was no embarrassment, he supposed, when he had the time to reflect on the shambles he had just quitted – or been allowed unaccountably to quit. Todd's permitting him, or rather instructing him, to accompany the now departed Gormley had felt like a free pass to escape the clutches of the English authorities but he had long ago come to the conclusion that nothing was ever quite what it seemed. And now it looked as if events would shortly be putting paid to his busy trafficking across the North Sea. One thing was clear – there was no explanation he could offer that would deflect the determination of the German police to lay hands on him after the events at the Speicherstadt.

There was perhaps one avenue still to be explored, and that was in the very heart of the Whitehall establishment – the one which, though he had never met directly, he had been fortunate enough to be able to communicate with via the auspices of Irish and German intermediaries. The most immediate problem to be dealt with, though, was what to do with the *Ineke* which by now was bound to be targeted by the Coast Guard, the Navy, the police and the security services. And if war did come there was no telling how severely the English judiciary would deal with a man who would without question be regarded as an enemy of the state. Having tossed his luggage ashore ten Berge sat disconsolately on the deck debating the future of his greatest financial and emotional investment which could so easily become the visible manifest of his location. He could leave her moored well offshore and row in on the dinghy; or set her on fire or sink her – though neither of these alternatives could disguise his presence unless he was prepared to take her well out into the North Sea. The prospect of destroying his

A DARKENING FIRE

pride and joy quickly became too offensive to contemplate, but to leave her moored where she was would attract undue attention. At a loss to decide on his next move he gave himself time to work to a decision by hurling his bags back on-board, sitting down on deck, lighting a cigarette and pouring himself a large brandy.

The afternoon sun enveloped him in a soporific glow and he was close to dropping off when he was sharply recalled to full consciousness by the roar of a motorcycle bounding and zigzagging over the low-lying, uneven grassland. Watching the vehicle's progress through half-closed eyes he waited until the rider brought the noisy machine to a spluttering halt a few yards from the bank against which the *Ineke* was tied to the bole of a solitary tree.

'A thing of beauty,' the newcomer commented as he dismounted, waving a hand at the yacht. 'But she'll be in trouble here when the tide goes out. The draught'll be too shallow for a boat that size.'

The Dutchman indicated to the man that he should come on deck and, with an engaging smile, conjured another glass which he passed to his guest.

'A brandy, yes? Of course you're right about the tide. I've been sitting here trying to decide what to do – drop anchor a bit offshore or just find somewhere else to moor her further up the coast.'

An older man than The Dutchman had taken him for at first, the bike rider accepted the tumbler with a nod of maritime fraternity, buckled down beside his host and peered around appreciatively at the *Ineke's* trappings.

'Now I'd say,' he said, 'that you're a good long way from home by the sound of you. You wouldn't be a German spy, would you? They're all the rage this summer according to the newspapers.'

'Just a sleepy Dutchman on a little holiday. And you, sir?'

'Just a Lakeland man on a little holiday. My daughter says I've obviously lost my mind buying a motorbike at my time of life, but I tell you, it's a grand way to see the country.'

'I used to have one myself,' The Dutchman said. 'And you're right – the freedom to go wherever you choose.'

'Exactly. Look at me – the nearest road is half a mile away and I thought – well, let's take in the bumps and go and have a look at the water. As you say – I can go where I like. Grand; it's grand.'

A DARKENING FIRE

The answer to ten Berge's problem had fallen gently into his lap.

'Another brandy? Here let me. So your daughter disapproves, eh? And your wife?'

'Widower. Long time. Just the girl now. Told her I'd see her again when I see her. Look at that – ' pointing at the bike ' – isn't she lovely? A Wanderer 2 horsepower. Side valve, 251 cc. Brand new, too.'

The Dutchman stirred and fixed his attention on the motorcycle.

'My God,' he said, 'that *is* a fine piece of machinery. Would you mind if I took a closer look?'

Flattered, the old man got stiffly to his feet, the two large brandies swiftly disposed of having already brought a hectic flush to his face and a slight confusion to his brain.

'Come on, my French friend, follow me.'

'Dutch,' The Dutchman reminded him from a yard behind as they stepped ashore.

'Aye, Dutch.'

In one sweeping movement ten Berge locked his arm round the other's throat and with his left hand plunged his long-bladed knife into his heart. Only when the body had stopped its violent agitation did he leave it to crumple to the ground, the blood pumping from the wound. After a break to smoke another reflective cigarette he hauled the corpse to the bank and tipped it into the reedy shallows several yards from the boat. He had too much luggage to carry on the motorcycle so he discarded most of it, tucked the rest into the dead man's haversack and with some difficulty started the machine and wobbled off towards the road with only the faintest notion of how to get to London. From Tillingham he rode to Southminster and on through a series of villages and small towns, asking occasionally for directions, until, as daylight faded, he reached Upminster where he found a room for the night.

The next morning he reached Stratford where he abandoned the Wanderer and took the short train journey into the city. Whitehall was alive with frantic activity that day as the international situation deteriorated and The Dutchman, confident that in this environment of heightened concern with more pressing matters his sauntering

A DARKENING FIRE

figure was unlikely to attract attention, ambled twice round the block of which Whitehall Court formed the eastern edge. The part of the building in which he had an interest now had a uniformed and discouraging commissionaire at the door but for most of the morning there was no sign of activity other than scurrying telegram boys with red-painted bicycles. Frustrated, he headed for St James's Park where he had previously gone to receive occasional instruction, payment or reprimand. In the absence of any personal contact the practice was for him to resort to the usual dead-letter drop hollowed out of the trunk of a plane tree behind a bench on the north side of the lake.

The Dutchman knew that he shared this means of transmitting information with German agents and dissident Irish, but today there was no message there either for him or the others. His hope was that at some juncture a familiar face would appear. The shot was not such a long one – he was familiar with a small number of the Irish seditionists and German agents whose activities he assumed would now be even more lively and requiring ever more urgent information exchange. Hungry, tired and on edge ten Berge lowered himself onto a bench and, fighting off the urge to drowse in the scorching summer heat, patiently scanned the crowds for a potential contact. After hours of stultifying boredom he was compelled to give up, scribbled a plea for an early interview along with the address he regularly used across the river in Lambeth, slid it into the usual hiding place as the numbers of leisurely passers-by shrank to a trickle and set off along the Embankment half convinced that every strolling policeman was eyeing him with deep suspicion.

If war did break out he was sure that every hotel and guest house in the capital would be providing the authorities with the details of alien citizens lodging with them. In the circumstances he saw no alternative to retreating to the flat located in a cul-de-sac off Pearman Street. He had used it intermittently over many years, the rent paid for by an anonymous absentee landlord. For some time he had feared that the place was no longer a safe haven – it was a facility which, like the dead letter drop, he shared with others and the threat of imminent conflict might have brought its irregular tenants under close scrutiny. But with nowhere else to rest up for

A DARKENING FIRE

what might be a protracted time he felt compelled to run the risk of lying low at the place where in the past he had sometimes run into agents of the Nachrichten-Abteilung on their way to or from the ports they had been dispatched to report on.

Approaching the narrow lane he took the precaution of studying from a distance the windows of the houses opposite and the posture of the few pedestrians strolling by or lingering in doorways or at corners. Satisfied that no unwelcome observer was lurking in the area he hurried up the stone-floored close, unlocked the black door to the ground floor flat and letting himself into the cool, dark little room, subsided into the embrace of a vast armchair smelling faintly of naphthalene. He was tired, hungry and wracked by tension but in minutes he was sound asleep and confronting in dreams the grotesque reality of the first murder he had committed.

Having raced north to attend to the simple matter of ensuring that Dr. Klein's supplies contained their unsought component Terrence Edwards had hurried back the following morning to London to be advised that the foreign agent called The Dutchman was ensconced in the Lambeth hideaway of which the security service had long been aware. Complying with a terse order he set off in haste across Westminster Bridge and was soon peering along Pearman Street and around the drab mews to confirm that no-one was paying any heed to his presence. The blinds were firmly closed at the flat where ten Berge had announced that he would be waiting for help and, quietly unlocking the street door, Edwards let himself into the unlit hall. He paused for a few moments to allow his eyes to become accustomed to the darkness. The door to the room in front of him was slightly ajar and, moving forward silently, he could distinguish the outline of a figure sitting unmoving in a low-backed chair, its back towards him. Bringing the wire garrotte from under his jacket and letting it dangle at his side by its wooden handle Edwards edged down the lobby and stepped between the door and the frame. Holding his breath he padded the last couple of steps until he was immediately behind the unmoving occupant.

'Good morning, Mr. Edwards,' the disembodied voice said from somewhere in the murky depths of the gloomy room, and a second later the door was softly closed and Edwards was propelled gently to the middle of the floor by a pair of large hands placed

A DARKENING FIRE

carefully on his scapulae. For a moment he was minded to resist, but as much out of curiosity as apprehension he allowed himself to be prodded into a worn wing-chair where he waited, the garrotte still in his fist, until the blind was wound up and the room was filled with the uncertain stream of sunlight that the geography of the building permitted.

'My evil twin,' Todd remarked from his place immediately opposite; and it was true that the two men had much in common physically. 'I expect you are keen to explain your arrival here with that interesting little implement you're sporting.'

Turning his head slightly Edwards could make out the presence of two tight-lipped hard cases looming over him, enough to dissuade him from his first instinct to make a lunge at the man he had seen only once before in a lane in the village of South Queensferry. On the point of offering a sarcastic answer he opted instead, after a swift glance at the expressionless Todd, for the truth.

'I was looking for ten Berge.' A pause. 'What's it to you?'

Todd ignored the question.

'I've no time to waste,' he told Edwards. 'We'll quite likely be at war with Germany very soon. The Dutchman is an enemy agent and he's safely behind bars. Tell me how you knew his whereabouts and who sent you to shut him up.'

Edwards shrugged. In the circumstances he could see no advantage in prevaricating.

'You're Todd – I remember you. We're on the same side. You know who I work for. I was sent here to look after this ten Berge. Extreme measures, I was told, what with that war coming.'

'Sir Derwent is sending out assassins nowadays? I hardly think so.'

'Couldn't care less what you think. Go to Whitehall Court and ask. And you're not the only one short of time, so if you don't mind I'll be on my way.'

Half-standing Edwards felt himself sharply returned to his seat by a second but this time less than gentle application of hands.

'I asked how you knew about this place,' Todd reminded him.

'Sir Derwent's office told me about it. And I'll ask you the same question.'

A DARKENING FIRE

'Not that it's any business of yours, but we've been watching this place for months. We followed a not very competent German agent called Protzman here a long time ago.'

Edwards made a small performance of winding the wire of his garrotte around the wooden handles and stuffing it back in his jacket.

'I'll say it again,' he muttered. 'Like your Harriet Nichols and your Colonel and the rest I'm for the same thing as you. I've got my orders and you've got yours. If you get in my way you'll answer to Sir Derwent himself.'

'Then you'd better tell me all about these little commissions of yours and we'll see if we *are* on the same side.'

A little later the same day and despite the traumas of the past several weeks Talbot House outside South Queensferry took delivery of one of Dr. Klein's occasional supplies of medication, laboratory equipment and reference works. The red and yellow crate emblazoned with the name Edina Pharmaceutical had become a familiar sight since the Germans had been closeted at Dalmeny but even this accustomed incursion was now being treated with wariness and a degree of suspicion. The vehicle was no longer to be permitted beyond the gates and the single wooden case was prised open to reveal nothing more sinister than the usual assortment of phials, books and surgical instruments.

'You better tack that lid back down,' the driver warned the officious Corporal of the guard. 'Your Miss Petzold will have the face off you if she thinks you've been interfering with the doctor's stuff.'

With a grimace the soldier nodded to Private Brandon to return the container to its pristine condition. Brandon went about sullenly hammering nails back into the damaged planks and diverted himself by recommending the driver to, 'Piss off with your French letters and de-lousers.'

Having satisfied his instinctive proclivity for giving offence he hefted the crate up to the house and as usual deposited it into stout Karoline's care.

'Any time you're ready, dearie,' he told her, patting his groin and then set off back to his post as a stone whizzed past his ear.

An hour later Rheinhold Sauer, hunched over a complex of

A DARKENING FIRE

equations set alongside carefully detailed illustrations, glowered across at Hanna Blindt and grated, 'Now what?'

Hanna too was distracted by the crash of glass from the tiny laboratory accompanied by a choking cry and the sound of someone barging into and upending the wooden table and chair there. Hanna was first to the door and found Karoline lying convulsing on the floor, her hands pressed against her chest, her laboured breathing interrupted by a rasping cough that suddenly gave way to a bout of vomiting.

'Get Klein, for God's sake,' Sauer shouted, making no effort to come any closer to this dire spectacle, but the doctor had also heard the commotion and in a moment was elbowing the others aside. While Klein knelt over the stricken Karoline, Hanna's attention was drawn from the grisly sight by an open cardboard box lying upended on the ground. Half out of the top was a small set of brass laboratory scales amid a pile of paper packing and a piece of felt padding from which protruded several short needle points.

'The clouds… the clouds are coming,' Karoline gasped between racking coughs, her eyes bulging, her heels drumming. 'They're crushing us… crushing…'

As Klein leaned forward to hold her writhing shoulders Karoline emitted a long sigh and lay still.

'Stillmark,' Klein muttered. 'Ricin.'

A DARKENING FIRE
CHAPTER 38: JULY 1914

Glancing back at the vehicle carrying McGarrity's party as it hurtled south at full speed Heller uttered an oath and slapped his driver on the shoulder.

'Get your foot down,' he said. 'I didn't spot that bloody thing.'

Quarter of a mile back Klieger's staff car was tearing after them, raising a cloud of dust that was drawing closer with every passing second. Heller had just finished boasting that he had ripped a tyre on each of the trucks at the Freimann site – but the Colonel's Opel had been out of sight while this act of sabotage had been performed. Whoever was at the wheel was driving with speed and skill and was gaining on the fugitives at an alarming rate. The road they were taking – east of the city and past the Speichersee – had been designed to disguise their intended route, bypassing Munich itself before turning back west once they had left the city behind. At the first junction Steinhoff's vehicle sped off down a narrow country lane but the Opel continued in hot pursuit of Schweitz's Mercedes and the Type C Audis that The Owl had provided. Flat out at their maximum speed of 90 kilometres per hour the two lighter vehicles were lurching dangerously on the uneven roadway despite the drivers' expert handling, and the faster pursuer was coming up on the rear car so quickly that McGarrity could see the five men jammed into it. The officer in the front passenger seat was leaning out trying to steady himself enough to aim the Gewehr 88 rifle.

'Let them go past,' Heller bawled at his driver, and as the car slowed a little he waved to McGarrity's Opel and Schweitz's car to overtake. 'This is my fault, but I'll fix it.'

'What's going on?' the terrified Dr. Fučić demanded as he sat rigid and grey-faced while Heller scrabbled on the floor to produce a long-barrelled Mauser C96 machine pistol with a wooden shoulder stock.

'Right!' he yelled at the driver. 'Brake and slew this thing round. Now!'

The Audi screeched to halt, throwing up a screen of gravel and

A DARKENING FIRE

the legionnaire leapt from the still swaying car. In a moment the pursuing Opel was no more than thirty yards away and braking fiercely to avoid a collision. As if casually practising on a firing range Heller took aim and pressed the trigger of his weapon. The officer brandishing the Gewehr died instantly and as the rear door of the Opel burst open the concentrated fusillade brought an emerging trooper tumbling to the ground screaming in pain. Unarmed, the driver threw himself out of his seat and went haring off into the long grass lining the roadside. Unaccustomed to the use of a gun, Helmut Protzman, still wedged in the rear of the vehicle, raised his M1883 Reichsrevolver in a wavering, untidy action and managed to fire off a single, wildly misdirected round before Heller put two bullets in his brain.

Dusting himself down with the air of a man mildly irritated by some minor inconvenience, Heller observed his handy-work for a moment, then climbed back into the passenger seat, patted the driver approvingly on the arm and with a negligent gesture indicated that their journey should be resumed. With the Audis bearing the pennants and badges of Schweitz's state-allocated military cohort Garrou was now more confident that they could successfully be conducted to their pre-arranged destination of Venice. Though a member of the Triple Alliance with Austria-Hungary and Germany, Italy had betrayed no sign of joining in the threatened rush to war and The Owl's agents in that country had concluded that her participation on whatever side – if it ever occurred – was unlikely to come any time soon. With both Germany and Austria on a war footing the escape route was flooded with army activity. In this environment there could hardly be a more effective disguise than the sight of a General and his entourage racing across the countryside in the direction first of Innsbruck and ultimately to the Brenner Pass. More than that, Schweitz's immense authority itself – evidently enough to keep the confused Brockmann in line – would be adequate to convince any suspicious officials in their way that they were engaged on an urgent mission to coordinate the resources of the two powers. However Colonel Klieger was dealing with the mystifying events at Freimann it soon became obvious that the arrangements made for their getaway had been formulated with a catalogue of potential

A DARKENING FIRE

hazard anticipated. The Owl had not spent the greater part of his life in Germany without acquiring or establishing a network of collaboration and the substantial funds allocated to the operation by the Deuxième Bureau had oiled the cogs of the covert machinery. And whenever it was required Heller's sheer arrogance combined with the fearful Schweitz's widely recognised eminence impelled them through check-points and patrols.

'Captain Brisse,' Garrou commented, 'is going to be far outranked by our beloved leader Heller when he returns to duty with the Legion.'

Having raced imperiously through western Austria it was only at the Brenner Pass and in Bozen that the convoy encountered a suspicious reaction, but the delay was occasioned by no more than a perfunctory interrogation by conscript troopers who were less inclined to questions than to pleas for informed assessment of the Empire's campaign prospects. The hundred miles to Verona took them down the east shore of Lake Garda through beautiful rolling scenery that came as an anti-climax after the nerve-racking trip through Bavaria and Tyrol. A little outside Mori the three cars drew up a hundred yards from a country inn from which Schweitz's wife Magda emerged in the amicable grip of a handsome Italian.

'Please be so good as to detain yourselves here for thirty six hours – no less than thirty six, you understand?' Garrou instructed the white-faced Schweitz when he had freed himself from his wife's hysterical embrace. 'Then you'll find your daughter strolling down the path there without a care in the world. You do understand, don't you?'

The tearful couple, watched over by the uncomprehending but complaisant Brockmann, could only nod and collapse on the grassy bank in a welter of relief and anticipation. Following an overnight stay at another of The Owl's pre-arranged stopovers the cars were changed yet again, this time to Fiats indistinguishable from most of the other vehicles they met. A further eighty miles at last brought them to Venice and to The Owl who had set himself up in an extensive and extravagant apartment within sight of the Basilica di San Marco. The exhausted drivers bid their passengers a muted *addio* and set off in their vehicles with their pockets stuffed with the money The Owl presented with professional formality.

A DARKENING FIRE

While the hasty retreat via Austria and Italy was being pursued Augustin Steinhoff was driving north with equal recklessness in the knowledge that his time to perform a last act of duplicity was now limited by the exhilarating occurrence at Freimann. He estimated the journey at no less than eight hours, by which point it was certain that Klieger would have been able to make some sense of his intrusion at Freimann and alert every police force in the country and, probably, his part in it. But he reckoned that nobody would for the briefest moment, expect him to travel back to the lion's den. So before his boss Conrad Schweitz was free to intervene the following day Steinhoff himself would have driven to Bremerhaven and boarded the 40 foot American-flagged power launch for which The Owl had, a week before, made provision in anticipation of Steinhoff's need to depart Germany in a hurry. A fast voyage would take him to Harlingen in Holland and, after a stop to refuel, on across the North Sea to the port of Lowestoft on the east coast of England where The Owl's personal Vauxhall C10 would be available to transport him at high speed to London.

In Venice an evening spent in high good humour at a noisy restaurant left Garrou and the others tipsy and triumphant and McGarrity coldly sober but more amiable than the rest had seen him. Later he and Taaffe, whose presence was explained as an act of benevolent liberation, excused themselves and found a quiet bar in the Calle Fiubera. Taaffe was still mesmerised by the apparent fact of McGarrity's having discovered his plight by some miraculous means and crossed the continent with the express purpose of freeing him from Protzman's clutches. The manner of his escape in the company of strangers who had hardly queried his presence all the way from Munich to Venice was too overwhelming for comment.

'You're a genius and a hero,' he told McGarrity as they clinked glasses of Fernet Branca. *'Aithnítear cara I gcruatán.'*

'Ah, well,' McGarrity answered with no intention of revealing to Taaffe the real reason for the expedition to Germany, *'Ní neart go cur le chéile.* If we don't hang together we shall surely hang separately.'

'Tell me this now, though – how in the name of Christ did you find me in yon fucking hole?'

A DARKENING FIRE

'You know how it is with ourselves and the Jerries. They're not all like your man Protzman. There are others that don't want to queer the pitch. We can't be falling out at a time like this.'

'I'll not lie to you, Leo. Come woe or weal I'm still your very man for the Cause, but, Jesus, I don't have a clue where I can turn that some bastard isn't going to belt my brains out. Boylan and his wee Council in Dublin had that Clarkson mess in Glasgow hung round my neck and on top of that he thinks I've buggered things up with the Germans. Then there was Gallagher getting shot in London that'll have been put down to me. Every bloody copper in Scotland and England is after my hide; and now the Jerries will want the guts out of me.'

McGarrity failed to suppress a wry grin.

'You're not usually this cheery, Ciarán. Have another drink.'

'I will, but there's no joke in this. Where am I supposed to go now, Leo? I swear you're looking at a dead man.'

The Inspector's instinct was to rain down a torrent of reality on his companion – to explain to him that the greatest of his burdens could be ascribed to McGarrity himself; that far from being the hero who meted out vengeance on the traitor Joey Butler, he was the Judas who had killed Joey Butler, the most loyal of Taaffe's lieutenants; that far from being the rescuer of some iota of Taaffe's credibility in the heel of the Clarkson hunt it had been he who was responsible for the disaster that had attended the project. But as he listened patiently to the despondent Taaffe he was unable to dispose of a burgeoning sympathy for the man whose entire life had been devoted to the cause of an independent Ireland and who was now, through no fault of his own beyond a blind patriotism and misplaced trust, at irrevocable odds with everyone and everything he had invested his ambition in.

'What do you want me to say, Ciarán? You must have had time enough on your hands to plan what you'd do if you got away from that Freimann place.'

'The truth, Leo – I'd given up altogether. By now my family will have it that I'm a treacherous fucker – Boylan'll have made sure of that. And there's not going to be a rebel in Scotland, England or any other damn place that doesn't think the same.'

McGarrity rubbed his mouth with the back of his hand and

A DARKENING FIRE

wondered at the wisdom of what he was about to do.

'You're still a sharp wee tack, *mo bhuachaill*. Where would you go if you got yourself on one of these ships in the harbour here?'

'Somewhere no bastard would ever find me.'

'Not back to Ireland then? Or Glasgow?'

'I've said it twice, Leo – I'd be lucky to last five minutes. No, if I had the spondoolicks I'd be bound for fucking Van Diemen's Land or right up the Orinoco. But I don't have two ha'pennies to rattle together.'

McGarrity leaned forward and assumed a confidential air.

'These folk I'm with,' he said, 'aren't the best for you to be too pally with. They're *drong gadaithe* – professionals and dangerous with it – a big international outfit. Set up a robbery in Hamburg that I was able to put them onto on condition that they helped me get you out. So now we're awash with money. But you've seen what they'll do to get it.'

'You'll not scare me, Leo. I've had years of looking out for myself.'

'Aye, well, you sound like a man scared enough already, *mo chara*. And I'll tell you this – I'm away out of here before the law catches up with them or they decided they've paid me over the odds.'

Taaffe was taken aback, having always assumed that nothing and nobody could put the wind up his titanic companion.

'Right,' he said after a moment's thought, 'I'll come with you.'

'To Glasgow?'

Taaffe grimaced. He'd already pronounced the city was not an alternative open to him. The two men sat in silence for a bit longer, then McGarrity, with a look of faintly ironic empathy, reached across to pat the other on the shoulder.

'You're still the resourceful wee fellow I knew,' he said. 'If you hurry to the port with your heels touching your head I bet you'll talk yourself onto a boat as quick as you like.'

A pause.

'So take this little token of appreciation and buy yourself a ticket for wherever you want.'

And McGarrity passed the bulging bag over the table. With a puzzled expression Taaffe undid the buckles and stared in disbelief

A DARKENING FIRE

at the pile of bank notes that The Owl had liberated from the Speicherstadt in Hamburg.

'What the fuck is this, Leo? I can't take it. There's enough here for us to bring the whole German army to the Coal Quay of Cork.'

'You're a patriot boy, still, but you've said it yourself: there's nowhere the other side of the Channel you'll be safe, and they'll not let you buy yourself back in. Boylan would as soon grab the loot and cut your throat in the one afternoon. Take it, Ciarán, and never turn your head. *Is fear rith maith ná droch-sheasamh*.'

'But, holy Christ, I couldn't spend this in a hundred years, and…'

'Keep your voice down, *tú leathcheann*. Now look – I've got to get back to that crowd and sort out where the rest of us go now. There's a war not far off so I'd say the police in Germany have more folks than us to worry about.'

Baffled by the other's generosity Taaffe continued to stare as if hypnotised at the bulging bag of currency.

'War coming on, is it?' he said finally, still unable to turn his attention from the treasure trove in front of him. *'England's difficulty…'* he went on but was instantly interrupted by McGarrity.

'Look to yourself, Ciarán, and shift your arse out there to New South Wales or Valparaiso or Vladivostok. Just don't tell me where. And find a boat for yourself before things get any worse here. *Go n-éiri an bóthar leat*.'

'I can't do it, man. If the boys won't let me hand it over, *you* give it to them.'

'I can't, Ciarán, and for a good reason I'll not let you have.'

'Then tell them they can have it off me any time they ask.'

'You'd be mad to let them know where you are. *Go dté tú slán*.'

And McGarrity stood up, emptied his glass and held out a hand to Taaffe who threw himself at the big man and seized him in a tearful embrace.

'You're the greatest of men, Leo McGarrity,' he sobbed. *'Go raibh míle maith agat*.'

And he subsided into a well of emotion as his gigantic saviour ambled out of the bar, half raising a hand in farewell.

Back at the apartment that The Owl had procured for the final stage of the operation it was plain that no-one was in the clearest

A DARKENING FIRE

frame of mind to render a full and accurate account of what had been extracted from Professor Rupprecht. Before the wine had taken effect Garrou had provided their host with a brief outline sufficient to allow a short telegram signal to be routed through his network and to be delivered to various desks in Whitehall and the Quai d'Orsay.

While the full detail of McGarrity's and Garrou's findings was tensely awaited in London and Paris an interview in less elevated surroundings was under way that would shortly have fatal consequences in the concealed depths of Whitehall. Terrence Edwards, having been detained unresisting at the safe-house in Lambeth was making himself comfortable under Todd's aegis.

A DARKENING FIRE
CHAPTER 39: JULY 1914

Late on the sweltering summer night McGarrity, Garrou, Heller and Fučić had caught the train from Venice to Turin. At their destination another of The Owl's proxies drove them at hair-raising speed the 160 miles to Grenoble. The guards at the French border were on high alert, but were duly compliant at the sight of Garrou's for-once-authentic diplomatic pass and Heller's military identity card. With hardly a glance at McGarrity or Fučić they waved the powerful Chenard-Walcker through and returned to their furious debate on the rapidly deteriorating relations between France and Germany. And while Garrou and the others were travelling by train via Lyon and Dijon to Paris The Owl was putting in place the arrangements for Lotte, the daughter of Conrad Schweitz, to be released unharmed. But aside from carrying out some hasty first-hand checks on outposts of his hidden empire he had another reason for risking his liberty and life by making his way sedately through Germany to Essen.

En route north to the French capital early the following morning Garrou, McGarrity and Fučić, closeted in the privacy of a first-class carriage, assembled into a coherent form the mass of information they had obtained at the Freimann site while the former "General", once again a Sergeant in the Foreign Legion, stood guard at the door. Arriving in Paris McGarrity and Fučić caught a cab from the Gare de Lyon to the Gare du Nord and took a train to Calais. Meanwhile, as a functionary still of the French government whose mission to Bavaria had been decreed in advance by his departmental head, Garrou along with Heller was waylaid at the station by a chauffeur and gendarme and driven in haste to the official presidential residence at the Élysée Palace.

Some hours later as Garrou and Heller were emerging from their audience at The Élysée Eckhart Fischer was inspecting his much augmented security staff at the Krupp plant in Essen. So critical to the German war effort was the Company that its protection from sabotage or attack had become the highest priority, especially following the cataclysm at Freimann. The stealthy hand-

A DARKENING FIRE

outs the now-departed Klausen had brought him had had the imprimatur of the secret state on them but now Fischer was having to turn elsewhere for such succour. So when The Owl materialised out of the summer dusk as Fischer tramped home whistling he anticipated recompense for some not too demanding undertaking. When The Owl suggested that they adjourn to a bar near the Altendorf-Cronenberg station Fischer had no hesitation in accompanying this prosperous but visibly agitated businessman whose proxy generosity had long fuelled their relationship. The Owl came to the point as they sat in whispered conversation in a darkened booth.

'When this accursed war comes,' The Owl said, 'it's going to destroy my business. The state will hardly look kindly on a dubious import-export outfit like mine. I'm going to have to close down my Hamburg operation and the only other place I have a lot of stuff stored is here in Essen. I'm going to have to make myself scarce so there's no chance of my being able to dispose of it at any decent profit. It's worth quite a lot, but the last thing I want is for the police to have a good look at it. I'm hoping I can rely on you, so here's my offer.'

Fischer's eyes lit up, caution and suspicion dissipated by The Owl's referring to their mutual friend Klausen.

'If I give you the keys to the place,' The Owl went on, 'can I trust you to sell off whatever you can to folk who will keep their mouths shut? You can keep all the proceeds for yourself so long as you get rid of absolutely anything in the place that might identify me as the owner. Just get shot of every last piece of it. If you handle that properly there could be more for you in a few months. As it is the market should land you enough to buy one of these fancy new houses out in the Moltkeviertal.'

Fischer reflected on the vagaries of an ill wind.

'One word of warning,' The Owl went on. 'I'm making this offer because I have only a couple of hours before I have to be out of the city. If the police were ever to find out that the store and everything in it are mine I would never be able to get set up again either in Hamburg or anywhere else. You understand? And believe me, I will be seriously disappointed in you if I discover that anyone has managed to find my name on anything in the place.'

A DARKENING FIRE

'I understand you perfectly,' Fischer insisted.

The Owl nodded and gave Fischer the address of the warehouse, slipping him a bunch of keys under the table. Then getting to his feet he extended a friendly hand, thanked Fischer for his cooperation and went out to mingle with the first shadows of darkness. Barely able to contain himself, Fischer glanced at his watch and decided he had time to perform his first inspection of the place before going home to boast of his imminent change of circumstance. The lane where The Owl's treasure trove was located was less than a kilometre away and at this time in the evening there was unlikely to be anyone around the place to query his interest. Letting himself into the building unseen he played the yellow beam of the tungsten bulb torch around the scattered boxes and crates. Prising open the nearest container he found nothing more than a miscellany of motor car parts, kitchen utensils and a collection of novels in Cyrillic script with peeling covers.

'Junk,' he muttered aloud. 'What's he up to?'

But then his searching gaze settled on something different – a wooden case on which had been stencilled the words PRIVATE – EXTREMELY FRAGILE – FOR THE ATTENTION OF DR. JACOB FENNER. Fischer frowned. The name was vaguely familiar but for some moments he couldn't put his finger on it. And then it came to him – all those months ago he and Klausen had been directed to allow Fenner access to some kind of papers in the Chairman's office and to make sure that he got no further than the plant's exit before dealing with him. Fischer had no idea why this ruse had to be played out, but it had hardly tested his conscience. The reward had been substantial, his later discretion he had sold cheaply and anyway he was an excellent shot with a rifle so the affair had been both trivial and lucrative. Yes – Fenner: it had to be this storage container that The Owl had been referring to when he spoke about the value of the warehouse's contents. Placing the torch so that the light shone on the top of the chest he cast around for some tool to force the thing open. By an apparent stroke of good fortune a short crowbar was lying on the stone floor at his feet. Rubbing his hands he picked up the heavy metal implement and in a matter of seconds had removed the lid. To his surprise he found that some coloured wiring was attached to the underside and

A DARKENING FIRE

ran down to what looked like a nest of wood shavings under which he could make out something that might have been a ball-like item made of iron. Curious, he let the lid of the crate drop to one side and leaned forward to examine his prize. He had perhaps five seconds in which to realise that the trailing wire had jerked a needle out of the half-concealed grenade before the explosion blew the upper part of his body to shreds.

A DARKENING FIRE
CHAPTER 40: JULY 1914

The house was in mid-terrace on London's Tufnell Park Road, a three storey building that looked very like all the others in the street except that it bore the conspicuous marks of desuetude. The paint on the door and window frames was peeling, the glass was cloudy, yellowing; and the stone steps and entrance were cracked and weeds grew luxuriantly out of the muddy patches. Heavy curtains were perpetually drawn and any coming and going tended to be late at night. Todd's nameless agency had acquired the property many years earlier and over that time had made many modifications to the interior. Even the loudest noise that sometimes filled one or two of the rooms was contained within its perimeter; and the cellar that ran the full length and breadth of the house had been extensively altered so that it had been translated into a row of tiny, self-contained chambers provided with no furniture beyond a comfortless bed screwed to the floor, and a basic, often fetid toilet facility. It was in the slightly more salubrious surroundings of a gloomy but less austere room on the ground floor at the rear of the house that Todd himself was at work.

'Harriet Nichols,' he was reminding Terrence Edwards. 'She was one of these people whose name or even existence was barely known outside this office. Please tell me how you came by it.'

'I didn't *come by* it. As I've said a hundred times already, I work for Sir Derwent Hartington. If something's happening in Whitehall departments that he doesn't know about, it can't be worth knowing.'

'In a very short while this country may be at war with Germany. So I would appreciate it if you could find it in your heart to cooperate with me.'

'At your service.'

'There are people whom I very much want to have a word with, but whom I have been unable to get hold of. I believe you can help me with this.'

'I only wish I could help.'

'You know of Talbot House of course. You turned up close

A DARKENING FIRE

behind Inspector McGarrity near there a while back.'

Again Edwards made a semi-apologetic gesture of dismissal.

'Never heard of it.'

'One of the occupants of Talbot House has been murdered. Poisoned. You know Edina Pharmaceutical, of course. That place where you deposited a set of lab scales addressed to a Dr. Klein.'

Edwards shook his head.

'Never heard of it either.'

'Norris Dyer has disappeared and ten Berge... what shall I say? A bit of housekeeping? A belated spring-clean, perhaps?'

'What's being tidied up? I don't follow.'

'And then one of the Edina chaps took delivery of the boxed scales from "a wee man in a raincoat" who turned up at the company not so long ago.'

'You and me to a tee,' he said.

Todd raised an eyebrow and one of his doorkeepers disappeared into the corridor outside to return with the smartly uniformed Private Brandon in tow along with an employee of the pharmaceutical company.

'Aye,' the soldier said as soon as he had set eyes on Edwards, 'that's the wee weasel.'

'The bastard promised me a bob or two for sticking his package in the Talbot House case,' the other man said. 'Never paid up a penny.'

Edwards half-turned to look at the pair with an air of vague recollection.

'Oh,' he said to Todd, 'I beg your pardon. I do remember now – some fellow asked me to hand in a parcel at that Edina place.'

'Some fellow?'

'No idea who he was. Just wanted a little favour. I'm an obliging type.'

'He's a lying little shite,' the newcomer put in. 'He taped the thing up himself when he came in the shop.'

Momentarily off-guard Edwards hesitated while one of Todd's men extricated the Edina driver and Brandon and waved another arrival into the room.

'I believe,' Todd said, 'that you are well known to Mr. Roland Tolley?'

A DARKENING FIRE

Whitehall Court's perennial sentry, the stolid former marine, stared down at Edwards for a few seconds, nodded once at Todd and stalked out.

'What's your point?' Edwards asked. 'I'm not denying I saw some fellow at Whitehall Court one night when Tolley was on duty there. He was injured and I got a taxi to take him to St Thomas' hospital. Didn't go along there myself, though.'

'Yes, I thought that might be your line so I've saved the best for last.'

And squeezing past Tolley in the doorway came the man whose treachery Edwards had not foreseen – his cousin, Albert Draper, the companion who had helped dispose of Dyer in the slick waters of the Thames.

'Sorry, Terrence,' he muttered, keeping his head down. 'But they was going to hang me for the thing. Better the jail than the rope.'

Edwards' assessment was that there was no point in pursuing the question of how Todd had identified and laid hands on his relation. There was only one resort open to him and he turned to it.

'Sir Derwent Hartington will confirm I was acting on his behalf,' he insisted. 'This was a matter of national security.'

'Yes, well, you can be sure we're checking that,' Todd said, signing one of his companions to remove Draper from the room. 'But maybe you'd like to clear your conscience and tidy up yet another case for us: one Eoghan Gallagher, deceased.'

'A Fenian and a traitor to this country I'm told. But if the man's dead that's nothing to do with me.'

'And a Mr. Thomas Beckett found in the River Almond at Edinburgh. Strangled with a garrotte, according to the police up there. The implement is familiar to you?"

Signalling his officers to remove Edwards to the sanctuary of a cell in the bowels of the building Todd unlocked the door to a neighbouring room where, his eyes screwed up against a brilliant, unshaded lamp, ten Berge sat manacled behind a bare wooden table.

'Bad luck, eh?' Todd said, settling himself opposite his prisoner. 'That motor-cycle – your mistake was to steal something so shiny and new. That model's been around for just a few weeks.

A DARKENING FIRE

Attracted too much attention, you see.'

A long pause followed during which The Dutchman tried to escape the insistent light and, licking his dry lips, swallowed two or three times.

'Terrible thing you did to that elderly chap up there at Tillingham. You'll know the penalty. I don't suppose there's anything you can tell me that might be shaped into a plea of mitigation?'

Nonplussed, The Dutchman stared back at him, caught between fear and vague hope.

'For instance,' Todd went on, 'if you knew how it's come about that so many of our nasty little secrets have ended up on the desks in the Wilhelmstrasse. No guarantees, of course...'

'There could be...' The Dutchman began, but then lapsed into silence in expectation of some guidance or enthusiasm from his interrogator.

'You see,' Todd explained, 'you may be unaware that there are some people close by who don't have your best interests at heart. People you probably took to be your trusted friends. In fact if I hadn't been so prompt in gathering you to my bosom the last of your blood would have leaked away into a smelly easy-chair.'

'I'll give you what help I can, but you must be more precise. And I must have... an undertaking that neither the rope nor the bullet will be at the end for me.'

Todd smiled.

'My dear sir,' he answered, 'you are a murderer. Make no mistake, you have one single opportunity to persuade me that the rest of your miserable life should be spent in jail rather than ended shortly on the scaffold. So please feel free to regale me with whatever you believe might be of consuming interest.'

'The house in Lambeth,' he began, but Todd waved that away.

'I know all about the place. It's no secret to us.'

'Guns for the Irish...'

'Turned up in Howth recently. Fifteen hundred Mausers. You know well enough that we tried to divert them – you were there at Benny Spiro's. So no secret to that either – the whole thing brought out quite a crowd.'

'But there was another plan...'

A DARKENING FIRE

'Miss Hagan was one of my people. And we know all about Boylan's sending the man Taaffe for another load of guns. If that's the extent of your...'

'No, no, wait,' ten Berge interrupted. 'There's the tree. That's how you can... that's how they do it all. The Irish and the Germans and... and your traitor in Whitehall.'

'Calm down, man. What in God's name are you talking about?'

'We... they pass messages. All of them. Hide them in a tree in St James's Park. It's the easiest thing to do – nobody would ever see...'

Todd raised a quizzical eyebrow. At last something was coming his way, no matter that it sounded comically, absurdly unprofessional.

'And this arboreal post box? Is it the haunt of wood nymphs and elves?'

'What does that mean? Listen, I can show you. You can lay a trap for your Irishmen and your spies.'

'And who leaves these messages for you – and all these others?'

'How would I know? When the system was set up I was told that if I tried to keep watch on it, that would be the end of the arrangement. And it was too good to take that risk. There was a lot of money to be had.'

'You were working with the Fenians and the Germans?'

The Dutchman shook his head impatiently.

'Working *with* them? Look here, sir, what I've done I've done for money. I admit it. I never gave any thought as to who else might be using the scheme. But I promise you, if you follow my guidance you will net whole gangs of your enemies.'

And so it almost stunned ten Berge when Todd, nodding gravely, said, 'Very well. This is not exactly the prize I was after, but it may spare you from premature demise. You will go to St James's Park and indicate this tree of hidden treasures. You will do it by an agreed sign. Do not stop at it, and do not break stride. Be assured my officers will have you well in sight.'

'And I have your word that I will not be facing an executioner over all this?'

'You have my word that I will do everything possible to ensure your future is a long, if not necessarily a happy one. I promise you

A DARKENING FIRE

– my voice is listened to in these matters.'

A pause.

'It's a pleasant afternoon out there. Why don't you go for a walk in the park?'

Hardly daring to believe what he had just heard, The Dutchman could only shake his head as if to clear from his mind some impediment to understanding and reach the happy conclusion that his imagination was not playing a foul trick on him. At a signal from Todd the guard, who had been indolently observing these exchanges through the half-open door, lumbered back into the room, bent forward and, without a word, unlocked the handcuffs by which The Dutchman was attached to the table.

'After St James's Park you can saunter off and make yourself at home at that place in Pearman Street. You'll be collected from there in a day or two after I've decided what's to become of you.'

'Of course, sir, of course. I thank you most sincerely for your...'

'This gentleman,' Todd said, stifling a yawn and waving a casual hand at the guard, 'will treat you to a fine lunch while the team make their preparations. Any questions?'

'None, sir. I am wholly at your disposal.'

'Indeed you are.'

When The Dutchman had left under the guidance of the taciturn warden Todd allowed himself a brief smirk before striding the length of the corridor to the stairway leading to the basement. In the half-light he slid open the well-oiled bolt on the single closed door and let himself into the malodorous cell occupied by Terrence Edwards.

'I believe we've seen enough of you, Mr. Edwards – for the moment anyhow. May I recommend that you spend the evening at that place in Lambeth where I assure you that you will be undisturbed by the minions of the law?'

A DARKENING FIRE
CHAPTER 41: JULY 1914

Ensconced in the Tir na nOg pub in Glasgow's Gallowgate Conor Fallon and Rónán MacInerney, now short of much of the companionship they had grown up with, were quietly going over recent events and current conundrums.

'What I don't see,' Fallon complained, 'is why we've been sitting on our arse all this time and doing fuck all about what's going on across the water. Look at this.'

And he passed to his friend a two day old Dublin newspaper reporting the death of three people shot dead by KOSB soldiers on Bachelors Walk in the city.

'One of them a woman,' he went on seething with anger, 'and one of them a lad of 18.'

'What's that to do with us? When the time comes for going back there we'll get word so – *caithfidh tú taithí na foighne a thabhairt duit féin*.'

'Jesus, Rónán, the guns that were coming in at Howth were German. That's what all the *coir thua* was about when the fucking army turned up and shot these folk. It's the Germans are trying to help us but will you believe this – my bloody brother's gone and joined the fucking British Army. *Cad é atá cearr leis*?'

'Keep your voice down, you *leathcheann*. We do what we're told. We're soldiers too, you know.'

'Aye, but the Germans, for fuck's sake. What if they turn on us now? Our fucking pals!'

'Joey Butler was our man with the Jerries. He's gone now, isn't he? Well, there'll be somebody else in a while. We've another fish to fry.'

'Aye – Joey Butler. Taaffe said he gave us all away to the coppers at Clarkston's.'

'And Boylan in Dublin says it was Taaffe who did the thing. Where's Taaffe now, eh? Fucked off somewhere and left Eoghan Gallagher and Tony Breslin dead and Brendan Keegan rotting in jail in London.'

'I can't make all this out at all.'

A DARKENING FIRE

'It's a safe bet the Brits are going to be at war in a day or two and Boylan says we have to bring their bloody war home to them.'

'Oh, aye – and we're off to invade Newcastle or something?'

'You've never met Boylan, have you? He doesn't make jokes and he doesn't like it if you don't take him serious.'

'Right so. What's the news for us then?'

'We have a good look at the comings and goings in London and see what's what. Asquith has made himself War Minister so it might be worth our while to have a *catsúil*. There's a chance of one of our lads getting a shot in once we know the setup.'

Fallon he was happy enough to spy out the lie of the land in London but not to start taking pot-shots at well-guarded Ministers of the Crown. There were other men conditioned to that sort of work.

'So it's off to *Londain*, is it? But we're not to do the thing ourselves, are we?'

'I'll not be up for that. There are better men with a rifle. All we need to do is spy out the land a bit. But let's see what comes our way, Conor, my boy. We'll get off tonight. Meet me at the station in time for the late train,' he said. 'For now get out to that flat of Taaffe's at Clydebank and pick up a couple of Brownings. But make sure that the place is safe enough first. If the coppers are on to it we'll have to go somewhere else. The stuff should still be under the floor in the bedroom.'

Fallon had a gift for sniffing out danger and MacInerney was confident that if their Clydebank retreat had been discovered his lieutenant would know it. But with several months having elapsed since the Clarkson catastrophe it seemed unlikely that the rundown property would still be under surveillance even if it had been uncovered at the time.

While these clandestine transactions were taking place in Glasgow Inspector McGarrity and Dr. Fučić, having been joined by Augustin Steinhoff, had gathered for a hasty conference at the Watergate office of Major Kell and the other heads of the security and intelligence departments. In McGarrity's absence Sir Derwent Hartington's office had instructed Superintendent Quinn of the Special Branch to have the Inspector present himself at Whitehall Court without fail the following afternoon. Kell's update was brief.

A DARKENING FIRE

The Dutchman ten Berge had been abruptly and fatally removed from the scene at a house in Lambeth; Norris Dyer, Thomas Beckett and Eoghan Gallagher all also either associated with or complicit in at least one way in spying, gun-running or the so-called atomic bomb plot, had come to a premature and violent end. And each of them might well have had critical insights had they survived long enough to enjoy the custodial and interrogatory comforts on offer. Plenty of trouble was brewing in Ireland which would wash over the shores of both sides of the Irish Sea. On the continent Russia had already embarked on mobilisation and Austria's ultimatum to Serbia had some days previously been succeeded by a declaration of war. Within the next few days it was probable that France would align herself with Russia in the face of the belligerent manoeuvring by the Central Powers and Britain would be obliged to look to the terms of her Entente.

'And now, gentlemen,' Kell said, addressing McGarrity and the others, 'I think our intrepid itinerants can shed some light on the darkness of this atom bomb affair. Dr. Fučić?'

Fučić outlined the technical aspects of what the Freimann safari had unearthed and concluded that there was no reason either to believe Rupprecht's vast dossier was a fake or that it had been doctored. Similarly Sergeant Heller had, without notice, expropriated Protzman's diary from the communications room at the site. It set out how the atomic project had been concocted and managed from the beginning. McGarrity's manuscript translation of the excerpts from the diary was passed around. The relevant entries had begun in mid-1910 and only the material that shed some light on the affair of the bombs had been extracted.

Monday 4th July 1910: Professor Rupprecht at Leipzig University brought that arrogant poser Graf von Schwabe to see me yet again. The pair of them overestimate my authority and underestimate my intelligence. Rupprecht is still harping on about this hare-brained bomb scheme of his. Of course the prize would be well worth having but the means of achieving it strike me as so far out of reach that it's not worth even daydreaming about. I suspect that the only reason they've come to me with this notion is that they're aware I have the ear of Conrad Schweitz in Berlin. But my judgement would surely be called into question if I went to him with

A DARKENING FIRE

a plan that would cost the earth and would be as much use as a glass hammer. If I understand the thing even vaguely Rupprecht's convinced – or he'd have me believe he's convinced – that that core of the atoms of certain elements could be burst apart and the result would be the release of a huge amount of energy that could be harnessed into an explosive device. It's all so far-fetched – how could something to tiny, if it even exists, have that effect? It's patent nonsense, but both Rupprecht and von Schwabe bear watching. They're up to something – probably trying to grab a mountain of funding from Wilhelmstrasse.

Wednesday 27th July 1910: a delegation this time, including Rupprecht and von Schwabe as usual and also an intense little man called Rheinhold Sauer who brought along a pile of diagrams and equations for my edification. For once I was able to make out what it was that these people were getting at – Sauer is much better at communicating the thing at a level closer to mine. He took me through quite a convincing history of this esoteric stuff. I can't pretend even to myself that I've got the hang of what they're doing, but I can tell by their demeanour that they really believe in this project. Anyway Rupprecht is an old chum of Schweitz's and he's pressing for a meeting with him to put his idea across. He's so keen on the thing that I'm coming closer myself to being persuaded there's something substantive to it.

Tuesday 9th August 1910: Schweitz isn't buying Rupprecht's plan, but he hasn't dismissed it out of hand. Not surprisingly he wants a lot more work done – including a submission to Gustav Krupp von Bohlen und Halback who has the clout to interest the Kaiser in it and also has teams of scientists with the expertise and background to validate the Professor's work. My inclination is to remove myself from all this but Conrad insists I act as intermediary between him and the physicists and chemists trailing along in Rupprecht's wake.

Wednesday 19th October 1910: unbelievably the Kaiser claims to have made sense of Rupprecht and Sauer's presentation – no thanks, I suspect, to Conrad's half-hearted advocacy. He has allocated the kind of funds that Rupprecht could never have imagined, so smitten is he with the notion of what the success of the project could bear. I've counselled Conrad Schweitz to distant

A DARKENING FIRE

himself somewhat from the operation – if it should go wildly awry or fail altogether it would be as well to have an alibi on hand. Wily as ever, Schweitz had anticipated as much and is content to take a back seat. He wants to know nothing of the progress of the affair until it's successfully completed. Krupp is enthusiastic: he has consented to the development of a suitable site for the work – probably in Bavaria. It seems that any establishment will have to be on an unimaginably grand scale so he's putting up much of the structural cost on condition that Berlin provides the rest, the bulk of the research and the actual building of the bomb – by far the larger investment.

Monday 12th December 1910: Rupprecht has turned up to see me in Berlin without giving notice. It was easy to tell from the outset that something had gone wrong. He was insistent that no-one should be aware that he had come. Work is already under way at Freimann – Krupp seems to be even keener on the project than Rupprecht himself, and it's been on his say-so that money has been pouring into the plan. I wasn't able to take in too clearly what had happened – last night I was drinking again to an ungodly hour with that Frenchman Garrou from whom I've been trying to extract any little secrets he might be harbouring. Unfortunately I must have become a bit too brazen about it a while back because he's got himself in hot water with Paris and he's been recalled. It looks as if he's about to be booted in the direction of some hellhole in Africa as a penance for his lack of discretion. Well, no matter how many Krupp scientists and assorted others have been working alongside Rupprecht, it's been he himself who's been leading the real research – maybe Sauer knows a bit more about it than the others, but the baby is to a great extent Rupprecht's. And now he's decided the time has come to admit that his Grand Plan has come off the rails – the theory remains a theory, and there just isn't the knowhow or the technology as yet to build this bomb of his. He wants my opinion on how to handle the situation. The whole thing is complicated by the fact that Wilhelmstrasse has embarked on a foreign policy predicated on the assumption that in a year or two we'll be able to brandish the thing in the face of all comers. The Kaiser is most concerned about the Russians. He's convinced that they're growing stronger every day and that the battle for the body

A DARKENING FIRE

and soul of Europe will have to be between us and them. And Rupprecht's wonder-weapon is the ace in his hand. I've warned the Professor to keep his own counsel about all this until I've had a chance to turn it over in my mind; so he's going to let me have the whole story before Christmas – nothing in writing, I've stressed.

Wednesday 21st December 1910: Conrad Schweitz and Krupp himself called me in two days ago to bring them up to date. Apparently the Kaiser is cock-a-hoop at the prospect of having this giant bomb in his arsenal, and already the military are planning how to deploy it to their greatest advantage when the day of judgement dawns. The Freimann site is well on the way to completion and it's Krupp's idea that it should be off limits to every living soul who is not directly concerned with the work. Schweitz has pronounced himself happy with progress, which I've had to misrepresent, and he's going to recommend to the Kaiser that unlimited moneys should be made available to sustain rapid development. Krupp, though, has a more acute insight into these matters and he obliged me to join him at his house in the city. He'd accurately read my reaction to his questions so I owned up to the truth. For a long while he said not a word, and then, over brandy, he sounded me out on a proposal that had come to him. It would be no difficulty for him to disguise the lack of genuine activity at Freimann – after all, nobody outside our minuscule group is supposed to know what's going on there. If he arranges for the place to be heavily guarded by the military – who will have no clue as to the purpose of the place – there's no need for anyone to discover that the work has been a failure. The most important thing is for the impression to be given that the weapon is under construction. If the nature and extent of its power are broadcast with sufficient assuredness it will make no difference whether the thing exists in reality or not. His suggestion is that Rupprecht and I set about spreading the gospel that we are on the verge of completing our research and embarking shortly on the actual construction. Krupp obviously has in mind that our potential enemies should be permitted an alarming glance into the hell we are prepared to unleash. I've no idea how we are going to prosecute this successfully though Krupp radiates confidence. At the same time though he's in no doubt that the Kaiser must be

A DARKENING FIRE

informed of the true situation. So Krupp will do that himself – what he intends is to stress to our Master that it will make no difference whether the bomb is real or a work of fiction so long as the rest of the world is led to accept that we have it when the right time comes. I can't conceal my anxiety about this approach – what if Krupp fails to persuade Wilhelm to it? We could all be facing a firing squad at the Plötzensee Prison. Anyhow, for the moment I have no alternative but to toe the same line.

Tuesday 10th January 1911: Blessed relief. Not only is the Kaiser happy to go along with Krupp's notion, he's actually rather pleased with it. Money will be saved and with any luck we'll still derive the same benefit from not having the bomb as we would have from having it! I have to hand it to Krupp – Wilhelm obviously believes the subterfuge is all his own work, so much so that he insists that everything should proceed as if the bomb is being constructed. Not even – or especially not – Schweitz is to be told the truth. The Freimann site is to be secured, all sorts of strange pieces of machinery are to be installed there – Krupp can make sure it looks and sounds authentic by bringing the stuff in from a whole wide range of sources. But the most important aspect will be the handling of the way in which a counterfeit report of the weapon's availability to us is to be leaked out. My own activities in England can be used to leave a door ajar for that purpose. Meantime I'm delegated to put together a whole series of incidents and fables in an appropriate chronology that will have the effect of turning our lack of success into a triumph. On no account, though, is the truth to spread beyond the Kaiser himself, Krupp, Rupprecht and myself. Even Dr. Sauer is to be kept in the dark as far as possible. At the moment I have no idea how to proceed with this but I have to admit to a degree of excitement. My French friend Garrou leaves in a day or two to face the music in Paris so I took the opportunity, when we'd plied each other with alcohol, to make some vague but, I hope, alarming references to our preparatory work on a mystery weapon that will change the world forever.

Friday 20th January 1911: all kinds of crated equipment are being stowed at Freimann and a rota of military security is being worked out. Most buildings are to be off limits even to them and the Krupp employees are to work on the plans for and construction of

A DARKENING FIRE

components of a gigantic artillery piece designed by Dr. Fritz Rausenberger. This is excellent cover because the work is to be spread the length and breadth of the establishment and everyone concerned has been warned that not a word about the work is to be said beyond the bounds of each individual area of the site. Rausenberger himself has told Krupp that the final design of his gun is still a long way off – he claims the thing will be able to fire a 106 kilogram shell over 130 kilometres, which sounds just about as convincing as Rupprecht's device now does to us privileged few. I've suggested we might enlist some convicts to carry out the low-level assembly work – they'd have no clue what they were really doing and having them set up there might convey the impression that what they're doing is so potentially dangerous that we've had to draft in a gang of expendables.

Monday 20th February 1911: a session with Rupprecht has set me on the right track. What his theoretical researches have shown is that the element that would be the necessary base of his bomb if it were ever to take shape is something called uranium – this for reasons that he tried without much success to explain to me. I think maybe it can be derived from pitchblende. There seems to be a quantity of that to be found in Saxony but I suggested that if we wanted the world to believe we really are putting together some kind of clandestine weaponry we should set about excavating huge amounts of the stuff where the mining could be witnessed by inquisitive foreigners. Rupprecht was enormously pleased at my proposal to make use of my former acquaintance Vincent Garrou who's now stagnating at an outpost of civilisation in Africa. Some selective reading has brought to my attention that considerable deposits of this stuff exist in Niger, the very location of my erstwhile drinking companion. If we make something of an inept song and dance about digging the stuff up and bringing it here Garrou's sure to report our efforts back to Paris. That should set the ball rolling, especially since we've agreed on the very man to lead the expedition – that swaggering clown von Schwabe. In his case there's little need to promote him as an inefficient liar, but some quiet briefing ought to do the trick. Krupp is happy, too, and has advised the Kaiser that things are under way. Wilhelm is impatient, so funds for this expedition will be immediately available. Von

A DARKENING FIRE

Schwabe will be flattered, and will never guess that the risks he'll be running out there will merely be a cover for deception. One thing concerns me a little, though – Rupprecht can't be dissuaded from keeping a detailed account of every aspect of this whole endeavour from beginning to end. Krupp, on the other hand, commends the idea and says the reason is that someday the means to complete the endeavour for real may be built on the foundations of his work. I suppose there might be something to that.

Monday 4th March 1912: hard to believe a whole year has gone by since I put the taper to what the Kaiser has elected to call Darkening Fire. Naturally I haven't been inactive for all that time, and I've unearthed another channel by which I might manage to convey the impression that there is substance to that project. It's clear to me now, and to most of those closeted in the Wilhelmstrasse, that war will be coming in the not too distant future. The Kaiser's fears about Russia's growing strength are widely shared – our potential foes have effectively caught us in a vice. The Generals see us being squeezed by Russia in the east and France in the west. While the rest of Europe's powers are busy gathering up colonies and dominions they are doing everything they can to throttle our own expansive national ambitions. When the showdown comes we will be at a great initial disadvantage in terms of numbers and economics. The obvious resort will be to dissuade one or more of our possible enemies from joining in a campaign against us. To that end they would, of course, have to be completely persuaded that our fictitious weapon would destroy their cities in the twinkling of an eye. Naturally this stratagem will work only if the fiction is sufficiently disguised as fact, but as Rupprecht point out, it needs to be believed only for so long as it takes for our military to achieve its initial objectives. After that it will be irrelevant – we will be more than strong enough to deal with any subsequent hostile coalition, if it were ever to be assembled. I'm ordered to consult the Professor on how best to follow up on this line and report back as soon as possible.

Thursday 14th March 1912: armed with Rupprecht's explanation of how the bomb would behave if it were real I'm going to put this idea to the Kaiser and Krupp for their consideration – the best scientists in France and England will definitely doubt that

A DARKENING FIRE

we've succeeded in giving birth to the thing; so we must be sure to saturate their intelligence networks with hints as to our progress and the effects of detonating a bomb created from this uranium material. Some of this will not be wholly unknown to them – I'm advised the work of Becquerel, Curie and Rutherford already points to the theoretical shape of the atom and, more remotely, how that could be harnessed and the longer-term results of breaking particular atoms apart. Oddly what might work in our favour is the fact the English scientists are quite far advanced in the theory of this atomic stuff so they might well be driven to accept that we have made huge strides in the field. I repeat – the whole business seems ridiculous to me – that shattering something so tiny could have such vast and catastrophic results as Rupprecht has asserted, but I bow to his superior knowledge. It's his opinion that not only would an immense explosion take place, but the impact on the neighbouring environment would remain appalling for years. In light of all this I suggested to the Kaiser that the best way of diminishing the odds against us would be to ensure that the English are gifted with a constant stream of misinformation about this device. It would then be a simple matter for us to rout the French and destroy their army so that we can deal unhampered with the Russians while the British have to sit fretting on the side-lines. We need to render them hesitant for just a few weeks or months and the continent will be ours.

Friday 29th March 1912: the Kaiser and Krupp have considered my plan and along with Rupprecht have come up with a rather clever elaboration. We need to spread the legend that this bomb is of such monumental power that setting it off either in France or on the borders of Russia would have devastating effect on our own territory. I agree that that would lend further weight to our account. It seems that if the British specialists in the field have even the remotest concept of what's being called atomic fission they will be more persuaded of our success in developing the weapon if this consequence is noised abroad. So the upshot is that for the next several months and possibly for the next few years we will continue to disseminate apparently inadvertent hints about the development of the bomb; and at the right moment we will lead the English to believe that, in the circumstances of its colossal power, it can be

A DARKENING FIRE

deployed solely against them. In the view of the Kaiser it will be quite enough to keep Britain at bay until both France and Russia have been defeated. Krupp believes that not telling Conrad Schweitz what the true situation is will foster an even more categorical conviction in the British that we really are in possession of the weapon. Schweitz's senior adviser Steinhoff is sure that the English are spying on the activities of his office. So much the better: we've kept him out of the picture too. The Generals have often made the point that the British army is practically non-existent, and such of it that there is, is busy lording it over their far-flung colonial possessions or keeping the Irish in their pathetic little place. But their navy is much too formidable to ignore. Anyway Schweitz's thinking is that the British may well, when confronted by our hegemony over the continent, opt to join forces with us in expanding our collective authority over the globe. I did question whether the English would manifest any great enthusiasm for doing so after their being duped by us into withholding assistance to their Entente ally, but this was a matter, I was informed, for another day. The Kaiser himself believes that, if the issue has to be thrashed out with the British, they can be convinced that the threat to deploy the bombs against them is as much a plot against us as against them – an attempt to alienate our two countries. I wonder! At any rate my job now is to set the rest of the strategy in motion. The Kaiser would prefer if Rupprecht and I kept our distance so as not to arouse any suspicion about what we're about. Wilhelm will be happy to examine our progress in due course via the record the Professor has been told to maintain.

Friday 11th October 1912: von Schwabe's useless mountain of ore from Niger has been stowed in various parts of the Freimann site and is heavily guarded if only to convince any interested party of its significance. Similarly Krupp himself has been busy bringing to fruition my suggestion that a most secret file containing details of Rupprecht's theorising translated into a fraudulent practicality should be compiled and held under the strictest security at the Krupp headquarters in Essen. It should be added to as time goes by until the moment seems ripe to allow its existence to become a sinister rumour among the intelligence communities of the Entente powers. Rupprecht himself is already hard at work on this, clearly

A DARKENING FIRE

enjoying a period of literary creativity. My role in the deception is child's play compared to that of the unfortunate Dr. Sauer who looks as if he is in danger of a complete nervous breakdown, so hard is he being driven by the Professor to make progress on a scheme which in fact has no prospect of success, but which Rupprecht claims for Sauer's benefit to be teetering on the brink of final resolution. We have decided to enlarge our magic circle a bit by recruiting a small team to aid the Professor and lend credence to his tireless activity. A couple of less eminent colleagues should be enough and it's been left to me to decide on who they are to be.

Saturday 4th January 1913: I've been diverted from Operation Darkening Fire – our elaborate untruth – by the need to make the most of my contacts in England, where I've been spending more time lately. The reason for this, though, is not unconnected with that operation. I have two irons in the fire there – first I've been doing what I can to stir some action into these Irish dissidents. If our real plan to keep the English out of the coming conflict is this grand bomb project, I still hold to the notion that stirring enough internal strife in the British Isles might also be relied on to discourage their participation on France's side. So I've been helping various discrete interests in the country to make as much trouble for the government there as possible – those suffragette harpies and the more volatile trade unions are our best bet. But if the Irish can be shaken out of their somnolence I'm confident that Whitehall will have so much more to cope with that the Entente will have to be relegated to a historical footnote. Next month I meet up again with the man Butler to keep that ball rolling. Mostly he'll be pressing for guns and ammunition – it's all so mundane given what we have in mind here. In that connection it's my intention to drop in his ear some poison about Darkening Fire. I'll have to phrase it quite carefully because I don't want him to think that we're more concerned about keeping the British out of a war on the continent than we are of supporting the Nationalist cause in Ireland. I repeat – the two might well seem mutually exclusive to him. I think I'll suggest to him that his people will be required to smuggle parts of the bombs into England in exchange for some of the guns he wants. With any luck he'll spill the beans to someone who'll let the English know that the bombs are being put in place in their cities. But even

A DARKENING FIRE

if he doesn't, I can make sure by some other means that some fearful hint is going to get out there.

My other – and far more important – contact in London is very well-placed and is going to be invaluable in misdirecting the British government as well as supplying me with such secrets as he can lay his hands on. It amuses me to bestow on him the codename "Casement." If any information about his very existence should come to the attention of the Security Service there that name ought to sow a little confusion. There's something quite amusing about these machinations of mine – I've made myself as well-known as possible to the English authorities to encourage them to the conclusion that I'm a hopelessly inept spy and that by keeping me at liberty they'll be led to bigger fish. Krupp is less than happy that I should be devoting so much attention to what he calls "these peripherals," and with the Kaiser's being cousin to King George there are some difficulties looming in Wilhelmstrasse too. I know too that Chancellor Bethmann-Hollweg still favours rapprochement with the British. But I go on ploughing my several clandestine furrows. Professor Rupprecht's team is now up to strength and I'm on the verge of putting out some further indicators of their alleged progress.

Friday 25th July 1913: over the past six months or so much has been done on Operation Darkening Fire that has demanded little of my attention. My planting with the man Butler in London the thought that the bombs were being transported bit by bit to concealment in the English cities has long since been approved. Krupp thinks that was the most convincing suggestion as to the mode of delivery. But as he points out it's essential that we don't try to hurry this business along. If we really were able to create these weapons it would be a long, slow process, so I shall be investing much of my time in keeping the people at Freimann separately guessing what their neighbours in the different parts of the site are really up to. And of course I'm keeping my pot of Irish stew bubbling quietly away.

Sunday 14th September 1913: the Kaiser has floated with us a wonderful idea for propagating Darkening Fire in Britain. It's an incredibly risky affair, and one that will place colossal demands on Professor Rupprecht and his coterie. Wilhelm proposes that the

A DARKENING FIRE

Professor should make known that he is horrified by what he has come close to achieving and is determined to share the secrets of his research with the British in order to counter the overwhelming advantage that it would endow us with. "A guarantee of universal peace" is how he should put it. If other countries have the kind of bomb that Darkening Fire is supposed to be the genesis of, then war between them would be out of the question. Aside from anything else this would give us the opportunity, if needed, to claim for example that the bombs reportedly planted in England are the work of a clique of rogue scientists or military whom we're trying to identify and deal with. We can say they've edged ahead of the weapon's original designers and completed the work. In effect we'll be absolving ourselves of perpetrating what could be cast as an act of war; and claiming that we're horrified at what's been done in our name. All this should render Rupprecht's alleged flight to Britain even more plausible. Rupprecht is in two minds over this, but His Majesty is insistent. The idea is that before the Professor's knowledge and alleged success can be properly tested he should be "abducted" and returned to Germany. The whole thing will need careful planning and skilful posturing by the Professor, not only for the benefit of the British but also for his companions who, apart from a woman called Karoline Petzold, will not be privy to the real nature of his desertion. Petzold will have certain specific instructions to follow once the group is installed somewhere in England. Much rehearsal is going to be needed – fine acting and impeccable timing are all and it's to be my responsibility to ensure this part of the plan runs smoothly. The stakes could hardly be higher.

Wednesday 24th September 1913: incredible! Rupprecht has taken to thespian deception with great gusto – and is thoroughly convincing with it, so much so that it rather worries me that he's been taking the rest of us for naïve idiots. Well, maybe I exaggerate for my own satisfaction because I think that I've inspired him and after all what he might achieve in Britain is beyond treasure. My particular nominee Karoline, too, though not in the same class intellectually or even theatrically, has been doing well. They ought to be ready well before the year is out so it's to me that the Kaiser is looking for the details of a plan not only to plant the Professor

A DARKENING FIRE

and his team in England but also to ensure that we have in place the means to extract them at the right time. I'm to consult the Imperial Navy and the Nachrichten-Abteilung about this and I'll probably enlist that small-time crook ten Berge to act as a go-between. I've got to say that this business has been quite rewarding and I'm enjoying the vicarious authority it has endowed me with.

Tuesday 25th November 1913: at last – a few weeks to relax before the next stage. Rupprecht, Sauer, Klein the physician (of whom more in a moment), Petzold and the fetching Hanna Blindt have "fled" the country and are being enveloped in the bosom of our offshore friends. I now have the leisure to consider how best to use my connections with the Irish dissidents to add convincing colour to the Professor's mission. It's all going to appear somewhat counter-intuitive to them and I'm going to have to tread carefully. The problem is that they're looking to us for conventional weaponry and all sorts of support that the Kaiser has no more than a little intention of providing. Wilhelm has toyed with the idea of stirring up plenty of trouble in various parts of the British Empire to divert their military, but the fact is he still hopes to keep the British on our side. So I must concoct a scenario that will give the Fenians succour while I pursue a line that really has nothing much to offer them but sounds as if it's designed all along to aid their ridiculous little cause. The thing is if we can goad them into action at minimal cost to ourselves they'll be giving us the means to keep the diminutive British army so busy that that, combined with Darkening Fire, will so preoccupy them that joining in any conflict on the continent will be out of the question. To sell this to these Irish won't be easy as they'll properly point out that it'll do their cause no good to have much of the British army encamped on them. I'm working on a line to take with them that should convince them we're still wholly on their side. Complicating life for me, of course, is – as I've said – the fact that Darkening Fire must absolutely persuade the English that their cities would be incinerated if they chose to deploy against us but at the same time believe that we ourselves have not committed an act of war against them in planting the bombs in the first place. Very tricky obviously – but as the Kaiser has suggested we'll just have to construct an alibi for ourselves which we can, if necessary, represent to the British. They'll have to be led to believe

A DARKENING FIRE

that the Kaiser's hands are temporarily tied but that he's working furiously to rectify the situation. It's a difficult balance to strike, but if the worst comes to the worst then we'll just have to counterfeit an acknowledgment that the locating of the devices in England is an action that can't instantly be undone. And Rupprecht, who had been consulting a few eminent chemists on some esoteric aspect to the plan, had in mind to give the impression that his work on Darkening Fire had led to his suffering from some obscure form of anaemia. He told me that this would lend even more credence to the story he'll be spinning to the English – and he wanted Dr. Klein along to "treat" him, keep the British medical people at bay and confirm the "condition" to be lethally degenerative. This means Klein had to be made aware of some, but by no means all, of the complexities of our scheme. Rupprecht assured me that chewing cordite – horrible thought – would be enough to give him the right appearance of a man slowly proceeding to death's door.

Friday 30th January 1914: I should shortly be on my way to London to confer with my contact Butler in the so-called Fenian movement but he seems to have disappeared for the moment at least and left me not a word as to what he's up to. Typical of these people.

Monday 16th February 1914: a fraught time of late – the British have become increasingly impatient with Rupprecht and Sauer who for obvious reasons have made little convincing progress with their continuing atomic "researches." Rupprecht has been adopting the line that, while he was in charge of the Darkening Fire project and was the lead scientist, the success of the venture was very much a team effort so there have been significant gaps in his own knowledge that he still needs to fill in. But it seems the British have well-informed experts in the field whose attentions are now starting to disturb the cover we've carefully laid over our duplicity. I flatter myself that we've managed to fend them off temporarily with a little trick of my own – I instructed Karoline by the usual means to have the Professor advise the British that his work would be greatly hastened along if he could get hold of certain secret papers held at Krupp's HQ in Essen. We know that they have a well-run secret intelligence service and we knew that they'd take any risk to obtain these

A DARKENING FIRE

documents. It's thought that the ring is conducted from somewhere in Hamburg and sure enough one of its agents has been trying to pump Krupp's man Klausen for information on the new guns being designed by Rausenberger. He's gone so far as to bribe Klausen to get someone into the plant to steal the alleged material. This turned out to be a triumphant holding operation – we made sure that the intending thief was shot dead in the act. And we had created some hopelessly blurred but quite realistic photographs of the documents which would need extensive poring over but which would lead nowhere. Klausen has consented to present himself as a traitor and to ensure delivery of these to London. What better way to have the British believe that these "secrets" were to be protected at any cost! But this gave us only a breathing space – the moment to effect the Professor's "abduction" was well and truly with us. Unfortunately an arrangement to get him away by submarine fell through, but Benny Spiro's connections at the Peacock Hotel in Edinburgh managed to work out an alternative. Some greedy and non-too reliable characters – Dyer, a local, and that tireless money-grubber ten Berge – who had been recruited to help with the escape succeeded, against expectations, in effecting an alternative. Rupprecht is now safely back in Freimann and out of the reach of the British. The others are still in Scotland and, with the exception of Karoline, little the wiser as to what has happened.

Thursday 2nd April 1914: at last back concentrating on Operation Darkening Fire but also combining these efforts with playing along with our Irish stooges. At my flat in Hamburg last month I had to entertain a profoundly unpleasant trio – Taaffe, Breslin and Keegan – with their non-too-clean hands outstretched for German alms. For good measure I told them a bit about The Dutchman and Dyer to convey the notion that my spy-ring is far more extensive than it really is. I also took the opportunity of hinting to them that Rupprecht had been brought back to Germany against his will – just in case the English ever got the chance to quiz these people about him. "Casement" is concerned that one of their unsavoury Irish colleagues could be about to expose him as a traitor, whether for money or some other motive. He wants this man – Gallagher – to be silenced and it occurs to us that there would be a pleasing irony about enlisting his Fenian comrades to do the job.

A DARKENING FIRE

I've made that part of the bargain for the rifles we're offering; and I've warned them that their funds are well below the level acceptable to the agent Benny Spiro, but that the shortfall would be made up by their getting rid of Gallagher and smuggling fuses for the non-existent bombs we claim to be planted in England. Of course these fuses have been carefully engineered at Freimann and their purpose has not one thing to do with the fictitious weapons. But I've been struck by some divine afflatus – I'm sure "Casement" is perfectly capable of disposing of this Gallagher by means closer to hand; and I can boost the credibility of Darkening Fire by arranging for two of the low-grade thugs charged with delivering the fake fuses to be identified by the authorities in England. Steinhauer's people can easily pour the necessary poison into the appropriate ear. For obvious reasons the British will want to follow the trail of these things rather than make sense of their contents so there should be no worry that they'll be prised open. We simply need somehow to ensure that that trail goes cold. All very satisfactory, and it would have been wonderful to have someone to share my ingenuity with.

Monday 6th^h April 1914: I've had to keep company with these Fenians all the way south to Freimann but I suppose the sacrifice has been worth it. Taaffe saw clearly enough that if we manage to keep the English out of a western front they'd be better placed to cope with an Irish insurrection. As a result I had to spin him a yarn to the effect that the bombs could be used at the same time to compel the British out of Taaffe's little island. Once Taaffe and his bodyguards have seen Freimann they're bound to be completely taken in by the Darkening Fire legend. And I've further elaborated the tale by subjecting them to the sight of the "ailing" Professor Rupprecht who, I claimed, would shortly be dead as a result of a condition brought about by his work; and I let them know that Graf von Schwabe is also there and working alongside the Professor – though God knows von Schwabe understands all this about as well as he could tell the time on Mars. Now these Irish toughs have gone off sporting what they think are detonators for the bombs they're sure are now planted in England. To make matters even more opaque I've supplied them with a number of these "fuses" while spreading the idea that only a tiny number of the bombs has been

A DARKENING FIRE

built for assembly – I like to keep everyone guessing. I've arranged for Keegan and Breslin to be put up at a house in London and for their presence with the "fuses" to be monitored – I hope with fatal consequences – by the British security service. I've made certain that Steinhauer understands that the pair must be detected arriving in England in possession of these items and if necessary for them to come to a sticky end – and at the same time make sure the "fuses" disappear. Yet more confirmation, it's safe to say, that there can be no doubt that the bombs are real and in situ.

Wednesday 13th May 1914: I know that the British are pretty sure that I'm up to no good, and indeed Conrad Schweitz himself counselled me to steer clear of further visits to England, but again my very presence ought to give them more cause for anxiety. Anyhow, I doubt they'll take any action against me just yet – they probably think it's worth their while to give me enough liberty to lead them to some enlightenment and "Casement" has done much to encourage them in that belief! When I caught up with my old acquaintance Vincent Garrou in London I made no secret of my desperate worry about the holocaust the Darkening Fire devices would cause and suggested to him that he warn the English about them and their devastating potential. I gave him some highly technical but ultimately useless information about them. Not a terribly subtle ploy but worth tossing into the cauldron. To muddy the seething water even further Krupp and I are going to propose that either the Kaiser or Conrad Schweitz respond to an approach by Cresswell at the British embassy by suggesting some malefactor is using the bomb "legend" to promote hostility between the British and ourselves. Perhaps an outright denial by Conrad of the weapons' existence would convince the English that the bombs really are in place at the heart of their Empire. I'll think a little more about that. Poor Conrad – under the impression that it's he who's running this affair and the truth is he's nothing more than a puppet. Still, a dignified, aristocratic and urbane one!

Thursday 23rd July 1914: I'm been comfortably settled here at Freimann now and am in a position, I would say, to sit back and relax a little after my efforts. Things are moving rapidly in the direction of conflict and the Austrians are planning to issue an ultimatum to Serbia very soon. The Kaiser will back them to the

A DARKENING FIRE

hilt, and I have every hope that my own work will mean that when war does come the British will hesitate long enough to allow us to smash both the French and the Russians. Their neutrality would be attributable to a combination of reluctance to become involved based on principle and the conviction that one or more of their cities would go up in smoke if they did choose to join their Entente partner. There was a minor annoyance today that at least had the effect of awakening a degree of satisfaction with my work over recent years – the Irishman Taaffe turned up here demanding my help – with what I neither know nor care. I had him locked away as much for my own peace as to inflict retribution on him for his insolence. But the incident did remind me that, apart from the more dramatic business of Darkening Fire, I've gone quite a long way to harassing the British by feeding the flames of division in Ireland: there should now be enough guns available to the two mutually inimical communities there to keep the British occupied even if the Kaiser's and Krupp's non-existent bombs should be exposed as a fiction – so long as that doesn't happen before our armies are successful on both eastern and western fronts when the war does break out.

Monday 27th July 1914: the Russians have embarked on what they call their "period preparatory to war." This suits us well – they certainly look like they are the aggressors now. I estimate that war can only be a few hours away. And what appears to confirm this belief is that a delegation of Conrad Schweitz and some of his brutes is on the way here to inspect the site. So far as I'm aware Schweitz is still in the dark about what really going on but with war in the immediate offing he's probably under orders to ensure all's well here. Rupprecht has been preening himself over his literary prowess in composing his confidential opus on the work he's undertaken so far, even if it apparently represents nothing more than theory which might one day in a distant future be translated into practice. He's been briefed also to cooperate with these people from Schweitz's private army. There's nothing much I can do about that, but if any secrets are leaked at this stage it hardly matters so long as they go no further than Berlin. And who knows – the time may be ripe to put my friend Schweitz wholly in the picture.

A DARKENING FIRE

Once Augustin Steinhoff had cleared up issues of detail Kell expressed himself satisfied that he fully grasped the nuances of the contents of the two files. The Prime Minister had ordered him to be at Downing Street the following morning to share with the Cabinet the most vital guidance they were ever likely to receive. Steinhoff and Fučić would accompany him and Professor Sir Earnest Rutherford had been summoned from Manchester and would also be present. The clouds of war were closing over Whitehall.

A DARKENING FIRE

CHAPTER 42: AUGUST 1914

On the day after Germany's declaration of war on France Sir Derwent Hartington, eyes drooping and shoulders hunched, was sitting at his desk pushing to one side a copy of Helmut Protzman's diary extracts and of the weighty tome that was Professor Rupprecht's *magnum opus* designed for the edification of Kaiser Wilhelm and perhaps of a future generation of physicists. Sir Derwent had gone without sleep since this great mass of papers had been brought to him in haste. Blessed with a remarkable facility for absorbing huge amounts of information at speed he ought by now to have been the focal point around which Whitehall's reaction to the Darkening Fire affair should be circling. And yet he had heard nothing from either Downing Street or any of the other offices of state. His exclusion from these inner sancta had been creating a tension more intense than he had ever experienced in all his years of service. Why at this late juncture he should have been afforded sight of these critical documents left him puzzled but relieved, unaware that in Major Kell's estimate it could only be to British advantage if it were now known in Berlin that the revelations they contained were informing policy in Whitehall even if the consequence of the assault on Freimann remained uncertain.

When the summons to Number 10 did come he found himself with Kell, Professor Rutherford, and Dr. Fučić, the latter still coming to terms with his own unlikely adventure in Bavaria. It was from the latter duo that the PM looked for a reaction on the purely technical aspects of the material made so dramatically available. In the few hours available to them they had pored over the contents of Protzman's and Rupprecht's extraordinary volumes and now presented themselves, unshaven and exhausted, for interrogation by Asquith himself and senior Cabinet members. More than three hours of close questioning concluded with agreement that what the papers indicated was in accord with the views expressed repeatedly by Rutherford and with some understandable hesitation by Fučić over the past several months. His views having been canvassed in

A DARKENING FIRE

the most perfunctory manner and having been dismissed before the PM communicated his conclusion to the others, Hartington returned to Whitehall Court more apprehensive than ever. Moments after his arrival his Principal Private Secretary Quentin Ackroyd brought in Inspector McGarrity whose presence Ackroyd had himself already arranged.

Sir Derwent didn't dissemble his unease.

'Frankly it's impossible not to see this Darkening Fire affair as anything other than an act of war. The PM said nothing in my presence but I assume we shall move quickly to comply with the terms of the Entente. But that's not the reason I wanted you both here.'

It was unclear to McGarrity why he should have been called on but he sat unmoved and unreadable as Hartington pressed on.

'It's no secret in Whitehall that I've been... exiled from the PM's inner circle. Am I to take it that I am suspected of some dereliction? I trust you both and I would hope that if you have cause not to reciprocate you will divulge it.'

Ackroyd fumbled with the pile of correspondence he had been sorting through and McGarrity remained silent, his face registering nothing.

'Come, Quentin. If I'm a traitor I'll be swiftly called to account now that we're on the verge of war. It can hardly do the nation any harm if I'm informed of the case against me.'

Finally Ackroyd, sensing that nothing was going to be forthcoming from McGarrity, said, 'I'm sure, Sir Derwent, you're misreading the situation. In all probability there has been concern that recent events have contributed to an unacceptable burden being placed on you. The PM has to be assured nothing is likely to distract you from your most critical duties.'

Hartington waved away this patently fatuous explanation.

'Your loyalty does you credit but leaves me unconvinced. Mr. McGarrity, you have the ear of our defenders of the realm. What do you say?'

'I'm a junior police officer, Sir Derwent. Nothing more.'

Exasperated, Hartington, patting the desktop repeatedly with both hands, said evenly, 'I'm aware of your rank, Inspector, but I'm also aware of the regard in which you're held by more senior

A DARKENING FIRE

officials. May I at least look to you for a direct and honest reply to my enquiry?'

'Very well. I have been told nothing about the matter.'

Struggling to contain an agitation wholly out of character Hartington dismissed the two men with an irritable wave, then as an afterthought called McGarrity back as he made for the door. When Ackroyd had left Sir Derwent, indicating that the Inspector should resume his seat and lowering his voice, said, 'I gather it was Dr. Ackroyd who wanted you to be here today. He seems to be uncomfortable in more elevated company for the moment. I can only surmise that he has no wish to be witness to my imminent perdition.'

Again eliciting no reaction from the impassive giant, he went on from his place by the window, 'If you have been enlisted to uncover my guilt I can only await the outcome of your scrutiny.'

'Are you confessing, Sir Derwent?'

'One of yours?' Hartington asked. 'Or of Mr. Todd's?'

McGarrity joined him and looked down at a nondescript figure, wearing a raincoat despite the brilliant sunshine, was lounging against the wall of a building opposite.

'He's been there most of the day,' Sir Derwent said. 'If I'm to be followed around perhaps it would be best done more surreptitiously.'

'You don't recognise him?'

'Good Lord, no. Should I?'

'I'll have a word with him. May I ask you something? You know my daughter is missing?'

'Dr. Ackroyd did say something about that, yes. Is there something I can do to help? The embassy in Washington...'

'No need to go on, Sir Derwent. I'll go and collar your friend out there.'

It took McGarrity little time to catch up with Terrence Edwards who made an unsuccessful effort to disappear towards Victoria Embankment.

'Still covering tracks?' McGarrity asked.

Edwards was not easily cowed but he took the sensible precaution of moving a little out of range of the other's casually flexing fists.

A DARKENING FIRE

'Not that it's any affair of yours, but I'm hanging on for orders from that office you just left.'

'Well, if I were you I would be relying too much on that. I've heard you disowned today already.'

'What do you mean?'

'Hartington has no idea who you are.'

'You don't think he's going to confide in a blood great lump of a stupid policeman, do you?'

'Enough to send me down with licence to beat you to a pulp if I was minded so you might want to reconsider what you just said.'

Uncertain how to take this but now on his guard, Edwards slipped his hand inside his jacket.

'If I thought you were reaching for a gun there I'd rip your wee arm off,' McGarrity warned him. 'Let's keep this amicable and have a little stroll together.'

And lightly but firmly touching Edwards' elbow led him in the direction of Westminster Bridge Road.

'My friend Mr. Todd – you know him, eh?'

'You know I do. What about him?'

'He tells me that all great Neptune's ocean is damned unlikely to wash the blood clean from your hand.'

Edwards looked blank.

'Mr. Todd tells me,' McGarrity went on, 'there are those in high places who are out for your blood and they'll have it. He doubts even he can give you protection from on high against his attentions.'

'Jesus Christ, I'm a government man. I get my orders and I do what I'm told, no more, no less.'

'Then tell me this – what is it that Norris Dyer, Tommy Beckett, Eoghan Gallagher, Karoline Petzold, and a fellow called ten Berge have in common that took them off to heaven in such a hurry?'

'You'll get no confession out of me. These are enemies of the state that you're on about. Our pal Todd seems to know about them. If you want more you'll have to get it from Sir Derwent.'

'And what was Karoline Petzold's crime against the nation? Would you know that? Or was it Dr. Klein that was the target.'

'No, it was Petzold...'

A DARKENING FIRE

'You know these people, then? Our German guests.'

'Heard the names. That's all.'

'Now if there's one man in the country with a conscience smaller than your own it would be Mr. Todd. He must have found a use for you, and here you go thinking it was out of the goodness of his heart that he let you walk away. I wonder what that was.'

'No idea what you're talking about.'

'The local police tell me they couldn't find anything incriminating at Gallagher's place. It seemed to have been cleared up by somebody in a hurry. That wouldn't have been you, would it?'

'Look, McGarrity, what the hell is it you want from me?'

A DARKENING FIRE
CHAPTER 43: AUGUST 1914

Catching up with his boss later the same day, Sergeant Hughes was taking direction as the pair sat in a pub in Wedmore Street. Like most of the other habitués of the place, they had mulled over the consequences that seemed likely to follow from the outbreak of a general war on the continent. Now the pair were drinking in melancholy silence for a minute until McGarrity turned to the real point he had in mind.

'This isn't really work for the Branch,' he said, 'so I'm going to ask it of you as a friend. Mr. Todd has been in a great hurry to bring Hanna Blindt, Rheinhold Sauer and Manfred Klein to that place of his over in Holloway. I wouldn't think he has their best interests at heart.'

'He's in the humour for battening down the hatches.'

'Aye. Well I don't see these folk as a danger to the state and I'd worry for their health over there at Tufnell Park. Pat Quinn has arranged this for me – ' McGarrity held out a warrant for the arrest of the three Germans, ' – and I'd appreciate it if you served it and corralled that trio.'

'No problem. What do you want me to do with them when I've got them tucked under my wing?'

'Don't be too relaxed about this. I've a feeling that Mr. Todd or his minions won't be so keen to let these people go. Take a couple of hefty local lads along and have a van ready.'

After a moment's hesitation, McGarrity went on in a low tone, 'There's a fellow who calls himself The Owl who was doing some good work in Hamburg and other places. As things have panned out he's now had to skedaddle from there but the thing is this – he has at his disposal a sizeable power launch called *Kalypso* that's tied up at West India Docks.'

'You want me to put Todd's guests on her and let them go? It could be that in a few hours they're going to be classed as enemy aliens.'

'I know that's possible, but I doubt they've done anything wrong. Likely they really did believe they were coming here to help

A DARKENING FIRE

us. Christ knows enough folk have suffered from all this already.'

'So I take them straight to the docks and put them aboard the boat? No fuss, no argument.'

'Not quite. Ask them if it's what they want. If they prefer to stay here, fine. Take them to this address first, but make sure nobody bothers to follow you.'

And McGarrity gave him an address near St Pancras station.

'If I'm not there when you arrive there'll be someone there to let you in and to look after our... fugitives.'

'All very secretive. Suits me.'

'I knew I could rely on you. Now get along to that police station at Blackstock Road. They'll be expecting you and they'll have a Black Maria ready for you.'

'Where are you headed yourself?'

'I'm off for another visit to Whitehall Court. I'm not sure how long I'll be but whatever happens let's meet up at that St Pancras place.'

Two hours later Hughes was slightly disappointed at the ease with which he gained access to Todd's sinister redoubt. His accompanying officers – fierce-looking men itching to make use of their truncheons – had been warned that serving the warrant might be met with resistance but in the event there was no sign of Todd himself and his underlings accepted the validity of the document without protest. Hughes instructed the driver of the closed van to take a meandering route in the direction of St Pancras while he himself kept watch from the rear of the vehicle for any sign of pursuit. Satisfied that they were not being followed he passed the address forward and sat alongside his beefy uniformed companions and silently eyed the three clearly confused and uneasy Germans.

When the van arrived at its destination Hughes hustled Blindt, Sauer and Klein into the nondescript ground floor passage under the gaze of the police officers and rapped on the door of the apartment whose number McGarrity had given him. When it was opened he took a step back in astonishment, confronted by McGarrity's daughter.

'Niamh! I didn't know you'd joined the force.'

Beckoning the party in, Niamh McGarrity shook her head.

'No – I haven't. Just doing what the old fellow asked. I think

A DARKENING FIRE

we can dispense with your bodyguards. I'm sure your friends here won't be any trouble.'

And she spoke quickly and fluently in German as she waved the trio into the neat living room. Telling the Blackstock officers to wait for him in the vehicle, Hughes carefully closed the door behind him and listened without understanding as Niamh exchanged what sounded like an urgent series of questions and answers with the threesome. This half-whispered conversation lasted for several more minutes until, apparently content with the responses, Niamh disappeared into the kitchen and five minutes later came back carrying a tray of teacups and cakes. The banal informality of the gesture and atmosphere left him puzzled. A little reluctant to convey his own mystification he resorted to the most casual tone he could muster.

'It's great to see you, but I thought you were on your travels in the States,' he said.

'I've been back for ages but dad wanted me to stay out of sight as far as possible – just for a while. He didn't say why, but you know him. It's easiest to go along with his whims.'

'And what now for Miss Blindt, Herr Sauer and the good doctor here?'

'I've asked them what they want to do. Obviously they know what's happening on the continent and Sauer and Klein want to go home to Germany. They both want to be there to help their own people in the war.'

'I'd have thought the chances would be good that they'd face a charge of treason or something back there.'

'There seems to be a lot we don't know about all this,' Niamh said. 'Anyway that's what they want to do. Hanna feels differently. She came here because that Professor Rupprecht told her what they were doing was to make war impossible. Now she's been told that the opposite was true.'

'Yes, your father told me about that, but how did these folk hear about it?'

'Some senior Civil Servant from Mr. Asquith's Private Office gave them all the details early this morning. It sounds as if the German army is on the Belgian border – I don't know, they may even be in the country already. And if that's the case…'

A DARKENING FIRE

'So the next step for us is what?'

'Dad wants the men to be given safe passage out of here. That boat is ready to go – it's American and there won't be any problem about its going on from here to Germany. Can you take them to the docks and make sure everything goes smoothly? Hanna's going to wait here with me until dad comes over.'

Taking Hughes by the arm she led him into the kitchen and asked in a low voice, 'What do you think of Hanna?'

Hughes restricted himself to raising an eyebrow.

'I'll get Klein and Sauer away, then,' he said. 'Am I to come back here after or what? Did Leo leave any orders for me once the deed is done?'

'Yes – some place in Whitehall Court. He said you'd know it. If you could get there as soon as you've unloaded these gentlemen. And there's somebody he'd like you to collect on the way – this is the address.'

While Hughes was transporting his charges to West India docks Inspector McGarrity was on his way to yet another appointment at the offices of Sir Derwent Hartington's unnamed little department. An oppressive air of unreality filled the streets and lay on the parks and squeezed between the banks of the Thames. The Bank Holiday crowds of the previous day had gone and were replaced by a population pretending to a summer normality. The paper boys were calling attention to ambiguous headlines and in Whitehall nerves were being tested by an unnerving uncertainty. While McGarrity and Hughes had been in conference in a pub the British Cabinet was deciding to send to Berlin an ultimatum requiring a reversal of the invasion of Belgium. This was to be wired to Wilhelmstrasse early that afternoon, giving the German government only a few hours to reply. As this high drama of international politics was being played out a far more intimate action was taking place out of the blazing August sunshine. Tolley, the former marine who continued to stand lugubrious guard over the entrance to Hartington's domain in the corner of the vast building and who had now re-assumed full uniform, officiously bent over a pad of handwritten entries and decided that Inspector McGarrity of the Special Branch did indeed have an appointment.

A DARKENING FIRE

'My assistant Sergeant Hughes will probably be joining us in a while,' McGarrity told the gangling guardian of the portal. 'Along with another chap.'

'You might have to wait for a bit, sir' Tolley announced. 'Sir Derwent is over at the House.'

'I'm not here for him,' McGarrity said, bestowing a friendly grin on the stolid Tolley and pushing aside the heavy door. At the sound of his heavy-footed approach Quentin Ackroyd, Hartington's Principal Private Secretary emerged from his luxuriously appointed office and beckoned the Inspector to join him.

'Very nice,' McGarrity observed, closing the door behind him.

Ackroyd offered only a vague gesture.

'Thank you for coming, Mr. McGarrity. Please sit down and I'll explain why I asked to see you this afternoon.'

'I would guess that you brought me here to add the few necessary touches to the case against Sir Derwent. The trail of clues to his treason has been spread like breadcrumbs right to his very desk.'

Ackroyd looked grave.

'We are talking about high treason,' he said. 'It's difficult to be sure how damaging his treachery has been but I assure you that in many respects the effects have been hardly short of catastrophic.'

'Right enough,' McGarrity replied, lounging back in his chair. 'So, bearing in mind that guilt of treason has the judge reaching for the *cie bais* I take it that you're about to add some absolute proof to what we already have?'

'I beg your pardon – reaching for what?'

'The black cap.'

Dr. Ackroyd pursed his lips impatiently.

'Now, if I may…'

'Timing, they say, is all. I arrived at Talbot House very soon after Rupprecht went missing. And damn soon, in fact, after Sir Derwent and his entourage had been there.'

'Yes. And don't you see how that points…'

'My daughter's name is Niamh. And my wife's name was Róisín.'

Looking entirely persuaded that the big man had lost his mind, Ackroyd struggled to say something in response that would pour oil

A DARKENING FIRE

on what sounded like potentially troubled waters rising between them. Licking his lips he stood up sharply and affected an air of calm as he retreated towards the elaborate Italianate cabinet where he kept an array of crystal decanters and glasses.

'Yes,' he said slowly, 'I was so sorry to hear that your girl had gone missing in America.'

'Aye. And you were sorry for me when you heard I'd started seeing my dead wife a few months ago.'

'You'll have a whiskey, won't you?' Ackroyd asked, waving a hand at his collection of spirits. 'Oh, yes, it must have been an unbelievably distressing experience.'

'The thing is, though,' McGarrity went on as if Ackroyd had said nothing, 'Niamh was never missing. I always knew where she was.'

'We're wandering off the subject, Inspector. Perhaps we could…'

'And I'm not given to any of that Celtic communing with the dead either. Róisín's not forgotten, but she *is* gone. She never has come back, and she never will.'

'Maybe,' Ackroyd managed, 'it would be as well to leave matters as they are for today. I'm sure there are other officers to whom I can pass…'

McGarrity swallowed some of the whiskey and nodded appreciatively.

'You see,' he said quietly, 'I'm a canny man. So I take wee precautions here and there. And the only person on earth that I told these tales of family heartbreak to was a friend of mine called Joseph Butler.'

Ackroyd's confusion was growing by the moment.

'Should I know…?'

'Oh, but you did. You told Sir Derwent the story about Niamh being lost in the States; and you told a man called Terrence Edwards that I must have been under a great strain to have been seeing my dead wife. So you were the one exchanging the time of day with Joey Butler.'

Regaining a fraction of his accustomed imperturbability Ackroyd sat down again and stared into space for a long while.

'Yes, silly of me to let that slip – it was something in Mr.

A DARKENING FIRE

Butler's very last communication. Obviously he was on the verge of rectifying a potentially fatal situation. He should have confided in his colleagues first, shouldn't he? In any event I'm afraid, Inspector, that your little tales of woe and the rest aren't going to be anything like enough to inconvenience me. What is required in this democracy of ours is something you ought to be thoroughly familiar with – and that's evidence. You might be able to tarnish my reputation somewhat, but life would go on.'

'So you were able to let our German friends know where Rupprecht was closeted. And later, when things began to fall apart, you needed to get rid of all those folk who could give you away. And that note that was "discovered" in Sir Derwent's safe was sent to you, wasn't it.'

Ackroyd replied with a thin smile.

'I can't think who or what on earth you're talking about.'

'Then there's the note Kell said he would be passing to Sir Derwent about security at the ports. The astute Major let me know he'd no intention of sending it. You overreached yourself there letting Berlin know about something that didn't exist. You thought that would be the final nail in Hartington's coffin.'

'I don't believe…'

'And that homicidal wee thug – Terrence Edwards – thought all along that his orders were coming from Sir Derwent, but they were all your own work, weren't they? In a way I have to admire the way you handled him – a rare prize, I suppose; a natural killer dedicated to defending his country at any cost. As a matter of interest, how did you recruit him? And get him thinking Hartington was directing him?'

Ackroyd, more relaxed as the conversation took on an amiable tone, affected one of his supercilious smiles.

'Terrence's father worked on my parents' estate in Buckinghamshire. He was Bulgarian by birth. Abominable accent, nothing much to offer but a surprisingly muscular strength in such a small man. Terrence's *praenomen* and *nomen* were indecipherable jumbles – hence our bestowing his current appellation. Unfortunately Terrence's psychological and emotional wellbeing proved to be not entirely secure.'

Irritated as much by Ackroyd's smirking flippancy as by his

A DARKENING FIRE

verbosity, McGarrity drained his glass and set it noisily down in front of him.

'I'm not here for biographical diversion. I asked how you got him on board.'

'Patience, Inspector. If you're minded to scupper my career surely I'm entitled to some leisurely latitude. The fact is I rescued young Terrence from numberless scrapes – so many that he became entirely devoted to me from the time we were infants. And in our teen years when Sir Derwent used to visit my father for advice the two of us were besotted by the notion that someday we would serve such eminent men. Terrence's natural inimical disposition towards the rest of humanity turned out to be constant, if unpredictable, but at least he had the decency to take lessons in elocution and became, orally if not sartorially, an approximation of an English gentleman. Or Frankenstein's creature.'

'That's still a long way from turning him into a murderer.'

'Not at all. For him killing is a pathological necessity. He actually enjoys his work. You see how mutually advantageous this is – he believes he's disposing of enemies of the state on the orders of the state. If his language skills had permitted it he would, I'm sure, have claimed "*je suis imperméable.*" And – I admit it – he was the tool to eradicate my steps in the miry path of high treason.'

McGarrity nudged his glass across the desk and Ackroyd obligingly filled it again.

'High treason true enough,' McGarrity said, 'but why? Why Germany? Why Ireland?'

'My dear chap, I should have though the Irish cause might at least have set you great heart aflutter.'

Ackroyd sighed as if explanation were redundant.

'Don't you see – Germany is the nation of tomorrow: she's vigorous, visionary and iron-willed. Our European civilisation is threatened by that imperial monstrosity of Russia, and while we British are wasting our resource on a ramshackle colonial agglomeration Germany is mustering the strength to deliver the continent from the Slavic hordes.'

'And the *Sean-Bhean Bhocht*? What has she done to deserve your patronage?'

'Oh, good lord, nothing at all. Your sympathy for her, if

A DARKENING FIRE

limited, is understandable, but she's a little outcrop of little people with one single redeeming feature: she has the capacity to deflect His Majesty's military from events elsewhere.'

'So through Joey Butler you orchestrated your double sedition?'

'Yes – orchestrated my double sedition as you call it via the laughably primitive device of a hole in a tree. Mr. Butler's idea. I had to desist for a while, of course, when Sir Derwent's internal enquiry made it unsafe to continue.'

'Well, why didn't you put Joey onto the fact that I was the copper sent to wreck Taaffe's outfit?'

'Oh, I would have done, make no mistake. But all I knew was a police spy was in place. No name, nothing more useful.'

'Obviously there's not much point in asking if you regret all the deaths you've caused.'

Ackroyd shook his head and after some thought asked, 'Tell me, Inspector, what happens now? As I've said I'm afraid your actual evidence is going to look a bit thin, but I imagine you'll manage to have me put out to grass. Should I draft my letter of resignation and retire disappointed but undismayed to Buckinghamshire?'

Before McGarrity could answer there was a tap at the door. Getting up he walked casually across the room and turned the handle.

'I don't think that'll be necessary,' he said. 'But you *are* right-handed are you not?'

Mystified, Ackroyd nodded and reached absently for a pen.

'Then I expect that'll be the hand they'll find the gun in. Some say it's the coward's way out but I'm not so sure.'

Ackroyd half-stood, staring blankly at the pen and mouthing something unheard as Terrence Edwards came in, patting McGarrity on the arm as the Inspector left for the brilliant summer afternoon. Sergeant Hughes was waiting for him at the entrance to the building, chatting to Tolley who in his old Marine uniform was looking every inch the veteran that he was.

'Niamh and Fräulein Hanna are waiting for you,' Hughes told the big man. 'Do you want a lift in the van?'

A newspaper vendor was brandishing a placard announcing that the ultimatum had been telegraphed to Berlin demanding a

A DARKENING FIRE

guarantee of Belgian neutrality. The heat of the day struck McGarrity full in the face.

'I think I'll walk for a bit, Niall, then catch a taxi.'

Then in a moment of uncharacteristic camaraderie he shook hands with Sergeant Hughes and was about to set off in the direction of Trafalgar Square feeling his own concerns submerge slowly in the approaching disintegration of the world around him.

'Inspector McGarrity, sir,' Tolley called, emerging in haste from his post, 'I know you're well thought of here. Would you be good enough to put in a word for me with Sir Derwent? I'm reckoned to be over the hill, you might say, but if there are strings to be pulled to get me back in the Service…'

McGarrity turned to exchange a double handshake with the old soldier.

'Look after yourself, Roland. You're a great man yet.'

And buoyed by the knowledge that a couple of miles away his daughter was waiting for his return he relinquished his usual vigilance to an unfamiliar sense of tranquil wellbeing.

It was by chance that Conor Fallon and Rónán MacInerney, scouring Whitehall for an entirely different purpose, witnessed McGarrity's exiting the building and exchanging warm words with the now armed doorman. Viewing this performance with stunned disbelief the pair fell in some distance behind him, hands close to the butts of their concealed revolvers, still locked in confused and whispered debate about Leo McGarrity's allegiance.

The breathless summer heat had brought the day to a torpid limbo. Soon it would be otherwise.

****